By Jude Deveraux

THE NANTUCKET BRIDES NOVELS
True Love
For All Time
Ever After

THE SUMMER HILL NOVELS
The Girl from Summer Hill

The
Girl from
Summer Hill

The Girl from Summer Hill

A SUMMER HILL NOVEL

JUDE DEVERAUX

BALLANTINE BOOKS

NEW YORK

Published in the United States by Ballantine Books, an imprint of Random House, a division of Penguin Random House LLC, New York.

BALLANTINE and the HOUSE colophon are registered trademarks of Penguin Random House LLC.

LIBRARY OF CONGRESS CATALOGING-IN-PUBLICATION DATA
Names: Deveraux, Jude, author.
Title: The girl from Summer Hill : a Summer Hill novel / Jude Deveraux.
Description: New York : Ballantine Books, [2016] | Series: Summer Hill ; 1
Identifiers: LCCN 2016001417 (print) | LCCN 2016005991 (ebook) | ISBN 9781101883266 (hardcover : acid-free paper) | ISBN 9781101883273 (ebook)
Subjects: LCSH: Man-woman relationships—Fiction. | BISAC: FICTION / Romance / Contemporary. | FICTION / Contemporary Women. | FICTION / Action & Adventure. | GSAFD: Love stories.
Classification: LCC PS3554.E9273 G57 2016 (print) | LCC PS3554.E9273 (ebook) | DDC 813/.54—dc23
LC record available at lccn.loc.gov/2016001417

Printed in the United States of America on acid-free paper

randomhousebooks.com

987654321

First Edition

Book design by Diane Hobbing

The
Girl from
Summer Hill

ACT ONE, SCENE ONE

Mr. Darcy is revealed

There was a naked man on Casey's back porch. She would have called the police or, at the very least, screamed if he hadn't been so damned beautiful.

Instead, without so much as a blink, she fumbled for the electric kettle and poured boiling water over the loose tea leaves in the silver strainer. Quite a bit of water missed the mug, went onto the granite countertop, and ran down to the tile floor, but she didn't notice.

It was so early that it wasn't yet daylight, and she hadn't bothered to turn on the kitchen lights. But then he'd turned on the porch lights, and in the misty morning, as she looked through the screen door, it was almost as though he were on a stage.

He'd dropped his T-shirt and sweatpants on the stone path, then, totally nude and facing Casey, he walked up the three steps, his full male glory in view. He came straight toward her, as though he meant to enter the house.

Casey had just woken up, and when she first saw him, she thought she was still asleep and having the best dream of her life. Not only was his body beautiful, but so was his face. Hair, eyes, beard stubble, truly luscious lips. His skin was a dark golden color all over, and he had long, sleek muscles. His hair was long, down his neck, and in the overhead light it was so black that it seemed to glisten almost blue.

When he got to the porch, he didn't open the screen door and come inside. Instead, he turned so she had a glorious view of his side.

Lord! Pecs. Abs. The curve of his backside, thighs like an Olympic skater's.

Casey managed to blink a few times. Surely she was asleep. Surely he couldn't be *real*.

He seemed to be doing something to the wall, and seconds later it started raining. That made sense. The deity who controlled the heavens *should* look like this man.

But, no, it was an outdoor shower that seemed to be attached to her little guesthouse. She hadn't noticed that it was there—for the few months she'd been in town, it had been winter. But yesterday had been so warm that she'd opened every door and window to let out the heat of her cooking. When she at last went to bed, the kitchen had been so hot that she'd just hooked the screen door and left the room open to the breezes.

She picked up her mug of tea and sipped it while she watched him lather himself with soap.

There was a tall stool near her, and without taking her eyes off him, she felt for it and sat down. As he ran his hands over his body, she was even more sure that she was dreaming. And she was just as sure that if she took her eyes off him she'd wake up.

She watched him soap his legs, and between them, then he moved upward. He had such trouble reaching the entire width of his back that Casey had thoughts of slipping out of her pajamas and joining him.

"Could I help?" she'd ask. He wouldn't say a word. He'd just hand her the soap and she'd get busy.

Of course, she could use some cleaning too, so he would do her back. Or front. Or wherever he wanted to.

Maybe it was the way it was dark where she was sitting and so very light where he was that made it all seem like a movie. She sipped her tea and watched him, dreamily smiling at the scene.

She'd been working in the kitchen until midnight and it was very early now. Kit said he wanted the food at the playhouse by eight, and she took that to mean he wanted it set up and ready to serve. Last night she'd called her brother Josh to ask if he'd please, please find some tables for her. "Use sawhorses or tree stumps, whatever your great manliness can find," she'd said in the voicemail she left for him. "Just so I have a place to put all this food. Kit said he's expecting half the town to show up for the auditions. Double please? I'll save you some of those cream-filled doughnut holes you like so much." She said the last in a voice as cajoling as she could make it. Considering that she'd been on her feet for fourteen hours, she wondered if she sounded more pathetic than persuasive.

But looking at the beautiful naked man was making up for yesterday. He was rinsing off now. He reached up to the shower-head on the wall, pulled it down, and began spraying water over his entire gorgeous body.

Casey held the mug of tea to her lips, frozen in place. All she could do was stare. His long hair was wet, plastered to his skull. His profile showed his strong features—and something about it seemed familiar.

He turned off the water, then looked around for something.

He needs a towel, she thought, and it ran through her mind that she could open the door and hand him one.

When he stepped toward the house as though he meant to enter, her heart seemed to stop. She was more fully awake now and she was aware that she'd just spied on a man taking a shower. Not exactly a polite thing to do. She certainly wouldn't like it done to her!

When he put his hand on the door handle, Casey's heart started pounding. She didn't dare move or he would see her.

He dropped his hand and went down the steps, picked up his sweatpants, and put them on—and she let out her breath. He would never know. Good!

But as he reached for his shirt, her cellphone rang. It had been charging and she'd forgotten it was on the counter. It kept ringing as she reached for it, then she fumbled and hit speakerphone just as it went to voicemail.

"Hey, little sis, I used a broadsword to cut down a couple of oaks and hacked out some tables. But I also borrowed a couple from the church. If you want me to pick you and your kettles up in my truck, let me know. If I don't hear from you, I'll see you at eight." He hung up.

Casey hadn't moved, nor had she taken her eyes off the man. When the phone rang, he'd dropped the shirt and turned to look at the door.

She was almost sure he saw her. She had on her white pajamas, the ones her mom had given her with the print of the dish running away with the spoon and the cow jumping over the moon. Too young for her, and they clung much too tightly to her curvy figure, but they were oh so comforting.

It had grown lighter outside and she knew she was probably visible inside the dark room. But maybe not. Maybe she could sneak upstairs and pretend she hadn't seen him.

As quickly as she could, she put her mug down and slid off the stool.

But she wasn't fast enough. He bounded up the steps and reached the door in seconds. When he tried to open it, the inside hook held.

Thinking she had a reprieve, Casey took a step toward the living room, but a sound made her turn back.

The man, naked from hip bones up, put his fist through the screen and unfastened the hook.

Okay, now she was scared. This man was big and he looked

furious. She glanced at her cellphone but it was between her and him. Her little house was set in eleven acres of garden and woodland. If she screamed, no one would hear her.

"Did you get it all down?" He stepped closer to her.

His voice was deep—and menacing. Maybe if she ran she could reach the front door and get out. But then what? The only house nearby was the big one, and it was empty.

She put her hands into fists at her sides, took a deep breath, and faced him. Minutes before, his size, the muscles, the sheer masculinity of him had been enticing, but now they seemed threatening. She didn't think she could escape him, but maybe if she didn't back down he'd go away.

"I live here," she said. "You're trespassing."

He stopped only three feet away. "Like hell you do! Who do you work for? Where is it?"

Casey took a step back. What a voice he had! Loud and deep. And what he was asking was thoroughly puzzling. "I work for myself. I cater and do private parties."

He took another step toward her. "And this is a sideline? Where are you hiding it?"

Confusion was replacing her fear. "What is 'it'? What do you want?"

He picked up her cellphone, the charging cord falling away. "Please tell me you didn't use *this*! I think I deserve better than a mobile phone." He put the phone back on the counter, then turned, his eyes roaming up and down her.

Casey knew she was looking far from her best. Who wanted a gorgeous man to see her wearing pajamas that were perfect for a five-year-old? And her hair was a rat's nest of tangles and probably full of flour and raspberry jam. She'd collapsed last night, not bothering to shower.

Maybe it was pride, but all sense of fear vanished. She put her shoulders back. "I don't know who you are but I want you out of my house. Now!" She grabbed her phone. "I think the sheriff would like to hear about a man stripping on *my* porch and tearing out *my* screen to get inside *my* house and threatening me. Unless you want to be in handcuffs, I suggest you leave immediately."

He stood there staring at her, saying nothing, but looking shocked. He opened his mouth to say something, but then closed it. Turning, he left the house, the door slamming behind him.

For a few moments, Casey stood where she was, her nails cutting into her palms as she watched him leave. He didn't stop to pick up his shirt but kept going, turned right, and moved out of sight.

Suddenly she felt exhausted. She made it into the living room and fell down onto the couch, her heart pounding in her ears. With her head back, she tried to use her breathing to calm herself.

The man had been so very angry!

When Kit had given her the little guesthouse to live in, she'd thought it was perfect. It had once been the kitchen of an old Virginia plantation, and the huge fireplace that had been used for cooking was in the living room. Years ago someone had added to the building, putting an excellent kitchen to one side and a bedroom and bath upstairs. There was even an herb garden just outside.

Kit had asked if she minded being so isolated, but Casey said no, that she loved it. The Big House—which had been renovated and decorated before she arrived—was locked tight and empty. For six years before she came to Summer Hill, she'd been the head chef of one of the busiest restaurants in D.C. After the noise and controlled chaos of that place, the quiet of the old plantation had been bliss.

But this morning had turned scary.

She was beginning to calm down, and she needed to think about what she was going to do now. All in all, she thought she should call the sheriff and report what had happened—including her embarrassing voyeurism.

She was still holding her phone and she saw that she had a voicemail from Kit. As she touched the screen, her hand was shaking.

"Casey, my dear," Kit's strong voice said, "I know it's late and I hope you've gone to bed, but I just wanted to tell you that the owner of Tattwell has returned. I know you think I own the place and I apologize for the subterfuge, but my cousin swore me to secrecy. Still, I feel I should warn you in case you see a couple of strange men on the grounds. The owner is Tatton Landers and he's with his best friend, Jack Worth. They are both very nice young men, so I hope you'll welcome them. I must go. I'll see you at the auditions."

Casey listened to the message twice to try to get all the information it contained. Jack Worth? she thought. That was the name of an actor she really liked. Her last boyfriend had been a fiend for his movies and had all the DVDs. They had never missed a new Jack Worth movie.

But he wasn't the man on the porch.

Casey took a breath. This was ridiculous! Jack Worth was a common name. Kit couldn't have been referring to the actor.

On impulse, she tapped the other name, Tatton Landers, into her phone's search engine, and it redirected her. There he was. The man she'd watched showering on her porch had thousands of photos on the Internet. Most of them were in period costume: a knight in armor, tight Regency trousers, a leather jerkin like Robin Hood would wear.

"Of course," she said aloud. "Tate Landers." She'd never seen one of his movies, but a friend of hers used to talk about him. She loved romantic movies and went to all of them. They'd never interested Casey so she'd only half-listened to what her friend was saying—and had teased her friend about them. "You have a Ph.D. in psychology but you drool over some actor who says, 'Oh, Charity Goodheart, your eyes are like emeralds. Please be mine.'"

"You don't get it, do you?" her friend said. "We live in a world of metrosexuals. Tate isn't like that. He throws women over the saddle of a horse and tells them to shut up."

Casey was aghast. "What would you say to one of your clients if she told you her boyfriend did that?"

"I'd give her the number of a center for abused women and make sure she went. But that's real; Tate is fantasy."

Casey shook her head at her friend. "This guy is an actor. In real life he probably wears pink shirts and gets his eyebrows waxed."

"Not Tate! I read that he—"

Casey had thrown up her hands. Her friend had tried to get her to go to romantic movies, but she wouldn't. With her workload she had little time off and she wasn't going to waste it on some drippy saga.

Now it seemed that she was living in a house on property owned by some big-deal movie star—who hated her.

And rightfully so, Casey thought. It was one thing to watch some half-naked guy mow the lawn, but when people spied on public figures they often ended up in court. And went to prison.

What was it he'd said? "Where is it?" And "Please tell me you didn't use *this*! I think I deserve better than a mobile phone."

"He thought I was photographing him," she said aloud. When he thought she'd snapped the pictures on a cellphone, his ego had been hurt. In spite of the gravity of the situation, she couldn't help smiling. No wonder he ran away at the mention of the sheriff. Wouldn't the tabloids love a photo of the romantic hero in handcuffs?

Casey stood up. "I have to fix this," she whispered. She needed to apologize and explain, then apologize some more.

She looked at the clock on the mantel. It was still early, so she could take about an hour to do what she did best. She was going to cook something wonderful and take it to him. She'd use her best I'm-sorry voice to make him forgive her. And she'd assure him that she had entered the room just as the phone rang, so she'd only seen him with his shirt off.

That's good, she thought. A few lies, some of her honey-glazed chicken, and a good strong mimosa, and maybe he wouldn't kick her out of her very comfortable little house. Or put her in jail.

She had a plan.

ACT ONE, SCENE TWO

Elizabeth doesn't tempt Darcy

An hour later, Casey arrived at the Big House—as everyone in town referred to it—with food. She'd used some of what she'd already prepared for Kit's group, then added a few things. In an insulated container she had strands of slow-roasted, honey-glazed chicken and sweet-potato hash with fried eggs on top. She'd buttered freshly made bread and grilled it.

It wasn't easy to think about what she had to do. Apologize profusely, explain that she didn't know about the showerhead on her porch, and— No! She wasn't supposed to know that he'd taken a shower. Her story was that she was in bed, heard the phone ring, and ran down the stairs.

There was an old brick path between her cottage and the back of the Big House. Most of the land was too overgrown to walk around, but during the past snowy winter, she'd explored the area near the house. She'd grown to love the uneven surface of the path, had even memorized the places where the bricks stuck up, so she wouldn't trip on them.

But right now she wasn't enamored of them. The big case was heavy and she was so nervous she was afraid she'd drop it. If she did, she was sure she'd be told to vacate the house. Then where would she stay? The lake people were beginning to open their houses in preparation for the summer, which meant that all the service personnel for the restaurants and shops were arriving. One-bedroom apartments would be packed with about six college kids each, all working in shifts.

Casey couldn't help shuddering at the thought. No, she liked where she was and wanted to stay there.

She'd never been inside the Big House, but during the winter she'd tried to look in some of the windows. They were mostly shuttered or curtained, but she knew where the kitchen was and that next to it was a glassed-in breakfast room.

She saw lights in the room and, like her, Mr. Landers had all the windows and doors open to the screens. As she approached, she saw him sitting at a white table, his head down. She halted. He was dressed in jeans and a plaid shirt and he looked . . . well, rather forlorn.

Casey stepped out of view. Please tell me I didn't do that to him, she thought. Poor guy probably came to sleepy little Summer Hill for some peace, but he was greeted by what he thought was a paparazzo taking photos of him *au naturel.*

She glanced at the heavy container she was holding. Maybe, possibly, this food would cheer him up—and make him forgive her. And later she could introduce him to some people so he wouldn't be so alone.

Putting on a smile, she turned back to the door. Would he welcome her or call the sheriff?

She shifted the container to free a hand so she could knock, but then she froze. Walking into the room was the actor Jack Worth, and all he had on was a pair of very low-riding sweatpants.

Casey flattened herself against the wall, and for the second time that morning her heart started pounding in her ears. She'd seen Jack Worth on the big screen, blown up to epic proportions as he tore through streets on a motorcycle, ran across buildings, rappelled down mountains—and saved the girl while doing it. His movies were nonstop action.

Whatever could be imagined, Jack Worth had done it onscreen—and usually while wearing the bare minimum of clothing. And she was one of his biggest fans! Meeting him had always been a dream of hers.

I must get myself under control, Casey thought. Calm down. No gushing or staring, or making a fool of myself.

But she wasn't succeeding at being calm. Two nude, or nearly so, drop-dead-gorgeous men in one day. Was the angel who'd been assigned to look over her a sweetheart or a sadistic devil?

She took a deep breath, straightened her shoulders, then turned toward the door.

But then Jack spoke. His voice seemed as familiar to her as her own. He was no smooth James Bond. Jack's voice was deep and gravelly, rough. Kind of dangerous-sounding.

She crept back against the wall. He really sounded like that! No sound adjustments—that was his actual voice.

"What are you so grumpy about?" She heard Jack's voice fade as he went toward the kitchen.

"Kit put some girl in my guesthouse."

Casey froze, her breath held. She was now going to hear her fate.

"That's good," Jack said as he returned to the breakfast room. "You need somebody to look after the place when you're not here. This refrigerator is empty."

"That's what happens when you leave your cook at home."

"Any hope for delivery?"

"In rural Virginia before full daylight?" Tate said. "Quit dreaming. There's coffee, so have some."

Jack poured himself a cup from the pot on the table and took a drink. "This is good. Who made it?" He glanced back at Tate. "What's on for today?"

"I made the coffee. Kit wants me to . . ." When Tate looked up, his eyes were bleak. "He's going to put on a play, even bought a big building and built a stage." Tate paused. "His first production is *Pride and Prejudice,* and he wants me to read with the women who audition for the role of Elizabeth."

Jack laughed. "Since you're the only Darcy who's been able to knock Colin Firth off his pedestal, I'm sure you'll attract a lot of would-be Lizzys, Janes, and all the others."

"I guess so. Kit said he wants to boost town spirit and to bring the people who have houses on the lake back to town. Seems they've started driving to Richmond to do their shopping, and local sales are falling. Since the proceeds from the play go to charity, I couldn't say no."

Outside, Casey suddenly realized that she was again spying. What was *wrong* with her today? She started to leave but then Jack said, "Think they'll have food at the auditions?"

"Yeah, and I think it's being cooked by that girl in my guesthouse."

Casey could no more walk away than she could have flown.

Jack gave a grunt. "What in the world happened to turn you into something like one of your characters? You look like you're about to draw a sword on somebody."

"She was spying on me."

Casey's heart leaped back into her throat.

"Oh. That's bad," Jack said. "Was she hiding in the bushes? Did you take her camera away from her?"

"No bushes," Tate said. "And no hiding. I don't think she took photos. But I believe she watched me take a shower."

Jack drew in his breath in horror. "She sneaked inside your house? We need to call the police. She can't—"

"No!" Tate said. "She was in the guesthouse and I used the shower on the porch. But I wouldn't have done it if Kit had told me someone was staying there."

Jack took his time before he spoke. "She's living in a house she probably pays rent on, you were naked on her back porch, and she saw you? So tell me what *she* did wrong."

Casey's heart settled. She had a champion! I love you, Jack Worth, she thought.

"It was just the way she did it that got me, that's all," Tate said. "Why don't you put some clothes on and go to this thing with me?"

"To a local play? No thanks. I think I'll fly back to L.A. tomorrow. This is about all the rural delight I can take. Empty refrigerators hold no appeal for me."

"You're getting soft. But I think I'll go back with you tomorrow—after I do those damned auditions, that is."

"So what's this girl like? And how old is she?"

Casey held her breath. What would he say about her: "She had jam in her hair but she looked good"? That would be nice to hear.

"Late twenties, I guess," Tate said. "She had on kid pajamas, so who knows what she looked like. I was too angry to see much."

"A grown-up girl in pajamas. I like it," Jack said. "And she cooks?"

"Either that or she's brilliant at making a mess in a kitchen. Pans and bowls were everywhere. And bread. From the smell of it, she'd been baking."

Jack groaned. "I think I may be in love with her. Pajamas and baking bread. Where is this guesthouse and what's she look like? Good face?"

"Okay, I guess. Nice eyes, but I wasn't tempted."

Yet again, Casey felt deflated. That's what she got for snooping. Okay, so she could stand to lose a few pounds, but other men liked her curves. But not this snooty movie star. As Jack pointed out, Tate had no right to be angry at her for being in her own house, but that didn't matter to this so-called celebrity!

Casey pushed away from the wall. She thought about leaving the container on the step, but she didn't. As snotty as Tate Landers was, he'd probably throw the food out. It wouldn't be good enough for someone so grand and glorious.

Jack was standing by the table, frowning down at his friend, when he saw movement outside. He went to the door and looked out.

A young woman carrying something in a wide container was quickly walking away. And from her pace, she wasn't happy.

She had on jeans and a T-shirt, and he liked her shape. Her backside curved roundly, and when she turned slightly, he saw that she was quite full breasted. He was glad to see a normal, healthy woman. So many of the starlets he worked with were emaciated. But then, the camera added pounds, so they were under pressure to be very thin.

Her dark-red hair was pulled back into a swishing ponytail and the early-morning sun glinted off it. Jack couldn't see her face, but if it was half as nice as the rest of her, he'd be pleased. All in all, he thought he should visit the guesthouse.

He looked back at Tate, who was glowering down at his cup of coffee. What in the world was wrong with him? In public, Tate was a very private person. When he had to attend something, he usually took his sister.

But when he was with his friends, he was nearly always relaxed and laughing. Jack knew Tate had planned to stay in Summer Hill for at least a month. Tate liked the company of his cousin Kit, who was old enough to be his father, but then, maybe that was why Tate liked him so much. And he'd talked about how he had other newly found relatives moving to the little Virginia town. It had all been good.

So why was he sitting at the table looking miserable? Why

wasn't he out exploring the place? And why was he dreading going to some local auditions? Tate was great with the armies of squealing females who followed him around.

Jack watched the girl disappearing into the trees. "What color hair does she have?" He purposely didn't say who "she" was.

"Kind of red. I think it was natural."

"Yeah?" Jack said. "Anything else natural about her?"

The glower left Tate's face and he smiled a bit. "From the way she jiggled when she ordered me out of the house, I'd say her upper half is quite natural."

Jack raised an eyebrow. "What were her pajamas like again?"

Tate smiled broader. "Very thin and half unbuttoned. And crumpled up from being in bed. She didn't have anything on under them."

Jack was working to keep from grinning. "Are you sure you want to leave here tomorrow?"

Tate gave a full smile, something only his friends saw. "Go get dressed. I have a script to read and Kit doesn't want me there until after lunch."

"I think I'll meet you there." As Jack went up the stairs to his bedroom, he was chuckling. "Not tempted, huh?"

Bingley defends Darcy

"Hi," Jack said from outside Casey's door.

She was putting food into boxes and coolers as she prepared to take it to the old warehouse where the stage was being built. Unfortunately, she was using so much force that she almost broke a Pyrex dish.

"Hello," Jack said louder as he knocked on the doorframe.

Casey jumped. "Sorry, I— Oh. You." Her eyes were wide.

"May I come in?"

"Of course, but it's a mess in here."

"When a place smells as good as this one does, it's beautiful to me."

"I have to—" she began, but stopped. Jack Worth, her absolute favorite movie star, was standing in *her* kitchen. Her first thought was how odd it was to see this man life-size. He looked good, but he also looked human, normal. And right now she recognized what she was so good at dealing with: a hungry person. "Would you like something to eat?"

"Please," he said.

Minutes later, Jack was seated on the far side of the island and before him was a feast. Casey had opened every container and dished out some of each to him. She warmed up the sweet-potato hash and fried fresh eggs to put on top.

"This is great." He was eating a maple-walnut muffin and looking around the kitchen at the rows of jars of home-canned jams, their tops covered with red-and-white gingham. On a side wall hung skillets from four inches wide to one that could feed a crowd. Three tall, narrow bookcases were between the big doors to the outside and they were packed with cookbooks, binders, and card boxes. By the big stainless-steel stove were shelves packed with bottles of oil of different colors, most of them with herbs and peppers inside. "I mean it, every inch of this place is great."

Casey smiled, pleased by his compliment. If she'd been told she was going to meet Jack Worth, she would have said she'd instantly turn into a fangirl. But as she watched him eat, she realized she felt the same way she did with her brother. "Excuse me, but I need to pack things."

"Go ahead," Jack said. "How are you transporting all of this?"

"I have to call my brother to come with his truck."

"Tate has a big pickup in his garage. I can get it and give you a ride."

She blinked at him. To ride with Jack Worth? All his stunts with cars flying through the air seemed to run through her mind.

"I promise I'll keep all four wheels on the ground."

"Then I'd rather go with someone else," she said solemnly.

Jack laughed. "Okay, next time I'll take the Jeep and we'll find some rough roads."

"You're on." She put a squash casserole into the cooler. "But you'd better not tell . . . him, the owner, who's in the truck or he might not let you use it."

"Bad first meeting, huh?" Jack bit into an apple muffin that had a salted-caramel top.

"Depends on if you like raging fury."

He held up the muffin. "This is . . . mmmm! Anyway, that sounds out of character for Tate. He's not like his screen image of the angry, brooding man. All I have to do is drive fast and a girl is happy. But what's Tate to do to impress her? Smolder?"

"What does that mean?" Casey asked. "Wait. Don't tell me. My friend used to say that Tate Landers only had to look at a woman and she'd start removing her clothes. I didn't feel that. He looked at me like I was something he found on the bottom of his shoe."

"That really doesn't sound like Tate."

Casey waved her hand. "Why are we talking about *him*? I loved that scene in your last movie where you grabbed the girl off the skimobile. I kept replaying it on DVD. What are you going to do next?"

"In September I start a movie about a spoiled, rich teenage boy who's been kidnapped. I save him and along the way I make a man of him. So what part are you trying out for in the play?"

"None. I'm not an actress. I just cook."

"This breakfast isn't 'just' anything. Listen, with your talents, I could get you a job in L.A. at—"

"Thanks, but no. Not yet." She was planning to say nothing more, but she couldn't help a bit of a brag. "Ever hear of Christie's in D.C.?" She knew he had, as she'd been told he'd visited, but she'd been too busy cooking to look.

"Yeah, of course. I've eaten there. That place was once great but it got to be a mess. You have anything to do with bringing it back to life?"

She didn't reply, just gave a modest shrug. Her boss had hired her straight out of school and had dumped the whole job of restoring the big old once-great restaurant onto her young shoulders. "You can do it. I have faith in you" had been his answer for every catastrophic problem. And he always said it as he was running out the door.

"I am impressed." Jack smiled the way he did at girls when the camera was on him.

Casey smiled back but thought that it wasn't the same as seeing him on a big screen. He just seemed like a hungry man, handsome but not overly so. Maybe real life took away some of the magic of a celebrity.

Bending, she put utensils into a box. "Right now I want some time off. I need to think about where I'm going and what I want to do. That's enough about me. Try these." She handed him what looked like doughnut holes but were actually Italian bombolini. Inside was a pastry cream with a touch of orange liqueur.

"Heaven," Jack said. "On second thought, forget the restaurant job. Move in with me and feed me every day."

"Now, *that's* a tempting offer," Casey said. "Do I get sex with that?"

"Honey, feed me like this and you can have any body part of mine you want."

They looked at each other and laughed because they knew in that age-old way that there would never be anything like that between them. He'd used his best smile on her and she'd felt nothing. As had he. They were destined to be friends and nothing more.

Bingley meets Jane

As Jack drove through the pretty little town of Summer Hill, he never took his eyes off the road and he obeyed all traffic signs. Casey didn't know if she was glad or disappointed.

At the first stop sign, Jack said, "I played Bingley in high school. It's what got me started in acting."

He'd been sitting in a way that seemed to take over the driver's seat, a kind of lazy, confident position she'd seen onscreen. But abruptly, he changed. He sat up straight, arms and legs close together, and quoted Mr. Bingley. "'When I am in the country, I never wish to leave it; and when I am in town, it is pretty much the same. They have each their advantages, and I can be equally happy in either.'"

"That's really good," Casey said in awe. "I've never been able to understand how actors can be someone else. What happens if you have to do a love scene with someone you detest?"

"Did you see *Runaway 3*?"

"Sure. Your girlfriend was trapped on a mountain and you parachuted in and let your plane crash. When that federal agent found you two in the cabin, the look you gave him was priceless. I was sure you were going to shoot him."

"I hated that woman. She complained endlessly."

"But you looked like you adored each other."

"That's why they call it acting. The nicest thing she said to me was that I drove recklessly just to mess up her hair."

"But driving like a madman is what you do."

"See? If you worked for me, you could have told her that and protected me."

"If I heard her being nasty, I would have put sweetened yogurt into her breakfast smoothie. The extra calories would get her back."

Laughing, Jack pulled into a big parking lot. Before them was a huge old two-story brick warehouse with about a hundred windows. There were a dozen vans outside, all of them with company names painted on the side: electrical, carpentry, heating/AC, plumbing, tile, and glass. It was early, but there was the sound of hammers and saws and men yelling orders.

Casey got out and went to the back of the truck to start unloading. "Hey, Josh!" she yelled.

A handsome young man in jeans and a T-shirt came over and kissed her cheek. He was tall, over six feet, and his shirt showed his muscular chest.

"Could you give me a hand here?" Casey asked.

"Nope," Josh said. "Not unless I get the bribe you promised me."

Smiling, Casey opened the container of bombolini and held it out to him.

As he took a couple, he glanced at Jack, who was standing to one side of the truck. "You look like that guy who—"

"He *is* that guy," Casey said. "Josh, meet Jack Worth, and Jack, this is Josh, my brother."

As the two men shook hands, Josh said, "I'm not really her brother. She's a half sister of my sister—who is also my half sister." He picked up a heavy cooler from the truck bed.

"Interesting relationship." Jack put a box on top of another cooler and picked them both up.

Josh put down the cooler he was carrying, set a big casserole dish on top of it, and picked it up.

Jack started to put his cooler down but Casey stepped between them. "Go, both of you. You can arm-wrestle later."

The two men started walking side by side toward the warehouse, but then Josh stepped forward and Jack went after him. By the time they got to the doorway they were nearly running.

"Now *there's* a bromance," Casey muttered.

"Do you need some help?"

She turned to see an older woman, quite pretty, with blonde hair and blue eyes. She was slim and looked fit.

"I'd love some help, but I believe in men making themselves useful." She turned to the vans, which were all open to reveal the tools and supplies inside; a few men were nearby. "I have food," Casey said loudly, "and as soon as I can get it set up inside, the sooner you guys can eat it."

Within seconds, half a dozen men were at the truck, picking up containers and carrying them inside.

The woman laughed. "I'm Olivia, and maybe I can help you set up."

"I'm Casey, and that would be great." They started walking toward the open doors of the warehouse. "Did you drive in for the auditions?"

"Oh, no," Olivia said. "I was born and bred in Summer Hill. I came with my daughter-in-law, Hildy. She's trying out for the part of Jane Bennet."

"That's good," Casey said. "I figured every female here would want to be Elizabeth."

"Hildy feels that her physical attributes predispose her to be Jane."

"What?" Casey asked, not understanding. "Oh, right, I see. Jane is very pretty. That's nice for your daughter-in-law." She glanced up at the warehouse. "I haven't been here since Kit bought this place. Half the windows were broken and the inside was full of trash. Looks like it's been cleaned up since then."

"Wait until you see the inside."

They went through a wide doorway toward all the noise of men and tools—and Casey gasped. The warehouse was in the final stages of renovation. It was a long, high-ceilinged space. A big stage was at one end, seats on raised tiers in the middle, and a closed-off area was for ticketing. What was especially startling was that a lot of one wall had been torn out and glass doors put in. Casey knew that when Kit bought it, the yard had been full of derelict pieces of machinery and some rather impressive weeds. That was all gone and in its place was a garden. As she watched, a crane lowered a twenty-foot-tall birch tree to two men who were guiding it into a big hole.

"Wow" was all Casey could say.

"Thank you," came a deep voice that she knew well. "I take it you approve."

She held her cheek up to Kit's kiss. He was tall and elegant, his thick gray hair like a lion's mane. "It's beautiful."

"I hear you had a bit of an adventure this morning," he said. "It seems that the question is whether you saw or didn't see." His eyes weren't on Casey.

"Do you know Olivia?" she asked. "And I'm not telling what I saw, but just so you know, fairy godmothers *do* grant wishes."

Kit laughed, a rich, pleasant sound.

But for all that he was laughing at Casey's joke, he hadn't taken his eyes off Olivia—who was studiously watching the men in the garden. Casey looked from one to the other. "Olivia is going to help me serve, and her daughter-in-law is here to audition for the role of Jane."

Kit dragged his eyes away from Olivia and consulted the clipboard he was holding. "And you are auditioning for what part?"

"None of them," Olivia said firmly. "I'm just here to help my daughter-in-law if she needs me."

The tables had been set up near the big glass doors, the boxes and coolers beside them. Three men were standing nearby, waiting for food.

"I better get busy." Casey went to the tables, Olivia behind her.

The two women worked well together, each seeming to know what the other wanted before it was done. Within minutes the big tables were covered with white paper, and breakfast items were set out. Kit had ordered dozens of pastries from the local bakery, so most of the food Casey had prepared could be saved for lunch.

As they worked, the big warehouse began to fill up with people, all of them carrying copies of the script that Kit had written during the winter with the help of Casey and her half sister Stacy. He had complained about the difficulty of translating *Pride and Prejudice* into a script. "She left out important dialogue and now I have to make it up." Since he was referring to the very perfect Jane Austen, Casey had groaned.

"Look at this," he said. "The pivotal scene of the book is paraphrased. She doesn't tell what Darcy said when he proposed, just that he insulted Elizabeth. How? What *exactly* did he say? Didn't this woman have an editor?"

They had laughed over Kit's complaints, but he got them back by making them read the lines aloud every time he rewrote them. They got to the point where they had memorized everyone's lines.

Smiling at the memory, Casey began filling mugs from the big urn, while Olivia opened more boxes of doughnuts. The tables were soon surrounded by workmen getting coffee and pastries—and they didn't seem to want to leave. "At this rate someone will have to make another run to the bakery," Casey said. "I think I'm jealous. What did they put into these that makes them so popular?"

"It's not the doughnuts, it's the Lydias. And the girls are here for Wickham," Olivia said. "Look."

A table had been set up by the exterior door, and names were being taken and badges handed out. All the *Pride and Prejudice* characters were represented, but Lydia was four to one. Many women had a badge saying LYDIA clipped to their shirts.

"What in the world is going on? I thought there'd be a lot of competition for the lead roles."

Olivia nodded toward the stage. There in the center, talking to Kit, was a very handsome man. Dark-brown hair, broad shoulders, all of it encased in the red uniform worn by the officers in Meryton.

"Another one!" Casey said under her breath.

"Another one what?" Olivia asked.

"Beautiful man. It's my day for them. I'm beginning to feel like a magnet attracting bits of very pretty steel."

"Hey, Casey!" Josh called from atop some scaffolding. "You gonna try out for Lydia?"

"No, but I think *you* should try out to be Wickham."

There was a collective gasp from half a dozen young women who gazed up at him with smiles and fluttering eyelashes.

"I'll get you for that." Grinning, Josh returned to plastering the wall, his back to the girls.

Eight of the Lydias hurried to Casey.

"Do you think Josh will play—"

"Will he audition with—"

"Can he wear a uniform?"

"Have no idea. Doubt it. Absolutely not," Casey said. "Who wants an eight-hundred-calorie pastry?"

All the girls backed away except for one. She too had LYDIA pinned to her top, but she didn't look like the other girls, all of whom had on enough makeup to start a business. This girl was pretty and blonde, tall and thin, and she kept her head down as though she was too shy to meet Casey's eyes. She took her dough-nut and a mug of orange juice and went to the side of the room to sit down and read her copy of *Pride and Prejudice*.

"What an extraordinarily pretty young woman," Olivia said in such a way that Casey glanced at her. She was about to ask a question that might get Olivia to reveal something about herself, but Jack came to the table.

"Where have you been?" Casey asked. "Hiding from the autograph seekers?"

"Are you kidding?" he said. "All the prettiest girls are chasing the uniform." He looked toward the stage, where the man in red was contemplating the girls sitting in the front row. It was a whole line of Lydias.

"You poor guy," Casey said, "but I'll tell you a secret." She leaned toward him. "I just saw Reverend Nolan's van pull up."

"What does that mean?"

She stepped behind him, put her hands on his shoulders, and turned him to face the exterior door. "Keep your eyes on that doorway and you'll see what I mean." She went back to the other side of the table.

"I take it this means Gizzy Nolan is going to audition," Olivia said. "Elizabeth or Jane?"

"Sorry," Casey said. "She's going for Jane."

"Poor Hildy," Olivia said.

Jack was watching the doorway but nothing was happening. He was about to turn away when an incredibly pretty girl walked in. She paused a few steps in and looked around. The bright out-door light was behind her and a breeze moved her long, thick hair. The shape of her was extraordinary, tall and slim but with a magnificent bosom. Small waist, curvy hips, and long, long legs. But her body was nothing compared to her beautiful face. She was like the princesses described in fairy tales: blonde hair, eyes like sapphires, full pink lips.

Jack, used to seeing spectacularly beautiful young women, could only stare.

"Darn!" Casey said loudly. "Gizzy didn't wear any makeup today. When she does, she's a knockout."

Turning, Jack looked at Casey in disbelief, then gave a little guffaw of laughter. "Is that local humor?"

Casey smiled. "It is. If you want to meet her, I suggest you get over there fast or you'll lose your place."

Three young workmen were putting down their hammers to go toward her. Jack covered the distance in just a few steps.

Olivia frowned. "That guy's a movie star. He'll leave soon. Gizzy's dad won't like that."

"I have an ulterior motive. In high school, Jack played Mr. Bingley, and he doesn't have a movie until the fall. If he could be enticed to stay here and be in our little local play, we'll be sure to have sold-out performances. And since it's all for charity . . ."

Olivia smiled. "So you're dangling Gizzy in front of him as bait?"

"Oh, yeah. There always have to be sacrifices for the greater good."

Olivia laughed. "Somehow, I don't think Gizzy is going to mind. But since you and Jack seem to get along so well, why don't you dangle yourself?"

"As much as I love Jack on the screen, seeing him in person isn't the same. Actually, I was wondering who the guy onstage is. He's not from around here. If I could act, I might try out for Lydia. Think I could pass for fifteen?"

"I think you should try for Elizabeth. Who's going to be Darcy?"

Casey lowered her voice. "Josh doesn't know it, but Kit plans to coerce him into playing the role."

"Josh has no idea what's in store for him?"

"None, but if I've learned anything since I've been in Summer Hill, it's that Mr. Christopher 'Kit' Montgomery gets whatever he wants. The owner of this warehouse said he would absolutely, positively *never* sell this place." Casey waved her hand. "You see what happened there. So anyway, if I played Elizabeth, I'd be pretending to fall in love with my brother. Yuck!"

Olivia smiled. "I can see your problem. Too old for Lydia, Lizzy is out, and Jane . . ."

"Will be given to Gizzy." She nodded toward the doorway. Jack and Gizzy were talking, and they made a very good-looking couple. As tall as Gizzy was, Jack was taller still, and her very feminine good looks were balanced by his rough handsomeness.

"I see you've done my work for me," Kit said from behind them.

Immediately, Casey understood what he meant. "You must know that Jack doesn't have a movie until September and you probably know he played Bingley in high school. Did . . ." She paused. "Did the other one tell you?"

Kit's eyes widened. "Are you referring to my cousin Tatton as 'the other one'?"

Casey shrugged. "Sounds like him to rat on his friends."

Kit made a sound of astonishment. "I thought he was the heartthrob of all women."

"Not this one," Casey said. "You want something to eat? I have some of those orange crêpes you like."

"No time now, but please save some for me." He was studying her in speculation, as though trying to figure something out.

"So how are you going to get Jack to agree to be in the play?"

"I'm going to wait until he comes to me and begs for the role." He looked at Olivia, lowered his voice, and spoke directly to her. "It was Elizabeth, but now it's to be Mrs. Bennet." Turning, he walked away.

"What was that about?" Casey saw that Olivia's face was red.

"Nothing," she said. "Do you think I should go buy some more pastries? Or cupcakes for lunch?"

"It's too early to know if we'll need them." Casey was staring at her, but Olivia wouldn't meet her eyes. "Did Kit mean he wants *you* to play Mrs. Bennet?"

"I have no idea." Olivia busied herself with rearranging food containers.

Three men came to the table asking for coffee and more doughnuts. Their conversation was full of "not fair" and "who does he think he is?" and "he should go back to Hollywood where he belongs." When they left, Casey and Olivia burst into giggles.

Jack and Gizzy had moved out of the doorway but were still talking. When he caught Casey's eye, he excused himself and came over to the table. "You have any more of those ..." He trailed off as he glanced at Gizzy, then back again. "She's smart and funny and as delicate as glass. I've never met anyone like her."

Casey glanced at Olivia, then back at him. "Look, Jack, we don't know each other very well, but you'll have to trust me on this: Gizzy is *not* made of glass."

Jack didn't seem to hear her. "She's trying out for Jane, and of course she'll get the part." He hesitated. "I was thinking I might audition for Bingley."

"What a great idea," Casey said. "Have you asked Kit yet?"

"Yeah, but he doesn't like it. He said some L.A. guy will call me and I'll fly away and leave them hanging. But I'm free until September and I could stay at Tate's house." He gave Casey a pleading look. "You'll cook for me? Fill that big shiny box in the kitchen?"

"I could do that." Casey tried to sound as innocent as she could manage. "If you can persuade Kit, that is. Hey! I have an idea that might help your case. If you have some L.A. publicity people, maybe you could get them to promote the play. Tell Kit they'll do it for free. After all, it is for charity."

"Brilliant idea," Jack said. "I'll make some calls and get it done. Wish me luck."

"I feel in my heart that Kit will consent to give you the role."

Smiling, Jack went back to where Gizzy was waiting for him.

Olivia was shaking her head. "I'm worried whether you and your co-conspirator are going to get into heaven."

"I think He forgives more when it's for charity. Besides, who knows? Maybe Jack and Gizzy will be a match."

Casey and Olivia looked at each other. A lot of men fell for Gizzy's outward beauty, but when they got to know her, they were turned off. She was a fearless daredevil inside the body of an angel. "Nah," they agreed. "It won't happen."

ACT ONE, SCENE FIVE

Lydia shows her true nature

At quarter to ten, the auditions began. The first was to be for the role of Lydia. Casting the part would get rid of twenty-some giggling, excited girls—and a few women who thought they could still pass for fifteen.

Kit, who would direct the play, told the girls that although the part of Lydia didn't have a lot of lines, it had to be believable that she had something about her that would attract an older man. True, she was giddy and frivolous. "But then, we men tend to like that," he said in such a suggestive way that everyone laughed.

All the girls with LYDIA on their badges went backstage, and as their turns came, they were helped into the high-waisted, low-cut dresses of the Regency era. Since the man playing Wickham was in costume, the girls would be too.

The first up was a local girl, a senior in high school, who was the head cheerleader and very popular. What she did and wore were constant topics of conversation among the girls at her school. The gossip was that three girls had dropped out because they were sure she'd get the role.

But she was awful! Olivia and Casey stood in the back, watching in horror as the girl showed what she thought was sexy. She played Lydia like a forty-year-old vamp from a black-and-white movie. All that was missing was a cigarette dangling from her lips.

When she finished, Kit graciously thanked her and she left the stage, smiling as though she knew she had the role.

Josh was standing by the food tables. "You have any more—?"

"Help yourself." Casey looked at Olivia. In silent agreement, they hurried down the center aisle to sit in the row beside Kit, who was behind a temporary desk.

"Did you come to watch a catastrophe?" Kit said under his breath.

"Oh, yes," Casey said. "So far it's more exciting than Jack Worth's last movie. Did you accept his offer of free publicity?"

"Of course. Next!" he said loudly, then removed an envelope from his pile of papers, reached across Casey, and handed it to Olivia.

She opened it, began to pull out a photo, then quickly put it back inside.

"What's that?" Casey asked.

"Nothing." Olivia's eyes were fixed straight ahead, on the stage.

Kit was also looking at the stage, where a girl was waiting. "Begin."

The second audition was as bad as the first. The girl stuttered over her lines and tripped on her skirt.

"My kingdom for some popcorn," Casey said.

It took two hours to get through all the auditions. They were mostly bad. The girls couldn't seem to disassociate real life from the character they were playing.

As for the man—Casey learned his name was Devlin Haines—he was excellent. No matter how many times he said his lines, they were always with feeling.

"Studied in New York," Kit said when Casey asked about him. "Gave up acting when he got married and had a kid. Said he needed the security of a regular job."

"Married?" Casey's voice showed that she didn't like that news.

"I believe he is now divorced."

"Interesting." Casey turned her attention back to the next audition. This Lydia—who was thirty if she was a day—said, "Shouldn't we kiss? That would make the scene more believable."

"Not in Austen," Kit said. "But maybe next time we'll do *Fanny Hill*."

"What's that?" she asked, but Kit didn't answer. Olivia and Casey had to bend forward to hide their faces so their laughter couldn't be seen.

By noon everyone was hungry and wanted a break, but Kit said there was one more girl they should see.

The girl who'd taken the pastry and juice came onstage. She had on the costume but wore a big cardigan over it, and she still looked so shy that they wondered if she'd speak.

"You're Lorraine Youngston?" Kit asked.

"Yes, and it's Lori Young," she answered rather timidly.

"She's spending the summer with her grandmother at the lake," Kit said to Casey and Olivia, then louder, "Begin, please."

Lori took her time removing her sweater and putting it on a chair. The stage hadn't been fully set but there were a few Regency-style props scattered about.

For the audition, Kit had written a scene that wasn't in the book and wouldn't be in the play—it was the first time Lydia and Wickham were alone.

Everyone watched as Lori walked across the stage to stand in front of Devlin. Then she changed. In a flash, she went from shyly slumping to shoulders back, her chest stuck out. When she smiled at Devlin, for a moment he seemed to lose his composure.

Her quick change in personality was similar to what Jack had done earlier. Casey looked at him, standing against the wall, and mouthed, "Like you." Nodding in agreement, Jack gave a thumbs-up.

Lori's performance was mesmerizing. She smiled and laughed—

and tempted. Devlin, who had been so in charge in all the other auditions, so perfectly in control, twice stumbled over his lines.

When Lori finished, she abruptly put her concealing sweater back on, resumed her shy expression, and stood there looking at Kit.

He took a moment, then said, "Thank you, Lydia. Shall we break for lunch?"

Lori left the stage, smiling in a quiet, unassuming way.

As they were serving lunch, Casey realized that she'd left six pies on the counter at her house. They were already having to supplement with food and desserts from local stores, so they needed the pies. Besides, she'd promised some people a slice of her berry custard pie.

She saw that Gizzy and Jack were sitting close together in a corner, full plates on their laps. She asked him if she could borrow the truck and said, no, there was no need for him to drive her there and back.

Jack handed her the keys and as she headed for the door, Casey told Olivia that she'd be back in a few minutes.

Darcy's pride suffers

Tate put his head back against the leather seat of the car and closed his eyes. Could this day possibly get any worse?

When he'd awakened early this morning, after a night of flopping around in bed, he knew he had to face his demons head-on. Even though it wasn't yet full light, he knew he must go outside and look around. It's what his sister, Nina, had been telling him to do for years.

Just three months ago, she'd again started in on him. "You spent all that money restoring the place but you've never even seen it. You have to go. Today. Now."

"I know." Tate was looking out the glass wall of his L.A. home. "I should go for a visit."

"Right!" his sister said. "Mom would have wanted you to spend time there. She—"

"Nina!" Tate cut her off. "I know all of this. You don't have to remind me."

She calmed down. "Stacy and Kit have done a magnificent job of restoring the house and garden. Emma and I love the place! It's so beautiful and peaceful. And everything Mom told us about is there. The barn, the pond, the chicken house. All of it. Remember the sour clover?"

"Of course," Tate said softly. "I remember everything."

"And Stacy did a great job of bringing Mom's little house up to date." Nina lowered her voice. "The old shower is there. Remember the story of the kids coming in from the pond and showering off outside?"

"And the tadpoles clinging to them," Tate said. "I remember, and I promise that I'll be there soon after you and Emma arrive. I bet the weather there is nicer than in Massachusetts."

"No," Nina said firmly. "You need to spend some time there by yourself."

"Does that mean you filled a room full of tissues for all my tears?"

Nina didn't laugh. "It won't be that bad. I promise. Once you're there, everything will be fine. You'll see the source of all the old stories. And you'll see what Stacy and I chose for the house. I'm sure you'll love it."

"Are there red flowers on the chair in the living room?"

"Of course," Nina said. "I sent you a fabric sample, remember?"

"Yeah, I do. Maybe Jack can go with me."

"That's a fabulous idea! Jack is always cheerful and he'll make you laugh. And Stacy stocked the house. She told me about going to a big warehouse store and filling the truck with supplies. There are paper towels, dishwashing detergent, and everything for the washer and dryer. You do remember how to use them, don't you? You haven't become such a big-deal movie star that you can no longer wash your own socks, have you?"

"I leave being a princess to Jack."

"I dare you to say that to him." Nina was beginning to sound relaxed.

"So how's Emmie, my beautiful and divine little niece?" He knew that mentioning her would change the subject.

That conversation had been months ago and now he was here— and every bad thing he'd predicted was coming true. He was in a car in the garage of the huge old house and everything had gone wrong. First there'd been the pajama woman this morning, then finding that there was no food in the house, and Jack was saying he was going to leave.

And that was the *good* part of the day! This morning he went upstairs to read a script that his agent had sworn was different from his usual movies. "No more sulking, sullen heroes," she'd said. "This is an action film."

When he started to read it, Tate had been smiling. But the "action" consisted of driving a six-horse carriage down a rough road at midnight in pursuit of a young actress who had nothing more to recommend her than a giant, artificially produced bosom. He'd met the girl and she had the IQ of a rabbit.

When he'd finished the script, he tossed it across the room. It was time for lunch, his stomach was growling, and he was ready to call a helicopter service to come and get him. But first he had to get something to *eat*!

When he got to the garage, he saw that the pickup truck he'd bought was gone. Parked beside its spot was a new BMW, and the keys were on a hook by the door.

But the damned car wouldn't start. He took a moment to think about how everything about this place had been a lie, then he picked up his cell and called his sister.

Georgiana persuades her brother

When Nina saw Tate's name on the phone's caller ID, she didn't want to answer it. She knew all this was difficult for her big brother, but she also knew she wouldn't help by babying him. When their mother died, Tate had taken her death very hard. Since he was nine, he'd helped support his mother and sister with his acting. And he'd always promised them that someday he'd make enough money to buy back Tattwell, the plantation that had been in their family for centuries.

But that hadn't happened while their mother was alive. She never got to see Tate's great success, and it was only after her death that he'd been able to buy the plantation.

After he bought the place, Nina and Emmie spent a lot of time there. Nina oversaw the restoration and Emmie explored the grounds. Nina hired a local interior designer, Stacy Hartman, to decorate the house as close as possible to what their mother had described to them. With Kit's help—and his memories of the place—furniture, wallpaper, paint, light fixtures were all put back the way they had been when Ruth Tattington was a girl.

Nina's problem had been getting her brother to visit the place. He'd been in one movie after another, filming in several countries, and he'd used that as an excuse not to go to the plantation.

She knew Tate dreaded the memories that Tattwell would

bring to the surface and also that he was angry at himself for not having been able to buy it sooner. But Nina also knew that the only way for Tate to let go of the past was to see the place.

It had taken a lot of work on her part to get Tate to promise that when he finished his last movie—in which he played yet another angry, brooding man—he'd spend a whole month at the plantation.

Nina refused to go with him because she knew that with her and Emmie there, Tate would stay with them and never venture out into the pretty little town of Summer Hill, Virginia. She'd even told Stacy that under no circumstances was she to put any food in the house. Maybe hunger would force Tate out to meet people.

And, well, okay, what Nina especially wanted was for her brother to meet Stacy, the decorator. The pretty blonde young woman was smart and funny and had a good outlook on life. She was exactly what her brother needed.

Taking a breath, Nina reached for her phone to answer her brother's call, but then the ringing stopped, and she smiled. Her six-year-old daughter, Emma, was home ill from school today and she was as restless a patient as Tate was. Nina had been up most of the night with her, and right now she had to see what her daughter needed.

Darcy runs afowl of Lizzy

When Tate's call to his sister went to voicemail, he gritted his teeth. "Just so you know," he said from his end, "that girl, Stacy, left only coffee. No food. I'd go get some—if this two-bit town has a restaurant, that is—but Jack took the truck and the car is dead. I'm starving but I have no transportation. And by the way, the new script my agent sent me is worse than the last two I got. Why can't I play a villain in a Batman movie? Jack's leaving tomorrow and I'm going with him. After I spend a few hours helping Kit find someone to play Elizabeth, that is. Then I'm free to get out of here. Call me when you can." He clicked off.

He got out of the car and pushed the button for the garage door. He was sure his sister was avoiding him, and he knew why. He'd promised her that he'd give the place a chance and he wanted to be able to say that he'd done that, but it wasn't easy. Look what had happened to him on his first excursion onto the property!

As the door went up, Tate was greeted with the sight of a truly gorgeous garden. Huge old trees shaded a pretty brick path that disappeared through tall shrubs that were beginning to flower.

Just as he knew it would, his mother's voice came to him as she used to describe the flowering bushes. "Pink for Letty and white for Ace," she'd say as she snuggled in bed between her two children. Nina often fell asleep, but Tate always asked to hear more about his mother and her childhood friend, Ace. And too, Tate liked that his mother's stories told of a time when the Tattington family had owned acres of land and had been senators and governors. "I want to hear about Ace saving the house from burning down," he'd say.

As she told the story yet again, he'd fall asleep, then she'd carry Nina to her own bed. From the time he was a kid, Tate said, "When I grow up, I'm going to be just like Ace."

The idea of becoming Ace had strongly influenced his becoming an actor. He liked the thought of pretending he was someone else.

Nina hadn't given him the caretaker's number, but if he could find the man's house, maybe he could get a ride into town or to the auditions. Pulling out his phone, he kept walking as he tapped out a text message to his assistant in L.A. He asked her to make plane reservations for Jack and him for tomorrow. AND HAVE A CAR DELIVERED HERE, he added, then sent the message.

He would return to L.A. and do what he could to get a role that was different from what he'd been doing for the last few years. Maybe he could get a part in the second *Avatar* movie. It would be nice to be tall and blue. Or how about a horror film? Or maybe Disney had—

He broke off when he looked up and saw that he was just a few feet from the pretty pajama girl's house. To his shock, the whole bottom of the screen door was torn out. There was a smaller hole in the upper half. He remembered doing that one, but had he been so angry that he'd also kicked in the bottom?

His cell rang. It was Nina and he touched the button to take the call. "Why did no one tell me some girl was living in Mom's house?"

"And good morning to you too," Nina said. "Maybe Stacy is staying there. Blonde, blue-eyed, and as pretty as a doll?"

"No, and stop trying to fix me up. This one is tall, red hair, really built. And she cooks. Or I think she does. She had no idea I own the place. I'm not sure she's ever seen me before."

"Good!" Nina snapped. "But if I'd known you wanted a fan staying in there, I would have advertised in *The Hollywood Reporter*."

"I don't want—" He let out his breath. "Okay, right, there's no reason she should know, but if I'd been told, I wouldn't have . . . I certainly would have thought twice before I . . ."

"What did you do?"

"Took a shower on the porch."

"Oh," she said. "Like Letty and Ace used to do? In a swimsuit?"

"Didn't have time to dress," Tate mumbled.

"You mean you had no time to put on a suit? So what did you do? Shower naked on her front porch?"

"The shower is at the back of the house, but, yeah, I did."

"Full frontal?" Nina was barely suppressing her laughter.

"Yeah." There was a hint of laughter in his voice. "I'm not sure but I think she sat on a stool and drank a cup of tea while she watched."

Nina laughed. "People usually have to pay to see you do that."

"In all my movies, there's been only one bathing scene. It was under a waterfall and it was shot from the side."

"But then you moved so they got your back and your bare chest, and afterward you walked around in a towel that wouldn't cover one of Emmie's dolls."

"Okay." Tate was laughing. "So I have to earn a living. Look, I need transportation and I have to get someone to repair a screen door."

"What's wrong with it?"

"I was sort of . . . well, unhappy when I saw Miss Pajamas in my house. I thought she was taking photos. I sort of put my fist through the screen. And from the look of the place, I may have accidentally kicked the bottom half out too."

Nina's voice was serious. "Tate, that's not funny. You're big, and when you get angry your whole face changes. Onscreen it's great, but in real life you can be frightening."

"I know." His voice was apologetic. "I've already heard this from Jack. And I will apologize to her. I'll probably see her this afternoon, but right now I need a car so I can get food. You think this town has a taxi service?"

"I doubt it, but I'll call the——"

"Holy crap!" Tate said.

"What is it?"

"There's something upstairs in her house. I think it's a bird. It's the size of a dog and I think it's trying to get out. It's pecking at the window screen."

"Oh, no!" Nina said. "It's probably a peacock or a peahen. I forgot to tell you that Stacy said the caretaker was releasing them today. The birds have to bond with their environment, so they've been in cages. Remember Mom telling us about that huge peacock and how she and Ace used to——"

"Nina!" Tate yelled.

"Right. Oh, no. Emmie is calling me. She's home sick in bed today. Why don't you go chase the pea-critter and let Emmie watch on her iPad? It'll entertain her while I call the caretaker."

Nina didn't wait for his answer but hung up and quickly left a voicemail for the Tattwell caretaker. He probably wouldn't get the message before evening, but Nina didn't mind. One great thing about having an actor for a brother was that he loved to entertain. He could make the most mundane of events seem spectacular.

Surely, chasing a peacock in a small house would cheer up Tate—
and watching him would occupy her daughter for a while.

She ran to Emmie's room and grabbed her tablet.

It took Nina just minutes to sync phone and iPad between her
brother and her daughter, and set it all to record. Sometimes her
brother gave his best performances for his family and she liked to
see them. She gave Emmie a bag of vegetable chips and some
juice, put the tablet on the stand, and headed to the bathroom. If
she knew her brother and daughter—kindred spirits if ever there
were any—she'd have at least half an hour to herself. She would
be within hearing distance, but she was going to soak in a tub of
very hot water for as long as she could manage.

Tate smiled at his pretty little niece, who looked unhappy at being
confined to her bed, even if it did have pink and white ruffles.
Since she was born, the two of them had had their own little
world. They understood each other. Tate said that entertaining
Emmie fulfilled his need to be writer/director/producer/actor all
in one. And he did indeed work to come up with new ways to
make her smile.

He put his finger to his lips. Today, he was going the way of a
silent film. The first thing he did was put on some music, and
he knew that for chasing a predatory bird, only Bizet's *Carmen*
would do.

Holding his phone at arm's length, he began tiptoeing toward
the house. When he got to the screen door, he showed her the
huge bottom hole and pantomimed a monster clawing its way
inside. He bit his nails in fear.

Emmie, in keeping with her uncle's silence, pantomimed opening a door and shrugged in question.

Tate gave an exaggerated look of embarrassment and pointed
to himself.

Why? Emmie asked, palms up.

Acting ashamed, Tate stroked long hair for a girl, then pointed to himself. He wore the scowl that was so famous in his movies, and he mimicked the girl putting her arms up in fear.

Emmie shook her head. That was bad of him to frighten her.

Nodding in agreement, Tate wore an I'm-sorry face.

Inside the house, he moved his phone around to show the kitchen, with spices and herbs hanging up and drying, tall bottles of oils, and fat jars of jam with their pretty cloth covers. He panned down the skillets hanging from hooks in the wall.

Emmie's eyes widened at the sight. Her mother barely knew how to make a grilled cheese sandwich. She pointed up and Tate took a jar off the shelf. The label said PEAR JAM WITH MANDARIN TEA. Smiling, she nodded vigorously. It looked delicious.

Tate put on a sad face and rubbed his stomach to show how hungry he was. As he filmed, he stopped at the big trash bin and saw two cold fried eggs on top. It took him a moment to come up with a reason for their being there. Was it possible that she'd prepared them for him? If she had tried to deliver them . . . He didn't like to think that she'd overheard what he'd said to Jack.

Emmie waved her hands to ask him what the problem was.

Tate showed the eggs, pointed at himself, then made tear marks down his cheeks.

Again, Emmie shook her head at him. He had been *very* bad.

On a countertop along a sidewall was a low row of something covered by white cloths. When Tate pulled one of the cloths back, he saw a pie with a crust made of long pieces of perfectly browned dough. The top looked like a flower. Underneath, berries oozed atop a golden custard.

Tate didn't have to fake his longing and hunger. He snatched away the other covers. There were six pies, each with a different top. They were works of art! One had meringue on it high enough to make a pillow. There was a tart with six fruits arranged in a pattern, another had peach slices baked in cream, one was topped with lots of little cut-out leaves, all perfectly browned, and on the end was a rolled-up crust filled with apricots and sliced almonds. The divine smell of the pies made him dizzy.

Tate's hunger and the beautiful pies were more than he could resist. There was a big spoon nearby and he grabbed it—but Emmie started waving her arms no. He could *not* steal the lady's food.

It wasn't difficult for Tate to silently show his hunger and his pure, deep lust for them.

But Emmie didn't give in. Her pantomime reminded him of what he'd done to the screen door. He did not deserve any of what the lady had cooked.

Tate sniffed hard and wiped away fake tears, but at last he put his shoulders back. He was going to be brave and strong and resist the food.

When there was a screech from upstairs, Tate's eyes widened. He looked terrified and as though he was going to run away.

But Emmie vigorously shook her head to let him know that it was just a bird. She silently encouraged him to proceed.

Holding his phone, he slowly went up the stairs, stopping three times to mimic fear. Each time, Emmie had to be firm to make him continue.

The stairs led to a landing outside the bedroom. Scattered around on the floor were objects that looked to have been on top of the dresser. By the window was a huge iridescent peacock, its long tail elegantly dragging behind it.

Tate plastered himself against the open door, his arms out-stretched in terror. The music was building in pace. Turning, he threw himself back over the doorway, too frightened to stay in the room.

It was Emmie's gestures, especially when she slapped her fist into her palm, that made him stay. She told him to go back in the room and close the door. This caused more fear from Tate; he was shivering all over.

The bird, now trapped in the room, leaped onto a chair by the window and tried to tear its way out through the screen.

Tate stood where he was and shrugged in puzzlement. Now what should he do? he silently asked of his niece.

Emmie made motions that he was to take off his shirt.

Tate showed shock and modestly crossed his arms over his chest.

Giggling, Emmie shook her head. He should take off his shirt and throw it over the bird.

There was more feigned fear from Tate, but he took off his big shirt, leaving a T-shirt on underneath. Like a matador in the bull-ring, he held his plaid shirt out, challenging the bird to charge forward. He had his shoulders back, his head cocked at a bull-fighter's angle, and his swagger was a perfect imitation.

Emmie was laughing and shaking her head no, no, no. Throw the shirt *over* the bird.

With reluctance, Tate quit the matador strut and fearfully held out his shirt toward the bird. After some elaborately missed attempts, he dropped the cloth over the bird's head, threw his arm around it, then looked at Emmie. Now what? he seemed to ask.

She pointed at the window in her own bedroom. He should let the bird out.

Tate nodded as though that was the wisest thing he'd ever heard. With one hand, he slid up a screenless window, lifted the bird, and tried to pull his shirt off its head. But to Tate's shock, the terrified creature leaped back inside. As Tate attempted to wrestle it into going in the right direction, its long tail slapped him in the face. His very genuine coughing fit made Emmie fall over in laughter.

When the chaos finally settled, Tate was sitting on the floor, the bird was on the roof of the front porch, and Tate's shirt was hanging by a button from the gutter.

Emmie howled in laughter.

Tate tried to get up, pretended to stumble, but when he reached the level of the window, there was the bird, its beak about three inches from his nose. The creature gave its loud, hideous scream right into Tate's face.

Genuinely startled, Tate fell backward onto the floor, and the bird ran to the edge of the roof and fluttered down.

A bit dazed, Tate got off the floor, closed the window, and dramatically wiped the sweat off his brow. A survey of the room showed that it was a mess. Emmie motioned for him to clean it up.

Tate gave an exaggerated, silent groan. He lifted his hands in a way to indicate that he was a man. He did *not* clean rooms.

Emmie shook her finger at him. He had to!

With a sigh, Tate straightened the bed, used tissues to wipe bird droppings away, and put things back on the dresser. The pajamas he remembered so well were on the floor.

He stepped back as though they were poison.

Emmie motioned for him to pick them up.

Tate, his face serious, shook his head no. He pointed to them, then made a motion of cutting his own throat. If he touched those PJs, the woman who owned them would murder him.

Emmie tried to get her uncle to put the pajamas away, but no matter what she suggested, he wouldn't do it.

As Tate went downstairs, he made motions that he was a hero—but then his stomach growled so loudly that Emmie heard it over the music. He rolled his eyes, showing that he was dizzy with hunger. In the kitchen, he looked at the pies on the side counter with true longing, then back at his niece, his eyes pleading.

She gave in and nodded. Yes, he had earned a slice of pie.

But Tate didn't get a plate and a knife and cut himself a piece.

He propped the phone up on the counter, then picked up a big cooking spoon. Grabbing the pie with the flower-like crust, he scooped out the entire center with the spoon. He ate with such gusto that he got dark-red juice all over the lower half of his face, pieces of berry lodging in his stubble.

As he chewed, he showed his ecstasy over the flavor with his eyes and smiles. He dropped down onto a stool and ate, enjoying every bite. Juice ran down his chin; berries fell onto his T-shirt. As he scratched his ear, he got pie filling in his hair. When there was only a shell left, he used both hands to break it apart and eat it, all while using his eyes to show how delicious it was.

Emmie was laughing very hard.

"What the hell are you doing?" came a woman's angry voice. The damaged screen door slammed behind her.

Nina sat straight up in the tub, and Emmie yelled, "No!" Tate slipped his phone into the pocket of his T-shirt, camera pointed out, as he stood to face the woman in whose house he'd just trespassed. Miss Pajamas Lady. The woman who hated him. And right now she looked so angry he was almost afraid of her.

ACT ONE, SCENE NINE

Lizzy's impression of Darcy is not sweet

"Look what you did!" Casey said. "You ate an entire *pie*! The whole thing. Or did you just tear it up for the sport of it?"

Tate stepped away from her. "Ate it," he said.

"Oh, really? From the look of you, you took a bath in it."

Tate put his hand to his hair and pulled out a couple of blackberries. Sometimes he felt silly having such long hair, but his contracts called for it. No wig, no extensions, just lots of real hair.

"I guess you did all this because you think you can. You own the place, plus you're a movie star, so you can walk into someone's home and steal her food. Is that what was in your mind?"

When Tate backed into a stool, he sat down.

Casey glared at the ruffle-edged pie plate. It was an Emile Henri, and her mother had given it to her for her eighteenth birthday. Last night she'd put her favorite pie in it, but now it was nearly empty. Just a piece of crust clung to the bottom. "I promised Josh and Kit some of that pie, but now it's gone." She looked back at him as he sat there in silence, watching her. "This morning I felt really bad about what happened. I should have told you I was there as soon as I saw you strip naked. But I didn't."

Tate raised his eyebrows.

"I sat there and watched you and later I was prepared to lie about it. I was so afraid that you'd throw me out of my house that I planned to deny being where I was and seeing what I did." Her motion included his entire body.

"But I can't take this," she said. "I have to have privacy." She went to a far cabinet and opened an overhead door, but the two big plastic pie carriers were at the top. She stretched but couldn't reach them.

Tate's arm went over her head, pulled the containers out, and set them on the counter.

"Thanks," she said, then corrected herself. "I mean, no thanks. I don't need your help. Look at these things. They were made to hold *six* pies. Six! But now I have only five of them."

Tate went back to sit on the stool.

Casey began putting the pies in the carriers and loudly snapping the clasps. "Okay, I will leave. Since you believe that owner-ship and your ... what? Celebrityship—if that's a word. No! Entitlement. That's what it is. Your sense of entitlement allows you to shower on my back porch and wander in and eat what I've cooked for other people. Since I can*not* live with that, I must leave. Where I'm going to find a house with a decent kitchen so I can cook for Jack, I don't know."

"Jack?" Tate asked.

"Yes." She glared at him. "While you were wandering about the grounds in your birthday suit, Jack and I became friends." She gave him a look of triumph.

Tate seemed surprised—and very interested.

"Get your mind out of the gutter. Friends! That's what Jack and I are. Not that it's any of your business, but Jack is falling for Gisele Nolan. But then, that's understandable considering that she's so beautiful." Casey waved her hand. "Not that anything in Summer Hill interests a big movie star like you, but anyway, your friend is going to spend the summer here so he can play Bingley.

And Gizzy will be Jane. Jack is going to live in your big, unused house, and I'm going to cook for him. It would have been perfect since I live close by, but now you've ruined everything. Can you drive?"

Tate's eyebrows were high on his forehead as he gave a single nod.

She took the truck keys off the counter and tossed them to him. "Good. Get what's left of the pies and put them in the truck, then drive us to the auditions. I don't know why he'd want you, but Kit expects you to be there."

Casey, still so angry she could hardly see, got into the passenger seat and slammed the door. When Tate got in beside her, she said, "I'd ride in the back but it's illegal." She looked out the windshield. "Please tell me that isn't your shirt hanging from my roof!"

Tate bent forward to look up. His blue plaid shirt was still caught in the gutter, waving in the breeze. He got out, grabbed the tip of it, pulled it down, and got back into the truck.

Casey's teeth were clamped together. "Were you in my bedroom?"

Tate was looking at his shirt. There was a big hole in the front. "Do you know how to sew on a button?"

That made Casey so angry her hands went into fists. She started to go after his throat, but what sounded like a child's laughter stopped her. "What was that?"

"Emmie. She's my six-year-old niece." Tate put his arm across the seat, backed the truck up, and headed toward the big gate. "Emmie truly loves it when someone yells at me. Her mother—my sister—does it all the time." He gave Casey the smile he used on-screen to make the heroine say she loved him. It was the one the fan mags said made women start removing their clothes.

But it did nothing for Casey. She glared at him. "You're an egotistical jerk, and turn off your phone."

She didn't say another word all the way to the auditions.

When they got to the warehouse, Casey started to get out of the truck, but Tate pushed the button to lock her in. She didn't look at him, just crossed her arms over her chest and stared out the front window.

"I want to say I'm sorry," Tate said. "I never meant to invade your privacy. I was wrong to get angry at you this morning, and you are right. Even though I own the place, I should *not* run around in my birthday suit."

Casey didn't meet his eyes. His apology didn't sound real. It was as though it had been scripted and rehearsed—and he was saying it all with a touch of humor. But worse was that his tone seemed smugly certain that she would immediately forgive him for whatever he'd done.

"I'm going to leave tomorrow." He sounded sad. "I'm going back to L.A., where ... well, I'm going home. Please remain in the house. If Jack stays here—"

She glared at him. "What do you mean? *If* Jack stays?"

Tate gave her a little smile. "I don't want to disparage anyone. I'm sure the girl he's attracted to is beautiful, but Jack has many obligations and people who depend on him."

"Ooooooh," Casey said. "*Important* people, who no doubt have barrels full of money. Jack can't possibly stay in little Summer Hill, Virginia, and be in a tiny local production and—"

"That isn't what I meant!" Tate said. "I just think that Jack won't stay. His agent will call and he'll—"

"Fly out on the next jet? For what? So he can spend more time with people like *you*? If you don't unlock this door and let me out of here, I'm going to start screaming."

Right then Josh came out of the building and Casey started pounding on the window.

Frowning, he came over, and as Josh touched the handle, Tate unlocked the door. "Everything all right here?"

"It is now." Casey slid to the ground.

Josh was glaring at Tate as though trying to figure out what was going on.

"Hi, I'm—"Tate began.

"I know who you are," Josh said. "Why was Casey hitting on the glass to get my attention? Did you lock her in the truck?"

"Josh!" Casey said. "The door stuck, just let it go. Besides, he's leaving our town tomorrow. Help me with the pies, will you?"

It took Josh a moment, but he turned back to Casey. "Kit and I saved room for your berry custard."

Casey gave a sound that was like a growl. "It's gone. Every bit of it was eaten!" She took a breath. "What happened while I was away?"

Josh got the pie carriers out of the back. "No surprise: Kit gave Jack the Bingley role, and Gizzy will be Jane."

The truck door was still open, and Casey knew Tate was sitting inside. She raised her voice so he could hear. "Has Kit persuaded you to be Darcy?"

"He's tried, but I'm not sure I can do it," Josh said.

She put her arm in his. "You'd be the best-looking man to ever play him—even better than *any* man in the movies." Casey spoke so loudly she was nearly shouting. She walked with Josh back into the warehouse.

Darcy's world is challenged

Tate sat where he was, his head back against the seat. He didn't think he'd ever felt so unwelcome in his life. Ever since he'd started acting as a kid, people would stop and point excitedly when they saw him. "Aren't you that boy on . . ." had been something he heard often.

From the time he was sixteen, he'd been greeted by squealing females.

When he'd been in the house with that peacock, in the back of his mind he'd thought how Miss Pajamas would forgive him for his earlier rudeness. But she hadn't even given him a chance to explain. She certainly hadn't acted like he'd thought she would!

He could almost hear his sister's voice. "What did you expect, that she'd say, 'Tate Landers ate my best pie! I am the luckiest person on earth!'"

Well, actually, maybe he had thought that. But then, maybe when he saw the peacock in her house he should have called animal protection. And he should have called Kit to come get him. He should have—

He ran his hand over his face. All in all, he did *not* want to go inside that old warehouse and face all those people. Was the entire town of Summer Hill made up of people like Miss Pajamas? When he got in there, would she have told them he'd eaten the pie everyone wanted?

He started the truck. Maybe he'd just drive directly to the air-port and take the next flight out. Instead, he moved the truck to the far side of the parking lot and sat there with the motor run-ning as his phone charged. When the passenger door was flung open, he wasn't surprised.

"Why aren't you answering your phone?" Jack got into the passenger side of the truck and closed the door.

"Dead battery."

Jack was looking at his friend. "You're scared, aren't you? You're so terrified of all those women that you're afraid to go in there. But I don't blame you. They're an excitable lot. They made fools of themselves over the guy who's playing Wickham. He's good, but the last girl who read with him is better. She may be a young Meryl Streep." Jack paused. "What's really eating you?"

Tate gave a half smile. "'Eating.' Perfect word." Turning, he leaned against the door. "What's this about you and the girl play-ing Jane? From what I heard, it was love at first sight."

"I bet Casey told you that." Jack was grinning in a silly way.

"Casey?"

"Miss Pajamas? Remember her?"

"Oh, yeah," Tate said. "I think maybe she carved a new spot in my brain just for her. But forget that. Who is this Jane?"

"She's beautiful." Jack's eyes seemed to look far away.

"Of course she is. The town beauty queen. Won all the prizes. Best swimsuit. But is there anything else about her that you like—or have you noticed?"

"No beauty pageants. Her dad is the local Baptist minister. We haven't stopped talking all morning. We tried out for the roles of Bingley and Jane and it was perfect. I really *felt* the lines!"

"I thought you were going home with me tomorrow."

Jack gave a snort. "No, I'm staying here. Kit didn't want to give me the role because he said I'd leave, but I swore I wouldn't. I don't have to be back until September."

"What about your training? You can't show up in the fall with a gut from eating entire berry pies for lunch."

"Who does a stupid thing like that?" Jack said. "I've already talked to the producer and he's sending a trainer here. He wasn't happy about it, but I told him this was the way it was and that's it. What about you?"

"I'm leaving at noon tomorrow and glad to go. Have you thought this through? You're staying here because you're hot for the preacher's daughter, but what happens after you get her? These small-town girls aren't usually happy with one-night stands or even summer affairs. They want to tie a man down with kids and complaints that you didn't call them for a whole three days. They—"

"Maybe I want that!" Jack said. "Maybe I'm sick of going home to an empty house. Sick of girls who ask me if they can sign autographs because they've slept with me a couple of times. They want the man they see on the screen, not *me*."

"What did this girl put in your drink?"

Anger flashed across Jack's face, but then he laughed. "This town is like where I grew up, except that no one is singling me out for a parade. Anyway, my point is that I'm staying here for the summer. I'm going to be a regular person for as long as I can manage it. I guess I should ask if I can stay in your big empty house. Casey is going to cook for me."

"Casey again," Tate mumbled. "You sure seem to have hit it off with all the women in this town."

Jack looked at his friend. "Okay, so what's the truth of why you're hiding out here in your truck? There are half a dozen women inside waiting to audition for Elizabeth."

"Did Kit tell them I'd be reading Darcy?"

"Of course not. If he did, you'd have to deal with every female in town. You should have seen the lineup to play Lydia, and all because the Wickham guy was okay-looking."

"What about whoever is playing Darcy?"

"Rumor is that it will be a guy named Josh Hartman. He's been building the sets, he's six two, and he looks good in a bland sort of way. But the girls seem to like him. By the way, Kit told me your costume for the auditions arrived and it's backstage in your dressing room."

"What about Miss Over the Moon Pajamas? What's she trying out for?"

Jack grinned. "She's not auditioning, but then, in my opinion, she's a contender for the world's best cook. She used to run Christie's in D.C."

"Nice place," Tate said, "but she hates me."

"Females don't hate you."

"*She* does. I, uh, well, I ate one of the pies she made to bring here."

"Some berry custard thing? With a top crust like a flower? Everybody's been saying it was missing. You didn't steal a pie, did you? I mean, really?"

Tate rolled his eyes. "Not you too! Yeah, I stole *that* pie. And, yes, I ate the whole thing. With a spoon. A *big* spoon. But after what I did for her, I deserved it. But she didn't even ask why I'd done it. She just assumed that I was doing something bad in her bedroom. It's a wonder she didn't call the sheriff."

Tate stopped talking and glared out the window.

"Casey was only gone for a few minutes. What the hell did you *do* to her?"

"Me?!" Tate said. "She was the one who—" He broke off because he realized Jack was laughing at him. This was one of the reasons they were friends. Jack could laugh at anything, while Tate could always see past the surface.

"What are you going to do?" Jack asked. "Stay out here and watch your phone charge? From what I've seen of that man Kit, he'll come out and drag you inside. Do you know what he did before he retired?"

"I have no idea. In the time we spent together, he didn't reveal much about himself. He said we're related through his mother's family, but I'm not sure how. I know he visited Tattwell when he was a kid because he helped Nina. Why?"

"Just curious. From the way he walks, I think he's ex-military." He picked up Tate's phone. "This is charged enough. You had a call from your sister, and Emmie sent you a photo of a peacock with its tail spread. What's that about?"

Tate took his phone from Jack. "I had to wrestle one of the beasts this morning at Casey's house and it almost won. Stay out of my messages. You ready to go in?"

"Think you can stand it? Want me to run inside and get you a piece of pie for energy?"

Groaning, Tate got out of the truck and they walked together to the front of the warehouse.

Jack halted. "Maybe Casey could make you a peacock stew. Are those things edible? Hey! How about some peacock PJs?"

Tate put his fists up like a boxer. "Maybe I should stay and be your trainer." He made a double left jab at Jack's face.

Jack easily ducked and sent a right cross to Tate's stomach.

But Tate twisted to avoid it and hit out with a left uppercut, which also missed its mark. Jack countered, and they went back and forth.

"Halt!" came a powerful voice.

Both men dropped their hands and came to attention.

Kit was standing in front of the warehouse doors with a scowl on his face. "Inside. Now." Turning, he went back into the building.

"Yeah, military," Tate whispered.

"Or dictator of a large country," Jack said.

Tate nodded in agreement. It was possible.

Mrs. Bennet reveals herself

When Casey got back to the food tables, Olivia had finished putting out the desserts from the local bakery and people were helping themselves. Since Kit had announced who was going to play Lydia, most of the high school girls had left. There were still some minor parts to cast, but most of the people were waiting to audition for Elizabeth. Since everyone in town was sure Josh was going to be Darcy, a lot of women wanted the part. Several of them had tried for dates with him, but few had succeeded. Hope for the future was written on their faces.

Casey opened the pie containers Josh had set on the table.

"I've heard about some berry custard pie you make that's supposed to be heavenly," Olivia said.

"It's not here. It was consumed in its entirety." Casey's voice was terse.

"Oh?" Olivia asked in an encouraging way. "What happened?"

"I guess his royal highness got hungry, but I still can't believe he ate a whole pie. He probably had one slice, didn't like it, and threw the rest out."

"Who?"

Casey waved her hand. "It doesn't matter, except that he's going to be here in—" She broke off because a woman hurried to the tables. She was tall and strongly built. Her face was long, her hair dark, and her eyes seemed to be flashing in anger.

"It's not fair!" she said to Olivia. "I wasn't given a proper chance to be Jane. If I'd known that sucking up to that B-movie actor would get me the part, I could have dealt with it. Or I could have tried out for Lydia. But really! To give the part of Jane to that wimpy little Gisele Nolan was ridiculous. She—"

"Hildy!" Olivia said. "This is Casey, and this is my daughter-in-law, Hildy."

She looked Casey up and down, as though appraising her. "What are *you* trying out for?"

Her tone of aggression, combined with her rather deep voice, made Casey blink. "Nothing. I'm just here to cook."

"Good!" Hildy said. "Stick to that, although I must say that your shrimp was a bit too spicy for my taste. You should call me and I'll give you my own recipe."

"I'll consider that." Casey stepped away to the end of the table.

"Hildy, that wasn't very nice," Olivia said.

Hildy turned her piercing gaze on her mother-in-law. "What are you doing back here at the food tables? People will think you're the maid. And what is this I hear about you trying out to be Mrs. Bennet? Are you showing off? You get a part but *I* don't? Is that what you want?"

Casey didn't like that this woman was taking her anger out on Olivia. Worse, Olivia was beginning to slump. Seconds ago her eyes had been full of laughter, and now her shoulders seemed to have fallen.

It wasn't any of her business, but Casey went to the other end of the table. "You aren't going to try out for Elizabeth?" she asked Hildy loudly.

Hildy glanced at Casey in dismissal. "This is a family matter." She looked back at her mother-in-law. "I don't think you should be in the play if I'm not. I'm sure this director will give you the part if you show him those ancient photos of yourself, but it wouldn't be fair to me. Besides, you're not exactly young, are you? This whole thing would exhaust you! I think—"

"Tate Landers is auditioning the Elizabeths," Casey interrupted.

Again Hildy turned to her, but this time her dark eyes were blazing in anger. "I told you that—" She stopped as she realized what Casey had said. "Who?"

"The actor Tate Landers. He owns Tattwell and he's a relative of Kit's. Landers is going to read Darcy with the women who audition for the role of Elizabeth."

Hildy blinked a few times, then she abruptly turned on her heel and left.

For a few moments it was awkward between Casey and Olivia, neither of them seeming to know what to say.

"I apologize for that," Olivia said. "When she's upset, Hildy forgets her manners."

Casey wanted to ask how often a bawling out like that happened and why Olivia didn't stand up to her. But it was too soon for personal questions like those. Besides, Olivia was so embarrassed that Casey thought she might leave. "What photos does she mean?"

"Oh, nothing," Olivia said. "It's just some long-ago history." She looked relieved that Casey wasn't commenting on Hildy's anger.

"Does it have anything to do with the envelope Kit gave you and how he called you Mrs. Bennet?"

When Olivia gave a bit of a smile, Casey was glad to see her shoulders begin to straighten. "Actually, it does. I did some acting when I was younger."

"You *have* to let me see!" Casey said. While it was true that she wanted to see photos of Olivia as an actress, she was even more interested in doing something to make her feel better. Hildy's words seemed to have taken the life out of Olivia.

Olivia took her handbag from under the table, pulled out the envelope Kit had handed her, and held it out.

Casey pulled out a shiny black-and-white head shot of a beautiful young woman, a younger Olivia. It was a three-quarter profile, and she looked like she was smiling at someone she loved. Her blonde hair was up in the back, with curls framing her face. The square neckline of her dress was quite low. "You're dressed as Elizabeth?"

"I was. I played her for twenty-four performances."

"Here in Summer Hill?"

"No." Olivia put the photo back in the envelope. "On Broadway. In New York."

"Wow!" Casey said. "You're a real live star."

Olivia smiled modestly. "Not at all. That was my only foray into that world, and it didn't last long."

"What happened?"

"Life. I had to return home to Summer Hill, then I met my late husband, Alan Trumbull, and . . ." She shrugged. "It didn't work out for me to go back to the stage."

"When was that?"

"Long ago. In the swinging seventies." She put the envelope back into her bag.

"But it looks like Kit saw you on Broadway."

"I guess he did. I didn't know that."

"But he remembers, so you must have been good," Casey said. "I think you should try out for—"

"Oh, no!" Olivia said quickly. "If I got a part and Hildy didn't, my life wouldn't be worth living." Olivia put her hand over her mouth. "Sorry. I shouldn't have said that."

Casey touched Olivia's hand. "My mother is a doctor, and she drilled it into me that half of abuse is the silence of the person who is on the receiving end."

Olivia stiffened. "Hildy isn't abusive. She just gets upset."

"Sorry," Casey said. "I overstepped, but I still think you should audition. Hey! If Hildy gets a role, will you try out too?"

"Possibly," Olivia said.

"Think of the smell of greasepaint and the footlights."

Olivia laughed. "It's not the 1890s, but that does sound good. I can do my work during the day, so most of my evenings will be clear."

"What's your job?"

"Actually, I live with my stepson and Hildy. I do what I can to help out."

Casey had to bite her tongue to keep from pointing out that Hildy had made a derogatory remark about Olivia being treated as a maid. But that's what Hildy seemed to think her mother-in-law was.

Casey saw Kit walking toward the exterior doors. "Excuse me, I have to ask Kit something." She practically ran to him. "You have to give Olivia's daughter-in-law, Hildy, the role of Lady Catherine de Bourgh. She thinks she's so pretty—which she is *not*—that she should have been chosen for Jane. She also thinks she's young enough—which she is not—to be Lydia. So now she's going to try for Elizabeth, but she won't get it. Who she is perfect for is that snobby, arrogant, bad-tempered Lady Catherine. If you, as the director, can reach Hildy's true personality, you'll have a great character. And best of all, if you give her that role, Olivia will audition for Mrs. Bennet."

Kit gave a bit of a smile. "Organizing the world, are you?"

"Just a few people. Do you agree?"

"Yes," Kit said. "Should I flatter this Hildy's ego?"

"Do anything you have to do to get her off Olivia's back."

Kit frowned. "What does that mean?"

"I'll tell you later. Just give Olivia the Mrs. Bennet role. That will help in many ways."

"I'd always planned for her to have it," Kit said. "Now, speaking of help, where is Tatton? I thought you were going to pick him up with the pies."

Casey bared her teeth. "I did bring him here, along with *five* pies. He ate one of them—so he says. But who knows what he actually did, since he was upstairs in my bedroom. And don't look at me like that! I have no idea what he was doing up there. He's the King of Entitlement so I'm sure he thought that because he owns the place he has a right to go anywhere he wants. He showers on my porch, eats the food in my house, and does whatever he did in my bedroom."

Kit was watching her with interest. "I don't think most women would object to young Tatton being in their kitchens. Or for that matter in their bedrooms."

"Whatever he is onscreen is *not* how he is in real life. Besides, I like to think women have more sense than that. To answer your question, I did my job and brought him here. Ask Jack where he is."

"Jack left the building twenty minutes ago. I can't believe he abandoned young Gisele for that long."

Turning, Casey saw the young woman in one of the seats. Already, there were two men sitting by her. "You think Jack and Gizzy could really make it together?"

"How much do you think Jack is like the characters he portrays in the movies?"

"You mean a reckless daredevil who risks his life every time he steps out the door?"

"That's about it," Kit said.

"I don't know, but since you've conned Jack into spending the summer here, it's my guess that Gizzy is going to make sure that we find out. Oh, look! There they are now." Outside in the bright sunlight were Jack and Tate. Jack looked happy, as though he was glad to be alive, but Tate was scowling. "I find it impossible to believe that women like that man."

"Think not?" Kit said, then his voice boomed out. "For today's reading of Elizabeth, the actor Tate Landers will play Fitzwilliam Darcy."

For a moment everyone in the building froze in place. It was like a sci-fi movie where a space traveler could stop time. A breeze whipped papers about, a bird called from outside, but inside, the people did not move so much as an eyelash.

Then, suddenly, it was as though the world started turning again, and the level of activity was like a dozen helicopter blades starting at once. World records were set in speed-dialing as every phone was attacked. It was a wonder the state's cell towers withstood the stampede.

"He's here!" screamed a voice into her phone. That was the only sentence that could be heard clearly. In the next second everyone was excitedly shouting into a phone. The voices of the people, male and female, as they called sisters, cousins, friends, spouses, everyone they knew, reached a decibel level that only a few merfolk could hear.

Kit looked down at Casey, his eyebrows raised as though to say, "I told you so."

She waved her hand toward the entrance. Tate and Jack were now in a fake boxing match. "Boys!" she mouthed to Kit, not even trying to be heard over the cacophony around them. Turning, she started back toward Olivia at the food tables.

But before she reached her, the room was filled with the sound of cars, trucks, and vans coming to an abrupt, screeching halt. Gravel was sent flying. In seconds, women ran inside, wearing clothes that ranged from dirty jeans to an evening gown with the price tag hanging off the low-cut bodice.

Minutes later, Jack had disappeared with Gizzy, but Tate was near the far wall with Kit. Around them were several women holding out scripts for Tate to autograph and staring up at him in adoration.

Kit looked across their heads to Casey with an expression that pointed out that some women did indeed *like* Tate.

Casey gave an exaggerated shrug. "Who can explain taste?" she seemed to reply.

Darcy takes the stage

"We're closing the food service down." Casey was standing by the tables. "Let people help themselves."

"Are you leaving?" Olivia asked.

"No. You and I are going to see the show." Casey rummaged inside a grocery bag under the table. "I sent Josh out for these." She pulled out two big bags of popcorn. "I thought that maybe there'd be fireworks when Kit announced who would help with the auditions, but this beats all my expectations. You and I are going to watch this fiasco in comfort."

"Surely with an actor like Tate Landers, things will run smoothly."

"Ha!" Casey said. "As far as I can piece together, Kit has used charity to shame the guy into performing. But Landers has made it clear that he doesn't want to do it. If these Elizabeths are half as bad as the Lydias this morning, I want to see his distaste and ar-rogance."

Olivia was looking at her in shock. "What in the world did that young man do to make you dislike him so much?"

"Let's see. Where do I begin? Bawled me out for sitting in my own house. Told Jack he thought I wasn't pretty enough for *him*. Broke into my house and ate one of the pies I made for my friends. And if all that weren't enough, I think he did something in my bedroom that made him take his shirt off and throw it onto my roof. Is that enough reason to dislike him?"

"I should say so!" Olivia said. "Come on, let's go and watch, and if he does a bad job we'll throw popcorn at him."

"Just so it isn't a pie. He'd like that too much."

Laughing, they went down the aisle to take seats by Kit at his desk.

The walls were lined with women who wanted to try out for Elizabeth, each one wearing varying degrees of fear and hope on her face. There was a two-page printout of the scene they were to use for the auditions, where Darcy says he wants to marry Elizabeth in spite of the fact that she is totally unsuitable to be his wife.

"None of them looks like she'd say no to him," Casey said. "From the way they keep glancing at the curtain, I think they're all hoping he asks them for real."

"I have to say that, even at my age, I was ready to run away with Mr. Landers when he played Heathcliff."

"You've seen his movies?" Casey asked.

"Of course. You haven't?"

"No," Casey said. "I've only seen *him,* and that was more than enough."

"But shirtless, he is—"

Casey snorted. "I've seen him with clothes and without them, and it's still no."

"How in the world—?"

"Quiet on the set," the stage manager shouted, and the curtain went up.

A young woman Casey had seen around town but didn't know was sitting at a desk and writing with a quill pen. She had on one of the prop dresses that had been used for the Lydia auditions, and she looked good.

From the right, Tate walked onto the set—and a collective sigh went through the auditorium. He wore a Regency suit, and from the way it fit it seemed to have been custom made for him. His tight trousers smoothed down over his heavy thighs and into tall boots. A vest clung to his flat stomach, and a black jacket showed off his broad shoulders.

Every eye was on the two people onstage.

When Tate spoke, his voice halted all motion. "'In vain I have struggled, but my feelings will not be repressed. You must allow me to tell you how ardently I admire and love you.'"

Everyone stared at him, mouths agape. He sounded like a man who was truly in love and torn apart by it. The angst, the misery, and the love were all there.

The young woman playing Elizabeth looked at him in open-mouthed astonishment—and said nothing.

Seconds clicked by and all she did was stare at Tate.

"'Sir, I thank you,'" Kit prompted. She remained silent. "'I believe I should express my gratitude for your sentiments,'" Kit said louder, "'even though I do not return them.'"

"Oh, yes," she whispered. "'I believe . . .'" she began. "I mean, 'I thank you.'" She straightened her shoulders. "'I'm sorry I caused you pain, but I hope it doesn't last long.'"

She had skipped lines and misquoted, but worse, as she spoke she stepped toward Tate until she was almost touching him.

Through all of it, Tate never lost his look of anguish and love. Even when she touched his chest with her index finger, he didn't break character.

"Cut!" Kit yelled.

Instantly, Tate stepped back from the woman, turned, and left the stage.

The young woman looked at Kit. "I'm sorry. I can do better. It was just such a shock that it really is *him*."

"We don't have time for second tries," Kit said curtly. "Thank you again, Miss . . ." He looked at the paper on his desk. "Miss Lewis. Please go downstairs and return the dress." There was absolute finality in Kit's tone.

One audition followed another. For the most part, the players were like the first young woman, so dazzled by being near Tate Landers that they couldn't get themselves under control. One woman made everyone laugh when she didn't even try to say her lines. She just held out a pen and paper to Tate and smiled adoringly at him.

When it was Hildy's turn, Olivia and Casey crossed their fingers. Three minutes later, they uncrossed them. Hildy remembered all her lines but delivered them in such an arrogant way that the scene made little sense. Tate was supposed to be the aristocrat, but Hildy acted as though she was of a higher class. It seemed that at any moment she would order him to get on his knees and kiss her ring.

At first the audience reacted to her interpretation in shock, then they began to twitter with barely suppressed giggles.

In spite of Hildy's bravado, Tate stayed in character, ardently professing his love for her.

Olivia didn't comment on her daughter-in-law's performance, but she called Tate a "true professional."

"Don't kid yourself," Casey said. "He's enjoying this. Just because he can keep a straight face doesn't mean he's a good actor."

When Hildy finished, Kit said he wanted to see her later. She walked off the stage with her head held high, seeming to think he was saying that she had the part. But Casey mouthed, "Lady Catherine?" to Kit, and he nodded.

After a couple of hours, Kit called a break and everyone headed to the food tables. He loudly suggested that the women who had already auditioned should leave. There were many calls made to husbands, babysitters, neighbors, et cetera, to pick up children, run errands, even to visit relatives in the hospital. The word "emergency" was heard often, but *no one* left the building.

Kit went to Casey. "Could you take something backstage for Tate to drink? And if you have any of those little cakes left, take those too."

"Maybe Olivia can do it," Casey said. "I'm busy."

Olivia gave a nod, prepared a plate and filled a glass, and took them toward the stage.

"He's good, isn't he?" Kit said to Casey.

"Who?"

He gave her a look.

"Yeah, I guess he's okay." In spite of what she'd said to Olivia, the truth was that they'd all been impressed by Tate. Every time he'd performed, he'd done it with feeling. Over and over. And no matter how the woman opposite him messed up, Tate never broke character.

A few of the women had made it through the entire scene, but none of them displayed the emotion that Tate put into the role. Again and again he looked like a man in love but fighting inner demons.

"Who are you going to choose to be Elizabeth?" Casey asked Kit.

"None of them. They're all dreadful."

"That Parker girl wasn't bad."

Kit looked at her in disbelief. "She kept fluttering her eyelashes at Tate. I expected her to ask him on a date."

"The Brickley girl?"

"Timid little thing. I think Tate's passion scared her."

"Maybe the second half will be better," Casey said.

"What I need is someone who sees Tate as a person, not as a movie star."

"Good luck finding that in this crowd," Casey said. "They're all making fools of themselves over him. The way they look at him is sick-making. 'Oh, Mr. Landers,'" she mimicked in falsetto, "'please look at me the way you do those women in the movies. If you do, I'll dedicate my life to you.' Truly disgusting. It's—" She broke off, as Kit had an odd expression on his face. "What's that look for?"

"I'm agreeing with you. I need someone who doesn't see him as some mythical being in a pair of tight pants."

Casey smiled at the image. "It's a good thing he's not going to play Darcy in the real production. Have you worked with Josh yet?"

"Yes, and I have to say that I have never seen anyone with less acting ability than that young man."

"Oh, no," Casey said. "What are you going to do?"

Kit gave a slow smile. "I think Tatton is doing a splendid job, don't you?" He didn't wait for an answer. "Five minutes to curtain call," he said loudly. "Places, everyone." He went down the aisle to take his seat at the desk.

"When I took the food to him, he was really nice," Olivia said from behind Casey.

Casey turned to look at her. "Please tell me you didn't fall for him too."

"No," Olivia said, "but it's sad that he has to sit back there by himself. His only friend here is Jack Worth, and he left with Gizzy. And the poor man is starving."

"I don't know how he can be, since he ate an entire pie. And for all I know, he cleaned out my fridge. I can't wait to get home tonight and see what he did in my bedroom."

"Perhaps, but he did look rather lonely back there. It couldn't be any fun having all those women act so silly around him."

"It's only for a few hours. Then he can fly back to glamorous Hollywood, where there are more people just like him."

"I'm sure you're right," Olivia said.

"Of course I am. How's Hildy?"

Olivia sighed. "On top of the world. Elated. She's already called Kevin, my stepson, and told him she has the starring role. When she doesn't get it . . ."

Casey took Olivia's arm. "Kit will fix it. He's good with problems."

"Not with all problems, dear," Olivia said in a tone she'd not used before. "Some things are too much even for him." Abruptly, she turned away and went down the aisle.

Casey was close behind her. "What do you know about Kit? He's a great mystery to all of us. He said—"

"The curtain is rising," Olivia said. "Shall we watch?"

For a moment Casey gazed at Kit. He was so tall, with such a commanding presence, that all he had to do was look at a person and any questions stopped. What did Olivia know about him other than that he'd seen her on Broadway?

As though he knew Casey was staring at him, Kit turned toward her, but his eyes revealed nothing. Feeling as though she was prying into something that wasn't any of her business, she looked back at the stage.

If anything, the second batch of women was worse than the first. During the break, Casey had heard the women explaining why they were there. When it was announced that Tate Landers was reading with women who auditioned for Elizabeth, everyone had been giddy. It was a chance to meet, even to speak to, a famous movie star. An unmarried, doesn't-even-have-a-girlfriend movie star.

Not one of the women had taken the idea of being in a local play seriously. With home and job obligations, they didn't have time for rehearsals, and certainly not for weekend performances.

The women began to admit that all they really wanted was to say they'd been among the people who'd tried out. The single women wanted to smile seductively at Tate, and the married women wanted to tell him how much they loved his movies.

Their shared confidences resulted in the second round of auditions going badly. Some of the women didn't even appear to make an effort in their performances.

It took only four time-wasting auditions for Kit to see what was going on.

First, he sent the stage manager to Tate to tell him to wait offstage, then, like the military commander everyone believed he had been, Kit ordered the women who'd already tried out to leave. There was a lot of grumbling, but they picked up their handbags and left. Kit told the women who were left to line up near the food tables.

With his hands clasped behind his back, Kit walked past them, his eyes blazing. "I want to make myself clear. Only the *serious* actors are to remain. If you are here for the sole purpose of making a fool of yourself in front of Mr. Landers, to show him that Summer Hill, Virginia, is the laughingstock of the entire country, to dishonor yourself, your entire family, and this state, then leave *now!*"

No one dared move. But then, who was going to admit to such low-life objectives?

"Everyone else is to get their scripts and memorize their lines. You have seen Mr. Landers, so you know what a true actor is supposed to do. When you go on that stage I want you to become Elizabeth Bennet. To clarify that: A man you thoroughly dislike has told you that he loves you. But at the same time he's saying that he can't believe he wants to marry you because you and your entire family are far beneath him in education, culture, good manners, and money. You are to react with anger to the dreadful things he is saying."

Kit looked at each of the dozen women standing in a line before him. "I want no more teenage, starry-eyed gaping at Mr. Landers. I want you to show him what Virginians can do. Show this actor what *you* can do!"

Olivia and Casey were behind Kit and saw the way the women stood straighter at his words.

He continued. "While you are going over your lines—this time with serious intent—another actress is going to show you how the scene *should* be played."

Nodding, Casey looked at Olivia. "He means you."

She shook her head. "I'm too old. Maybe it's that girl who played Lydia."

"She's a kid," Casey whispered back.

Kit stepped aside so the women could see Olivia and Casey.

"It *is* you." Casey was smiling.

Kit held out his arm. "Coming to us from our nation's capital, I give you Miss Acacia Reddick." He sounded like a circus ringmaster.

Casey blinked at him. Smiling, Olivia stepped away, and when the applause started, she joined in.

"I can't—" Casey began, but Kit took her arm and led her toward the door to the backstage area. When they were in the hallway that led to the lower level, she halted. "Are you crazy? This is ridiculous. I've never acted in my life."

"Sure you have. Haven't you heard that all of life is a stage? I know you know the lines, so there's no problem."

"I can't do this. And besides, I can't stand the actor. I've never met a more arrogant, self-satisfied—" She broke off, her eyes wide. "Like Elizabeth thought Darcy was."

"Exactly," Kit said. "And wouldn't you just love to tell him off? To break that cool smugness he has on the stage? All these women fawning over him haven't made him so much as hesitate. Tell him what you actually think of him—in Austen's phrasing, if possible. Think he could handle that?"

"I . . ." Casey began, but then a slow smile took over. "He would be shocked if he walked out there and saw me, wouldn't he?"

"He'd probably completely lose his composure."

Casey's smile broadened. "Seeing that would make it worth getting up there."

"You can show the players someone who isn't awed by a man just because he looks good in front of a camera."

"Yes!" Casey said. "Where do I change?"

"Straight down there. First door on the right."

"Corset, here I come!" She hurried down the corridor.

Smiling, Kit turned away. He'd always meant for young Tatton to play Darcy. He just wasn't sure who would be Elizabeth. But now he was almost certain that he'd found her.

ACT ONE, SCENE THIRTEEN

Wickham makes himself known

"Hello" came a male voice from the doorway.

Casey was sitting at the dressing table putting on a third coat of mascara. She had on the costume, but she wanted to look her best when she went onstage. Turning, she saw the man who was to play Wickham holding a pretty bouquet of spring flowers. He had on dark trousers and a white shirt with rolled-up sleeves. He looked really good!

"These are for you." He rather shyly stepped forward and put them on the edge of the table.

She thought how refreshing it was to meet a man who seemed humble rather than acting as though he owned the earth. When he started to leave, Casey said, "Wait!"

He turned back, smiling, but he didn't step inside the little room.

"If you got those for the winner of the role, that isn't me," Casey said. "I'm just supposed to ... Well, I'm not sure, but I think my job is to give Mr. Landers a hard time."

The man's handsome face instantly went from shy happiness to appearing almost afraid. "Are you sure you want to do that? Landers is a big name in Hollywood."

"Maybe he is," Casey said, "but for me, telling him off is going to be easy."

His face relaxed somewhat, but the man still seemed worried.

"I understand wanting to do that. By the way, I'm Devlin Haines and I've been cast as Wickham."

She liked that he didn't assume she knew who he was. "I saw you perform and you're very good."

"That's kind of you to say."

Casey got up and went to shake his hand. It was big and warm and he had truly beautiful eyes. Wish *he* had showered on my porch, she thought, and reluctantly pulled her hand away.

Politely, he stepped back from her. "I don't mean to put my nose where it doesn't belong, but you should be careful of Tate Landers."

"From the sound of it, you know him well."

"Unfortunately, I do. He used to be my brother-in-law."

Casey's eyes widened. "Are you Emmie's father?"

His words came fast. "Yes, I am! Have you seen her? Is she going to be here soon? What did she say? Did she mention me?" He took a breath. "Sorry, it's just that I haven't been allowed to see my daughter for weeks. Excuse me." For a moment he turned to the side and Casey thought maybe he was wiping away a tear. When he turned around, his smile was forced. "I apologize for that, but I'm a bit daft when it comes to my daughter. How do you know her?"

The deep emotion of the man, his sense of loss—his tears— seemed to fill the room. "I just heard her over the phone. She laughed, that's all."

"Ah, yes. The sweetest sound on earth. The music of the angels. It's been so very long since I heard it."

"Casey," the stage manager said from the hall, "they're ready for you upstairs."

"I'm coming," she answered, then looked back at Devlin. "I don't mean to pry, but what do you mean that you haven't been 'allowed' to see your daughter?"

He took a deep breath, as though trying to gather his courage.

"I guess the most diplomatic answer is that my famous ex-brother-in-law is a very rich and powerful man. He could afford to give his sister, my wife, the very best of lawyers. I'm sorry. I came back here to wish you luck. I don't know what is causing me to bare my soul. But there's something about you ... Again, I'm sorry to be rambling on. You must think I'm an idiot."

"I don't." Casey was solemn as she thought about what he'd just revealed about Landers. It was one thing to trespass but another to use the legal system to take away a man's daughter. She smiled at Devlin. "After I get this done, why don't you come to my house for dinner—if His Royal Highness hasn't thrown me out because he owns the place, that is. We can talk about ... things."

"I would like that very much." Life seemed to be coming back into Devlin's eyes. "You know, there aren't many people—especially women—who are perceptive enough to see beneath how Tate presents himself to the world."

"Casey!" the stage manager shouted. "You need to come *now!*"

"Tell His Majesty Landers to keep his shirt on. And I mean that literally. I'll be there in a minute." As she plucked a little blue flower from the bouquet Devlin had given her and stuck it into her hair, she smiled at him warmly. "This isn't Hollywood and he doesn't rule here." She started down the corridor, walking backward. "Eight P.M., my house. You know where Tattwell is?"

"I rented a house here for the summer just to be near it. I'm hoping that my daughter will visit and I'll get to see her."

"You will," Casey said.

"The moment I saw you standing by the food tables and laughing, I knew you were special. I felt it." Devlin was grinning, but then he grew serious. "But be careful of him. Tate doesn't like to be crossed, so tread lightly."

Casey gathered her long skirt and ran up the stairs. "No, I don't think I will be careful," she said quietly as she took her place on the stage.

Lizzy and *Darcy dance*

Casey didn't look at the audience. But then, it was mostly the women from town who'd come to drool over a movie star. Besides them, there were a few workmen who were still planting the garden and some electricians in the rafters, putting in the lights. She didn't know if Josh was around or not. And there was Kit, behind his desk and watching, with Olivia not far away.

For a moment Casey smoothed her skirt and composed herself. She knew her lines well, since she and Stacy had helped to write them. And for the last few hours she'd heard them many times.

Right now, foremost in her mind was what she'd just heard about Devlin's dear little daughter. Why had Tate Landers done something like that? But she seemed to know the answer. She'd seen his sense of possession. He owned Tattwell, so he believed that gave him the right to enter her house when she wasn't there.

As for his niece, it was almost as though he carried her in his pocket. Did he consider his sister and niece his property? Something he owned? Is that why he'd used his wealth and prestige to get rid of Emmie's father?

As she stood there, she could feel her anger building. Right now he seemed to be delighting in making everyone wait for him.

I must remember that I am Elizabeth Bennet, she thought. I'm supposed to be from a time when women didn't stand up to men and tell them off.

To her right the people were, yet again, waiting for HRH to appear onstage. When the stage manager yelled, "Quiet on the set," Casey knew he was about to appear. What? No drum rolls? No trumpets playing "God Save the King"?

As Tate Landers stepped forward, there was a wave of female sighs and it was all Casey could do not to roll her eyes. He did look like the proverbial tall, dark, and handsome, but as Devlin said, she was perceptive enough to see beneath his exterior.

When he saw Casey, he didn't react as she thought he would. She'd expected a frown and for him to emit an annoyed "You!" Instead, there was a bit of a smile, as though he was glad to see someone familiar.

I bet he sees me as something he owns, she thought, and her expression almost turned into a glower.

"Sorry for the delay," he whispered when he was a few feet from her. "Wardrobe problems. My—"

"Shall we get on with this?" she said curtly.

"Sure." He took a step back. "Where do you want to start?"

"How you think I'm an inferior being to you."

He was staring at her as though trying to figure something out. "I really am sorry for all that's happened today. Maybe tonight we could—"

"You can begin now," Kit said loudly.

Tate turned to him. The stage was so brightly lit that by contrast the auditorium was almost dark. "Sure," Tate said. "Give me a second, would you? I need to channel Darcy." He turned his back to them, but Casey could see his profile—and he was *not* trying to get into character. "Let me take you out to dinner tonight and explain what happened."

"No, thank you," she said with a smile in her voice. "I have a date with a man named Devlin Haines." Casey had the great satisfaction of seeing him look at her in horror. She didn't give him time to recover his composure. "'Sir!'" she said loudly. "'What is it that you wish to say to me?'"

Instantly, he went from looking horrified to wearing Darcy's lovesick expression, which had become familiar to all of them. He faced her.

"'I have fought against my feelings.'" Tate's voice was full of longing. "'But your inferiority of birth and circumstances and your lesser family have not swayed me from what is in my heart. You must allow me to tell you how ardently I admire and love you. I ask you to marry me.'"

Casey was glad she'd rehearsed this scene when Kit was writing the words. She gave Tate a look of pity. "'I see by your countenance that you expect a favorable answer, and I should like to give it. But, sir, I cannot accept your proposal. I am sorry to give you pain, but I daresay you will have little difficulty in your recovery.'"

Tate stepped back as though she'd struck him. "'This is your reply? Am I to have no reason why I am rejected with so little civility?'"

Casey lost her expression of pity, and a bit of anger glittered in her eyes. That she felt real anger at him helped. "'And may I ask why you offend and insult me by declaring that you care for me against your will, against your reason? Even against your character! If I liked you before, I do not now!'"

"You have misunderstood me. I should like to explain myself. I—"These were not the words in the script.

Casey wasn't about to give him a chance to talk his way out of what he'd done. "I have every reason in the world to dislike you. You have invaded my privacy, falsely accused me. You have stolen what is mine." Her eyes were now blazing in anger. "You have tried to take a father away from his child."

"I have what?!"

This was Tate Landers speaking, not Mr. Darcy, and Casey

couldn't help a bit of triumph at having penetrated his complacency. "Do you deny that you used your wealth and power to obtain legal counsel for your sister?"

She saw enlightenment come into his eyes and he stiffened. "Do you refer to my former brother-in-law?"

"I do. To the man who will be Wickham. What say you to this? Did you or did you not interfere in what was a private matter?"

In the audience, everyone had come to a standstill. The electricians sat down on the overhead beams, legs dangling as they watched what was happening on the stage. One of them adjusted a spotlight so the two players were better highlighted. The women who were to try out next halted, eyes fixed. Who dared to speak to a movie star like this?

The only person in the room who didn't seem shocked was Kit. He was sitting behind his desk and smiling—as if this was exactly what he'd hoped for.

"Wickham?" Tate said under his breath, then he put his shoulders back. "I did." His voice was proud. "I used all that I possessed to get my sister away from a man she did not love."

"And so you admit that your niece was a pawn in your attempt to control a family? It seems that, as with me, you assumed ownership of those around you."

Again, Tate's face changed, only this time he went from anger to what appeared to be amusement. "I have never owned you, even though you first appeared to me in a nightdress that was from a child's fairy tale. Was your intent to seduce me into an illicit liaison?"

Casey's anger increased. "Seduce you? Why you vain, arrogant—" She glared at him. He was *not* going to make her forget where she was! "You, sir, are the villain in this. When you first showed yourself to me, you were as bare as the day you were born. You conjured rain from above and soaped parts an unmarried woman should not see."

Tate almost smiled. "Then why did you not make yourself known? Why did you not flee the scene?"

"It was a matter of fear. Does not the maiden fear the attacker?"

"That you held still in utter silence to watch said soaping makes me question your maidenhood."

Casey's lips curled up in a snarl. "Shall we compare the multiple losses of physical virtue? Perhaps a recording of names would suffice. Is there enough paper in this small town for such a long list as yours would be?"

For a moment he turned away from the audience. Only Casey could see that he was truly enjoying himself. When he turned back, the audience saw "that" look, the one he used onscreen. His dark eyes seemed to exude lust and desire. His voice was a low, seductive rumble. "Perhaps your protests are intended to add yourself to that number." He reached out to touch her cheek.

But Casey lifted her hands and blocked his touch. "I wouldn't have you if—"

Tate had taken both her wrists in his hands. Slowly and seductively, he kissed her palms. He looked at her with heavy-lidded eyes, as though he expected her to fall into his arms and forgive him all.

Casey felt nothing. His action was so false, so meant-to-impress, that she had no response. She gave him a cool gaze. "Sir! I demand that you release me."

Tate was so shocked that she knew she'd struck home. He'd used his most seductive acting maneuvers on her and had failed.

He dropped her hands and stood there staring at her, seeming to have no reply.

Casey couldn't resist an extra punch. "Tonight I will enjoy dining with the brother-in-law you have discarded." When she saw that she'd rendered him speechless, she went back to the script—and there was genuine venom in her voice. "'From the first moment I heard you speak, I have seen your arrogance, your conceit, and your selfish disdain for others—all of which have built within me an unbreakable dislike of you.'"

She stepped so close to him that her breasts were almost touching his chest, and she looked up into his eyes. She was glad to see that she'd erased the smugness from them. "'Sir! If you were the last man on earth, I would not marry you.'"

Tate stepped back from her. "'That is enough! I understand your feelings and am now fully ashamed of my own. Forgive me for taking so much of your time. I wish you health and happiness in your life.'" Turning, he left the stage.

Casey stood where she was, watching him walk away, his steps angry, then she started to walk toward the other side to leave.

That's when the cheering erupted. Startled, she turned toward the audience and saw that everyone was applauding and calling out. Electricians in the rafters, gardeners from outside, all the women, everyone was clapping and shouting.

"You go, Casey!" they yelled.

"Tell him for us!"

"Brilliant!"

Casey felt blood rushing to her face. During the . . . whatever it had been, she'd forgotten about the people watching. She had only been aware of shooting barbs back and forth with that detestable man.

However, the applause and the cheers did feel good. She gave a bit of a curtsy, then ran off the stage.

Lizzy and Bingley differ in perception and knowledge

Jack opened the door of the Big House.

"I'm sorry this is such a simple meal, but the auditions ran late." Casey was standing outside the entryway. "Plus, I have a dinner guest coming soon, so I didn't have much time to prepare." She held out a big basket to him.

He took it and opened the door wider. He was grateful for his own acting experience because he was able to keep smiling. Tate had returned to the house looking like he wanted to murder someone—and it was a toss-up between his ex-brother-in-law and Casey. All Jack had been able to get out of him was that Haines was going to play Wickham and Casey was his champion. Jack wanted to hear everything that had happened.

But when he asked Casey to come in, she backed away, her hands raised in horror. "No thanks. I have to get ready for dinner, and besides, it's been a very long day."

"Mind if I walk you back?"

"Please do," she said.

He put the basket down and they walked toward the guest-house. "I heard that you auditioned for the role of Elizabeth Bennet."

"Not really," she said. "I mean, I did sort of."

"What did Kit say about it?"

Casey stopped walking. "Sorry, but ... Men! The audition was a fiasco. I got really angry and was embarrassed by what happened, but people cheered and—" She waved her hand. "Kit loved it. He was ecstatic. I was still in the dressing room when he came in and told me I was going to be Elizabeth. Then he left. Just like that! He made an autocratic decree about me, and added—like it meant nothing—that the movie star was probably going to play Darcy. Then Kit just walked away like it was a done deal. I ran after him and told him I'd sooner cook with aluminum pans, let my knives get dull, whatever, than be in a play with Tate Landers. I said— Oh." She looked at Jack. "Sorry again. I know he's your friend, but he makes me furious. But then, if you spend a lot of time around him, I'm sure you're used to women saying that."

"No, actually," Jack said, "you're the first."

They were at the guesthouse. "I suspect the women were too dazzled by his good looks to notice what he's really like. If he were ugly, women wouldn't have anything to do with him."

"Isn't that always true?"

"So now you're saying that all women are superficial and are attracted only by a man's pecs and abs?"

Jack raised his eyebrows in a way that made Casey laugh in spite of herself. "Okay. You have a point," she said. "Come in and I'll make you a drink. How about some twelve-year-old Scotch on the rocks?"

"Sounds great." He sat down on the same stool as he had before and she poured him a drink. While he sipped it, he watched her move about the kitchen as she put things away. "Are you going to take the role?"

"I'm no actress. All the passion I put into the lines came from my anger at Tate Landers." She turned to Jack. "Do you know what he was doing in my bedroom?"

"I have no idea." He wasn't being entirely truthful.

She dropped two stainless bowls into a drawer, making a clatter. "I think he undressed, because his shirt was hanging off the porch roof. All day I was dreading what I'd find up there when I got home."

"And?" Jack asked.

"My pajamas were on the floor, and everything on my dresser had been rearranged. It's as though he went through all my things." She looked at Jack. "There was a peacock feather sticking out from under the bed. Bright green with an eye on it. Finding that in my bedroom was really creepy! Tomorrow Josh is going to put some dead bolts on my doors, and I'll have to close all the windows and lock them."

Jack was frowning. "None of this sounds like Tate."

"I guess we can never see the truth about our friends." She went back to cleaning.

"Casey," Jack said tentatively, "I think I should say something about Devlin Haines."

It didn't take much to know what he was going to say. "Do you know the man personally or have you just heard what Landers says about his ex-brother-in-law?" Her eyes were challenging his.

"Just what I've been told," Jack said. He put his drink up to his mouth and said nothing more.

Casey took a breath. "That's enough about me. You seemed really taken with Gizzy."

Jack looked down at his drink. "She's nice, very sweet. She makes me feel like I should put on armor and protect her."

"Um . . . Jack . . ." Casey leaned across the island toward him. "Maybe you know that Gizzy is my half sister. We share some things, but we're also very different."

"What does that mean?"

"Gizzy is as beautiful as a spring day, I'll give you that. Men follow her wherever she goes."

Jack didn't seem to notice that she hadn't answered his question. "I heard that her dad is tough on men who try to date her. But I understand. She needs to be protected."

"Actually, Reverend Nolan tries to protect the men."

"Oh, no." Jack groaned. "Tell me she's not insane. In the last two years every girlfriend I've had has been crazy. One danced for three days with no sleep, then spent six days in bed saying she hated life, then she got up and did it all over again. And if you tell the press that, I'll sue you."

"No, Gizzy isn't crazy. She's quite sane. I don't know how to explain. You know how movie princesses used to stand around and wait for a man to rescue them? But now they grab a sword and fight their own way out?"

"Yes, but that's good. In my last movie the girl saved me twice."

"I loved that part. Was that really you climbing up that wall and later hanging from the helicopter? Did *you* dive into the ocean from that cliff?"

"All me. I was told the insurance guy fainted at the dive, but I did it anyway."

"Then you'll be fine with Gizzy. Now, I don't mean to run you out, but I need to shower and change. I have a date tonight."

Jack stood up. For a moment, he looked like he might say something else, but he didn't. "That's great. He's a lucky man."

"Thanks," Casey said.

Jack started for the door, but then he turned and kissed Casey's cheek.

"That'll get you squab for dinner tomorrow night."

"What's that steak two people share?"

"Chateaubriand," she said.

"Keep that in mind. I'll tell you when I need it."

"Gladly." Smiling, Casey watched him walk away, then closed and locked the door. "If Gizzy doesn't decide to catch some grasshoppers and fry them," she muttered as she glanced toward the stairs. She'd only spent a few minutes in her bedroom earlier, but she'd been so creeped out by what she saw there that she'd run back down. She'd quickly prepared dinner for four and taken two meals to Jack. She hated including enough food for Tate as well, but he was her landlord and he was staying there. Besides, she couldn't bear to let anyone go hungry.

At the foot of the stairs, she took a breath before going up. Maybe she should burn some sage sticks to get his presence out of her house.

In her bedroom, she again looked around. Earlier, she'd hastily put things back to the way they had been. The little red jewelry box her mother had given her went to the left; her two awards for Best Chef went on the right. The photo of her with her mom in Appalachia, surrounded by a dozen grinning children, went in the center. Her big hairbrush was on a linen cloth beside her comb.

She'd checked the insides of the drawers, but nothing seemed to have been moved. As she'd picked her pajamas up off the floor and thrown them into the clothes basket, she wondered if she'd ever wear them again.

While locking the bedroom door and checking that the windows were secure, she again wondered what he'd been doing in her bedroom. Was the answer one of those creepy male things where a man just liked to touch female possessions?

She showered quickly and got ready for Devlin's arrival, putting on a cotton dress with a little pink shrug and pale sandals. Not too daring, but modest and demure. As she gave a last glance at the mirror, she told herself that tonight she was not going to even mention Tate Landers.

Her head came up. What if she played Elizabeth and Devlin played Darcy? Josh could be Wickham. Not a bad idea, she thought. Tomorrow, she'd be firm and tell Kit that the only way she'd play Elizabeth was if Devlin could be Darcy.

Smiling, she went downstairs to set the table with candles and her prettiest wineglasses.

Darcy defends himself

"You should have been there!" Tate said.

It was after dinner and he and Jack were in the library of the old house. Jack was sitting on the leather chesterfield sofa, sipping the espresso Casey had made and put into a thermos.

Tate was pacing the floor like some predatory animal. "She assumes I'm full of myself, swallowed up by my own ego. But she knows nothing about me, especially not the hell all of us went through with Haines." He put his hands in his pockets and sat down on a red-and-green plaid chair. An hour earlier, while Tate was upstairs, Casey had delivered their dinner. When he saw the basket, he was sure there'd be nothing in it for him, but there were two of everything. While they'd eaten trout braised in whiskey, he'd been mostly silent, looking at his excellent food as though it might be poisoned.

"If this is what she does in a hurry, I can't imagine what she cooks when she has time," Jack said, but Tate hadn't responded. When they got to the library, Tate nearly exploded and told Jack what was going on.

Jack had been shocked to hear that Tate's ex-brother-in-law was in town, even more surprised to hear that Haines had the role of Wickham in the play. He'd only seen the man once before today, so earlier, when Haines was onstage, Jack hadn't recognized him. "Appropriate," Jack had mumbled, but he'd been knocked speechless when Tate said that Casey's date was Devlin Haines.

"I tried to tell her about the man but she wouldn't listen," Jack said. "And she was right. I don't know him. *You* have to tell her about him."

"Go to her with my tail between my legs and beg her to believe me? I don't think so." Tate got up and went back to pacing. "I wonder when she met him? She was at those food tables all day long. And through all the auditions she sat there with that blonde woman and they laughed at everything. Not that they made any noise. She was very respectful of those poor women who stared at me like I was from another planet, but I saw her. She laughed exactly where I would have. There was one time when a woman left out the word 'not.' She was supposed to say that if Darcy were the last man on earth she wouldn't marry him, but she said—"

"I get it. An amateur messed up the line."

"Yeah, but it was funny, except that nobody else laughed. Only she did."

"Casey."

"Yeah, PJ Lady."

"You ever call her that to her face and you may not live."

"No danger of that, since I'm leaving tomorrow. Anyway, I cut a glance at her and she and the woman were nearly falling out of their seats—but silently. Who is she?"

"The blonde or PJ?"

"I've had all the ridicule I can take today."

"The other woman—the blonde—is named Olivia something, and she's going to play Mrs. Bennet."

"There were auditions after I left?" Tate asked.

"I have no idea. Gizzy told me. By the way, before you open your mouth and insert your foot, Gizzy is a half sister to Miss PJ—I mean Casey. So don't complain to her about Casey. You want some of this coffee?"

"No."

"What are you going to do about your brother-in-law?"

"Ex," Tate snapped. "I pay him enough that he's supposed to stay out of our lives."

"That's not possible, since he's Emmie's dad."

"Why couldn't my sister have played around? It would be great if a DNA test would show that Emmie's real father was some nice accountant. Or a clown who did children's birthday parties. Or—"

"She didn't, so stop fantasizing. He's probably in the guesthouse with Casey right now, telling her what an egomaniac you are. And I know you mentioned it, but what exactly were you doing in her bedroom?"

Tate gave a little snort of laughter. "This morning the caretaker released a peacock and his ladies on the property, and the big guy tore through her screen door and went upstairs. It turned her bedroom upside down. I had to throw my shirt over the beast to get it out the window, and even then it nearly bit me in the face. I'm looking forward to a peacock barbecue."

"When I was just there, there was no hole in the screen door. Maybe the caretaker fixed it. You should tell Casey that story."

"Before or after I give her a list of the women I've slept with? It's something she asked me for while we were onstage. In front of everybody."

"I am definitely sorry that I missed this afternoon's perfor-mance. What was your reply?"

"I, uh . . . I gave her my best look of . . . of, you know, and she said no."

"What does that mean?" Jack asked, then his eyes widened. "You—the great romance hero—came on to her and she turned you down?"

Tate sighed. "Yeah, that's just what happened. I used the full-blown, come-to-me look of the hero. The one I get paid so much to do. But she curled her very pretty upper lip at me and told me to drop dead. More or less." He paused. "You know, the irony of all this is that when I walked out onto that stage I was really glad to see her. At least she was familiar-looking." He sat down on the couch so hard, Jack's coffee sloshed.

"Okay, so you've made a fool of yourself from the moment you met her and she's slapped you down at every step. But you still like her. A *lot*."

"That's ridiculous!" Tate snapped, and got back up.

"Is it? She laughs at the same things you do. She gives it back to you when you take potshots at her. Didn't you drop your last terrifically beautiful girlfriend because she had . . . let me see if I remember exactly what you said . . . 'the IQ of a doorknob'? Is that right? And your complaint about the one before her was that she adored you."

"Yeah, well, she kept saying how fabulous it was to be Tate Landers's girlfriend. I told her *I* was Tate Landers, but she had no idea what I meant."

"So now you're mad because Casey is smart and she sure as hell doesn't 'adore' you. Sounds perfect to me. The question is, What are you going to do about your ex-brother-in-law?"

"Nothing. What can I do? She hates me so much she wouldn't believe anything I said."

"So you're going to fly back to L.A. tomorrow and leave Casey to date Haines? How long will it take her to find out what he's really like? Before she's crying as hard as you told me Nina was? Think Casey will be put under a doctor's care as Nina was? Given little blue pills? Or were they green?"

"Both!" Tate said loudly. "Okay, I get it. You don't have to—"

"And then there's Emmie. If Haines is in the play, that means he plans to be here all summer. You told me how much Nina and Emmie love it here. I know! You could buy your niece a pony. But you'll have to do it from L.A., because that's where you'll be. Maybe her daddy can teach her to ride since he'll be here with

Casey day after day. That's his MO, isn't it? Court them, make them fall for him, then dump them? After he cleans out their bank accounts, that is. But don't you worry about anything. When Haines leaves and Casey is crying her heart out, I'll be here for her. Hey! Maybe while you're in L.A. you could send me some—"

"Shut up!" Tate said. "Just damned well shut your mouth." He took his phone off a side table and began punching buttons.

"Calling anyone I know?"

"Texting my assistant to cancel my flight tomorrow. I'm staying here and I'm going to play Darcy in a two-bit small-town play. Damn! The things I do for my family!"

Jack couldn't hide his smile. He hadn't looked forward to living alone in the huge old house for an entire summer. But now things were looking up. Tate, Nina, Emmie, and his new friends Gizzy and Casey would be here. Life was looking good!

He watched Tate scowling at the empty fireplace. Jack hadn't said so, but he had a suspicion that if Tate had been watching Casey, Haines had seen it. Jack meant no offense to pretty Casey, but if that man was going after her, it was probably to get back at Tate.

As Jack sipped his coffee, he thought that Tate sure had canceled his flight quickly. And that was good, because if anyone was going to persuade Casey that Tate was a good guy, it had to be Tate himself. Jack had an idea that that's exactly what his friend was going to try to do.

Jack put his empty cup down on the coffee table and stood up. "This has been a long day and I'm meeting Gizzy for breakfast tomorrow. I'll see you in the morning."

"Long day—that's it!" Tate said. "If there's one thing Haines can't resist, it's anything he thinks is luxurious—paid for by someone else, of course. Didn't I see some bottles of wine somewhere?"

"Yeah. In the pantry off the kitchen."

"Great!" Tate said. "Before you go to bed, could you do me a favor and take two bottles over to the guesthouse? I'll stick a card on one saying 'Congratulations.'"

"You're sending Haines wine?"

Tate gave a slow smile. "Casey has been on her feet since before daylight. Let's see how much she can drink and stay awake."

Jack laughed. "It's a gamble, but let's hope it works. You write a card and I'll get the booze."

Mrs. Bennet is concerned

"Casey?" Olivia looked down at the sleeping woman on the couch and worked to keep from frowning. It wasn't any of her business what Casey did in the privacy of her own home. "I don't mean to disturb you, but people are arriving, and . . ." She gave a quick glance at Casey's disheveled state.

Casey winced at the crick in her neck. Olivia, clean and coiffed, was standing in her living room.

"Are you all right?"

"Sure." Casey sat up, feeling stiff, with aches all over her body. She had that swollen feeling from having slept in her clothes. A bra strap was cutting into her skin. "What time is it?"

"A little after nine," Olivia said. "I didn't mean to intrude, but I knocked several times. I could see your foot and when you didn't move I got worried. Mind if I ask why you slept on the couch? If it's a hangover, I can get you some aspirin. Or if someone is upstairs I'll leave."

"No hangover. I only had half a glass of wine, but after the day we had, it was enough to do me in. I fell asleep on the table, and I woke up about midnight. I meant to go up to my bed but I couldn't manage the stairs, so I flopped here. What time do rehearsals begin? I need to start cooking."

"That's why I'm here. The stage manager called me to say there will be no rehearsals today, but there's a lot of work going on and you're needed. It seems that it's been posted on the Internet that Tate Landers is going to play Darcy. People have started camping out in the parking lot. We can't work there."

When Casey rubbed her eyes, her hands came away with dark streaks. She hated sleeping in makeup. "Someone should tell them that it's not true."

"I think it is. Gossip is that Tate is staying, with his friend Jack, and since his sister is coming to visit, he said he might as well be in the play."

Casey stood up and stretched her back. "So who's going to play Elizabeth?"

"Last I heard, you are. If so, I'm sure your excellent performance yesterday is a big part of why Tate wants to stay. You challenge him as an actor."

"I'd like to challenge him with a crossbow," Casey muttered, then looked at Olivia. "I need to take a very long shower and— Oh, no! I forgot Jack's breakfast."

"I saw him on the way here and he said he's going out with Gizzy."

"Alone?"

"I got the impression they were meeting someone. I don't think they've been alone yet." Olivia glanced through the doorway at the kitchen. "I'm still curious as to why you were sleeping on the couch. There are two place settings on the table. Didn't your dinner companion help when you fell asleep?"

"I guess it wasn't very flattering to him when I put my head down on the table and dozed off. Poor guy."

Olivia didn't smile. "I would have thought Tate had better manners than that. He should have helped you—"

"I didn't have dinner with Landers. I was with Devlin Haines. You know? The guy playing Wickham?"

"Oh, sorry, I didn't know you'd met him. Is he new in town?"

"He's here only temporarily. He's Landers's ex-brother-in-law. You should hear his horror story! Or better yet, not hear it. Anyway, Devlin came to Summer Hill hoping to see his daughter, who is Landers's sister's kid. I bet that man is staying here all summer just to keep Devlin from seeing his own child."

"That's a strong accusation," Olivia said. "Why don't you go upstairs and take a shower? Or soak in the tub? I know I did last night. Your hair is a mess. Elizabeth doesn't deserve that."

"If Landers is Darcy, I am absolutely *sure* that I am *not* going to play Elizabeth! After what Devlin told me yesterday, I never want to see Tate Landers again. In fact, I may move off his property."

"Good idea," Olivia said. "I hear that Pizza Hut needs a new head chef. Or maybe you can cater weddings this summer—as soon as you spend weeks trying to find a kitchen you can use."

Casey was blinking at her. "You're sounding like my mother."

"I am honored. Now, go!"

"Yes, ma'am." Smiling, Casey ran up the stairs.

ACT ONE, SCENE EIGHTEEN

Mrs. Bennet understands Darcy

Olivia was frowning as she cleaned up Casey's kitchen. The dinner table still had bowls and platters with the remnants of what looked like it must have been a delicious meal. The unrefrigerated food had to be thrown out, and she didn't like waste. There was a half-empty wineglass but no bottle. Where was the other glass? And the candles had burned down to the base.

It looked like the guy playing Wickham had just walked off. Casey, exhausted from the long day, had fallen asleep, and he must have grabbed a glass and the wine and left her there. He hadn't so much as blown out the candles.

"Hello."

She looked up to see Tate standing outside the screen door.

"I don't mean to bother anyone, but Jack left my truck here when he gave Casey a ride home. The keys aren't in it, so they must be inside, and I need to go get some food." His voice was tentative, sounding apologetic.

Olivia opened the door to him, but he didn't step inside.

"I just need the keys."

"I don't know where they are. Casey is upstairs, but she'll be a while. Come in and I'll make you some breakfast."

"Would you?" There was gratitude in his voice.

His exaggerated meekness annoyed her. "Yes, and if Casey starts to come downstairs I'll help you escape out the window. I think she's after you with a crossbow."

Tate groaned. "Has she heard that I'm staying for the whole summer?" He sat down on a stool.

"Yes, she has."

"And?"

"She says she will not play Elizabeth and I think she's going to move out and get a job at Pizza Hut." Olivia was cracking eggs into a hot skillet while bacon fried in another one.

Tate hung his head and let out a sigh. "Sounds like she's been listening to my ex-brother-in-law. No matter what I do, I cannot rise above his accusations of me. But then, my honor won't allow me to disparage the father of my beloved niece."

"Hmmmm," Olivia said as she dropped bread into the toaster. "'Disparage' is too much and definitely don't use the word 'honor.' Too old-fashioned. And tilt your head a little less to the side. You're much too pretty to pull off such deep despair."

When Tate laughed, his voice changed completely. The misery was gone. "Oh, no! Not another actor. I thought I'd be able to escape the breed here in Small Town, Virginia."

"No, we're here." She put a plate of bacon, eggs, and toast in front of him. "Now go choose a jam and tell me the truth of what's going on."

Tate got up and went to the rows of pretty jars of jam, but he hesitated. "If I take one of these she'll accuse me of stealing."

Olivia went around the island, grabbed a jar, and put it by his plate. "Wimpy men *never* win the girl."

Tate sat back down and picked up the jar. "Nectarine with lemon verbena. My favorite. I have it every morning. What makes you think I'm trying to win her?"

"Puh-lease. Yesterday you fooled everyone else, but I was on Broadway before you were born. You acted by rote. Half the time you didn't even look at whichever girl was drooling over you.

Instead, you kept stealing glances at Casey and me. Since I don't think I was the one you were getting into a slow boil over, it must be Casey. So what's going on with you and the ex-brother-in-law?"

"If I tell you, you won't rat on me, will you?" He sounded serious.

"This will be between us."

Tate took a bite, nodded, and lowered his voice. "Devlin Haines is a bastard. I assume he's here to try to get more money from me. Emmie, my niece and his daughter, probably told him she and her mom were going to be here this summer. No doubt Haines decided to come here to sweet-talk my sister into finagling extra money out of me. It's worked in the past, so why not try it again?"

Tate lowered his voice even further. "I'm a little concerned that he also saw me, uh, looking at Casey, and that's why he's going after her."

"To get back at you?"

"That's my guess. But I could be wrong. Maybe he's developed a genuine liking for her. I know they had dinner together last night, so maybe—" His head came up, alarm on his face. "Is he upstairs? Did they spend the night together?"

Olivia smiled, glad to see a real emotion. No acting but a genuine look of . . . what? Horror? Fear? She couldn't tell if he was on the verge of slamming out the door in a rage or running up the stairs and throwing his ex-brother-in-law out the window. "No, he's not upstairs. In fact, it seems that Casey fell asleep during the dinner and your sister's ex left her there. Her head in the soup, so to speak. In my day—"

"The man would have carried her up the stairs. I would have."

"That's nice to hear. So what are you going to do to get her to forgive whatever you did in her bedroom yesterday morning?"

"I chased a peacock out," he said, "but there's no way she'd believe that. And if I told her the truth about Emmie's dad, she wouldn't believe that either. How do you disprove something that a person is absolutely *sure* is true? Casey has made up her mind about me, and I don't know how to change it."

"That is a tough one. My advice would be to let her spend time with your ex-brother-in-law and stay out of it. They'll have some great bed romps and eventually, in a year or two, she'll figure out that he's a cad. Afterward, she'll be so down she'll finally look at an unattractive, cowardly guy like you. Problem solved."

Tate blinked a few times, then laughed. "You have to meet my sister. You two will get along well. No advice for me?"

"None at all." She leaned across the island toward him. "I don't know either of you young men, so I'll have to decide which of you to give the most votes to, but right now you are ahead in the polls. I don't like that the Wickham guy went off and left Casey to find her way to the couch. He should have—"

"I sent the wine," Tate said, sounding sheepish. "I sent two bottles because I hoped he'd drink too much and I knew she'd had a long day and . . ." He shrugged.

Olivia laughed. "Clever use of your enemy's weakness, and that gets you another vote. Uh-oh."

There was a step on the stairs and Tate immediately stood up. "I better go."

"Who's going to cook for you all summer? And don't you have trouble learning lines?"

"Actually, I'm not a bad cook. I had a single mother, so it was necessary. And I have a bit of a photographic memory. At least for lines, anyway. I can—"

Olivia was glaring at him.

"Oh."

She picked up her handbag and went to the door. "Be nice and don't do the wounded-hero act. You're not onscreen. Got it?" She waited for Tate to nod before she hurried out the door.

Darcy and Lizzy dance some more

"What are you doing here?" Casey asked as soon as she entered the kitchen and saw Tate sitting on a stool at her island—the stool she'd already come to think of as belonging to Jack.

"Olivia let me in, fed me, and now I'm trying to think what I can say to get you to cook for me this summer. Any suggestions?"

Casey went to the dishwasher to unload it, but it was empty. "Did Olivia clean up the kitchen?"

"I guess so." He was watching her, waiting for her to make a decision. "It wasn't me, but I would have done it. Although if Olivia hadn't been here I would have been too terrified to enter your house. She grabbed me by the shirt collar and pulled me inside. She is extraordinarily strong."

Casey didn't smile at his joke. Turning, she glared at him. "So it's true that you're spending the summer here?"

"Looks like I am. Jack's director is sending a trainer for him so he'll be in top shape for his next movie. I thought I'd use him too. The garage is being converted to a gym. If you want to join in, you're welcome."

"No thanks." She took a breath. "Has Kit found someone to play Elizabeth?"

"I think he means for you to do it."

"No!" Casey said. "Absolutely *not*." She started for the door. "I will tell him that I'm not going to be in his play."

"Please?" Tate asked loudly.

Casey hesitated, her back to him.

"I know you don't like me and I'm sorry for that, but I promised Kit I'd help out. You were the only one in those auditions with me who had any talent. If one of those girls who think I'm some fairy-tale hero from my movies takes the role, the play will be a flop. Critics will come and butcher it all. Sales will fall off and it will be the charities that suffer. Maybe they're impersonal, faceless organizations, but they still—"

"No, they're not." She looked at him. "The charities aren't impersonal or faceless to me. A third of those proceeds will go to my mother's clinic."

"I hadn't heard that. What kind of clinic is it?"

"Medical. In Appalachia."

"That's great," Tate said. "The more tickets we sell, the more money your mother gets, right?"

Casey tightened her lips.

"Does your mom know how good an actor you are?"

Casey stepped away from the door. "I'm not good. It was an angry scene and I was furious. At *you*."

"I know," he said, "and I'd be sorry for that if it hadn't been some of the most powerful acting I've ever seen."

She narrowed her eyes at him. "Why are you piling praise on me?"

Tate started to give a little smile and lower his lashes at her. It was a trick he'd been using since he reached his full height and women began really looking at him. But then he thought of Olivia's words and stopped. His head came up. "Because I want a good summer. I haven't had even two weeks off in years. My sister and her daughter are coming here and I want to spend time with them. I had no plans to be in some local play, but Kit ..." Tate threw up his hands. "I honestly don't know how I got rooked into doing this and I already regret it, but on the other hand, if I don't *do* something while I'm here I'll go nuts with boredom. So what about it?"

"What part?" Casey asked.

"Cook for Jack and me and when Nina and Emmie get here, add them to the list. And play Elizabeth. But only if you swear that you won't look at me like I'm some chocolate statue you want to devour."

At that, Casey had to turn away to cover the tiny smile that came to her. "You want me to play Elizabeth because I don't like you?"

"Pretty much," he said. "But then, in my last three movies the lead actresses couldn't stand me."

"Understandable," Casey muttered.

"Ouch! Can I give Kit your answer?"

"I will," Casey said. "Next time I see him——"

"He's here. Everyone is here."

"Who is everyone and where is here?"

"At Tattwell. The whole cast is here, and the property is being fenced in. Guards have been hired to patrol the place. That guy Josh has half a dozen workmen putting the old gazebo back together. He and Jack have developed some kind of rivalry. Do you know what that's about?"

Casey was scrubbing the sink. "I have no idea."

"I was afraid it had something to do with the girl playing Jane. What's her name? Glenda?"

"Gisele, but we all call her Gizzy."

"Jack's really taken with her."

"It won't last," Casey said as she folded her cloth. "I have to ask Kit how he's planning to feed the cast and whether he needs me for cooking." She went to the door, but Tate stayed where he was. She could see that he was waiting for her to answer his questions. "All right, I'll cook for you. I'll deliver three meals a day."

Tate didn't move.

"And I'll talk to Kit about being in the play."

Tate smiled but he still didn't get off the stool.

"What else?"

"It's my niece, Emmie. My sister doesn't cook. Never has. The last time she tried to scramble some eggs, she set the skillet on fire. Emmie thinks a Pop-Tart is a good breakfast."

For the first time since seeing Tate Landers in her kitchen, Casey's eyes came alive. "Pop-Tart? You start a child's day with processed flour and pure sugar?"

"Not me. My sister. Emmie is a very picky eater. Think you could get her to eat something that didn't come out of a delivery box?"

"Yes," Casey said as she opened the screen door. "I'd like to go now and see what's being done. But I guess you don't have to leave since you own this house."

Tate got off the stool and went to stand near her. "How about if I swear that I'll never again enter this house unless *you* invite me in? No one else, just you."

"You mean like a vampire?"

Tate gave a laugh that was part groan. "If they remake *Dracula*, think I should try out for the part? I'd bite beautiful necks right there." Reaching out, he lightly touched the side of her neck with his fingertip—and an electrical current shot up his arm and ran through his chest.

Casey jumped away from him. "What the hell was *that?*"

"Static electricity, I guess. You okay?"

"Fine. But from now on, keep your hands to yourself."

"Sure," he said, then held the door open for her. "No touching, no trespassing, no anything. I got it." He followed her through the gardens toward the big gazebo—and he was smiling. Static electricity, like hell! That was pure sexual desire in its most basic form.

ACT ONE, SCENE TWENTY

Lizzy confides

Casey had put her phone in her pocket before she left the house, and she could feel it buzzing. She stepped back to let the movie star pass, then answered it. "Stacy!" she said in happiness at hearing her half sister's voice. "When will you get here? Want me to meet you at the airport?"

"No. I'm, uh, Casey, please don't be mad at me, but I'm not coming back. Not for a while, anyway."

"But you're supposed to dress the sets and take care of the costumes. The play can't be put on without you."

"I know you think that, but it can. I called Mom, and her book club is going to give up dissecting the latest prizewinner that they all hate and get their sewing machines out of storage. They're going to make all the clothes for the women. And Dad is going to get the clothes for the men from some place in L.A. My drawings for sets and costumes are fairly complete, so they can be used. And I got an upholstery shop to do the curtains and slipcovers at a really good price."

"It sounds great," Casey said, "but I will miss *you*."

"Sure about that? From what I heard, you and Tate Landers are the talk of the town. Did you really bawl him out onstage in front of everyone?"

"Sort of." Casey didn't want to talk about that. "Why are you staying in D.C.?"

"Because I'm falling in love with a man."

"What?! Who? Where? When? How?"

Stacy laughed. "Remember I told you that I was going out to dinner with Kit's son Rowan? He picked me up, but he brought his cousin Nate Taggert with him. And well, Rowan was a bit too serious for my taste. But Nate was funny and charming and very interesting."

"I take it he's the one?"

"Yes! It's only been a week, but we've hardly been out of each other's sight for the whole time. He's wonderful! He got me a job decorating an apartment here for another of his relatives. I'm sorry, but I can't leave now. Please tell me you understand."

"Of course I do—and I envy you."

"You're living a few feet from Tate Landers and you envy *me*?"

"He's a jerk."

"Oh, no. Tell me that isn't true. His movies are so great. He makes the whole theater sizzle. What dreadful thing has he done? Has he come on to you?"

"No. I mean, he nearly electrocuted me, but it's more what he's done to someone else. His brother-in-law is here and—"

"What do you mean, he electrocuted you? With what? A Taser gun? Casey, this sounds serious."

"It wasn't like that. I sort of called him a vampire and he put his hand on my neck and it hurt, that's all."

"Choking? I'm calling the sheriff. You need protection."

"No!" Casey said. "It was just his fingertip. That's all he used."

"Oh," Stacy said. "Tate Landers touched you with his fingertip and you tingled so badly you were in pain?"

"That isn't the way it was. Not exactly, anyway. It was—" Casey laughed. "I do miss you! Bring your boyfriend here. You can redecorate your mom's sunroom. It's looking a little shabby."

It was a town joke that when Stacy was studying interior design she'd practiced by redoing every room in her parents' house—
repeatedly. "All of you will do fine without me. And Casey ..."
She paused. "I know you can handle the props."

"Oh, no! I can't cook and play Elizabeth *and* deal with the
props."

"Did you just say what I thought you did? *You* are playing
Elizabeth?"

"I think so. Tate asked me to and I—"

"Tate as in Landers? *That* Tate? He personally asked you to play
Elizabeth to his Darcy?"

"Yes, but it wasn't like what you're thinking. Yesterday he broke
into my house and ate an entire *pie!* The whole thing. Plus, he was
upstairs in my bedroom."

Stacy was silent.

"Are you still there?"

"Yes. I think you have just lived my every fantasy. Casey, I can
see that this guy has impressed you in the wrong way, but when it
comes to your cooking, you should have some mercy on us mortals. Remember those little hazelnut orange cakes you made and
they disappeared? We said Josh must have taken them. But it was
me. I ate every one of them and I lied about it. So cut this guy
some slack, will you? I have to go. Nate will be here in minutes
and I need to get ready."

"Wait! What did Kit say when you told him about all this?"

"Kit? Oh ... I ... You're such a diplomat that I think you
should— Uh-oh. I think I hear Nate. Gotta go. I love you bunches
and heaps and I'm really, really glad you're my sister. Call me later.
Bye." She clicked off.

"She didn't tell Kit." Casey's teeth were clenched. "Crap. Double *merde*. I'm going to kill her!"

"Anything I can help with?" Tate asked. He had returned to
check on her, it seemed.

"No. It's none of your— Oh, just go away."

But Tate didn't move. "Did you get bad news?"

Casey was pacing.

He held out his hands as though he meant to put them on her shoulders, but then he dropped them. "Tell me what happened."

Casey stopped walking. "My sister isn't going to help with the play."

"You mean Jack's girl?"

"That's Gizzy, and she doesn't belong to Jack or to any other man. It's Stacy."

"Blonde, very pretty? Interior designer?"

"When did you meet her?"

"I didn't. My sister knows her and has spent the last several months trying to fix me up with her." There was a wooden bench nearby and Tate motioned to it. "Sit down and tell me what's going on."

Casey sat. "You're too late. Stace is falling in love with some guy in D.C. and she's staying there. She's turned over the costumes to her mother and she wants *me* to look after the props. And absolutely worse, I don't think she's told Kit about any of this."

"You're afraid of him?" Tate sat down at the far end of the bench.

"Not like you mean. He's a great guy, but this is too much—for him and me. Cooking, acting, props. I didn't even get breakfast this morning."

Tate reached into his pocket and withdrew a fat bar in a wrapper that proclaimed it was all protein and gave a person limitless energy.

Casey took it, tore off the paper, and bit into it. "I hope you know that these things are mainly sugar and very bad for you. They're downright lethal."

"Sounds like what my publicist says about me."

Casey couldn't help a laugh, and that made her relax a bit. "Kit is going to be one unhappy director because he really likes Stacy. They worked together in D.C. and here in the Big House. He even introduced her to his son in D.C."

"That she's staying to be with Kit's son should make him happy."

Casey looked at Tate. "He showed up at dinner with his cousin and she liked the cousin better."

"Ah," Tate said. "The plot thickens. Maybe I can—"

He was cut off by the squeals of four girls who sprang out of the bushes. "You *are* here," one said. "My mom auditioned to be Elizabeth."

"And my sister did," another said. "Is it true that you went to her dressing room and tried to French-kiss her but she told you no?"

"My cousin said you pushed her down on a sofa and tried to put your hand down her dress."

Two men wearing tan uniforms came rushing forward. "Sorry, sir. They got past us. The fence will be up by tomorrow."

The men took the arms of the girls and began to pull them away.

"Wait!" Tate got up and walked to them. "In the house, I have a whole box of DVDs of my last movie. Any of you want a copy?"

The girls started squealing and talking at the same time.

Tate looked over their heads, gave an apologetic shrug to Casey, then led the group toward the house.

Casey stood up, tried to gather her courage, and went down the path to the gazebo.

Mr. Bennet is disappointed

Kit was barking orders to Josh, who was on the roof of the gazebo, a hammer in his hand. "I want no leaks!" he yelled.

Josh was his usual smiling self. "Too bad, because I always leave holes in every roof I repair."

"Smart-ass," Kit said under his breath as he turned and saw Casey. "Did you finally get out of bed?"

"Wow! You're in a bad mood."

"That I am," Kit said. "Rehearsals can't be held in the theater because there are a dozen giggling girls waiting outside to get a glimpse of Tatton."

Casey decided that now was not the time to tell him about Stacy. In fact, she was going to make her sister break the news to him. "Send Landers back to L.A. That'll solve everything."

"If he goes, then I'm stuck with your brother for Darcy, and he has the acting ability of that tool he's holding."

"I heard that!" Josh called.

"I meant for you to." Kit was gazing at Casey with steely eyes. "You look like you have something you want to say to me."

"No, not really." She took a step backward. "I just wanted to say that we'll all do our best to help out." Kit's eyes were boring into hers. "I'll be around so, uh . . ." She turned on her heel and started to leave so quickly that she was almost running.

"Halt!"

"Damn," she said quietly, then forced a smile as she looked back at Kit. "Need something?"

"Yes. When will Stacy be here?"

Casey could feel her entire back turning yellow—not just a cowardly stripe, but every inch going Technicolor. When—if—she lived through this, she was going to murder her sister. "She's not, uh . . ." She gave Kit a little smile.

"Not what?" Kit bellowed so loud that all the workmen looked at them.

"Coming," Casey said.

"Stacy isn't going to show up?" Abruptly, Kit's stormy face calmed, and he smiled. "She's with Rowan, isn't she?"

"I've been meaning to tell you what a great name I think that is. He sounds like a hero from the olden days. I think you should call her *right this minute* and let her tell you everything." Casey was slowly walking backward. Yes, she was definitely going to annihilate her sister.

"*You* will tell me everything," Kit said.

Behind him were nearly a dozen people. Hammers and saws had stopped. Josh had come down off the roof. Who needed an old play to watch when they had such great real-life drama?

Casey took a very deep breath and let it all come out in one big gush. "Stacy is falling in love with some guy named Nate Thomas so she's staying in D.C. and can't do the props. But the good news is that she's turned the female costumes over to her mom's reading group and her dad is getting the clothes for the men, so you see, everything will be fine. I have to go, uh, cook something." She turned at warp speed and started walking.

"Acacia!" Kit said in a way that made Casey stop.

Slowly, she turned toward him.

"Was it Nate *Taggert*?"

All the anger about the bad day had left Kit's face. He seemed defeated. As Casey walked toward him, she glanced at Josh. "Don't you guys have something else to do?"

"Not anything as exciting as this. Could somebody get us some water? Drinking out of the hose has lost its country appeal."

"Sure." Casey looked back at Kit, who had sat down on the edge of the gazebo. She sat beside him. "I'm sorry about this. We'll find someone to deal with the props. Stacy's mom—"

"Stacy is falling for the wrong man. Nate isn't right for her."

"Oh." What could she say to that? "Love is blind, so maybe . . ." She trailed off.

Kit took his phone out of his pocket, and with it came a folded brochure that he handed to her. "Stacy was to go to that tomorrow and buy things to use onstage."

It was for an estate sale that was about a hundred miles away.

"You'll have to go instead of her."

"I don't know anything about buying props. What would I get? What's needed?"

"Stacy has a list. Get her to send it to you. She can—" Kit moved the phone to speak into it. "Rowan, this is your father. Call me immediately." He touched the off button. "Not that anything I say will do any good. He's as stubborn as his mother." He turned to Casey. "Of course you can buy props. Take Tatton with you. He knows about sets."

Casey stood up. "No, but I'll find someone. Right now I'm going to get food and water for the guys. I'll be back by lunch. If you need anything while I'm out, call me." She started to walk away.

"Casey," Kit said and she looked at him. "I apologize for my bad temper."

She smiled at him. "That's okay."

"By the way, did the caretaker find you? He asked if the peacock had done much damage inside your house and if the door was okay. He said the bird tore through the screen so he put in a new one. And oh, yes, he congratulated you on getting the creature out. He said they can be devils." When Kit's phone rang, he looked at the ID. "The prodigal son doth call." He clicked the phone on and took long strides to get away from everyone.

ACT ONE, SCENE TWENTY-TWO

Wickham apologizes?

By six P.M., Casey gave up trying to find someone to go with her to the estate sale. Stacy had previewed the items a month before, and she sent Casey a list of everything she'd planned to buy for the production. She wrote that she'd tried hard to get the late owner's grandson to sell to her before the official sale, but he wouldn't.

"Is that supposed to make me feel sorry for you?" Casey muttered, glaring at the email. She'd made half a dozen calls to her sister, but Stacy—wisely—didn't answer.

Casey had called several people and asked them to go with her. But her preference for someone with muscles and a big truck was limiting. There were two settees and six chairs on Stacy's list, plus some small tables, four boxes of knickknacks, a trunk full of old clothes, and a crate full of fabric. But Kit had everyone she knew working on the play, and no one could spare a whole day away.

Except for Landers, she thought. After the squealing girls had shown up and he'd led them away, she hadn't seen him again. Which was good, because she knew she had to say something about whether or not he'd rid her house of a berserk peacock. If he had, she might, well, owe him an apology.

When her cell rang, she grabbed it. Please, please let it be someone who can go with me tomorrow, she thought. And let them own a truck so big it could star in a Transformers movie.

When she saw Gizzy's name on the ID, her shoulders slumped. "Hi, Gizz, what's going on? You and Jack having fun?"

"Oh, yes," Gizzy said. "He's wonderful. Fabulous. He's so smart and he's been so many places, and can we go with you tomorrow?"

"Sure." Casey's shoulders straightened. "Can you bring a truck?"

"Yes, and Jack can drive it. He's great behind a wheel."

"I know. I've seen all his movies. Gizzy, will you promise me that you'll behave? My heart hasn't recovered from the last time I was out with you."

"Of course. I let Jack lead in everything. Did you know that he likes motorcycles?"

"Does he know that you also like them?"

"Not yet. I have to go. Oh, I nearly forgot. Jack said to tell you that Tate is going out to dinner with us tonight, so you don't have to cook for him. And, Casey, thanks for letting us go with you to get the props. It's really difficult to go anywhere with Jack. People constantly want to talk to him about his movies. We have to hide, and poor Tate is a prisoner. He spent today alone in his house. He said he didn't want to cause anyone any problems."

"Or maybe he didn't want to be around us," Casey said under her breath.

"What was that?"

"Nothing." She was looking at the food bubbling away on the stove. It would have been nice if she'd been told earlier that she wasn't cooking dinner. "I'll see you at seven tomorrow morning. Okay?"

"We'll be there. And thanks again."

Casey put down her phone and looked at the food. Tenderloin with a red-wine glaze. She'd finish cooking it, then store it for tomorrow, but it wouldn't be as good. She planned to tell Tate

Landers what she thought of his lack of consideration in not informing her earlier that he—

"Hello," came a tentative voice from outside her door.

It was Devlin, and she smiled. "Come in. You wouldn't like something to eat, would you? I've been left with a full dinner and no one to share it with."

"Stay for *your* cooking? Yes! Definitely. If it were nails on a bed of rocks and *you* had cooked it, I'd eat it."

Laughing, she unlatched the door for him.

"I feel bad about leaving last night so I brought you something." He handed her a small package prettily wrapped in white paper with a silver ribbon. "I hope it's all right. It's not anything new, but it did belong to my grandmother."

She opened the gift and took out an antique tin chocolate mold. It was about the size of her hand, in two pieces, hinged on one side, with a handsome rooster in the middle. "It's beautiful," she said. "Really lovely." She looked at him. "But if this is something from your family, I can't take it."

He stepped away. "That's okay. The woman I love isn't interested in cooking, so . . ." He shrugged.

"Do you mean Tate's sister, Nina?"

"Right!" Devlin's eyes were wide. "Don't tell me he told you about her? If he talked about his family to you, then he must think very highly of you."

"Not at all." She opened the oven door to pull out a tray of crisp wafers of Gorgonzola and ground piñon nuts and slid them onto a cooling rack. "Help yourself. I can't save these for tomorrow."

"Got stood up, did you?"

"I did," Casey said. "If you want a drink, everything's in that cabinet."

"How about if I make you a gin and tonic?"

"Love it." She tended to the pots on the stove.

Minutes later, Devlin handed her an icy cold, perfectly made drink.

"Thank you."

"I need to explain about last night," he said. "Tate came by, and I'm ashamed to say that I turned coward and ran away. It wasn't very manly of me. I'm sorry."

"It's okay. I understand. But I think you should explain to Olivia what happened. She found me sleeping on the couch and didn't like it."

"Now I am *very* sorry! After all the therapy I've had, I'm still scared of what that man can do to me. I just want my daughter and . . ." He trailed off. "I'm sure you don't want to hear about my life. Can I help you do something? Mash potatoes, maybe? I'm no cook like Tate is, but I can beat the heck out of spuds—if they're soft, that is."

She turned to him. "I didn't know he could cook."

"Didn't you know that Tate Landers can do anything? He can act, he can cook, he can memorize lines at one reading. Hell! He can even *sing*. The rest of us mortals don't have half his talents."

"Would you please open the bottle of wine by the sink? You wouldn't know what happened to my wineglass from last night, would you? It's part of a set that was a gift."

"No, I don't. It was on the table when I left. You were sleeping so peacefully that I didn't dare wake you, and besides, I was hurrying out the front to escape Tate's wrath. You don't think he— No, no, of course not. He's not a thief. Now I realize that I should have stayed here to protect you."

Casey was stirring the glaze and frowning. "He was in my bedroom yesterday and I think he was chasing a peacock out. Kit said—"

Devlin gave a derisive snort. "That doesn't sound like him."

Casey began to plate the food. "Why don't we sit down and have our meal and not so much as mention Tate Landers?"

"I'd love to do that. It's just that usually, when people hear who my ex-brother-in-law is, he's all they want to talk about." He held out a chair for her.

"Not me," Casey said.

"I'm very glad to hear that." He smiled so warmly that she couldn't help returning it.

Darcy and Lizzy do a long, slow dance

When Tate showed up with Gizzy and Jack, Casey knew she shouldn't be surprised, but she was. He stood there looking at her, his eyes a bit sad.

"If you don't want me here I'll leave," he said. "But Kit called and said you might need a couple of men, so here I am."

"Tate got us a bigger truck." Gizzy was encouraging.

The three of them were lined up and staring at Casey in a way that made her feel like the Bad Parent. "Cut it out!" she said. "All three of you! I'm sure it's too much to hope that any of you have eaten. No? I thought not. Get the coolers."

Grinning, Gizzy and Jack went toward the Big House. "I told you she'd have breakfast for us," Gizzy said. "Food surrounds Casey like mosquitoes in a swamp."

Tate stayed where he was, watching her. "I'm serious. If you can't stand a day around me, I'll go. Jack is quite capable of doing whatever you need."

She turned to face him. "Did you get a peacock out of my house?"

"Yes." There was a bit of a smile on his face.

"Why didn't you say so?"

"I felt bad about the pie, and it was kind of nice to be thought of as a villain. Always playing the hero gets tiresome. I shouldn't admit it, but throwing women across saddles is exhausting."

Casey didn't laugh. "I guess I owe you some food. As for today, what are we going to do when you're recognized by squealing girls?"

"I brought a fake mustache and a baseball cap. And I figure that if I keep my clothes on, even my most rabid fans won't recognize me."

At the memory of their first meeting, the blood rushed to her face. His smile showed that he'd seen her blush—and he enjoyed it.

"What about Jack? Doesn't he need a disguise?"

"Fewer people . . ."

"Oh, I see. His movies have a select clientele, while yours are seen by the masses."

"Except for you." He looked at her for a moment. "I better go help Jack with the coolers. He's a puny little thing, and I'd hate for him to collapse under the weight."

Casey went back into her house. After Devlin left, she'd stayed up until midnight making apple cranberry muffins, and she'd put ingredients into her bread machine and set the timer. This morning she'd boiled eggs and made crêpes and packed everything.

"We're ready if you are," Tate said from outside the screen door. "When does the sale start?"

"Ten, but they open for previewing at eight. My sister sent me a long list of items that we need to buy. Could you get this box? It's full of ropes and bungee cords so we can tie things down."

Tate didn't move, just stood there.

"If you'd rather not carry it, I can," she said stiffly.

"There is no way on earth that I'm going to enter your house without a specific invitation. Something like, 'Landers, please come inside.'"

Casey rolled her eyes. "Okay. You may enter. Please come inside and pick up that box while I get the first-aid supplies."

He still didn't move. "Are the pies securely hidden away?"

With a groan, Casey flung the screen open. When he passed her, his arm grazed hers, and electricity shot up her arm and into her shoulder. "Ow!"

Tate smiled as he picked up the box.

"Have you had yourself checked out by a doctor?" she asked. "There must be a reason why you shock people."

"Since it only happens with you, I haven't felt the need for an exam. Besides, since I'm pretty sure it's just old-fashioned sex, I think my doctor would laugh at me. Anything else you need carried?"

"No," she said, frowning. "But I'm sure the electricity has nothing to do with—" She broke off, because Tate had left.

This is bad, she thought. First he reminded her of the idiocy of watching him take a shower, then he said . . .

As she straightened her shoulders, she told herself that she wasn't going to dwell on any of that. She picked up the last of the boxes and went outside, closing the solid door behind her. A closed door would keep out whatever critters were running around, human or otherwise.

The truck they'd brought had a big double cab and a closed back. It was from a major rental company and Tate was standing by the open doors. "Where did this come from?"

"Kit called me yesterday," Tate said. "Let's see if I can quote him verbatim. 'Since you're wasting your life doing absolutely nothing, why don't you call somebody and get a big truck so you can help Casey?' He seemed to be in a bad mood."

She handed him boxes to put into the back. "He is. It's what I told you about Stacy and Kit's son. Kit seems to think she's falling in love with the wrong man."

"Been there, done that," Tate said in a way that made her give a little snort. "Sounds like you have too."

"Not really. My only long-term boyfriend was perfect. He was an altogether nicer, kinder person than I am."

"So you didn't rage at him and falsely accuse him of crimes he didn't commit?"

"Absolutely never."

"Poor guy," Tate said, his eyes sparkling.

"I've been meaning to ask how you and Kit are related."

"I think it's that his maternal grandmother and my great-grandmother were sisters. Or was it my great-great-grandmother? I can't remember which."

When Tate closed the back door of the truck, Casey's eyes widened at what she saw. Standing under a nearby tree, Jack and Gizzy were wrapped around each other and kissing with great enthusiasm.

Tate took a step to the side to block Casey's view.

"How long has that been going on?"

"Since about five minutes after they met. They rarely come up for air. My house has become like a Roman orgy. Underwear is hanging from the chandeliers, and peanut butter is everywhere. What do you think they *do* with all that peanut butter? Make sandwiches?"

She narrowed her eyes at him. "You're not funny. Gizzy's dad won't like this."

"I think that's part of the reason they're trying to hide out. In public they barely lock pinkies, but when they're alone at my house . . ." With a shrug, he turned and yelled, "Jack! We're packed and ready to go. I'm driving." He looked at Casey. "You get shotgun beside me."

Minutes later, the four of them were in the truck, Jack and Gizzy in the back. As Tate left town and pulled onto the highway, Casey began handing out food and drink. After they ate, Gizzy snuggled up to Jack and the two of them immediately fell asleep in each other's arms.

"You're looking at them like you're the disapproving school-marm. They don't have sex in Summer Hill?"

She started to defend herself but didn't. "How would I know? I'm sure you can answer that better than I can. How's Angela Yates?"

"Have you been reading the fan mags?"

She didn't tell him that last night Devlin had mentioned the starlet. They'd been talking about themselves, comparing stories of education and relationships, when he'd said that he had dated Ms. Yates, who was a very pretty, up-and-coming young actress. But then she'd met Tate. "And that was the end of *me,*" Devlin said. She'd left a Christmas party with Tate, and Devlin never saw her again.

When Casey didn't answer his question, Tate glanced at her and the teasing look left his face. "I've never met the young woman. Don't you know that most of what you read in those magazines and see on the Internet is a lie? If I'm seen at the same restaurant as some starlet, the next day they'll say we were meeting in secret and she's going to leave her husband for me." He changed lanes. "We've got a long drive ahead of us so why don't you tell me about yourself? I heard you used to run Christie's in D.C. What made you quit?"

"How do you know I wasn't fired for being a bad cook?"

"That pie I stole," he said. "It was as addictive as a drug. Not too sweet, a bit tart. It had a cream base but was also crunchy. The owner of a restaurant would *never* fire somebody who could cook like that. So you must have left for some other reason. My guess is that your leaving had something to do with the perfect boyfriend."

For a moment Casey looked out the window at the passing scenery. Virginia really was a beautiful state. The only person she'd told the truth of what happened to make her leave the restaurant was her mother.

But right now, being isolated in the car with a man she hardly knew—but who sent electricity racing through her—with the couple cuddled in the back, was making her feel like telling the truth.

"Who was the one who did the dumping?" All humor was gone from Tate's voice.

"He was."

"Hurts, doesn't it?" He sounded sympathetic.

"I don't know." She paused. "I wasn't there."

Tate waited, but when Casey said no more, he said, "I love stories. It's a lot of why I got into acting. My mother used to tell my sister and me fascinating stories about her summers at Tattwell. I—"

"Your family owned the place? I didn't know that. Did you—?"

"Oh, no, you don't. You first. Tell me how he broke up with you when you weren't there. A Post-it note? Email? Twitter? What was it?"

His tone was lightening the mood. So far she'd only been able to cry at the thought of what happened. One night over a glass of wine she'd started to tell Stacy, but wine on an empty stomach had dulled her senses so much that she didn't continue. "None of the above," Casey said.

"Phone message? Skywriting? He had someone else tell you?"

Casey was beginning to smile. "He didn't tell me at all." She looked at Tate. "I didn't know he was gone until ten days after he left."

Tate glanced at her with what was supposed to be a concerned look, but he couldn't keep it. He let out a burst of laughter so loud that Jack and Gizzy stirred.

"Shhhh, you'll wake them up."

"Then they'll start kissing again and I'll start looking at you and we know how that ends. I thought you were going to hit me with a spoon over a pie. If I stole a kiss you'd probably use a tire iron. You have to divert my mind. Move to the middle and tell me everything."

"I don't think— Why are you slowing down?" She knew the answer. "Okay, I'm moving. But don't *touch* me."

"Wouldn't dream of it. Fasten your seatbelt. Now, tell me."

"It was all my fault," she began.

"Let me judge for myself."

"I took on too much, and that caused the problems. You see, Mr. Galecki—he owns Christie's—wanted someone to bring the old place back to life."

"So he wisely chose you."

"Actually, I was fifth on his list of possibles, but I didn't know that until three years later. He's a wily old man and I think he figured me out in an instant. He told me he thought I was too young to do the job."

"And his words lit a bomb of determination inside you?"

"Exactly," she said. "Everyone, even my mom, told me not to take that restaurant on. I thought she doubted that I could do the work, but no, she saw through Lecki."

"My guess is that he hired you because you were young and alive with the old I-can-do-it attitude. And you were probably very cheap."

"That's exactly right. I was determined to show them all that I *could* do it. So anyway, back to my boyfriend, Ben. We'd been dating off and on since college. For most of the time, I was in culinary school and he was getting his law degree. After we moved in together, he started his new job and I began at Christie's. We hardly saw each other, but it was okay. We were both young and ambitious and . . ." She shrugged. "It worked. At least I thought it did."

She took a breath. "But last fall Lecki booked me for three weddings in ten days. He just kept telling the brides, 'Oh, Casey can do that.' Whatever those girls could come up with, he told me to do it. Port-wine sauce, check. Every chicken deboned, check. I had to do everything!

"I was working sixteen-hour shifts, with a full crew, but after the first wedding, two of my cooks came down with the flu. I knew they were lying. They were like me and exhausted."

"You were gone so much that the boyfriend decided to leave? After which wedding?"

"Uh ..." she said. "I don't know when he left, because I didn't notice that he wasn't there. I was coming in at midnight and falling onto the bed. I thought he was asleep beside me. Each morning at six I'd take a three-minute shower and talk to him the whole time. He didn't reply, but it was early and he'd never been a morning person."

Tate glanced at her with lips that seemed to be holding in laughter. "He'd moved out?"

"Yeah." For the first time, Casey began to see humor in it all. "After the reception of the third wedding, I collapsed onto a chair and I called him. He answered right away. I told him I was fed up with all that Lecki dropped onto me and that I wanted us to go on a long vacation to somewhere warm. We'd have two weeks of wine and moonlight and fabulous sex."

"Sounds great to me."

"That's when he said, 'Casey, I moved out of the apartment over a week ago, and last weekend I went out on a date with a paralegal. I like her a lot.'"

Every time Casey thought about that night, about how bad she'd felt, tears had come to her, but when she looked at Tate, with his dancing eyes, she smiled. "It's not funny. What kind of insensitive woman doesn't notice that the man living with her has moved out? Gone. His closet was empty but I didn't see it. And I'd been *talking* to him."

Tate couldn't hold his laughter in. "He must have been a real dud. He was so boring that you didn't know when he wasn't there."

"Actually, he's a tax attorney and he's quite interesting."

"Oh, in that case I understand. My tax attorney is fascinating. He's always telling me I need to file document 8A6X-12, or whatever."

Casey tried not to, but she laughed too. "So maybe sometimes his conversation did get a bit technical, but Ben was a good guy."

"Sounds like it. Spontaneous and fun, was he?"

"Will you stop it?" When she made the mistake of slapping him on the shoulder, electricity shot through her body. She unclicked her seatbelt and moved back to the far side of the truck.

"Damn!" Tate said. "Maybe I should buy a lightning rod. So what happened after your jealous boyfriend ran away?"

"Ben was *not* jealous."

"You, just a kid, single-handedly brought back an old restaurant to its current glory, and you could handle three weddings in ten days even when your staff was depleted. Unless he's some legal phenomenon, he was jealous. Was he a genius, rapidly on his way to IRS heaven?"

"No," Casey said. "He had some setbacks, but we agreed that he would eventually make partner."

"While you were going straight up to success. Forget him. What did you do after you found out he was gone?"

She hesitated. "I took a look at my life and realized that I didn't have one. I'd worked so hard to prove that I could bring the old restaurant back to life that I was left with only one friend and my mom. I called Mom. When I picked up the phone I was crying and at the lowest point of my life. I'd never felt so alone. But, as always, she helped me make a plan, and when I got off the phone I was smiling again. The next day I gave two weeks' notice at the restaurant. I knew my sous chef could take over and would do a good job. I packed up everything I owned and I left."

"And out of everywhere in the world, you chose to go to Summer Hill, Virginia?"

"Yes and no. My mom suggested that it was time that I met my father, and he lives in Summer Hill."

"Let me guess. Your mother had a torrid affair with Kit Montgomery."

"Heavens, no! Kit isn't my father. Dr. Chapman is. I'm a donor baby. I have eleven half siblings—that we know about, that is. There could be more."

Tate gaped at her in astonishment. "Who— What—"

Smiling, Casey said, "Look, we're here."

"I want to hear more about this Dr. Chapman," Tate said.

"You will, and you'll meet him too. He's going to play Mr. Bennet. Turn here."

They followed homemade signs that pointed the way to the sale and led them down a rutted gravel road. Weeds grazed the underside of the truck, and Tate had to repeatedly jerk the wheel to miss the big potholes.

The jostling woke Jack and Gizzy. Leaning forward, Jack looked out the windshield. "I got the idea this place was a mansion. Doesn't seem like the entrance to one."

Casey handed him the brochure. On the front was a photo of a sprawling house that was part Victorian, part Queen Anne, and more than a little creepy.

"Beautiful," Jack said, then leaned back, and he and Gizzy began kissing.

"Give us a break, would you?" Tate said. "My envy is getting the better of me. There it is."

As the house came into view, everyone looked out the front. It seemed to be as long as a football field, with turrets with witch's cap roofs, and its windows looked like they hadn't been cleaned in years. The house was in such bad repair that it had an air of abandonment about it.

"Looks just like home," Jack said, and they laughed.

The huge old house was surrounded by what appeared to have once been a beautiful garden. But now only a few trees were left, along with the stony remnants of flower beds. Around the house was endless farm acreage that had been plowed and was ready for planting. To their left was a parking area, with a few pickups and SUVs already there.

"Dealers," Casey said as Tate parked the truck. "Stacy said they'd be here early and that if we want things we have to act fast." She'd printed out what Stacy had sent her, so each item had a color photo with it. She divided the pages into four groups and handed them out. "I think the best thing would be for us to separate and stake claim to what's on each list." She gave them envelopes of cash. "This is from Kit and the prices are estimates, so try to keep in the budget."

Tate turned off the engine, then reached across Casey to the glove box and pulled out a baseball cap and a little packet. She watched him tie back his hair and slide the cap down over his eyes. Next went a huge, bushy mustache, which didn't seem to want to stay on, and aviator glasses.

"I should have shaved," he said.

"And ruin your image?" Casey said, making him smile. "Okay, everyone know what to do?"

"Sure." Jack handed his pile of papers to Gizzy. "We work together." He opened the truck door.

"But that's not—"

Tate took Casey's papers and put them with his. "Sounds like a good idea to me."

Casey started to protest, but the truth was that she didn't look forward to wandering about the ratty old place by herself. She got out of the truck and joined the others. "If anyone gets hungry or thirsty, food is in the back of the truck."

They left the parking area, and when they rounded the corner they looked up at the house. Up close it was downright scary. A gutter hung down, some of the windows were cracked, and a roof at the far end appeared as if it might collapse at any second.

"Welcome!" said a little man standing by a table where a woman sat with a cash box. "There's a twenty-dollar-per-person cover charge to see it all. If you buy anything, it's refunded, but I have to get something from the looky-loos."

"This is your house?" Jack asked.

"It is now. My great-aunt's family owned it. Monster, isn't it?"

"What are you going to do with it?" Gizzy asked.

"Sell everything I can, then bulldoze the house and plant kale. This whole country is kale-mad. There's money to be made in anything kale." He was staring at Tate. "You look like—"

"Don't say it," Tate said in a heavy Southern accent. "Come on, let's go."

Jack handed over four twenty-dollar bills and they went through.

In front of the house were tables covered with dusty items. Chairs and small tables were set around on the grass, which seemed to have been freshly mowed. The couples separated.

"Big stuff is in the house," the little man called to them. "The prices are on everything, and I won't sell anything before ten A.M. But I might be persuaded to bargain."

"He dreams of bidding wars," Tate said and Casey agreed. "Come on, let's go inside. I'd like to see this place before the hordes get here."

Casey knew she should start searching for the items they needed, but she stuffed the papers into her pocket and followed him. He didn't go in the front door but through the side. They came out into what seemed to be a basement passage with lots of doors leading to side rooms.

"It looks like a movie set," Casey said.

"My thought exactly. Can't you imagine a guy with an ax chasing the pretty girl through here?"

"He wants her kale?"

Tate laughed as he went through a doorway into the kitchen. A row of copper saucepans hung over the big stove, and against a wall were a dozen copper cake molds.

"Ooooh," Casey said.

"Your idea of heaven?"

"Close to it."

They wandered about the old house, all four stories, and found most of the items on the list. High up was a bedroom that looked to be the master. An old inlaid-wood jewelry box caught Casey's eye, but the price was too high. She and Tate agreed that it was sad that the house was to be torn down.

They lost track of time and only realized the sale had begun when people began arriving. Tate and Casey raced down the stairs. Jack was already at the sale table, handing over a stack of hundreds to the little man.

"You find everything?" Tate asked.

"Most of it. There are some small items we didn't see."

"Your voice!" the man said. "You *are* him." His small eyes glittered. "I forgot to tell you that some of this stuff has been priced incorrectly. The sofa you want is an antique. It's about three hundred years old. I don't know who priced it at four hundred dollars, but they left off a zero. It's four thousand dollars."

"Listen, Buster—" Jack looked as he did in the movies, like he was about to punch the man in the face.

The screams of a woman cut him off.

ACT ONE, SCENE TWENTY-FOUR
Jane Bennet is exposed

They all turned in the direction of the sound. At the far end of the house, a woman stared up at the roof, her face showing her fear. Sitting on the edge, three stories up, was a little boy, smiling, his chubby legs hanging down. It was as if he was getting ready to leap down into his mother's arms. But then, the roof seemed almost too rotten to hold him.

Tate looked at Jack. "You go. I'll get the rope. I hope you don't have to play catch."

Casey's mind raced. "Where is Gizzy?" She ran to the back of the truck.

Tate flung open the doors, climbed inside, and got the box of ropes and bungee cords. "I have no idea where she is. Call 911 and get the fire department here." He took off running.

"You can't go out on that roof," she called after him, but he didn't hear her.

Casey took her phone out of her pocket. The signal was weak, but she got through to 911.

The dispatcher answered right away. "You're our third caller," she said. "The truck is on its way, but it's going to be twenty to thirty minutes before they can get there. Can someone talk the child into holding still?"

"We'll try," Casey said and hung up.

"What happened?" Gizzy asked from behind her. "I was look-ing for—"

Casey grabbed her sister's hand and started running. "They may need you." People were gathering around the front door and blocking it, so Casey ran to the side. "We'll take the back stairs. I hope I can remember how to get there."

There was a big man at the head of the main staircase, and he was keeping people from going up. A flash of a badge showed that he was a deputy sheriff.

Casey turned to Gizzy in question and she nodded. While the deputy was distracted by some guy with a camera, the two women sneaked past the crowd and ran down the hallway.

"I think this is it." Casey flung open a door to reveal a narrow staircase leading up. There were a lot of footprints in the thick dust.

"Those are from Jack's boots," Gizzy said. "I recognize the print."

At the top was a closed door, but when Casey tried it, it was locked. She knocked. "It's us. Let us in."

"Wait for us in the truck," Tate said through the door. "Jack's going out on the roof to get the kid."

"He's too heavy!" Casey shouted. "He'll go through. Landers, if you don't let us in—" She couldn't think of a good threat.

"Please," Gizzy said. "Please."

Her sweetness made Tate open the door. Jack was by the wide window, with a rope looped about his waist, one end on the floor, the other end in Tate's hands.

Tate was frowning. "We're handling this."

"No," Casey said as she looked at Jack. "You're too heavy. Gizzy will go."

"Absolutely not!" Jack said.

Ignoring him, Casey asked Gizzy, "Can you move in those skinny jeans?"

"No." She unzipped them.

"What the hell are you doing?" Jack spat out.

Casey knelt to unbuckle Gizzy's tall wedge sandals. When Casey stood up, Gizzy was wearing only her pink underpants and a shirt. Her long, trim legs were bare.

Tate was standing to one side, still holding the end of the rope. He seemed to understand what the women were doing because when Casey looked at him, he stepped forward. This wasn't a time to argue. As he looped the rope around Gizzy's waist, he talked to her in a calm voice. "The roof is in bad shape and the old tiles are falling off. You need to step carefully. Test every tile with your foot before putting your weight on it. Understand?"

Gizzy nodded.

"Jack will keep the rope around him and he won't let you go. If you fall, he'll hold on and all of us will bring you up." Tate put his hand behind him, and Jack handed him something they'd tied together out of a bungee cord and another piece of rope. "The stunt coordinator on one of Jack's movies made a harness like this for a scene. You need to get it around the kid, then fasten it to you. That way—"

"If I drop him, he won't fall."

"Yes, exactly." Tate nodded at her. "You ready?"

"Yes," Gizzy said.

Jack's face was solemn as Gizzy came to him. He kissed her, then helped her out the window.

Tate was standing beside Casey. "What the hell were you thinking?" he said quietly. His calm, soothing voice was gone. "This is dangerous. She has no training. She can't—"

"She can!" Casey said. "Gizzy can walk a tightrope, race motorcycles. Whatever. She inherited Dad's inner bad boy."

"Whatever that means," Tate said.

Casey went to the open window beside Jack. He was talking Gizzy through walking on the roof. The child had lost his smile and was now clearly afraid. His mother was still below, talking to him and telling him not to move. Around her was a growing crowd of onlookers.

"Watch the pretty lady," his mom called up to him. "She's going to get you down, then I'm going to buy you so much ice cream you can go swimming in it. Would you like that?"

When the child twisted his body to look at Gizzy, half a dozen tiles fell to the ground and the crowd below gasped.

"Stay calm and test the tiles," Jack said.

Gizzy stepped carefully, but she didn't seem to be afraid.

Tate stood behind Casey, looking over her head. "She's good. Just so she doesn't freak when she gets to the edge."

"She won't. She never does. She's helped the Summer Hill Fire Department many times."

They all watched as Gizzy slowly made her way to the boy. Every time tiles fell, the crowd reacted loudly. Gizzy would pause and wait, then take another step. She smiled at the boy. "Hi," she said. "Want me to get you off this roof?"

The child nodded, but when he held up his arms to her, more tiles fell down.

"His name is Stevie," Jack said. His hands were white from gripping the rope so tightly. He was very aware that this wasn't the movies. There were no nets a few feet away, no crane on standby.

Stevie began to cry, and when he did, he moved just enough to make everyone gasp in fear.

"I need you to hold absolutely still," Gizzy said to the boy. "Can you do that?"

The boy gave a nod, but he was beginning to shake.

Gizzy changed tactics. "Isn't this *fun*?" Her voice was happy, full of adventure. "I love walking on roofs. But I guess you do too or you wouldn't be sitting on the edge."

The child stared at her in surprise—and his trembling slowed down.

"When I was your age I climbed on every roof there was. I scared my mother a lot." Gizzy stopped as half a dozen tiles tumbled to the ground and loudly smashed into pieces. Through the ensuing noise, she kept her eyes on the boy and never lost her reassuring smile. When it was calm again, she held up the harness the men had made.

"Stevie, I'm going to slip this around you so the men in the window can pull us inside. How does that sound?"

The child nodded. There were tears glistening in his eyes, but he seemed stronger, more determined.

"I just need for you to sit very, very still. Don't move your arms or your legs. Okay?"

Again he nodded as Gizzy slowly slipped the rope over his head and down to his waist. It was harder to get the bungee cord between his legs and fasten it. Twice Gizzy had to wait for falling tiles to settle. When the old gutter broke off and crashed to the ground, the gasp of the onlookers made the child throw his arms around her.

The unexpected weight almost made Gizzy lose her footing, but she balanced and managed to sit down.

Below them in the crowd were Mr. and Mrs. Johnson from Tucson, Arizona. They were one of the few remaining retired couples who could afford to spend their summers driving around in a gas-guzzling RV. Mrs. Johnson liked estate sales and had an eye for a bargain. She shipped lovely things back home to her sister, who sold them in her antiques shop. Mr. Johnson's passion was photography, and the RV was fitted with deep drawers full of equipment. Right now he had his new Nikon Df equipped with a 200- to 400-mm lens, and he was recording the rescue. It was his wife who'd identified Tate Landers, while he loved Jack Worth's movies. The Df didn't have video, but it did contain a very fast

256GB memory card. Mr. Johnson put the camera on continuous shots and kept snapping.

Gizzy's grip was strong, and she was able to hold on to the sturdy little boy and stand up.

Now that Stevie was with Gizzy, Jack began talking to her, his voice encouraging. "Just a few more steps, baby. I'm right here." He was steadily pulling on the rope, taking up the slack as she came forward.

She was almost to the window when the tiles under her feet flew out from under her. Gizzy and the boy went down. Her arms stayed around him and she made no attempt to catch herself. She had absolute faith that Jack would hold her—and he did.

Tate grabbed the rope behind Jack and helped hold the weight of Gizzy and the boy.

Immediately, Casey saw what needed to be done. It was going to be impossible to pull Gizzy in with only the rope without removing a lot of her skin. The tiles were so loose that she'd never get a foothold. Casey ran to the door and shouted down the stairs for the deputy to come up: "We need you." The big man was there in seconds, and he relieved Tate at his end of the rope.

Casey looked at him. They both knew what she had to do, and his eyes asked if she was willing. She nodded.

She pulled off her tennis shoes, then went to the open window, Tate behind her.

"I won't let you fall. You know that, don't you?"

"Just stop the electricity. For right now, don't be a movie star in hiding."

In an instant, Tate pulled off the cap, unfastened his hair, and tossed the mustache into a corner. "Better?"

"Yes," she said as she climbed into the window, then put her hands down onto the roof. She was going out headfirst. Tate clasped her waist, and as she inched onto the roof, he slowly worked his way down her body to her knees.

"Somebody's been working out," he said.

Casey was looking at Gizzy, who was hanging by a rope around her waist, a heavy, frightened toddler clinging to her. "Can you believe that he's flirting with me?"

"Yeah. He likes you."

The sisters smiled, trying to reassure each other. Yes, Gizzy was a daredevil and seemed to be fearless, but Casey saw the worry in her eyes. The rope was around Gizzy's waist and cutting into her with the pressure. She was bleeding in a dozen places and must have been in pain. It was clear that the boy was holding on so tightly that Gizzy could hardly breathe—but then, she was holding him just as tightly.

When Casey held out her hands, Gizzy clasped them hard, hands to wrists. "You ready?"

"Yes," Gizzy said.

Casey yelled, "Now!" and the three men began pulling, two on the rope, with Tate holding Casey's legs and drawing her in. It hurt. The rough surfaces of the tiles and the old window took off a layer of skin on Casey's arms. She couldn't imagine what was being done to Gizzy's bare legs.

When Casey was nearly inside, Tate pulled her the rest of the way through the window. She never let go of her sister's arms, didn't break eye contact with her.

Jack leaped forward to grab Gizzy's arms.

The door burst open and the boy's mother ran in, her arms outstretched, her voice hysterically calling her son's name.

Only when Gizzy was standing in the room did she finally loosen her grip on the little boy. He fell into his mother's arms.

Behind them, Tate pulled Casey to him. Her heart was pounding and she was shaking. Tate's hold on her was comforting—with no electricity.

He bent his head so his cheek was on her hair. "You didn't inherit your dad's love of adventure?"

"None of it. I'm a total coward." She knew she should break away from him, and she could hear Jack and Gizzy and the deputy talking. They said they were taking Gizzy to get medical treatment. Casey knew she should go too, but she didn't move out of Tate's arms. They seemed to fit together perfectly, and it had been a long time since a man had held her. Tate's laughter at the story of her breakup had made her remember things that she'd blocked out. Maybe it was what she'd just been through or Tate's humor, or maybe it was being held after so long without, but she thought about what had happened with her and Ben. Months before he moved out, he'd made some very unpleasant gibes about how Casey was the only one who could run the restaurant. She knew he'd been passed over for promotion, and she'd done her best to make it up to him. There had been fabulous dinners followed by great sex, followed by days of ego-boosting, but nothing she did stopped his endless little snipes.

Before she knew it, tears came to her eyes, and she tightened her arms around Tate. He buried his hand in her hair and held her, saying nothing, just standing there with his arms around her.

The tears lasted only seconds, then she became aware of where she was. It was silent in the room. Had the others left or were they watching?

When Casey gazed up at him, Tate kissed her forehead—and electricity shot through her.

She pushed away from him and glared. "You had to ruin it, didn't you?"

He didn't look the least bit apologetic. "I did. My arms around a beautiful woman who I like very much turns me on. Sorry. My weakness. Are you okay?"

She took a breath. "Yes." Except for deep embarrassment, she thought. "We better go. The owner will sell everything and we'll have a bare stage for the play."

"No. Jack will take care of him. That fierce act he shows in his movies is real. Are you sure you're all right?"

"Yes, I'm fine." As he opened the door for her, she looked at him. "I'm sorry about falling apart."

His eyes were serious. "You were very courageous. If I'd let you go, you would have slid down the roof and hit the ground head-first. It takes a lot of trust, as well as faith, to do what you did." He smiled. "And a lot of muscle on my part. Where did you get quads like that?"

Casey went into the hall. "You make me sound like an Olympic lifter. I just haul big, heavy pots off the stove, and I run around the kitchen for sixteen hours at a time."

"The trainer gets here tomorrow. Maybe you can tell him your technique. I want muscles like you have."

"Why, you—" She started to smack his shoulder but drew back.

"Wise," he said. "That electricity you put out hurts weak little me."

"That *I* put out? It's *you* who thinks he's Benjamin Franklin."

"Is that the Ben who was so jealous of you that he left in a very cowardly way?"

Casey stopped at the head of the stairs. For months she'd been living with guilt, thinking that she'd been terrible to a really nice man, but Tate was making her see things differently. She smiled at him. "Thanks," she said softly. "Thank you for not dropping me off the roof and for making me feel better about Ben. It was very kind of you, especially after I . . . I . . ."

"Bawled me out after I saved your house from total destruction by a rampaging bird the size of a bear cub?"

She laughed. "More or less." When she went down the stairs, Tate was close behind her.

Laughter, she thought. It's what she most needed after the harrowing experience on the roof.

At the foot of the stairs, she started toward the kitchen, but Tate stopped in front of her. He nodded toward her bare forearms. They were bleeding. Tate had so distracted her that she'd forgotten about them, but the sight of the blood brought it all back and she felt her knees giving way.

Tate caught her with his hands under her elbows. "Let's go to the truck and clean you up."

She nodded and followed him out the side door to the parking lot.

Gizzy was sitting on the grass by the truck. She had a bandage on her forehead and gauze around her left hand. Her legs were now covered by her jeans, but Casey guessed there were bandages under there.

"People know you're here, so we need to leave," Gizzy said to Tate. "Jack had a talk with the owner about his increase of prices. Seems like it worked, because everything we wanted is going to be put into the truck. We just need to wait until they bring it here."

"Actually," Casey said, "I want some things from the kitchen before we go."

Tate was using wipes to clean the scrapes on Casey's arms. When he put a bandage on one of them, she didn't dare look at him. What he was doing now, this tender caring for her, and what he'd done earlier were having an effect on her.

"There," Tate said. "It wasn't as bad as I thought. I need to speak to Gizzy for a moment."

Casey stayed on the truck while he went to Gizzy and squatted down beside her on the grass. They are a truly beautiful couple! Casey thought. Gizzy was tall and gorgeous, the same as Tate. Her blondeness matched well with his dark hair and eyes.

Casey was appalled to feel a rush of jealousy. Ashamed of herself, she left the truck and went toward the house.

Tate caught up with her. "I thought I'd play pack mule and help carry the copper pans you want."

"You'll be recognized."

"After what you did today, you're more likely to be asked for an autograph than I am."

When Tate smiled at her, Casey remembered how it felt to be in his arms—and how good he looked with Gizzy. Turning away, she tried to get her emotions under control. She told herself that the trauma she'd just been through would make any man look good.

There were two women in the kitchen checking out old implements. Tate waited until they left before he entered the room. "So, which pieces do you want? Or shall we make a bid for all of it?"

"I thought I'd hunt for chocolate molds. I might start collecting them."

"What do they look like?"

She described them, and Tate began examining the highest shelves, moving things around as he searched. "You have a lot of them?"

"Only one. Devlin Haines gave it to me."

Tate's back was to her and for a moment he halted. She couldn't see his face, but she knew he'd been affected by the name. "Did he?"

"It belonged to his grandmother. I said he shouldn't give me something of such great sentiment, but he did. What's between you two, other than being ex-relatives, that is?"

When Tate turned around, his face was expressionless. "He is my niece's father."

"I know that, but what—"

"I think I better go back to the truck and see if Jack needs any help." He left so fast he almost raised a cloud of dust.

Casey stood there blinking at the space where he'd just been.

Obviously, he didn't want to talk about his relationship with Devlin. Tate Landers would flirt, but it didn't seem as if he'd share his real feelings.

She stayed in the old kitchen for a while, trying to settle her thoughts and emotions. There wasn't anything for chocolate, but there were two copper cake molds that had good tin linings. After paying for them, she started back toward the truck.

Gizzy met her halfway and held out the inlaid jewelry box that Casey had so admired. "Tate had me buy this and he asked me to give it to you. I don't know why he didn't give it to you himself."

"This is what you two were whispering about?"

"Yes. You didn't think Tate was making a pass at me, did you?"

"Of course not!" she said as she took the pretty box. "But you looked so good when you had your jeans off that I wouldn't blame him."

Laughing, Gizzy took Casey's arm in hers and lowered her voice, but she couldn't contain her excitement—or her wonder. "Jack wasn't turned off by what I did. And he wasn't scared of me. Oh, Casey, I think this may be *real*." Turning, she ran back to the truck.

"Please be careful," Casey said to no one. She needed to have a talk with Gizzy about not falling head over heels for a guy who would probably drop her when he went back to his home in Los Angeles. Gizzy was a small-town girl, a pastor's daughter who went to church three times a week, while Jack was a movie star— and everyone knew what that meant.

She got to the truck as Tate and Jack were closing the back doors. Jack walked away with Gizzy.

"Thanks," Casey said to Tate as she held up the box. "I didn't realize you knew that I liked it."

He was smiling, but she saw that it was without warmth. "You're welcome. Are you ready to go?" He didn't wait for her answer, just turned away.

"I'm sorry," she said loudly.

He glanced back at her. "For what?"

"Being a Mean Girl. I know you and Devlin aren't friends and I shouldn't have mentioned him. But I'll be honest and tell you that I've shared a couple of meals with him and I like him."

"Like him how?" There was such a deep scowl on Tate's face that she took a step back.

"We're friendly," she said. "That's all. He talks about Emmie a lot."

That statement made Tate snort in derision. "How the hell would he know about her? She——"

"You two ready to go?" Jack yelled. "Gizzy knows a place where we can picnic. Casey, did you bring enough food for lunch?"

"We could feed a town with all she brought." Tate opened the side door and held it for Casey. "You're stuck in here with me."

She was glad that his anger seemed to have disappeared, but when she looked inside the truck, she halted. Half the seat was taken up by two huge boxes. "What is that? A piano?"

"Just a few extra items Gizzy wanted," Jack said.

"And so did you!" she shot back.

"Are you saying that you two filled the entire back of this huge truck and this is the overflow?" Casey asked.

"Well ..." Gizzy glanced at Jack. "Kit did say his cousin Dr. Jamie and his wife are coming to help Dad out. They're going to need furniture, and our sister needs some for her shop, and I saw a bed that Josh would love, and ..." She shrugged.

"Looks like you're going to have to sit close to me," Tate said, and there was happiness in his voice.

"Hmph!" Casey said. "I just need to find the switch to turn off the electricity."

"You didn't see the switch on that first morning?" His face was all innocence. "Now, Mean Girl, you've really hurt my feelings. You didn't see *any* switches?"

Casey's face turned red but she couldn't help laughing. "I can't remember very clearly. Besides, what you do with soap is none of my business." When she threw a leg up to get into the backseat, Tate put his hand under her backside and pushed.

As she went up, he said softly, "I'd like to show you what I can do with soap."

When they got on the road, Jack and Gizzy began to quietly talk. In the back, by necessity, Casey sat close to Tate. Even if they weren't actually touching, she could feel his warmth.

She looked away from him, across the boxes, and out the window. Now that it was quiet, she was beginning to think about what had happened. She remembered that little boy sitting on the edge of the roof and Gizzy dangling from a rope. As the images came back to her, Casey thought of her own part in the rescue. If Tate had let her go . . .

"Thinking about what happened?"

"Yes." She changed the subject. "I'm glad we got all the things Stacy picked out."

But Tate didn't let her avoid the issue. "I know it was scary hanging down the roof like that, with your body supported by someone you hardly know. Have you ever done anything like that before?"

"Never. I'll probably wake up at two A.M. in a panic."

Tate looked serious. "I could stay with you tonight and . . ." He gave a suggestive shrug.

"Thanks for your generous offer, but I'll pass."

"If you change your mind, you know where I live."

She couldn't keep from laughing, and Tate smiled. She knew he'd been teasing her on purpose and it had worked to bring her back to the present. "Thanks." She lowered her voice. "If I'd had time to think, I'm sure I would have been too scared to do anything. But it all happened so fast. But then, Gizzy was the real hero."

"No," Tate said. "She loved it. There wasn't any real fear in her. When you're afraid but do it anyway, that's courage." He could see that Casey was getting serious again. "Like me. At the auditions, all those women were looking at me like I was supposed to fulfill their every dream. But I got up there and performed anyway. Now, *that* is courage."

Casey was smiling again. "Until I got on the stage."

"Do you think I'm shorter today? I could swear that your delivery of Ms. Austen's lines cut me down by at least four inches."

"You? It was all new to me. You're used to it."

"Ha! You turned down my best invitation. You so wounded my pride that I may never be able to get another woman in bed with me. I think *you* are the only one who can heal me. How about eight tonight?"

"You are incorrigible." Casey was laughing so much that she didn't realize the truck had stopped.

Jack and Gizzy had turned around and were staring at them.

"I hate to interrupt your rom-com banter," Jack said, "but we have reached our destination. Last one out has to carry the metal cooler." He and Gizzy got out of the truck.

Casey looked across Tate at the door, but he didn't open it.

"I'm serious," he said. "If you have any aftermath from today, let me know. If it's in the middle of the night, I'll come. I've had my share of trauma in my life and I know how to handle it. And I'll keep my hands to myself. Okay?"

"Yes." She gazed into his eyes. "I think I'm all right. If there hadn't been a happy ending I would be a mess, but I feel good about it all."

"If you wake up screaming from a nightmare that I dropped you, call me. Give me your cell."

She handed him her phone, he typed in his number, then he opened the door and helped her out.

Darcy's dancing gets dirty

Casey and Tate were sitting on an old quilt by a pretty rushing stream. Huge rocks glistened and the sun sparkled on the water. Over them was a dense canopy of trees. On the quilt was a feast of Casey's cooking: jicama and citrus salad, olive tapenade, three kinds of bread, and a selection of cheeses.

Their backs against a wide boulder, they were munching on coconut-lime cookies and watching Jack and Gizzy argue. Casey and Tate were too far away to hear what was being said, but they could see them clearly.

"What's that about?" Casey asked.

"I was going to ask you the same thing. But my guess is disillusionment. You fall for a delicate flower, then she does what?"

"Beats him on a motorcycle," Casey said. "Jumps out of a plane. Whatever. Men can't take it."

"Jack can. I have confidence in him."

"Bet you another berry custard pie that he'll leave her."

"If by some freak chance you win, what do you get?"

She started to say, "Another shower show," but didn't. "The satisfaction of having won."

Tate groaned. "What a cop-out. There must be something you want. Your own restaurant? Boyfriend back?"

"I haven't decided yet. Not about the boyfriend but about

my future. What about you? Anything you want that you don't have?"

He stretched out on the quilt, his hands behind his head, all six feet plus of him lying beside her. "I want to be in a comedy or a mystery or a horror movie. I'll take anything besides brooding hero."

"But you're so good at it," Casey said. "Just today when you glowered at me, I felt like a princess in a tower."

"Yeah?" When he looked at her, he saw she was teasing. "I'm going to get you for that. I—" His cellphone rang. "It's probably my agent telling me I'm going to be in the next Wolverine movie. . . . Nope. Better. It's Emmie." He touched the phone on. "Hi, sweetheart. Are you still making your mother crazy?"

He paused and listened. "Right now I'm lying on a quilt, watching Uncle Jack argue with a very pretty girl. I think he's losing. Beside me is Casey. She made the pie I ate. . . . Oh. Okay." He handed the phone to her. "Emmie wants to talk to you."

Puzzled, Casey took the phone. "Hello?" She listened. "Yes, I can make grilled cheese sandwiches. I grill the bread, then put the cheese on the toasted part and re-grill the whole thing. Makes it very crunchy. . . . No, I never use the kind of whipped cream that comes in a can." She handed the phone back to Tate.

"Does she pass?" Smiling, he nodded at Casey. "Emmie wants to know where you got the hey-diddle-diddle pajamas and would you please marry her uncle—that's me—and cook for all of us?"

Casey blinked a few times. "My mom got them. I'll ask her where, and no."

Tate went back to the phone. "Yes to the cooking, but sorry, she won't take me as part of the deal. Story of my life. When will you be here?" He paused. "Yes, I'm sure Casey can make a pie that tastes like an Oreo." He looked at her and she nodded. "I hear your mom calling you. . . . Yeah, me too. Lots. Do try to behave, but feel free to nag to get here sooner." He laughed. "No, you can't ride the peacock. Go on, now. Kiss your mom for me." He turned off his phone and looked back at Casey. "You were telling me the plans for your life."

"No, I wasn't. You've told me very little about yourself. How did you get started in movies?"

He took a while to answer. "The official story is that I was discovered by a director when I was nine years old. That's true but it's also a lie." He rolled over and stood up, his long body unfolding like a great cat. "Let's walk, or we may see what we don't want to."

Jack and Gizzy had stopped arguing and were now kissing.

"Besides, my libido can't stand the torture. You wouldn't want to ..." He wiggled his eyebrows to let her know what he was thinking.

Maybe it was his ability as an actor, but he seemed able to project images into her mind. Lazily making love on the quilt. Sharing a glass of wine. Her lips on his sun-warmed skin. His mouth caressing her. Her—

"Stop it!" Tate said in a low voice. "Your face gives everything away and I can't take it. You're too desirable. The day is too warm, the air too fragrant, and I've had too much wine."

Casey looked away from him.

"Come on," he said. "I saw a path nearby." He held out his hand, but before Casey could take it, he drew back. "Better not risk it. With our mutual thoughts, if we touch we might start a forest fire. How would we explain that arson to the fire marshal?"

What he said was so ridiculous that she laughed. "Okay, no touching, no anything but what friends do. Lead and I will follow you."

Tate put his hand on his heart. "To a man, those are the sexiest words a woman can say."

"How about this? Stop the melodramatic acting and *go*! Jack and Gizzy seem like they might start on the peanut butter."

Tate began walking down the path. "Just so you know, the bad-acting hit was a good turnoff, but mentioning the peanut butter is enticing. Makes me think of you in those PJs with absolutely nothing on under them. Did your mother really give them to you? What was she thinking?"

"That I'm still a little girl who likes fairy tales. I thought you were going to tell me how you became an actor."

They'd come to a shallow stream that they were going to have to wade across. "You ever see the movie *Dirty Dancing*?"

"A hundred times. Do you do the lift? Even I saw the movie where Ryan Gosling—"

Tate gasped. "Don't put a dagger in my heart with my competition's name."

"You're better-looking than he is," she said seriously.

"You've made my day. So how about it?" He was pointing to a big tree that had fallen across the stream.

She knew what he meant: the scene in *Dirty Dancing* when Patrick Swayze and Jennifer Grey balance on the log while he talks about how he came to be a dancer. "Nope," Casey said. "I'm not Gizzy. I don't do logs. How about if we—"

Tate took her hand, but no electricity shot between them, just warmth and encouragement.

"How do you do that? Turn emotions on and off?"

"I have no idea. Some kind of control, I guess." He started toward the log, but when Casey didn't move, he put her hand to his lips. His voice dropped to a low growl. "The scent of you runs through my body. It delights me, excites me, drives me mad with desire. To touch you, caress you, to . . ." His voice was a whisper. "To kiss you, I would give my all."

Casey was staring at him, unable to move or to speak.

He dropped her hand. "The log? Wanna try it?"

She had to shake her head to clear it. "Did you make that up?"

"Nah. Lines from one of my movies. It's either more of that or you walk across the log with me."

"Tree!" she said, and pushed past him. "Give me a boost, and watch what you do with your hands."

He lifted her up so she was facing him. He did watch his hands—as they ran down her body. In the next second he was on the log with her.

Casey tried to hide it, but she really was afraid of the height, the narrow roundness of the tree, and maybe a little scared of Tate Landers. If he'd kept on with his hand-kissing and his words, she might have fallen into his arms. She tended to take lovemaking seriously, but it seemed to be a game to him. He could turn the seduction—the electricity between them—off and on at will.

Tate held both her hands as she stepped backward on the log. No matter what else she felt about him, she trusted him to not let her fall.

"We needed the money," he said. "My dad died when I was four and Nina was just a baby."

"I'm sorry."

He shrugged. "It was a long time ago. I grew up seeing my mom struggle to pay the bills and raise us. I wanted to help, but how could I? I was only a kid." They were in the middle of the log, and he let go of one of her hands.

"We were living in California, and a kid at school said his mom was taking him to try out for a role in a movie."

"And you went too and got the job, which means that you were born talented."

"Just the opposite. My mom took me to the audition and it was a cattle call, with over three hundred kids. Most of them were eliminated before the director saw them."

"He only wanted pretty boys?"

Tate gave a half smile. "Physical appearance has a great deal to do with how you're cast."

"A diplomatic answer. But I guess you were the cutest child there."

"I was certainly the most scared kid. But not by the audition. That morning my mother had one of her asthma attacks. It was so bad I thought she was going to die."

"Oh," Casey said. "I really am sorry."

"Thanks. Anyway, that day I was pretty gloomy. The director put all the kids who were possibilities on a stage. He wanted to see if we could follow directions, so he told us that we weren't to laugh no matter what we saw. He then paraded people past us. They did pratfalls, funny dances, made faces, et cetera. One by one, the kids were eliminated."

"But not you."

"No. I was so worried about my mother that nothing on earth could make me smile. After a while there were only three boys left and the director told us to cry. One kid couldn't do it, one faked it, but I . . ."

"You cried for real."

"Oh, yes. The director joked that I was either a great actor or one seriously unhappy kid. He said, 'Okay, so let's see which one it is.' He told me to smile. I don't know if it was fate or what, but just then my mother walked in and gave me a thumbs-up. She had recovered from her attack."

"And you smiled."

"With all the joy I felt. The director said, 'You're hired. And it's my guess that we have a star in the making.'" Tate stopped talking and looked at her.

"That's a wonderful story."

"Think so? To my mind, I got the job on false pretenses. I had no idea how to act, so I had to learn. For years I used my emotions about my mother to portray whatever the director asked for. But eventually I learned to cry, laugh, whatever, without having to tear out my guts to do it. That wasn't easy."

"What about the smoldering that I've heard about?"

"That is a natural talent. Want me to show you?" He was leading her backward, toward the end of the log.

"No thanks."

"My loss."

"Tell me, do you come on to all women as you're doing to me?"

"No." His face turned serious. "The truth is that since I was a
teenager I've just stood still and women have come to me. Being
the predator is a new experience." He smiled at her in a very
sweet way. "As much as I hate to say it, we better go back. Jack
wanted to go over lines for tomorrow."

"Don't mention the play! If I hadn't been so angry at you, I
wouldn't be stuck doing something I'm no good at."

Tate jumped down off the log and held up his hands to her. He
caught her by the waist and swung her down. "Ha! The way you
shot Mean Girl barbs at me shows you have a lot of talent. And
don't kid yourself about Kit. I think he meant for you to have the
role from the beginning."

"I don't think so. Last winter Stacy and I helped him write the
script, and we talked about who could play the parts. Neither
Stacy nor I was ever considered as an actor."

They were walking back to the picnic area, Casey in front.

"Stacy again!" Tate said. "She and my sister became friends."

"I know. I used to hear them on the phone. We knew Nina was
related to Kit and that she was overseeing the decorating of the
house, but we didn't know her family used to own the place. You
bought it back because ..."

"Mom loved Tattwell so much. When she was a kid, she spent
summers there with her family. She and a little boy were inseparable. They used to shower on the back porch of the house Mom's
family stayed in."

"I guess that's my house," Casey said. "So you wanted to do that
too?"

"I did." They had reached the picnic area. Gizzy was sitting on the quilt, her back against the boulder, and Jack was stretched out, his head on her lap. She had a copy of Kit's script of *Pride and Prejudice* in her hands.

Jack turned to them. "Here they are. You two look too happy. Lizzy and Darcy are supposed to hate each other."

"No," Tate said. "She hates me but I love her. Most true-to-life role I ever had." He sat down on the quilt and picked up a bottle of water. "Is there any lemonade left?"

"No," Jack said, "but I found some beer in the bottom of a cooler. Casey, it wasn't nice to hide that."

"There's a difference between hiding and saving. If you'd drunk it with lunch, you wouldn't have it now. Did you find the green-chili crackers? No? I'll get them." She opened a plastic container that she'd hidden under some empty ones. "Did you two settle your argument?"

Gizzy smiled, but Jack grimaced. "I lost," he said. "Completely and totally *lost*. So which scene are we doing first?"

"The opening one?" Casey sat down near Tate.

"No," Tate said, "we have to do ours out of order. Jack and I will have to go back to L.A. for a few days, probably next week, so we'll miss some rehearsals. He needs to reshoot some scenes and I have to be fitted for armor."

"Really?" Gizzy said. "What's the movie?"

"It doesn't have a name yet," Tate said. "The final script isn't done and there's a big argument about the title. I'm playing an Elizabethan knight who comes forward in time, meets a pretty lady in distress, and we fall in love. Then I go back to my time and she follows me, but I don't remember her, so we have to fall in love a second time."

"Who's the lead actress?" Casey asked.

"No idea. So what scene should we rehearse first?"

Gizzy looked at the script. "At Netherfield, when Darcy is

writing to his sister. I'll be Miss Bingley, who is mad about Darcy. Casey, you have to quit smiling at Tate and look at him as though you can't stand him."

"I'll try," Casey said. Her lips weren't smiling, but her eyes were.

Tate picked up one of the scripts and found the scene. "Jack, do you have the number of that blonde we met at Marty's party? I thought I'd suggest her as the lead for my next movie. I need to do something to make the sex scenes enjoyable." With a smile, he looked back at Casey.

She knew what he was doing and she wanted to say that his words had no effect on her, but damn it, they did! "Okay, you got it. I am in Darcy-is-a-jerk mode."

Jack stayed seated while the other three got up. Since she had helped write them, Casey knew the lines, and Tate demonstrated his ability to quickly learn them. For a while, Gizzy held the script, but Jack took it from her.

Gizzy was good. She batted her lashes at Tate so convincingly that Casey was astonished. The realism of Gizzy's performance spurred Casey so that by the time she delivered her line to Darcy that she'd never heard of so many accomplished women, there was venom in her voice.

At the end, Jack and Gizzy applauded and Casey took a bow. She glanced at Tate, who seemed to be gazing at her in speculation.

He picked up a copy of the script, flipped through it, and handed it to Casey. "Let's do this scene."

"But this is where Mr. Collins proposes to Lizzy," Casey said. "Who will play him? Jack?"

"I am wounded," Jack said. "I can play a loser but ol' Landers can't?"

Tate stepped to the edge of the stream and to Casey's astonishment, he poured handfuls of cold water over his head. He ran his hands over his long hair to slick it down, then his body slumped.

When he turned back to them, the handsome hero was gone. In his place was a sleazy man who had a bent back and eyes that moved around a lot. He looked Casey up and down in such a lecherous way that she stepped back from him.

He gave her a creepy little smile and began telling how his patroness, the condescending Lady Catherine de Bourgh, said he must marry so he had chosen Lizzy. "'I will overlook your lack of dowry and I will make no demands on your father. And my further concession is that after we are married I will not remind you that your station in life is much inferior to mine.'"

"My what?" Casey's upper lip curled into a sneer.

"Psst! 'You are too hasty, sir,'" Gizzy quoted.

Casey knew she was in a play, but she couldn't make herself remember that the odious creature in front of her was a man she was beginning to like. Her delivery of the refusal to marry him showed her revulsion. When he said he knew she didn't mean her words, she told him again, this time in a tone that was unmistakable.

Tate's eyes turned cold and seemed to glitter with animosity. He told her that her lack of income, as well as her failure to be a great beauty as her sister was, would ensure that she would never get another offer of marriage from *any* man.

His words about her sister's beauty and her lack of proposals hit too close to home. It was as though he was throwing what she'd told him about her personal life back in her face. "Why, you—" She was too angry to be able to think of a clever putdown.

Tate stood up to his full height, picked up her hand, and kissed it.

"Did you get that?" Jack whispered to Gizzy.

She looked down at the video on her cellphone. "I did."

ACT TWO, SCENE ONE

Darcy feels; Lizzy sees

Casey was smiling as she rolled out the pie dough. It had been days since the trip to the estate sale, and it had been a glorious time. She and Tate and Jack and Gizzy had become a happy foursome.

Well, maybe not a real foursome, as there were big differences between the couples. Jack and Gizzy were lovers; Casey and Tate weren't.

But the discrepancy hadn't caused problems. When Jack and Gizzy's physical actions became too much, Tate and Casey would walk away.

They'd all had a very busy few days. Casey had a lot of cooking to do to prepare three meals a day, plus she'd had a children's party and a dinner for eight to cater.

One afternoon, they'd all crowded into Casey's kitchen and iced cupcakes. After the cake and snacks were done, Tate helped her put them into his truck and he drove her to the party. He'd stayed in the cab, his head down, while Casey unloaded.

"Is that . . . ?" the child's mother whispered. Everyone in Summer Hill knew Tate was in town and that he and Casey were the leads in the play.

"Of course not," Casey said, but she'd never been a convincing liar.

When she slipped into the seat beside Tate, she said, "It's like being around a criminal on the run from the law."

"The price you pay. So where to now?"

"Back to the stage, I guess."

They both groaned. For days, Kit had not seemed able to get over his bad mood, and he'd directed them with scowls and complaints.

It hadn't helped that Casey was by far the worst actor. She found it nearly impossible to laugh with Tate, then ten minutes later be onstage and treat him with disdain. Even though she'd read *Pride and Prejudice* a couple of times and had seen every film production, she'd not thought about how oblivious Lizzy was to Darcy's growing love. Kit's idea was that Tate had to let the audience see that he was falling for Lizzy.

This meant that every time Casey so much as glanced away, Tate gazed at her with love. When she spoke one of Jane Austen's famous lines, Tate stared at her blankly, but the second she turned her back, the audience saw Tate's face soften. Sometimes he smiled in a dreamy sort of way. Other times, his whole body leaned toward her, as though in surrender.

Casey wasn't supposed to see, but she *did*. One time she whipped around and saw his eyes so full of warmth and longing that she reached out her hand to him.

"Stop!" Kit yelled. "Acacia, you are *not* to look back. Lizzy is *not* to see what Darcy is feeling. You are—"

He broke off because Olivia had put herself in front of Casey. She didn't say anything, just stood there and glared at him. But that was all it took to make Kit back down.

"Don't look," he'd mumbled, and turned away.

Later that day, the foursome had lunch at Casey's house. She put out sandwich makings and homemade bread.

"All I can say," Jack said, "is that I wouldn't want to be on the receiving end of Olivia's evil eye. Is there any more of this stuff? Tate ate it all."

Casey got a jar of mango–blood orange chutney off the shelf and handed it to him. "What's going on between them? They've been odd since the first day."

Jack and Tate were having a tug-of-war over the jar of chutney.

"I have no idea," Gizzy said. "Anyone up for a swim this afternoon?"

Jack released the jar. "Not if you plan to jump off the roof into the pool again."

When Casey went back to the stove, Tate joined her. Behind them, Gizzy and Jack were arguing.

"Are you all right?" Tate asked her.

"The acting is hard for me. Saying and feeling what I don't mean goes against my nature."

"Lying versus honesty."

"I guess so. The emotions you show when you look at Lizzy seem so real. How could she not see what he was feeling? How would she not know that Darcy was falling for her?"

"In the book, I don't think Darcy sneaks glimpses of Lizzy behind her back. That's all from Kit's direction, but I like it. It lets the audience see what's in Darcy's mind and adds some sex to the drama."

"You do it all so well, but knowing what you're doing behind my back makes it hard for me to look at you with . . . What is it? Cold disdain?"

"Just think of me rummaging around in your bedroom with your PJs on the floor."

That image made her smile.

"Definitely the wrong expression," Tate said. He straightened his shoulders, then stared down his nose at her, his eyes full of contempt. "Perhaps, Miss Reddick, you should stay away from the pies."

"Are you saying I'm fat?"

Tate's eyes changed in an instant. He looked her up and down again, but this time in a way that made her take a step toward him. With a wicked grin, he moved away. "Jack! Leave some of that ham. Save it for the stage."

"Are you saying I was hamming it up?"

With a wink at Casey, Tate went back to the table.

His teasing spurred her into wanting to do a better job on the stage. In the afternoon, Jack, Gizzy, and Tate went to the Big House to work out with the trainer who'd arrived from L.A.

"Come with us," Tate said. "If you don't want to hit the weights, sit and watch."

"So I'd be the fat girl who sits on the sidelines? Is that what you mean?"

Tate seemed startled. "You are *not* fat. Girls in L.A. work to look like you. I didn't mean that for real. I was just showing you an acting technique. You—"

Casey grinned at him.

"Good one! I certainly did walk into it. Come meet the trainer. He's five foot four and has never smiled in his life. Kit wants him to play Mr. Collins."

"I have cooking to do and Olivia is coming by. And I have to figure out how to make an Oreo pie."

Tate was walking backward toward the Big House, his face one huge smile. "Nina will come here after I get back from L.A. Emmie wants me to buy her a pony."

"And who will take care of it when you're on some faraway location set clumping around in a suit of armor?"

"Think Kit would like to muck out the stables?"

Casey groaned. "He'd tell the poor creature it was wearing the wrong expression. 'Pony! I want to feel what you do!'" she quoted in a deep voice. "'Don't just stand there munching the hay, *emote!*'"

Tate looked behind Casey, and suddenly his face changed to horror.

Her whole body seemed to drain of blood. Obviously, Kit was behind her and he'd heard. But when she turned around, it was Olivia and she was suppressing a giggle.

Casey whipped back to glare at Tate, but he'd disappeared down the path and she could hear his laughter. "I'll get you for that," she called after him.

"I look forward to it," he yelled back.

ACT TWO, SCENE TWO

Wickham sweetens the pie

Casey and Olivia had spent a lot of time together, but whenever Casey tried to find out what was between her and Kit, Olivia had politely but firmly changed the subject.

The day after the estate sale, while Olivia helped her bake pies, Casey had told her about rescuing the little boy.

"You weren't worried that Tate would drop you?"

"I don't think it crossed my mind. He is rather muscular, you know."

"A veritable Colossus of Rhodes. How about if we go over your lines for tomorrow? Let's see if we can prevent Mr. Montgomery from complaining so much."

"Do you know what's wrong with Kit? I spent a lot of time with him this winter and he was one of the calmest people I've ever been around. Stacy and I said that he was like those men on the *Titanic* who gave their seats away to women and children."

Olivia was looking at her script. "How about if we go over the scene where Wickham says that Darcy is a man without honor? I think you might have trouble there."

Casey was blinking at Olivia. She had completely ignored the question.

"I'll be Wickham. Will that be too difficult to imagine? Should I paint on a chocolate mustache?"

Olivia was smiling, and Casey had wanted to ask her questions, but she didn't. "Sure, let's work on that."

Now that everyone was settling into a routine, Kit's bad temper did seem to be calming down. Casey was getting better at pretending Lizzy didn't know what Darcy was doing behind her back, but tomorrow they were going to start on the scene where Darcy asks Lizzy to marry him. She was to tell him what he could do with his proposal. Casey had played the scene in the audition, but then she'd been in a very different mood.

"Hello."

She turned to see Devlin Haines standing outside her screen door. She hadn't spoken to him—or, for that matter, thought of him—in days. "Hi. Would you like some pie and coffee?"

"Love it."

He came in and when Casey motioned to a stool, he sat down.

"How about raspberry cobbler?" She took a plate off the shelf.

"Exactly what I wanted. Would you mind if I had a glass of milk instead of coffee? I know it's childish, but I'm missing my daughter so much that I need it."

"You must be excited about seeing her."

"Will she be here soon?" His eyes were eager, but when he saw Casey's startled expression, he looked shy. "Sorry. That's something I should know, but to get to my daughter I have to go through my ex-wife. The only word I ever hear from her is 'no.'" He gave a little shrug. "Yet again I'm dumping my problems onto you. How have you been?"

"Great," Casey said. "I've been learning that acting is really difficult. Here, have some almonds. I bought them to use in a pie crust, but Olivia told me she's allergic. How have you been?"

He took a bite of cobbler. "This is delicious! Actually, I may have a job. At least, I've got a chance to try out for a new cop show that will be on FX. I won't be the lead, but I could be the lead actor's best friend. If I get it, that is."

"Congratulations! Or do I say 'break a leg'?"

"I'll take either one." He looked down at the pie, then up again. "Town gossip is that you and my ex-brother-in-law have become a pair."

"Hardly that!" Casey didn't meet his eyes. "I do cook for him and Jack, so of course . . ." She trailed off.

"Do you know anything about boats?" he asked, changing the subject.

"Only that they shouldn't have holes in the bottom."

"That's the extent of my knowledge too." He was smiling.

Casey thought what a good-looking man he was. And simple. He seemed to be open and cheerful, as though he'd smile no matter what happened in life. She could imagine him laughing while his daughter rode a pony.

Since Devlin and Tate were so closely connected, Casey couldn't help comparing them. Devlin didn't seem to have Tate's way of going from darkly glowering to smiles within seconds.

He began to tell her an amusing story about the house he'd rented on the lake. There was a small wooden boat stored in the garage, and he'd taken it out to make space for his car. But he'd found that the boat was such an annoyance to mow around that he slipped it into the water.

He made Casey laugh when he said he didn't know what was wrong with him—maybe it was the romance of a boat on the crystal-clear lake—but he'd stepped into it. That he hadn't tied it to the shore didn't enter his mind.

Devlin was a good storyteller, and he acted out his arm-twirling attempts to get back to land using a single oar. The other oar was lying on the lawn, and he told how he'd watched the neighbor's dog carry it away. "All while I was standing up and cursing at it," he said.

"You stood up in a rowboat?" Casey asked, her eyes laughing.

Devlin shook his head at his stupidity. That's what he'd done—

and that's when he'd fallen in and found out he was in only four feet of water. He'd slogged back to the shore, pulling the rowboat behind him.

As he finished his story, Casey took the last of the pies out of the oven. Devlin said the boat was now back in the garage and his car was sitting in the driveway.

"I should be going," he said as he stood up. "Maybe you could visit me. Come out to the lake one evening. I make a mean frit-tata, and I'm good at opening bottles of wine."

Casey hesitated.

"It's okay," he said. "I understand. You've met Tate."

He sounded as though she'd dropped him at the mere sight of another, more handsome man. "That's not how things are. I—"

"Sorry again," Devlin said. "Tate Landers is a great guy. Has he told you how he came into acting? About his mother's asthma attack?"

"He did, actually."

"Mmmm," Devlin said as he went to the door. "The talk shows love that story, and it's a good one. I guess Letty and Ace will be next. My silly little boat story can't compete with Tate's tales of childhood bliss."

Casey was frowning, but she wasn't sure why. Because she'd thought Tate had never told his story to anyone else? That he saw her as someone special?

Devlin had his hand on the door. "Casey, I'd never dare tell you what to think about anyone, but please, I beg of you, don't tell Tate about my coming audition. He's a big-deal movie star, while I'm a jobless TV actor. All he'd have to do is make one call and . . ." Devlin took a breath. "Not that he would, but anyway, would you please not mention my audition to him? In fact, maybe it would be better if you don't tell him that you've seen me." He stood there looking at her, his face sincere.

"I won't," Casey said.

Devlin smiled in relief. "Thank you for the pie, for laughing at my story, and especially for your friendship in spite of what you've been told about me."

"I've heard no gossip about you from any source."

Devlin's face brightened. "Yeah? That's great. Maybe things *are* changing. I better go. Thank you, and I'll see you at rehearsals." He gave a little grimace. "One thing I hate about playing Wickham is that I got stuck romancing a kid. How old is that girl playing Lydia?"

"She wrote on her application that she's eighteen. I thought she was great in the audition."

"If you like a kid playing a seductress, yeah, she was excellent. I tend to like grown-up women." He gave Casey a look so hot that the hairs on the back of her neck stood up. "If you ever get any time off, I'm at the end of Barton Road. Thanks again for the pie."

With that, he closed the door behind him.

Wickham tells all

As Devlin left Casey's house, he was smiling. He'd found out what he needed to know and he'd planted seeds of doubt in her pretty head.

Security, with Landers's blessing, had decreed that people not rehearsing that day couldn't hang around, but Devlin liked to know what was going on. As always, it was because of Landers that Devlin had been forced to hide. He found places in the bushes near the stage where he could watch without being seen. One of the things he wanted to know was if his big-shot ex-brother-in-law would show his disdain for small-town theatrics. Would he take direction from some guy who didn't know a script from the instructions for a can opener?

Devlin's hopes were dashed when Landers acted as though he were performing in an Oscar contender. Why? he wondered. But then he saw the looks Landers was giving Casey.

At the auditions, he'd seen Landers watching her, but now the looks were deeper. Much more serious.

Why did the best of everything happen to Landers? Devlin wondered. Whatever he did was touched with good fortune. It was as if some great cosmic force had decreed that each family was to be given a pot of luck, and in their case all of it had gone to Landers.

But maybe today Devlin had been able to take away a little bit of that golden touch. He knew that Landers had told only his sister that story about his first audition, but when he and Nina were married, Devlin had worked to get information out of her. He liked to know secrets about his enemies. And right now the work had been worth it, just to see the look on Casey's face. His insinuations had made her trust of Landers go down a few notches.

When his phone buzzed, Devlin frowned at the ID. It was the private eye he'd hired. "It's about time! What happened?"

The man's voice was gravelly from years of cigarettes and whiskey. "Keep your pants on. I told you I'd get them and I did. But they're going to cost you twenty thou."

"What?" Devlin yelled, then lowered his voice. "You paid twenty grand for those photos? From some tourist with a long lens?"

"Don't blame me. It's the Internet. The guy knew pictures of Tate Landers and Jack Worth saving some kid's life were worth a bundle. I talked him down from fifty, but then, you can't really tell for sure who the men are. They're back inside the house in deep shade."

"Can you see the girls?"

"Oh, yeah. That blonde is loved by the camera! But I like the other one better. She's got meat on her in all the right places. If you're planning to use these photos to blackmail Landers, you're going to have a hard time proving it's him."

Devlin gritted his teeth. "It's none of your business why I want them. Just send them to me." As he clicked off, he could hear weights clanging together, and he stepped off the path to the Big House's garage, into some tall bushes. In the weeks that he'd been in the nowhere town of Summer Hill, he'd become quite familiar with Tattwell. After all, the place should have been his. With Landers always in L.A., what did he need with a house in Virginia?

And all Nina had to do was ask for something and her brother gave it to her.

As he peered through some branches, he saw Landers and Worth with the ugly trainer and the girl playing Jane. They were a cozy little group, looking like they'd known one another for years.

That Devlin had been thrown out of the rich, easy life of Tate Landers renewed his rage. He had worked hard to be part of it. In fact, he was the one who'd foreseen what Landers was going to become. Didn't that count for everything?

Years ago, right after he'd first arrived in L.A., he was young and hungry and living with six guys in a one-bedroom apartment, all of them going from one audition to another.

One night when they were out for midnight pizza, their good looks attracting a lot of attention, Devlin noticed an "older" woman, late thirties maybe, watching them with interest. The other guys ignored her as she sat there in her plain little car and put away a large pizza all by herself. But Devlin was sure he'd seen her before, so he smiled at her—and ended up going home with her.

He'd been right that he'd seen her before. She was a top executive at a major movie studio and had a mansion up in the hills. The cheap car was only used when she didn't want to be recognized.

When Devlin moved in with her, he knew it was temporary. And she told him that if he tried to use her name to get an acting job, she'd throw him out. She said, "You're here for sex and that's all. And when I get bored with you, you're out. Got it?"

He did get it, so he kept his ears and eyes open for anything he could use to make a future for himself. One night he heard her on the phone talking about who they were going to get to play the lead in some big-budget romance movie. She said she favored a grown-up kid actor named Tate Landers.

Devlin didn't have anything to do while she was at work, so he watched every show Landers had ever been in. Devlin had to admit the kid was good, and when he reached his teen years he'd developed an angry air that the camera seemed to magnify.

As Devlin watched the shows, he began to think of the advantages of being the best friend of a superstar. He just needed to establish the friendship while Landers was still unknown. Later, there would be big houses, trips together, opening nights. "Did you meet my best friend, Devlin?" he imagined Landers saying. "He taught me everything I know. I owe it all to him."

He sought the guy out. Like Devlin, Landers was living with roommates in a small apartment and going to umpteen auditions. He had no idea he was being considered for a major motion picture.

Devlin did his best to befriend Landers, but it didn't work. Since he was a few years older, he tried to set himself up as a mentor, but Landers didn't go for it. They were cordial, but they never got past the superficial.

It was only by accident that Devlin met Landers's weak spot: his younger sister, Nina. She was quiet, shy with strangers, and looked to her big brother for everything. In an instant, Devlin changed his plans. If he couldn't crack the brother, he'd go after the sister. But his intuition told him that Landers wouldn't like him dating his precious sister.

It had taken a lot of talking and many lies—both of which Devlin was good at—to get Nina to agree to see him in secret, but he managed it. He conducted a courtship that should have been put in the history books. Flowers, chocolates, laughter, stuffed animals—and sex. Lots of great sex. Nothing kinky. No tying her to the bed, as the woman he lived with liked, but still good. Devlin was kind and considerate, respectful and affectionate. So what if he punched a few holes in the condoms? It was all for a good cause.

But still ... something was wrong, and she began to talk of breaking up. When Nina told him she was pregnant, Devlin was apologetic, said he couldn't understand how it had happened. He'd been so careful. With big, slow tears, he offered to do whatever she wanted. He loved her and wanted to marry her, but if she didn't want him, he'd get out of her life. It was her choice. He just begged to please, please be allowed to see his child now and then. In the end, Nina couldn't stand up to his tears and she accepted his proposal.

After the wedding, things went well for a while. Landers got his movie role and used some of the money he received to buy his pregnant sister a modest house in an L.A. suburb. Most of the time, Landers was away on movies, Nina was a wife who didn't ask too many questions, and the kid was quiet.

It was all great—until Landers began to interfere. Why couldn't he have left things alone? It was true that he paid for things, but he could afford it. Devlin wasn't greedy. He didn't demand a mansion in a gated community, as the sister of Tate Landers deserved. And Devlin did go to auditions. Maybe not as many as he said he did, but enough to say he was trying to get a job.

It all started collapsing after some blabbermouth told Landers that Devlin hadn't even tried out for a part that he'd said he was sure he was going to get. There'd been loud arguments and threats from Landers, who afterward used his connections to get Devlin a serious audition. It was because of Landers that Devlin got the lead role in a new cop series on a cable network.

The work was grueling! Twelve-hour days. Devlin was in every scene, so they demanded that he stay in shape. If he wasn't in front of the camera, he was in a gym being yelled at by some thick-necked jock to lift more and more weight. And if the work wasn't bad enough, Nina and the kid spent the money as fast as he made it.

Devlin put up with it for one whole season, all while imagining his coming multiple-month vacation. But he had only two weeks off—most of which he spent in bed with one of the extras—then they wanted him to start all over again.

It took a while, but he got out of it. A few tantrums, a few fights, too much booze, and they threatened to kill his character off. As Devlin knew he would, Landers paid to keep it out of the media, and in apology Landers starred in two episodes. But the series still flopped.

Afterward, Devlin put on his best act of contrition. He cried to everyone and even spent six weeks in rehab. But it wasn't enough for Landers. He said he'd be damned if Devlin was going to go back to sitting on his ass and doing nothing while Tate supported him. In private, he yelled about the women. Devlin defended himself by saying that Nina cared more for the baby than she did for him. Landers said, "Damned right she does! Emmie's the only good thing you've ever accomplished in your entire freeloading life."

The divorce had been bad, and Devlin had a difficult time getting awarded any money. He'd had to cry to the judge that it wasn't right that he was being separated from his beloved daughter and that he deserved compensation.

The L.A. judge mumbled, "I hate actors," then he'd looked at Tate—who by that time was a major star—and said that sometimes justice and pride had to be put aside for the good of others. "Please don't drag that little girl through this filth."

In the end, Landers had selfishly and begrudgingly agreed to support Devlin for a few more years—until he could "get on his feet again."

Landers was now talking about hiring lawyers to get out of paying any more. If he did that, Devlin didn't know what he was going to do next. During his once-a-month call to Emmie, she'd told him that Uncle Tate—how Devlin hated that name!—had bought the Virginia plantation and her mom had fixed it up.

"You mean that old place Nina used to go on and on about,

with those two kids?" He was annoyed that he hadn't been told this useful information earlier.

"Letty and Ace," Emmie said with enthusiasm.

"I didn't think that place was real. Will *he* be there?"

As young as Emmie was, she knew who "he" was. "Mom wants Uncle Tate to come, but she says that if he does, he'll only stay for a day. My uncle is a celebrity and he can't—"

"Yeah, yeah," Devlin said. "I gotta go," and he'd hung up.

It had taken him a while to swallow his anger over that news. He was having to scrimp on everything, from clothes to his car, but Landers was buying plantations. How was that fair?

Devlin did some investigating and found the town of Summer Hill, where the old plantation he'd heard too much about was. When he read of the auditions for the local play, he thought that maybe, for once in his life, his luck had changed. He'd go there, be in the play, and he'd work on getting Nina back. They could live on that lovely old plantation in the little town and he'd become ... what? The mayor? He imagined town meetings with everyone lined up, asking for his autograph.

But his long-term plan wasn't working out. As always, everything good was given to Landers. He'd shown up with Jack Worth—the B-movie actor who had been chosen for his friendship instead of Devlin—and taken over the whole town. That was all anyone could talk of.

And now it looked like Landers might be falling for some local girl. Sure she could cook, but who the hell was she? Nobody!

Devlin knew that if he were given what fate had dished out so generously to Landers, he'd go after some rising starlet—or three. Not some cook in a nowhere town in Virginia.

As he made his way to where he'd cut an opening in the fence at the back of the property, he thought about the photos he'd bought. He wasn't yet sure what he was going to do with them, but he'd figure out something. His goal was to do to Landers what had been done to him—and it looked like that would involve this local girl.

Smiling, Devlin went back to his Toyota, which was hidden at the side of the road. His next car was going to be a dark-green Jaguar.

ACT TWO, SCENE FOUR

Lizzy follows her heart

"Good morning."

Casey looked up to see Tate standing at the screen door. The early-morning sun behind him made her remember the first time she'd seen him: wet and naked.

What she was thinking must have shown on her face because Tate's eyebrows raised in a way that made her blush.

"Maybe now's not a good time," he said as he turned away.

"You don't have to leave." She took the two steps to the door and held it open.

As Tate went past her, he lifted his arms as if he were in a holdup, and stepped sideways. She knew he was making a point of not touching her, so no electricity would pass between them.

She ignored his theatrics. "Where are the others?"

"Richmond. Gizzy said she had to go there to get something for her dad, and Jack asked to go with her. My guess is that they'll spend the night. That means I'm . . ." He shrugged.

"That you're all by yourself and I'll bet you're hungry. Sit down. I made breakfast burritos, so we can eat before the rehearsals start."

Tate straightened his shoulders. "Actually, I told Kit I needed a break and whether he liked it or not, I was going to take the entire day off."

Casey gave a derisive little snort. "He called off rehearsals today, didn't he?"

"Oh, yeah. His relatives are moving into their new house and he's spending the day with them. This whole place is going to be free of people, so I thought I'd go exploring. You wouldn't want to go with me, would you?"

"Love to!" Casey took four stainless-steel buckets out of a closet. "I was told there's a stand of blackberry bushes on this property, and I'd like to find it. Wrap up a couple of burritos and we can eat as we walk."

"Walk, ha!" Tate said. "I live in L.A. We drive from the kitchen to the living room." He quickly wrapped two burritos in foil, grabbed bottles of water, then held open the door. Outside was a little red utility truck.

"Perfect." She set the buckets in the back.

Tate put the burritos and water on the seat, then returned to the house. Moments later he came out with a big plastic pie carrier and a huge spoon. "Must feed my addiction."

Casey laughed as he put it in the back, then got in beside her, turned on the engine, and drove across the lawn. "So who are Letty and Ace?" A flash of something she couldn't read went across his eyes, then it was gone. It looked like he'd guessed that Devlin had first mentioned the children to her. Was he jealous?

"My mom spent summers here until she was ten. Her real name was Ruth but she asked everyone to call her Letty, short for Princess Colette, because she thought that was the most beautiful name she'd ever heard. The boy she played with every summer was called Ace. When Nina and I were kids, Mom told us stories about what they did."

"Anything about peacocks?"

"Oh, yes. Ace covered a piece of cardboard with aluminum foil and used it as a shield. He used to run a particularly big peacock away from the well house, where he and Letty had their most secret hideout. My mom said Ace was a true hero, fearless and brave."

"Like you were with the peacock?"

"No. I didn't confront the beast. I was a total coward. Threw my shirt over the creature, gave it a push, then ducked down under the window—and he still almost pecked my face off."

"And Emmie saw it all?"

"Every second of it. It entertained her immensely, but then, she thinks her uncle Tate is fairly ridiculous. So what made you decide to become a great chef?"

"I haven't reached that level by any means. Ow!" Tate had hit a pothole so deep that her head hit the ceiling.

"Sorry. We are now going into uncharted territory. But you've been here for months, so you must know the place better than I do."

"There was too much snow this winter for me to get out much, and besides, Kit got me quite a few jobs so I was busy. I cooked for him until he dragged his former housekeeper out of retirement. She wasn't happy about it, and every day she says she's leaving. What's that?"

She was pointing at a ramshackle building under a big oak tree. The roof looked fairly new but some windows were missing.

"Probably the old chicken coop." He stopped the truck. They opened the burritos and began to eat.

"This place has a lot of memories for you, doesn't it?"

"From my mother's stories, yes," he said. "After my father died, I couldn't understand why he wasn't there to toss me around and throw a ball to me. My mom did her best, but she was grieving too. She had a baby and a rambunctious four-year-old, and lots of bills."

"It must have been awful for all of you."

"It was." He looked back at her. "But that's when Mom started telling me the Letty and Ace stories. The kids vowed to be best friends forever and ever."

"Was Ace his real name?"

"I don't know. I've always wished that I'd asked. At first I was too young to question the name, then later I was too busy with my own life to think about it."

"Your mom . . . ?"

"Died just before I got my first major role."

Casey could hear the pain in his voice, and she reached across the seat to put her hand on his.

"Thanks," he murmured, then in the next second a charge of electricity went through both of them.

Casey snatched her hand away and started to make a sharp retort, but instead she laughed, and Tate joined her.

"Shall we explore the henhouse? I'll tell you how Letty and Ace made a ramp to roll the eggs down. It worked perfectly— except that every egg broke. They were— Bloody hell! There he is!"

Casey looked up to see a huge peacock, long tail trailing behind him, strutting in front of them. He disappeared into some rhododendron bushes.

Tate tossed his empty foil to the floor and handed Casey his water bottle. "Hold on! I'm going to get that creature."

She grasped the doorframe of the truck as Tate drove around the huge shrubs, but on the other side was a tangle of what looked to be young trees. They could see the peacock making his way through them.

"He's going somewhere," Casey said. "He's not just wandering; he has a destination."

"Are you up for following him?"

"Oh, yeah!" Casey braced her feet and tightened her hands. The ground was rough, with ditches and holes and stumps.

"Nina said that when she first saw the place, it was all like this. She had a couple of acres around the house cut and smoothed."

"My brother Josh did the work," Casey said. "Yeow!"

"Okay?"

"I'm fine." The peacock turned left. "Maybe he's leading us to the blackberries. I was told they're hard to find."

Tate jerked the wheel around so hard that Casey almost flew out the side, but he grabbed her arm and pulled her back. "Tell me how you came to be a chef."

"Thanks. My mom and I found my career by accident. Since she's a doctor, she was gone a lot."

"Sorry," Tate said.

"No! No! It was okay. She's a bit intense, so . . ." Casey shrugged.

"Got it. Serious, dedicated doctor. Great in a hospital but overpowering to live with. I've played that role before. So who took care of you?"

"Nannies. I had a Jamaican woman for the first seven years of my life and I loved her very much. When she decided to go back home, my heart was broken." She paused while Tate drove around a magnificent magnolia tree. Casey looked back. "There's a big statue under that tree."

"Probably where Letty and Ace made contact with outer-space demons. They conquered them and saved the world. How did you put your heart back together?"

"By not repeating that error. I told Mom I never wanted to hurt like that again, so we decided to hire a different nanny each year. Mom suggested we find people who could do specific things, like art or teaching me how to swim. She especially wanted me to learn some lifesaving techniques. She never said so but I knew she wanted me to be a doctor. Anyway, that's what we did. Mom and I would think up things that I wanted to learn, then she'd find someone to teach me."

The peacock had found something on the ground and was

pecking at it, so Tate stopped the truck. "That was either a lot of fun or a nightmare."

"Exactly! One of the artists once said she needed a few puffs of her special herbal smoke-sticks to be truly creative. My mom came home to find her eleven-year-old daughter rolling marijuana joints in origami paper and the nanny stoned. I was rather good at it, and I thought they were very pretty. Quite colorful."

Tate laughed. "My guess is that nanny was fired."

"Right that moment. After that, Mom hired a retired woman who had worked in a bakery for twenty-some years. I learned a lot from her. The next one was an Italian man who showed me how to make pasta. After those two, I realized I liked cooking the best, so the rest of my caretakers were in the food industry. By the time I was in high school, Mom and I changed them every six months, and I got interested in the cuisines of different nationalities. French, Basque, Hungarian. I loved Mexican cooking! When I left for college I could make my own tortillas, cut sushi, and decorate a wedding cake."

"And roll joints."

"In tortillas?" Casey sounded confused. "I don't think they would burn properly."

Laughing, Tate put the truck in drive. The peacock was on the move.

"Was that . . . ?" Casey asked as they passed a group of gravestones.

"My ancestors' private burial plot," Tate said. "Uncle Freddy is buried there. He lived here for many years with his caretaker, Mr. Gates, and when he died he left the whole place to Mom. By the way, Nina told me it was my job to see that the family cemetery was cleaned up."

"What did Letty and Ace think of that place?"

When Tate turned to grin at her, he almost hit a tree stump. They were near the back of the property, and it looked as though it hadn't been trimmed in a century. "Of course they said it was haunted. One time they sneaked there at midnight, but Mr. Gates caught them, picked them up, and carried them back to the house. I've always wondered what he was doing outside at midnight." Tate backed the truck up and went to the left, but there was a clump of thorn-covered bushes.

"I'm not sure, but I think those are gooseberries," Casey said.

He was backing up again and glanced over at her. "Aren't they pie material?"

"They are. Pies and tarts and jams and— Look out!"

He slammed on the brakes just in time to not hit a family of opossums. The mother glared at him, then started walking again, her two babies following her.

"Now we see who really owns this place." He turned off the engine. "I think we should walk. Or if you don't want to, I could take you back to civilization."

Casey got out. "Remember that I'm good at following."

"And you know that idea sends me into spirals of lust."

She frowned. "I thought I was pledging to follow the peacock."

"That's cruel," Tate groaned as he got the pie carrier out of the back. "Speaking of the devil, where is he?"

Casey, holding the buckets, crouched down enough to see the long tail disappearing into the bushes. "He's going that way."

It took them another thirty minutes of following the peacock, sometimes fighting their way through six-foot-tall overgrown patches of weeds, before they found the blackberry tangle. It was tall, with branches twisted together to make what appeared to be an impenetrable clump. Not far away, plants had been cleared for the newly erected fence. They were at the very back of the plantation.

The peacock—who had not deigned to acknowledge their presence—was lazily pecking at the ground.

Casey started pulling blackberries off the vines while Tate looked around.

"See that?" He pointed.

She had to stand on tiptoe, but she saw the point of a roof. The little building was surrounded by a mass of thorn-covered branches.

"Maybe I should go back and get a chain saw."

Casey looked at him in horror. "And destroy wild blackberry bushes? Are you out of your mind? These need to be pruned professionally, not by some redneck with a chain saw."

"I grew up in California. How do I get labeled a redneck?"

"Ancestry can always be told," she said seriously.

"I—" He broke off because the peacock, beak in the air, had strolled between them, arrogantly ignoring them. It lowered its head and went into the bushes. Tate crouched down to see where the bird had gone. "There's a tunnel here. Someone has bent sheets of galvanized steel to make it. It's old, but . . ." He stood up. "I think we may have found Mom's hideout. If I have to slither like a snake, I'm going in."

"Tunnel or not, those thorns will tear you apart. You can't—" A crack of thunder cut her off and she felt the first sprinkles of rain.

"The keys are in the truck and it's that way. No. Wait. It's over there. No, that's not right. I'm sure it's that way. Or maybe—"

"Go!" Casey said. "I'm right behind you."

"If we end up crawling on our bellies, I'd rather get behind you and watch."

"No." She motioned for him to go first. Under her breath, she said, "And I'd rather see you naked and wet." She spoke so quietly that he didn't hear her.

Tate went in front of her, the pie container before him. "The path is a bit overgrown," he said over his shoulder.

Pebbles and dried, thorny branches littered the ground, and, above them, blackberry stalks had found their way through the sheets of metal. It took a while to get through the tunnel, and the rain was coming down harder.

But before they got to the center, the rain hit them. It came down through the canopy of crisscrossed branches and gaps in the old tunnel. By the last few feet, they were soaked.

In front of Casey, Tate attempted to stand up, but the branches were too intertwined to fully separate. He helped her stand halfway up, her back against a wooden wall, while he wrestled with an old door. He managed to get it open a few inches, and Casey slipped inside, Tate behind her.

It was a small building, about the size of a walk-in closet, and to one side were remnants of some machine.

"Well pump," Tate said, as he ran his hands through his hair to get the water out.

"For what well?" Casey was wringing her shirttail out. There was a little window in one wall, but between the rain and the blackberries, there wasn't much light.

"I have no idea. I was told about this place from the point of view of a child. I doubt if Mom asked what the big machine was used for. If I remember correctly, and if no one has moved it ..."

She could see his silhouette as he ran his hands along a wall until he reached the corner.

"Aha!"

She heard a match strike, saw a flame, then he lit a candle and they had light. Tate held aloft an antique pewter holder with a shield on the back.

Behind her was a stack of rugs and cushions that looked as though they'd been pilfered from the Big House. They ranged from a couple of dark velvet ones, probably Victorian, to one that had big red lips with a cigarette hanging from the corner.

"Mom didn't mention that she and Ace were bandits. Want to sit and wait this out?"

"Sure." As they moved the pillows, they coughed from the dust, but it was better than sitting on the hard wooden floor.

Casey leaned a fat pillow against the wall, put more on the floor, then sat down. Tate was still standing. The light of a single candle was behind him, and his wet T-shirt was plastered to a body she remembered well.

When she looked at him, he wore the most genuine expression of emotion she'd seen on his face. No acting, no trying to entertain, no teasing. Neither was there a sense of protecting himself. He was open and vulnerable—to her.

It was easy to see what was in his mind. He was waiting for her answer.

Scenes from the last few days flashed through her mind: his anger because she'd spied on him while he showered; how he'd sat quietly while she bawled him out for eating a whole pie. When he'd first stepped onto the stage and seen her dressed as Elizabeth Bennet, a light had come into his eyes. He'd been glad to see her. Later, he'd held her life in his hands as she dangled down on a steep roof. Most of all, she remembered how many times he'd made her laugh. He'd even made her feel better about Ben. For months all she'd felt was guilt. How could she have been so insensitive to a man she loved? But Tate had made her see a different side of it all.

When she gazed up at him with a smile of welcome, he grinned in understanding—and in such deep happiness that she laughed.

He peeled off his wet T-shirt and flung it to the side. The candlelight played off the muscles of his body, and for a moment he stood there looking down at her.

She expected him to pounce on her, but he didn't. Instead, he stretched out beside her on the pillows, barely touching her. She'd braced herself for an electrical shock, but there was none. Instead, her body seemed to hum.

He reached out to run his fingertips down her cheek. "You're a very pretty girl," he said, his voice low and husky.

Her heart was beginning to beat faster. "You see starlets and—"

He pressed his lips to her temple. "You're prettier, and I *like* you. Big difference."

She started to reply, but he began to kiss the side of her face. Her eyes closed as she gave herself over to the pleasure of his lips and his skin pressing against hers. He kissed her eyelids, then slowly moved down toward her mouth.

His lips touched hers, softly at first.

The gentleness slowly deepened so that her mouth opened under his and she felt his tongue. Her arms went around him, her hands on his warm skin, caressing the hardness of the muscles beneath.

The humming inside her seemed to increase.

Tate drew back to look at her. "Feel that?"

"I do," she said.

His lips moved to her chin, down to her neck. It was only as he reached her throat that she realized he'd unbuttoned her shirt. He easily slipped it off her shoulders. Her bra came next, and when he pulled her bare chest to his, she gasped. Her skin was cool from the rain, but his was warm to the point of being feverishly hot.

His face was in her neck, kissing, his tongue touching the sensuous cords. His hand moved up her ribs, his thumbs caressing her breasts.

"I've wanted you since I saw you in those pajamas."

"You yelled at me."

"It was either that or throw you across the kitchen table."

"Too bad I wasn't given a choice."

When Tate laughed, she could feel it all over her body. "Not you," he whispered. "You hold yourself in too high esteem for that."

"Do I?"

Casey leaned her head back. His lips moved down to her breast. With his tongue on the tip, the humming that ran through her body grew too loud for her to remember words. All she was aware of was this man and this moment.

She wasn't sure how it happened, but all their clothes came off. When their nude bodies touched, she thought she might die if he didn't come to her completely.

But he didn't. He continued to kiss her, to touch her, until it was as though her very soul left her. She was all sensation, all desire.

She ran her hands over his body, caressing each muscle and its contours.

His hands moved down between her legs and parted them. When he moved on top of her, she was more than ready for him, and he slipped inside her with velvet ease.

Tate took his time, slowly building, his strokes gradually increasing in strength and speed. His breath was by her ear. She could hear him, feel him, sense him, smell him.

When he came, she was ready for him, and her release went through her entire body. Waves of pleasure passed through her, making her body convulse.

Tate held her close to him, not moving off her, and the weight felt good. The hardness of his taut, muscular body was a perfect contrast to her softness.

It was a while before he rolled away and pulled her over so her head rested on his chest. "I wasn't prepared for this, so maybe we should talk about my lack of protection."

"Pill," she murmured. Right now she didn't want anything to ruin this magic moment.

He kissed her forehead and snuggled her to him, her leg across his. The rain kept coming down, isolating them. When it grew cool, Tate pulled an old lap robe across them, and when the dust flew up, they coughed and laughed, but they didn't detach from each other.

"I want to thank you," Tate said softly, his voice barely a whisper.

"For this?"

"No, but yes. Thank you for taking my mind off my . . . my fear of seeing this place." He paused before continuing. "Nina and I kept track of Tattwell since we were kids. We knew it changed hands twice after my mother had to sell it, and both times the owners wanted to subdivide the land and put in mass housing. The town of Summer Hill fought them and won. But the place was virtually abandoned for about ten years."

"Why didn't you want to see it?"

"My goal had always been to make enough money acting to buy it and present it to Mom as a gift, but she died before I could afford it. I felt guilty and . . ." He shrugged. "I told Nina there were too many memories attached to the place and that I didn't want to be taken back to the stories of the past. Or I didn't want the press to find out. Whatever. I came up with a thousand excuses. But then one day Kit Montgomery showed up at my trailer on set and told me we were related. Nina said that it was fate that Kit had shown up, so I could buy Tattwell through him without the press knowing."

"Maybe it was fate."

"Nah. It was Kit's secretary. Someone in Kit's family works on genealogy and found out that we're related. When he made an offhand comment to that fact, his secretary said that if he didn't get her an autographed photo of me she was going to quit."

"Did you give it?"

"Of course. Kit and I spent a weekend drinking and bellyaching about relatives and employees. When I got sober—which took a while, as that man can drink!—I went to his office in D.C. and had photos taken with everyone. And . . ."

"And what?"

"I had a friend, an assistant director, who I'd told Kit about, and he said I should bring him. Kit arranged a blind date with my friend and the secretary's widowed daughter. They're married now and expecting their first child."

She looked up at him. "That's a wonderful story. Was the matchmaking your idea or Kit's?"

"His. He likes to manage people's lives."

"Like yours? And mine?"

"Exactly. But this time I like it. How did you meet him?"

"I opened the back of my car. I was—"

"Wait," Tate said. "I think this story calls for pie."

When he moved away from her, Casey sat up to watch. Although he was totally nude, he didn't seem the least bit shy or inhibited. As for her, she held the dusty old lap robe under her arms.

Tate got the pie carrier and the spoon, then moved back to snuggle beside Casey. He opened it, scooped a huge spoonful from the middle, held it out to her, and she took a bite.

"You do know, don't you, that pies are usually sliced and served on plates."

"I used to think so too. But then I fought a mad beast in a girl's bedroom, and later I ravenously dug a spoon into a pie so good it must have been made in heaven. Then a very pretty girl yelled at me, and all I could think of was that her cheeks were pink and every part of her body was bouncing, so I changed my mind. Since then I've liked pies and spoons. Brings back good memories."

Casey blinked a few times. "In that case, I understand." He fed her another bite. "Back to Kit. Remember I told you that I packed up everything and drove to Summer Hill? In my case, that meant one suitcase full of clothes and the rest of my car packed solid with cookware and cookbooks."

"You could have shipped it all. No! Let me guess. You feared that it would be lost. Too precious to trust to strangers in big trucks."

"Exactly. But it was all a bit much for my little car, because when I parked in front of the local B&B and opened the back, a lot of things came tumbling out. The owner of the inn helped me repack, then she made a call, and ten minutes later Kit was there."

"Then what?"

"He looked inside the open back of my car and hired me as his cook, without my having so much as made a biscuit. The next day he put me in the guesthouse on an old plantation I thought he owned. Over the winter he introduced me to half the town and used Stacy and me as readers for a play he was writing."

"All while planning to have you perform as Elizabeth."

"Maybe. I'm not sure about that. That all seems to have just happened. My guess is he wanted you and Stacy together. But then, he also wanted Stacy for his son."

"At least we agree that Kit was up to something."

They had eaten half the pie. Tate licked a tiny bit of chocolate-tipped pecan off the side of her mouth, then kissed her. He seemed about ready to do more, but his head came up. "Treasure."

"I agree," Casey murmured, her eyes half closed.

Tate sat up straighter. "Mom used to talk about the treasure box she and Ace put things in. She never said where they kept the box hidden, but this was their hideout, so maybe it's in here somewhere." He picked up Casey's hand and was kissing her fingertips. "Put on a child's thinking cap. Where would you hide a treasure box?"

"I think you already found it," she murmured.

He turned his attention back to her and his voice lowered. "I don't think so. I'd better keep searching."

Casey slid down on the pillows and he took her in his arms.

It was nearly an hour later that they flopped back on the pillows, sweaty and sated. Above them, the rain had stopped and the candle had burned to a nub.

"Weren't we looking for something?" Tate asked.

"Trust me. You found it."

"Did I?" He turned on his side to face her, picked up a strand of her hair, and held it up to the light. "I've always liked red hair."

"When I was a kid, it was much redder and I wanted to dye it."

"Speaking of red, what is that?"

Turning, she looked at the wall. Their energetic lovemaking had knocked loose a piece of wood that covered a little opening. Tate reached over her and pulled out a metal candy box. It was red on the sides, the top painted with a scene of a peacock with its tail in full flourish.

"Maybe it contains a recipe for peacock pie," Tate said enthusiastically as he set the box on the cushion between them.

When he put his hand on the lid, Casey covered it with her own. "Are you sure you want to see what's inside? This box probably belonged to your mother."

He met her eyes. "You know, I think being here, where my mother was so very happy, and with you treating me like a real person, is healing me."

"That's a very nice thing to say. Thank you."

"But again, it might be your pies that are doing the most damage repair."

Laughing, Casey removed her hand.

Tate got up to get what was left of the candle and set it by them. It was lighter outside now and they could see.

Inside the box were little things that would fascinate children.

There was a silver tiger's head that looked to have been broken off an old cane. Tate held up a strange dried-up item.

"Chicken claw," Casey said, and he set it aside.

There were three marbles with gold-colored centers, two silver dollars dated 1910, and a long bullet in a brass casing.

"M-One, World War Two," Tate said.

"Learn that from a movie?"

"Yeah. I died from one of those. But it was in the arms of a woman I loved, so it was okay."

"Did you love her? I mean the actress."

"For the first half of the movie, I made an effort to. In the second half I found her in the director's trailer. Funny how quickly love can disappear at the sight of legs in the air."

"Or being told your boyfriend is dating his paralegal and he *likes* her. I took that to mean that he'd never actually *liked* me." She pulled out three matchbook covers from the box. They were from local businesses that no longer existed.

"I'm sorry he took his inadequacies out on you."

"I should have—"

He leaned across the box and kissed her. "Don't say that. You were working hard. You did nothing wrong." He smiled. "On the other hand, I'm glad he was such a douchebag. If he hadn't been, you wouldn't be here with me now."

"To share an afternoon of truly wonderful sex?"

"Thanks, but that's not what I meant," he said. "I was talking about outside of here. I dreaded coming to Tattwell, but you've made it a joy."

She kissed him in thanks, then looked back at the box. "What's this?" She held up a scrap of black velvet, so old the fuzz was mostly gone. "Something's inside it." Slowly, she opened the fabric. Inside was a ring that appeared to be an antique. It was white gold, with a large round clear stone surrounded by cutwork and tiny brilliants.

When she held it up to the light, it flashed and sparkled. "This looks real."

"I think it might be."

"We have to find the owner of this ring." Even as she said it, she knew it was a ridiculous statement. "Wonder how long it's been in here?"

"Thirty, forty years, something like that."

Casey was peering inside the ring's band. There was no engraving. "Why did your mother's family stop coming?"

"My grandparents taught school, so they had summers free and came here to work for Uncle Freddy. But the winter my mom turned ten, Granddad got a job in California as an engineer in a shipbuilding plant. It was a year-round job."

"Did they visit Uncle Freddy?"

"Once or twice, but not often."

"Poor man. He must have missed them very much."

"I guess so, because when he died, he left everything to Mom. She never told me about it, but one time I heard her on the phone saying that Uncle Freddy's brother and the other relatives were so angry she thought they might hire a hit man to go after her."

"So why didn't they buy the place from her?"

"My guess is that they wanted it for free, not to have to pay for it. What's your extended family like?"

"Don't have one," she said. "Mom was an only child, and her parents died long before I was born. She was forty-three when she had me."

"And that's why she used a donor." He smiled. "You must have been a much-wanted child."

"Yeah, I guess so. Sometimes I envied other kids having fathers, but you make the best you can out of what you have."

"I agree," he said.

When they looked into each other's eyes, understanding passed between them. Their childhoods had been alike, with single mothers struggling to do the best they could. And by necessity, both children had grown up quickly. When Tate was just a kid, he'd looked for ways to help support his family. Casey, instead of complaining about her mother being gone so much, had figured out a way to make her time alone into something educational and fun.

Neither of them had had the childhood luxury of a world that revolved around them. Casey'd had to adjust to no father and a mother who was rarely there. Tate had dealt with the death of his father and the adult problem of putting food on the table.

"You should have this," Tate said. There was a black lanyard in the box with a plastic ornament on it. Tate slipped the ornament off and put the ring on the cord, then hung it around Casey's neck.

"I can't take it." But even as she said it, her hand closed over the ring. It was quite beautiful.

"Think of it as a gift from Letty and Ace. They hid it away, just waiting for us to find it."

"I bet whoever they stole it from wasn't very happy about it."

"I wonder why Mom never told me a story about the ring. I think that if she knew who it belonged to, she would have returned it. Do you have any idea what time it is?"

"Noon maybe?"

Tate groaned. "I have to go. That trainer they sent came through the doors of hell. If I'm not there soon, he'll send a SWAT team after me."

"I'm on his side."

"What?" Tate frowned so hard his eyebrows met, then he understood. "Yeah?" He flexed his biceps. "You don't think I'm getting too bulky?"

Smiling, Casey set the box aside and opened her arms to him. "I think you're just right."

They made love again, this time very slowly. The only thing they had on was the ring around Casey's neck.

"From the first day, I've wanted to give you a ring," he whispered, but Casey was sure she'd misheard him.

Afterward, they reluctantly put their damp clothes back on and slithered out through the tunnel under the fierce blackberry bushes. Standing outside like an angry guard, was the peacock. This time, instead of ignoring them, he gave a very loud screech of protest. Casey thought it sounded almost like the cry of a human in distress. Hearing it from only a few inches away was nearly enough to injure her eardrums.

At the deafening sound, Casey jumped back, and for a second Tate put his body protectively in front of hers.

But he couldn't resist an opportunity for drama. He leaped behind her, hands on her shoulders, and ducked his head. It was as though he were terrified and using her as a shield.

"Come on, Ace," she said in a deep voice. "You know I'm wearing the magic ring so no one can hurt us. Now stand up straight and tall and face your fears."

He took a deep breath and stood up, but he stayed behind her.

"Look, he's just a bird and he's probably lonely," she said.

"Actually, he's so mean no one can stand to be around him." Tentatively, Tate stepped around Casey and took her hand. "I think we better find the truck and get out of here."

But Casey didn't move. Still holding Tate's hand, she took a step forward, her other hand extended toward the bird. "I'm sure he's a very nice guy. He just needs a little TLC."

The big bird suddenly put its magnificent tail up in a glorious circle—and pecked Casey's hand hard.

"Ow! That hurt!" There was blood on her hand. "I think—"

Tate didn't give her time to say any more because the peacock, its five-foot tail flashing in the sunlight, was going after Casey.

With the expertise of having done it in many movies, Tate

threw her over his shoulder and began to run, the peacock on his heels.

Casey lifted her head enough to see the bird. "He's gaining on us. Run faster!"

"You sound like my last director." He swerved around two tree stumps, brushed tree branches out of his face, and jumped over a fallen log.

"I could walk, you know," Casey said, but Tate ran a caressing hand over her curvy rear end, which was right by his ear. "Actually, I think my ankle is broken and I may never walk again."

Tate laughed. "Is he still charging us?"

"Oh, yeah. You think that tail is up for you or me? You're by far the prettier one."

Tate sat her down with a *thunk* on the seat of the little truck and kissed her quickly. "He wants you. You look and feel and taste like a girl." He said it with such a leer that Casey came close to giggling.

Tate started to run around the front, but the peacock pecked his ankle, so he climbed over Casey—with lots of hand–body contact—into the driver's side, started the engine, and drove as fast as the vehicle could go.

She was watching out the back. "You outran him."

He slowed down the truck, looked at Casey, and they burst into laughter.

Mrs. Bennet tells of the past

"Hello," Olivia said.

Casey was putting buckets and mixing bowls in the utility truck. After she and Tate got back, she'd asked to borrow the truck so she could try to find where fruit was growing. He'd warned her to watch out for the livestock, then they'd kissed goodbye, and he'd run to the Big House and the trainer.

"Enjoying your day off?"

The thought of just how much she'd been enjoying the day sent blood rushing to Casey's face. "So far, it's been one of the best days of my life. What about you?"

Olivia smiled. "I take it you spent the morning with the master of the plantation."

"I did," she said.

"Judging by the new scratches on your forearms, I'd say that you were at the back of the property."

Casey looked at her in shock. "I forget that you grew up in Summer Hill. Did you spend a lot of time on Tattwell?"

"In the summer of 1970, I was the housekeeper for Uncle Freddy. He wasn't my uncle, but everyone called him that. What are you doing with all these containers?"

"I'm going to search for food. Tate drove us around this morning and I saw several possibilities. It's early in the season, but I think there are a few things I can preserve. You wouldn't like to go with me, would you?"

"I'd love to."

As they got into the little truck, Casey focused on Olivia. She wasn't sure, but she thought maybe she'd been crying. "Everything okay at home?"

"Fine," Olivia said. "Did you check the cherry trees? A few of them used to bear fruit very early."

"Tell me where they are."

Olivia gave directions and Casey drove.

"It's changed so much since I was here," Olivia said. "All of this used to be beautifully kept. Uncle Freddy gave jobs to so many people in Summer Hill—which is probably why he died broke."

There was a sadness in her voice that made Casey frown. Earlier, Casey had been so happy that she called her mother to tell her everything—well, maybe not all of it. Her mother had been delivering a baby, though, and couldn't talk.

But now Casey didn't feel right talking about her happiness when Olivia looked so forlorn. And she had an idea that her daughter-in-law, Hildy, was behind it. Why in the world was Olivia living in the same house as that rude young woman? Maybe she could find out by starting at the beginning. "Were you madly in love with your late husband?"

Olivia let out a loud laugh. "No, I wasn't."

"Oh," Casey said.

"Turn here. I shouldn't have said that. I did come to love him, but when I married him I didn't love him at all."

Before them were half a dozen cherry trees, some of them dead, all of them in desperate need of pruning. There wasn't much fruit, but there was some. Casey turned off the engine. "I'll get what I can while you tell me the story."

Olivia seemed to consider that for a moment. "All right," she said as she got out of the truck.

They walked through tall weeds and trees with broken branches, to one that was laden with ripe cherries. The sun was shining, and everything was glistening from the morning rain.

"It was 1972, and emotionally I was in a very bad place. I had recently been told that I couldn't have children."

Casey gave a gasp.

"It's okay," Olivia said. "It was a long time ago." She took a deep breath. "My Broadway career had failed and I was at home in Summer Hill, living with my parents. I loved them, but they were older and they hated any noise. You ever play the Rolling Stones at whisper level? It loses a lot."

Casey laughed.

"I got a job as the bookkeeper at Trumbull Appliances. The owner was a man named Alan, and he was in a mess. For one thing, his wife had died in childbirth and left him with an infant son."

"Oh," Casey said. "And there you were with baby lust."

"It was eating up my soul," Olivia said. "My childless future made me want to lie down in the road and let trucks run over me. Anyway, there was Alan with this motherless baby and a thoroughly incompetent, lazy live-in housekeeper who pestered him all day with her complaints."

"Perfect for you to step in," Casey said.

"At the time I thought so. Besides Alan's domestic problems, the store was failing. He'd inherited the place from his father, who had been a great salesman, but Alan took after his quiet-tempered mother. By the time I got there, he had only two employees and they did very little work."

Olivia began to fill a stainless mixing bowl with cherries.

"For three whole months I stood back and watched as things fell apart, but then one day Alan was at his desk, eating a bologna sandwich and pulling strands of the housekeeper's long dark hair out of it, when she brought the baby in. She handed him to Alan, said she had a headache, and left. He had a desk piled high with papers, the phone was ringing, and he looked like he was going to cry."

Olivia took a breath. "I'm ashamed to say that I didn't ask permission, I just took over. I put the baby on his desk and changed him, all while telling Alan what to do. I'm afraid I was very bossy. 'Answer the phone.' 'Tell them you can deliver it by Tuesday.' 'Call the newspaper to repeat last week's ad, but say that this Saturday you're having a one-day fifteen-percent-off-everything sale.'"

"It sounds like you'd thought about it." Casey put a full bucket of cherries in the truck.

"I had. From the first day, I'd watched and thought about what I would do if the business were mine. Anyway, six months later Alan and I were married, and twenty-plus years after that we owned five appliance stores that did very well."

"And you came to love him?"

"Yes, I did. But not . . ." She smiled. "Not in that way of young love, the kind where you rip each other's clothes off at first sight."

Casey smiled at the clothes-ripping image. It's where she and Tate were. If he weren't with the trainer, she would be with him now. As it was, she was planning a special dinner for the two of them to share. She made herself stop thinking about Tate. "I don't mean to pry, but why do you now live in your stepson's house? Did the stores fail?"

Olivia took a while before answering. "Alan willed the stores to his son, but I had our house and a good retirement plan, so I would be quite comfortable."

Casey's eyes widened. "Are you saying that your husband left the businesses that you had helped to build entirely to his son?"

"Yes, he did."

Olivia looked away, but Casey saw a flash of pain go across her face. She had saved Alan Trumbull's business, yet he'd left everything to his son. "His" being the key word. "What happened?"

"Kevin was always like his father, even in that he married a woman who was stronger than he was."

"Like Alan married you? Olivia, I don't mean to disparage anyone, but I've seen enough to know that Hildy is *not* like you."

"Thank you. I don't think she is either." Olivia waved her hand. "That doesn't matter. What happened was that as soon as Kevin got his inheritance, he and Hildy joined a country club, traveled, bought an expensive house, some cars, et cetera. Unfortunately, the stores suffered. By the time my stepson realized what was going on, they were almost bankrupt."

"How did they recover?" Casey asked. "But wait, let me guess. You sold your house and emptied your retirement plan to bail them out."

"I did," Olivia said. "And I'm afraid it all shook me up more than I thought it would. I've been living in their house for about a year now and I need to do something else."

"I think so," Casey said. "I'll ask Kit—"

"No!" Olivia said.

Casey started to ask more but the closed, final look on Olivia's face made her back off. She knew that Kit had visited Tattwell when he was young. And he had handed Olivia the photo of her when she was an actress. Onstage, it didn't take much to see that there were some deep feelings between them. Even talking about the rotten things her late husband and his family had done to Olivia hadn't seemed to bring out the intensity of feeling that erupted at the mention of Kit Montgomery.

She decided to change the subject. "You said you worked at Tattwell in the summer of 1970. You wouldn't remember a couple of little kids, would you?"

"Letty and Ace?" Olivia's face lost its angry look. "They were quite unforgettable. They were into everything. If I baked cookies and walked out of the room for two minutes, half of them would disappear. There were times when I wanted to strangle both of them—except that I was laughing at their antics too often. Uncle Freddy loved them so much! He was in a wheelchair and everyone treated him as if he were glass. But not those kids! They used to turn off the chair's brake and push him down every path on this property. One time he rolled into the shallow end of the pond, and that's when Uncle Freddy found out that he could still swim. So he had the pool put in."

Casey tried to be serious but couldn't. She started laughing, and Olivia joined her.

"In retrospect it is funny, but it wasn't then. They were the brattiest kids on earth."

"I know Letty was Tate's mother, but who was Ace?"

"He grew up to be Dr. Kyle Chapman."

Casey was so shocked she nearly dropped the bucket of cherries. "My *father* was Ace?"

"Yes." There was a twinkle in Olivia's eyes. Everyone in town knew about the children that Dr. Kyle's donations had created. "Poor kid. That summer his mother was dying of cancer. His dad needed time to be with her, and that's why Ace pretty much lived here. People in town said the child didn't know what was going on, but he most certainly did! When his dad brought him back from visits to his mother . . ." Olivia didn't seem able to go on.

"What happened to the children at the end of the summer?" Casey asked softly.

"Tears and screaming. It was awful. Their misery made all of us cry. My mother wrote me that the next summer they were just as inseparable. Ace's dad, Dr. Everett Chapman, was grieving for his wife, and he was the only doctor in Summer Hill. When Uncle Freddy asked him to please let Kyle stay at the Big House, he said yes. After that, the children's summers together became the normal thing."

"Until Letty's dad got a different job and quit coming here."

Casey put the last bucket into the truck. "I wonder why Dad didn't seek her out when he was an adult?"

"I have no idea. Why don't you ask him?"

"I will. You ready to go? I'd like to go to the blackberry patch."

"The one that surrounds the well house?" There was an odd tone to Olivia's voice.

"Yes." Casey pulled the ring on its black cord from inside her shirt. "Have you ever seen this before? It was in the kids' treasure box."

Olivia held it for a moment. "No. Never. I bet they found it in the attic. When it was too rainy to go out, the kids disappeared inside the house. We would hear them tramping around up there. There was a windup Victrola and they used to play Caruso records. You should have that ring appraised. It looks valuable."

"I think so too. Ready to go?"

"Yes," Olivia said.

Lizzy makes a decision

They didn't make it to the well house. Olivia suddenly remembered that she had things to do and couldn't go, but Casey wondered if the problem was some memory of the little building.

She drove to the front gate, where Olivia's car was parked, and let her out, then went back to the guesthouse to take care of the fruit and start dinner. But all she could think of was that she was dying to tell Tate what she'd learned.

It seemed that she may have stumbled on a mystery. What—if anything—had happened between Kit and Olivia during the summer of 1970? Some great love affair that ended badly? If so, who dumped whom? From the way Olivia's lower jaw went rigid at the mention of Kit, Casey felt sure he'd left her. For the woman who became the mother of his son? Was the breakup caused by Olivia's infertility?

At that thought, Casey's heart clenched. Her mother, an OB/GYN, had talked to her about baby lust. "When it attacks a woman, she will move heaven and earth to satisfy it."

"Like you did with me," Casey would say, then she'd again be told the story of her conception.

Her mother said she'd thought that someday she'd meet a man and they'd marry and have babies. "I thought it would all just sort of happen, but on my fortieth birthday, it hit me that if I wanted it, I had to *make* it happen."

"Baby lust," Casey would say. Her mom had chosen a donor from a catalog: six two, blond, blue-eyed, studying to be a doctor. It wasn't until Casey was an adult that she'd found out the information in the catalog was a stretch of the truth. Yes, Kyle Chapman was a beautiful, healthy young man, who did become a doctor. But at the time he'd made the donation that would become Casey, he was cooking in a food truck that he drove around New York City.

When she'd told her mother that, they laughed. "It was meant to be," they said, meaning Casey's love of cooking.

Dr. Kyle's other children had inherited other traits. He'd spent a year riding a motorcycle in a metal sphere in a tiny circus. For six months he'd worked with a fabric manufacturer. The sisters had all agreed that Gizzy and Stacy had talents and temperaments that appeared to come from those traits of Dr. Kyle.

Casey looked at the buckets full of cherries. She should get started on them. But in the next second she was running out the door. Maybe her father had adventurously gone from job to job and country to country for so many years before starting med school because of Letty, Tate's mother.

At the Big House, she walked along the back path toward the garage at the far end. Her mind was bubbling with all she had to tell Tate. His mother and her father had been best friends!

Casey had read the online bio of her father, that his mother died when he was five and he'd been raised by his dad. When Kyle—aka Ace—was eighteen, he'd left home and for years had gone from one job to another, never staying anywhere very long. But then there'd been an accident and he'd saved a man's life. The next day he went back to school and eventually became a doctor.

When Casey had read the story, it sounded romantic, but now

the reality of it was hitting her. A little boy who'd lost his mother when he was only five. Forever after that he must have feared that something awful was about to happen to him. And no wonder he acted up by being naughty.

She wondered if all that had been behind why her father had run away from home when he was eighteen. But then, as the child of a doctor, Casey knew the pressure to follow in her mother's footsteps. If she so much as glanced at a stethoscope, someone would remark that it was obvious Casey was going to grow up to be a doctor. When she said she didn't want to be one, people laughed at her. It was almost as though she *had* to become a doctor.

Oh, yes, she well knew the pressure to follow parents into a medical career. Had her dad felt it so strongly that he'd escaped, at least temporarily?

And then there was Olivia. She'd been there that summer with the children.

Casey had a vision of her and Tate sitting down with Olivia and Dr. Kyle and hearing about Tate's mother. There'd be funny stories and information gathered. Casey and Tate had found the well house where the kids played, but what about other places? She imagined exploring the attic with Tate. They'd play Caruso records on the old Victrola—then they'd make love on the floor.

As she got to the garage, she heard Tate's voice. Damn! He was still with his trainer. Poor guy. They'd been at it for hours.

She leaned back against the building. Should she interrupt them or wait until later to tell Tate? If she met the trainer, how would Tate introduce her? As his girlfriend? That thought made her smile.

"Meryl Streep wants to play my mother?" she heard Tate say.

The illustrious name made Casey stay where she was. It seemed that he was on the phone.

"Right. Dench got an Oscar for nine minutes as a medieval

queen, so there might be a statue for her. Got it. So who am I bedding in this one?" Tate paused. "You're kidding. . . . No, I've never seen her TV show and I'm sure it's hilarious, but this girl is supposed to be smart and *serious*. Can she do tears? . . . All right, I'll give her a try, but she'd better be worth it. And what's this about Romania? I can't go there. . . . Yes, it has to do with the play I'm in here!" Tate gave a snort of derision. "No, I'm not wasted on a small-town stage, and, yeah, I have something good going on here. None of your business. I'll be there next week and we can talk about what you have planned for me. I want to play out what's going on here for as long as I can." He laughed. "Yeah, there's a female involved. I gotta go. That trainer they sent is a sadist. Call me if you hear anything."

Casey turned back toward the path to her house, this time walking slowly. What in the world had she been thinking? Tate Landers lived in a completely different world than she did. He was surrounded by flashing lights and red carpets and the "statue." An Oscar.

By the time Casey got home, she knew she had to make a decision. One thing for absolute, positive *sure* was that there was not, and never would be, a "relationship" between her and Tate Landers. Their worlds were too far apart. She was the cook; he was the star.

To him she was "something good going on here." She was "a female." Nameless.

Whereas she . . . She shut her eyes in memory. She had done the ultimate girl thing. After a happy afternoon of fabulous sex, she'd thought they were a couple. She winced when she remembered wondering how Tate would introduce her to someone. As his girlfriend?

In her kitchen, she sat down on a stool, picked up the cherry pitter, and began on the fruit. Her choice was whether to go on or to back away.

What would make her stop was the fear of being hurt. Again. She could imagine herself in a daze of romance. Lovemaking under the cherry trees. Laughing as they held hands and ran away from a ferocious peacock. Sex against a wall. Kissing while summer rain splashed on them.

Casey had to stop to catch her breath. Did she want to forgo that so she wouldn't be hurt? Would she give up all that so that when he went back to his world of movie stars and gorgeous starlets whom he "bedded," she would be saved from a few tears? Right now tears didn't seem to weigh much when compared with sex under a cherry tree.

But maybe she should tell him that she would never again have sex with him. She could hear herself saying, "It was a mistake. It shouldn't have happened."

Right. The best, most marvelous, wonderful, exquisite sex she'd ever imagined shouldn't have happened? Was she crazy?

Of course, there was another choice. She could have a purely sexual friendship with Tate. If she knew it wasn't going to last, she could enjoy it while it did. There'd be tears—hers, anyway—when he left, but a person tended to cry at the end of any great vacation.

What she didn't want, and knew she wouldn't be able to bear, was humiliation. She'd had enough of that from her last boyfriend. Not that Tate Landers would ever be an actual "boyfriend," but she didn't want outsiders to think that he had been. She liked Summer Hill, and she didn't want to have the town whispering this coming winter about how she'd been used then dumped by a famous movie star. She couldn't bear their looks of pity.

If she did continue with this summer fling, she wanted to keep it a secret. He was an actor, so he could carry that off. They'd work on the play during the day, keep their hands off each other in public, and at night when they were alone . . . Well, let happen what may.

ACT TWO, SCENE SEVEN

Darcy doubts

"Hi," Tate said from outside the door. "Want some company, or have you had enough of me today?"

"No, please come in, I'm just frying a couple of peacock legs. Want one?" Casey joked.

"My favorite." He gave a groan of pain as he sat down on a stool.

"Was your workout bad?"

"Horrible. I have to learn to use a sword."

She glanced over at him. "You don't look like you're suffering. You enjoyed it, didn't you?"

He laughed. "Caught. But I wish Jack had been there. He texted me that they won't get back until tomorrow." He paused. "I know you haven't lived in Summer Hill long, but how well do you know Gizzy?"

"Actually, not well at all. The first time I went somewhere with her, the siren for the volunteer fire department went off and she drove nearly a hundred miles an hour to get to the fire. She put on a big black coat, and ten minutes later I saw her sliding through a narrow window to search for people to rescue. She scared me."

"But it didn't frighten her." Tate was staring down at his hands. "You don't believe she thinks of Jack as just a source of . . . excitement, do you?"

"No, I don't. I think she genuinely likes him."

Tate nodded. "I hope so." He looked at her. "Maybe tonight you and I . . ."

Casey knew what he was hinting at. Where were they going to spend the night? His place or hers? She knew that if he'd mentioned it while they were still in the well house, she would have said his. Or hers. Or by a campfire under the stars.

But now that she wasn't pressed skin to skin with him, she could think more clearly—and she remembered things. There were Devlin's words about Tate and secrecy, and the phone call she'd overheard. He wanted to "play things out" as long as he could.

Smiling, she said, "Would you mind if you and I kept our"— she couldn't really call it a relationship—"intimacy secret? Until we see how things go?"

For a second his eyes flashed with something that she couldn't read, but it was quickly gone and he smiled sweetly. "If the peacock doesn't tell, I won't. But Jack and Gizzy will guess."

"I'm sure they will. And Olivia knows. But if possible I'd like to contain it within that group."

He gave a nod. "You got it. Whatever you're cooking, it smells great."

"Quail with apricots from Ottolenghi's latest cookbook. The man is a genius. Oh! I'm about to forget my news. Pour us some wine and I'll tell you how close you and I came to being brother and sister."

"That would have been a tragedy. How could it have happened?"

"Ace grew up to be my father."

"Yeah? Tell me everything."

She told him Olivia's story of Letty and Ace and Uncle Freddy, but she didn't tell what Olivia had said about her marriage. Nor did she tell him about her suspicions that Olivia and Kit may have known each other quite well in the past.

Maybe it wasn't fair of her, but she felt that even though Tate owned the old plantation, he was an outsider. Maybe she wasn't ready to give up the physical pleasures of their friendship, but she needed to do what she could to protect herself from the inevitable pain she was going to feel when he left.

Lizzy begins to live with her decision

Hours later, Casey had just stepped out of the shower and was drying off when her phone rang. It was Stacy. "Hello, traitor."

"I knew you'd forgive me, and from what I hear, you did great with the props. And you had some serious excitement. Did the fabulous Tate Landers really hold you as you hung down a roof?"

"He did," Casey said. "I want to hear every word of what you know about Kit. And tell me about Olivia Trumbull and her husband, and the son, Kevin. What do you know about his wife, Hildy?"

Like Gizzy, Stacy had grown up in Summer Hill. Her father was the mayor, and he prided himself on knowing everything about the private lives of the full-time residents. "I heard that Olivia's husband had financial troubles and that she pulled him out, but not much more than that. As for Hildy, isn't she ghastly? She runs half the committees at church. What have you heard?"

"The same thing. So how's the new boyfriend?"

"Splendid. Divine. I am falling in love. What about you and Tate?"

"Puh-lease," Casey said. "He's an actor. I never know what's real and what's not."

"I'm glad to hear you can see that. I was worried about you

having a second heartbreak so soon after your breakup, if he returns to L.A."

"Why not? For three days I can eat masses of ice cream and chocolate and tell myself I deserve it."

Stacy laughed. "You'll want to do that after you see Nate and realize that I have landed the only perfect man on the planet. I feel sorry for all other women."

"I bet he looks like a frog."

Stacy sighed. "No, he is utterly beautiful. You should see him shirtless! He is the most gorgeous—"

As Casey listened to her half sister extol the virtues of the man in her life, she couldn't help wishing she could reply in kind. She wished she could tell about her and Tate in the little red truck, and about the peacock, and about what happened in the well house. But she said nothing about any of it, not even their dinner together. Any of it would cause too many questions. "What does this guy do for a living?"

"That's the oddest thing," Stacy said. "I'm not sure. I know it has something to do with whatever Kit did before he retired, but I don't know what that is."

They stayed on the phone for another twenty minutes, but Casey didn't reveal anything else about her and Tate. After she hung up and got into bed, she wished he were there beside her.

ACT TWO, SCENE NINE

Lizzy keeps secrets

"You don't think people are going to be suspicious when we both disappear for lunch?" Tate asked. They were in the well house, their own secret place, and they had just made love on the pillows of Letty and Ace. It had been nearly a week since they first made love. During that time, unless it was for the play, he and Casey had done their best to not look at each other. But the moment there was a break, they met in a predetermined place, usually in the well house.

"I think people see you as untouchable." She ran her hand down his bare chest. "Still leaving tomorrow?"

He kissed her fingertips. "I have to. It shouldn't be more than a couple of days. And while I'm gone, you guys can rehearse in the theater. You'll be glad of that. No peacock screeching."

What she didn't want to say was how much she was going to miss him. She didn't even want to say that to herself. "You'll probably get asked to star in another big-deal movie and never return. Poor Josh will have to play Darcy."

"Probably," he said seriously.

In alarm, she looked up at him. When she saw that he was teasing, she put her head back down. "From what Stacy said, Kit's nephew is a real beauty. Maybe he'll come here and play Darcy."

"For the first time, I'm glad there are no kissing scenes." Laughing, they began to kiss, their bodies close together.

"We better go back." Casey's lips were against his.

"Definitely." But they didn't stop kissing.

Something hit the roof of the little building, making Casey jump. "What was that?"

"Him," Tate said. Draped in front of the window was the tip of the peacock's tail. "Guess he decided to try to fly."

Casey was quickly getting dressed.

"We have a few more minutes."

"I better go."

Reluctantly, Tate sat upright. "I don't understand why we have to sneak around. I feel like some teenager from the wrong side of the tracks and you're the good girl who—"

She stopped buttoning her shirt to look at him. "Is that the plot of one of your movies?"

"I'm too old to play a teenager, but it's a script I turned down." He put his hand on her arm. "I want to take you out to dinner. I want to go to a movie together. I want us to sit on a park bench and eat ice cream."

"You'd cause a riot wherever you went."

He didn't reply, just looked at her.

"Okay, so yes, you can disguise yourself quite well, but . . ." She couldn't think how to finish that. Every day of the past week he'd asked her the same question, but she'd never come close to telling him the truth. What was she to say: "I want to protect myself from what I know you're going to do to me"? She didn't want to put those words into the open, because then there'd be a discussion about the future. In September he'd return to his own world and she'd stay where she was.

But hey, Jack had offered her a job cooking, so maybe Tate would too!

She didn't smile at her own joke. She wanted to be sophisticated about this. She was having a summer affair with a beautiful man. That he was also kind, funny, thoughtful, and a truly great lover was just something good for her to look back on.

ACT TWO, SCENE TEN

Darcy expresses his fears

"Ready to leave in the morning?" Jack asked as he sat down in the lawn chair next to Tate. They were several feet away from the big gazebo so their talk wouldn't disturb the players in their rehearsal. Casey and Gizzy were in costume and laughing over horrid Mr. Collins, who was being played by the ugly trainer from L.A.

"I'm not packed, if that's what you're asking," Tate answered. "But then, I'm not taking anything with me."

"I guess that means you're planning to return."

Tate looked at his friend to see if he was serious and saw that Jack's eyes were laughing. "Yeah, I might come back. Not sure if Casey will care."

"Whoa! Where did that come from?"

"I don't know. I think it comes down to first-grade wisdom. I like her more than she likes me."

"You're talking about the secrecy thing, aren't you?"

Tate shrugged. "I guess. She certainly doesn't want anyone to know about us. How are you and Wild Woman doing?"

Jack let out a long sigh. "She sits in church like an angel dropped onto earth, then we go out and she walks along a cliff edge so steep my hair stands on end. I think I may be in love with her."

"Does she like you or the movie star?"

"Me. I think. We don't have a lot of in-depth talks about feelings—which is another reason I adore her. She's never asked me what I'm thinking or feeling or even what my favorite color is. She's like my best buddy in the most beautiful package ever created."

"Good for you."

"So out with it," Jack said. "What's eating you?"

"Something happened with Casey, but I don't know what. Things were going great, then . . . she changed."

Jack took a moment as he watched Gizzy on the stage. To his mind, she was so beautiful she might as well have a halo around her. When she smiled at him, it seemed that his insides grew soft. In bed, out of it, he wanted to be with her every minute. But it looked as if his friend wasn't finding the same happiness. "Maybe the whole movie-star thing scares her off."

"Casey? No way. She's never seen me like that, and I've been careful that she doesn't see that side of my life. I want her to see me as a man, not as a product of my job."

"Good philosophy. Hope you can pull it off. By the way, I've been meaning to tell you that I think I saw your ex-brother-in-law hiding in the bushes on days he's not rehearsing."

"Can't be. I had the place fenced and I pay a couple of guys to ride around the perimeter."

"And a couple of hours ago they found where the fence had been cut."

Tate sounded alarmed. "Why didn't they tell *me* that?"

"Because you tend to disappear for hours at a time. What was I supposed to tell them? To look for you in the blackberry bushes? And I didn't tell security to search for the intruder because I knew he might be your ex-brother-in-law. The press wouldn't be kind to a story of you and him in a fight."

Tate was still staring at him. "You really think it's Haines who's been sneaking in?"

"The guard was sure it was him by the fence, and I've seen Haines in the bushes. So what's he after?"

"Money," Tate said. "He'll do anything to get out of having to work to support himself. Damn! He wants to get to Nina. All he has to do is look tearful and say he misses Emmie and she softens."

"Why is he breaking in now, before they get here? Maybe he's taking photos of you and Casey and planning to sell them. How secure is that shed you two hide out in?"

Tate's eyes were on the stage. "We can hear anyone approach. I don't know what Haines is up to, but I do know that he's seen Casey in private a few times."

"She tell you that?"

"Yes," Tate said, but he didn't elaborate.

"Your snake of an ex-brother-in-law is sneaking around and seeing your girlfriend, she's not giving you any details, and to-morrow you're leaving. Didn't you say that you might have to go with the director to the wilds of Romania to scout locations? They have cell service there?"

"Doubt it," Tate said, frowning deeply.

Onstage, Kit called cut and said they'd take a thirty-minute break.

Darcy and Wickham hear a secret

"Exactly where did you see him?" Tate asked.

Jack didn't look around. "Behind me. To your left. After my last scene, I went over there and the bushes had been trampled down."

"Do me a favor, will you?" Tate asked. "Take the girls some-where. Get them ice cream, whatever. Tell them I had to ..." He waved his hand. "Make up something."

"Want me to run back to the house and get a sword?" Jack was trying to lighten the moment.

"For this, I want to use my bare knuckles." With one last glance at Casey, who was laughing with her sister, Tate sauntered down the path toward the Big House. He wanted to look as though he had all the time in the world. Like he wasn't upset or worried about anything.

As soon as he was out of sight of the stage, he doubled back. Thanks to days of exploring, he knew how to get through the tangle of old shrubs. Silently, Tate made his way to the place Jack said he thought he'd seen Haines. In the center of some tall shrubs was a circle of flattened weeds, and, through the bushes, there was a clear view of the makeshift stage.

What was Haines after this time? Tate wondered, remembering how much money he'd poured into the man. There'd been years of supporting him while he was married to Nina. Cars, clothes, booze. Just paying off his AmEx bill each month had been a killer. Nina, always the softhearted one, would sometimes quote her husband to Tate, saying that Devlin just needed a good acting job but that he couldn't get one because he lived under the shadow of Tate's great success.

At first, Tate had made the mistake of thinking his brother-in-law was like him. When Tate had been out of work and frantically searching for acting jobs, he'd waited tables, tended bar, driven a truck. "Really?" Nina said at the suggestion. "You expect Devlin to do that? Can't you see the tabloids? There'd be a big photo of Tate Landers's impoverished brother-in-law washing dishes."

In the end, Tate had "invested" in a TV show, with the stipulation that Devlin Haines play the lead. After her husband got the role, Nina had been jubilant. She and Emmie at last had a chance at being part of a normal, happy family.

And for a while, Tate had also been content. He was shooting on location, and every night he thought of his family's perfect little life and how Haines was now supporting them. It made him feel good that he'd been able to give it to them. When he talked to Nina and Emmie via Skype, there'd been nothing but smiles and gratitude.

Then one of the show's producers had called him with the complaints. Haines was drinking on the set, groping every female. He was belittling the other actors onscreen and off. *He* was the star. *He* was the reason they had a job. Worst of all, with every episode, his performances got more wooden.

"Nobody can stand him," the producer told Tate. "Last time I was on set he told me to go get him some coffee. We would all put up with him if his attitude didn't carry over onto the screen. Did you see the *TV Guide* quip about the man's ego eating up the script? Devlin Haines has become a joke! Tate, as much as I respect you, you can't—"

"How about if I do a couple of episodes?"

"Yeah?" the producer said. "Can I announce that to the press?"

"Sure," Tate said. "Just give me twenty-four hours to break it to my manager. I'm sure you'll hear her screams."

But even that hadn't been enough. At the beginning of the second season, Haines's behavior and acting were so bad the writers killed him off in an attempt to save the show. But it was too late. By that time the whole series had become a punch line to late-night comics.

Tate wished he could have paid Haines to get out of their lives, but the man was Emmie's father, so Tate felt he had to back off. As part of the divorce, Tate agreed to support the freeloader for a few more years, the case to be reviewed later. But now what? As far as Tate could tell, the man had made no attempt to get a job.

He could almost hear Haines telling Emmie, "I can't get a job because your uncle Tate won't let me, so I'm living out of my car."

As Tate stood in the tall bushes, he closed his eyes for a moment. When he'd heard that Haines was in Summer Hill, he'd been shocked, but at the same time he knew he should have expected him. He was sure the man was there to get to Tate's bank account through Nina, and probably through Emmie. But they weren't here yet, and his rehearsals weren't until next week, so why was Haines skulking around in the bushes now?

Tate ran his hand over his face. There was no use trying to figure out the way Haines thought. All Tate knew for sure was that the man had been sneaking around Casey, no doubt gaining sympathy from her. He had a knack for making women feel sorry for him.

Whether Haines was up to something fairly innocent, like trying to win Casey away from Tate, or if he was taking photos to use for blackmail, Tate didn't know. What if there were pictures of him and Casey naked in the well house? Tate knew he'd pay to keep them out of the press. He wouldn't want Casey embarrassed that way.

As he looked through the shrubs, he saw that the stage was quiet. Olivia was to one side, sitting on a chair they'd bought at the estate sale and reading the script. Kit was at the bottom of the stairs, talking to the caretaker. No one else was about.

Tate saw a movement behind the stage. It was just a flash and it could be the peacock, angry to have so many people on the property, but it could be something else.

Feeling a bit ridiculous at sneaking around on his own land, Tate circled the gazebo while staying hidden. Twice he saw broken branches, as though he wasn't the first one who'd walked through there.

At the back corner of the gazebo was a trellis covered with dense honeysuckle vines. It was so thick that it blocked that corner of the stage from sunlight, and from view. A person onstage couldn't see through it.

Standing in the shadows was Devlin Haines. Silently, Tate walked up behind him. "Stay away from her," he said.

Devlin turned and there was a second of surprise, but then his face calmed and he gave his small smile, as though he was in control. "I have no idea who you mean. Jack's hot little blonde number?" His phone was in his hand and he held it up for Tate to see. It was a photo of Gizzy with her arms around a fireman, kissing him on the mouth. "This was taken two days ago. I thought maybe Jack would like to frame it so I sent you a copy."

Tate was inches taller than Devlin, and as he used his height to glare down his nose, he did his best to ignore the photo of Gizzy. "I want to know what you're up to. What lies have you been telling about me?"

"How do I know what are lies? You kicked me out of my own family, remember?"

"The chocolate mold from your *grandmother?* You hardly know who your mother is." Tate leaned forward. "If you hit Nina up for money, I'll get lawyers on you."

"So they can take away everything I own?" Devlin shot back. "You already did that. How's it going to look to the press if famous, rich you sues someone as broke as me? And don't forget that I'm the father of your niece, who you love being photographed with."

"You always twist things around to your advantage."

Devlin smiled again. "I'm just trying to earn a living, that's all. You help me out, and my daughter will give you all that great family publicity that you need. I especially liked seeing you with her at Disney World. You two looked so cute together."

Tate's hands were forming into fists. "Why are you stalking Casey?"

"She's one juicy morsel, isn't she? And not a bad cook. I've seen you two crawling through the bushes. What's she like in bed?"

When Tate raised his fists, Devlin stepped back and put his hands up, palms out.

"Aggressive, aren't you?" he said, still smirking. "I bet the police would love to hear that I came to this adorable town because my daughter was coming. And I volunteered my professional services to help in a local play. But what happened was that my rich, famous ex-brother-in-law showed up and *hit* me. No reason. Just punched me in the face. Wait until dear, sweet little Emmie hears what her uncle Tate did to her daddy."

Tate dropped his fists, but his anger stayed. "What do you want from Casey?" he repeated.

Devlin hesitated, as though he was deciding whether or not to answer that question. His eyes turned dark. "I'd like to take everything away from you, exactly as you've done to me. A few more tears from me and I'll have her clothes off."

"You—" Tate began as he stepped forward. But a voice from the stage above them stopped him. Someone was behind the screen of vines.

Tate didn't want someone seeing them arguing, then innocently sending out a text message that would alert the media. In a lightning-fast move, Tate grabbed the man in a choke hold and held him just tight enough that he couldn't speak. "Not a word!" he said.

"Don't touch me!" It was Olivia's voice, professionally trained and carrying clearly.

"Livie." Kit's voice was pleading. "Please listen to me. You must know that I did all of this for you. Building a stage, putting on a play—it was all to attract you to me."

"Trap me, you mean," she said. "So I'm here. What do you have to say?"

"That what happened wasn't supposed to."

"You mean your walking away from me? Leaving me?"

"I didn't have a choice. The government came for me. I had to— Damn! They're back already. Please, tonight let's talk."

"No. The time for words is past. I'm here because of my son and daughter-in-law. I'm playing a part because—" She raised her voice. "I'll be there in a minute." She paused. "Stay away from me, you ... you worthless boy."

Kit's voice softened. "You used to say that in a different tone."

She gasped. "You ever touch me again and I'll walk off this stage and never return."

"Like you did the last time?" There was deep anger in his voice.

The slap she planted on Kit must have hurt because the vines shook as though from a strong wind. She stomped away.

Tate, still holding on to Haines, waited until Kit left, then he released the man. He glared at him. "You ever tell anyone a word of what you just heard and I won't care about the tabloids. I'll go after you with an army of lawyers. You understand me?"

"Of course. You can do that. You're successful, while I'm—"

"Spare me!" Tate said. "Keep your mouth shut and stay away from Casey."

Devlin didn't reply. Instead, he clicked his heels together and gave Tate a straight-arm salute.

Disgusted, Tate walked away.

★

Devlin rapidly headed to the front gate, while dialing his PI. When the man answered, Devlin didn't bother with preliminaries. "I think I have a story. Find out about Christopher Montgomery and Olivia Trumbull. He's from Maine and she lives in this two-bit town. I already did some searching and I know Montgomery is from a mega-rich family. I want to know what happened between those two. You have anybody who can help you find out about this? I want info *fast*."

"Yeah, I have people, but who's paying for it?"

"Landers will. He's related to this guy Montgomery, and he'll pay to keep him out of the media, so don't hold back."

"You still owe me from last time. You—"

"Listen, you moron! Montgomery hires people like Landers to entertain at his kid's birthday party. I want to know what he's been up to. Go back years on this one. I know it has something to do with this town, but it may also be connected to this vermin-infested plantation. Landers's great-uncle Fred Tattington owned it. Find out about him. Send somebody here to ask questions of the old-timers. Not you, but somebody clean and decent-looking. You have people who can to do this?"

"I can send an army, just so you can pay for them."

"For once in my life, money is no object. I've *earned* this! I'll call you tonight and see what you've found out."

"I don't know if I can do anything that fast. I need—"

Devlin hung up, not wanting to hear the man's excuses. Like all extremely lazy people, he expected others to work backbreakingly hard.

Darcy makes a proposition; Lizzy misunderstands

It was morning and Tate and Casey were in her bed, the first night they'd slept together. She had on just her pajama top, while Tate wore nothing at all.

"I'm glad I bought this place," he said. They were snuggled together, her head on his chest. There'd been a few women before he was successful, but back then all he'd thought about was getting a job that could pay the bills. After his name had been on a couple of movies, there'd been more women, but they'd only been interested in him as a star.

Casey was the first woman who didn't seem to care about his movie-star status or even his looks—except to make jokes about them. She was interested in him as a man.

"I'm glad you didn't try to make it modern," she said. "No odd-looking sculptures in the garden. Do you mind if I put some more plants in the herb garden? I could use a patch of cilantro. And I need more lemon verbena."

He kissed the top of her head. "Sure. Buy whatever you want and give me the bill."

"Or send it to your accountant?"

"Nina takes care of that and she'll be here soon. She's doing some charity work now, and as soon as she finishes, she and Emmie will come."

Casey smiled up at him. "I can hear the anticipation in your voice. Why don't they live in L.A. with you?"

"They did, but after the divorce, Nina moved to Massachusetts. L.A. had too many bad memories for her. Speaking of which, Nina says I need a house in California that isn't all steel and glass." He stopped talking and waited for her to say something, but she didn't. "What kind of house do you like?"

"One with a kitchen," she said. "Walk-in pantry, big marble island. Or stainless steel—I can't decide."

"Any rooms attached to it?" He was laughing.

"Bedroom." She ran her bare leg down his.

"Sounds good to me." He kissed her, his hands on her face. He didn't want to leave. Last night he'd talked to the director of his next movie, saying he'd rather not leave the country to go look at sets.

The director had not been understanding. "You want to blow off a multimillion-dollar production for some local play?"

Tate hadn't said any more.

He looked into Casey's eyes. "After the play is over, maybe you'd like to see my house in L.A. If you don't like the kitchen, we can find another house."

"That sounds good. I bet there are fabulous grocery stores in L.A. Now I have to order some ingredients online. Tamarind was in the quail dish. I had to do overnight shipping to—" His cellphone was ringing. "You better get that."

Tate stuck out a long arm to pick the phone up. "It's Jack." He clicked it on. "Yeah, yeah. I'm dressed and ready and waiting for you. I'll be there in seconds." He turned the phone off and rolled back to Casey and started kissing her neck.

She pushed away from him. "You told Jack you were dressed, so now you have to get up."

"I am up."

Casey gave a giggle. "Not like *that*. Stop kissing me." She was leaning her head back as his lips began to move down her shoulder. "Tate! We don't have time for this. You have a plane to catch."

"It'll be a quickie."

"You don't like quick. You like long and slow and . . ." She was sliding down in the bed.

"I'm an actor. I'll pretend I'm your last boyfriend and it'll all be over in seconds. Just lie very still and think about tamarind and cilantro."

Casey started to laugh, but he kissed her as he moved on top of her.

Bingley begins to doubt

Jack and Tate reached the car at the same time and they grinned at each other across the car's roof. It had taken a lot more than seconds to get there. Inside, they sat on opposite ends of the leather seat and told the driver to go.

"So where's your suitcase?" Tate asked.

Jack shrugged. "I left everything here, maybe even my heart. What about you?"

As the car pulled onto the street, Tate looked out the window. "Mine but not hers." He turned back to Jack. "I practically asked her to move in with me in L.A., but she just wanted to know what the grocery stores carried."

"That sounds good. Maybe she is thinking about living there."

"No, she isn't," Tate said. "What about you and Gizzy?"

Jack took a moment before answering. "You know how I was glad she didn't ask me a lot of questions? Now I'm a little concerned that she doesn't want to know anything about me."

In spite of himself, Tate remembered the photo Haines had shown him of Gizzy kissing a fireman. "What's her boyfriend history? Has she had a lot of them?"

Jack frowned. "I don't know. As much as I love her nonstop action, sometimes I wish we could have a heart-to-heart. What do you know?"

Tate hesitated. Should he show Jack the photo that Haines had sent him or not? Maybe it was all a lie, but he and Jack had been duped by ambitious women before. He took out his cell and clicked on the photo. "I was told this was taken two days ago, but that could be wrong."

Jack glanced at the picture, then handed the phone back to Tate. "That's what I was beginning to suspect."

The two men looked at each other.

"We'll see how things stand when we get back," Tate said, and Jack agreed.

Lizzy listens to others

"So how have you been?" Olivia asked Casey. "Anything interesting happen?" They were wearing pretty Regency-era dresses and sitting on chairs that had been set up outside the gazebo. Onstage, Lori was flitting around Gizzy and teasing about how wonderful the soldiers were. She seemed very young but at the same time quite seductive.

"That girl is really talented. I hope she does something with it," Casey said.

"I found out that she's staying in a lake house with her grandmother, Estelle, who I knew in high school. I want to talk to her about getting Lori into Juilliard." She took a breath. "How lucky Estelle is to have a granddaughter like her."

Casey reached across to squeeze Olivia's wrist.

"Actually, I was asking about you and Tate," Olivia said. "He's been gone for a whole twenty-four hours. How are you holding up?"

"Very well. I don't have three meals a day to cook, and I don't have him hanging around my kitchen all day. He isn't bugging me to go everywhere with him in his little red truck. Did I tell you that one day he went to the grocery with me? It was a fiasco! He bought three dozen grapefruits and challenged me to make a pie with them. I didn't, but when we got back I put up some jars of a rather nice marmalade with a stalk of tarragon in the middle. Using the whole stalk was his suggestion, and he cleaned the grapefruit for me. Well, anyway, I can now do my summer canning without him underfoot."

Olivia was smiling. "You told me that story. Twice. You miss him a lot, don't you?"

"I do, but I wish I didn't." She blew out her breath in exasperation. "I've always prided myself on functioning on my own. Even when I lived with someone, I stood on my own feet."

She paused, then said, "I'm confused about what's going on between Tate and me. Before he left he talked about my being his cook in L.A. I guess I'd be his sleep-in chef. But I—" She put her hands over her face. "I really, really *like* him and I miss him—but I don't want to. I *like* being independent. I grew up with a mother who was gone all the time, and I learned to rely on myself. But then, that's what drove my ex-boyfriend crazy. He used to say he didn't feel needed."

"When you were a child, there must have been times when you wanted your mother to be there."

"Yes, but I knew she was helping other people." She looked at Olivia. "But sometimes I wanted her to help *me*. Sometimes I wanted to be like the other girls and complain about how my mother wanted me to choose a truly hideous prom dress. When I chose my dress, my mom was in Mumbai at a medical conference, and my caretaker at the time was a retired butcher. I now know how to field dress an elk, but sometimes . . ."

"You wish you could have had a normal teenage fit."

"Yes." Casey glanced back at the stage. "This is stupid, but I miss Tate even more than I used to miss my mother. I didn't think that was possible. But I don't know if I can trust him. Devlin says—"

Olivia cut her off. "Are you basing part of your judgment on what someone else says? Casey, you can't do that. You have to use your own instincts, what *you* want."

"I know," she said, "but I can't dismiss information from someone who knows Tate so well. Uh-oh. Kit wants us onstage. I may be off in this, but are you and our illustrious director angry at each other?"

Olivia stood up. "He made a pass at me and I turned him down. Come on, we have lots of scenes to rehearse." She started toward the stage, but Lori stopped her.

"I was wondering about something, and Kit said you could help me. There's a scene where Lydia gets to go on a trip, but her sister Kitty can't go. The girl playing Kitty and I are friends—or used to be—and . . ." She gave Olivia a look of helplessness.

"You want to know how to play it so you're glad but not shoving your triumph in her face."

"Yes!" Lori said. "That's exactly what I want."

"Let's go over to the side and we'll figure out how to run the lines so you don't hurt your friend's feelings."

As Casey watched the two of them walk away, she thought how sad it was that Olivia would never have her own grandchildren. Then she thought of Kit. He was older, but he was a really good-looking man. "Why in the world would you turn him down?" she said under her breath.

Wickham turns up the heat

"Hi."

Casey looked up from the pot of bubbling blackberries to see Devlin standing outside the screen door. She couldn't help the frown that flashed across her face. With three dinner parties to plan and prep for, she needed to get the jam into jars. She didn't have time to hear Devlin's snide remarks about Tate.

As soon as she thought that, she felt guilty. The man had confided in her in friendship and she should have sympathy for him, not wish he'd go away.

"I don't mean to bother you, but I was wondering if I could hire you."

"Oh!" She put down her spoon. "Sorry. Come in." She felt even more guilt for what she'd thought. Be nice to customers, she reminded herself.

He came inside, but he didn't sit down. "Today I'm rehearsing scenes with that kid Lori. I don't know how Jane Austen could write about a grown man going after a fifteen-year-old girl."

"There was no 'politically correct' then." Casey glanced back at the pot.

"I won't keep you," he said. "A friend of mine, Rachael Wells, is flying in on Saturday morning and she wants to go on a picnic. Could I hire you to make something wonderful to take with us?"

"Sure." Casey wiped her hands on a towel as she picked up a pen and notepad. "What do you two like to eat?"

"I, uh, I ..." He gave her a helpless look. "You wouldn't go with us, would you?" As though he weighed a thousand pounds, he flopped down on a stool. "I'm in a bit of a pickle. This woman has a crush on me. She was the co-star of my TV show, played my girlfriend. It was on cable, so we did some nude scenes together. Hazards of the trade. Anyway, I'm afraid Rachael took it all seriously. She said she's coming here Saturday morning and she's demanding that I take her on a picnic. I know she wants us to be alone in the country, but frankly, the idea scares me. So would you please go with us?" His eyes were as pleading as a hungry dog's.

Casey didn't want to go, and her instinct was to say no. But then she thought of this man being Tate's niece's father, and she found herself nodding.

Devlin got off the stool, his face one huge smile. "You are a great, great friend. Thank you so much." He went to the door.

"What about the food?"

"Anything you like," he said as he left. "I trust you."

The moment he was out of sight, Devlin began cursing. The bitch had forced him to change his plans! Landers was gone, so what was the frown she'd given Devlin when he showed up? What hold did Tate Landers have over women?

This morning Devlin had rehearsed what he'd say to Casey, about how Landers had ruined his TV show. He planned to use her sympathy to get her to go on a picnic with him. Yesterday he'd heard of a nearby sheer rock face beside a stream. Devlin thought he'd take Casey there, then fake a nearly fatal accident and let her save him. Women so liked a helpless man. While she was nursing him back to health, they'd just naturally end up in her bed.

He loved thinking about telling Landers that he'd enjoyed his new girlfriend. It wouldn't be as great as when Devlin had taunted him about his sister, but it would still feel very good.

But when Devlin saw Casey frown, he knew that wasn't going to work. Landers had certainly done a number on her! He'd played the hero and made her believe it.

As always, everything was given to Landers, but Devlin had to work hard for what he got.

For a few moments, he'd had no idea what to do. But then he thought, I'll have to get someone else to tell her.

The story about the girl and the picnic had been impromptu—and if he did say so himself, it was some of his best work. Just that morning he'd been thinking of Rachael. On the TV show, their sex scenes in front of so many people had turned him on so much that he'd been eaten up with desire. Uncontrollable. He'd pulled her into his dressing room and not given her a chance to say no. But then, what could she say? Devlin was the star of the show. His word was law. If she refused him, he'd just tell the producer that Rachael wasn't right for the part, and she'd be killed off—which is what he'd ended up having to do.

Even though today hadn't gone as planned, Devlin had spontaneously come up with the idea of Rachael and a threesome picnic. His acting had been so good that he wondered why he'd never before realized how brilliant he was at improvisation. Really quite remarkable.

Smiling at the discovery of yet another talent, he took out his phone, found her number, and touched the call button.

"Rachael? It's Devlin," he said into the phone.

"What the hell do *you* want?" she snapped.

"Come on, baby, don't be like that." His voice was low and coaxing.

"You got me fired! That TV show was the best job I ever had. A regular paycheck. And all I had to do was look at you like I gave a crap whether you lived or died."

"I'm sure you don't mean that. I hear you haven't found another job yet."

"Nobody will hire anybody who was on that show you ruined. It's like you put a curse on all of us. The guy who played your boss won't even put it on his résumé. I wouldn't but—"

Why did people always blame *him*? Devlin wondered. He cut her off. "How about if I make it up to you? I have a job for you. It'll only take a couple of hours. I'll fly you out here to the glorious state of Virginia, you'll play a part, then you can go home the next day. I'll even shell out for a night in a hotel. How does that sound?"

"Like you're up to no good."

"Do you care?" he shot back.

"Not when I owe three months' back rent, I don't. Except I won't do anything that'll get me put in jail."

"I wouldn't do that to you, baby. How well do you know Tate Landers?"

"We're great buds. He hangs out around my pool. We have drinks together every Friday."

Devlin gave a little laugh. "I miss your humor. Then you haven't been one of Tate's millions of girls?"

"If he used to be your brother-in-law, how come you know nothing about him? Word around town is that it's easier to get a front-row seat at the Oscars than to get into Tate Landers's bed. Some girl I know tried, but—"

"Do you want the job or not?" Devlin snapped. "Or are your scruples going to get you thrown out on the street?"

"How much are you paying?" Rachael asked through clenched teeth. "And what exactly is the job?"

"You're going on a picnic, so wear something conservative. No cheeky shorts." He paused. "You can wear them later. For me."

"You ever touch me again and I'll make you sorry. Now, talk to me about money and what I have to do to get it."

ACT TWO, SCENE SIXTEEN

Lizzy hears an awful, terrible story

Casey glanced at her phone yet again. There were emails from her mother, Stacy, and a couple of friends from Christie's, but nothing from Tate. It had been four days now and she'd not heard a word from him.

Yesterday at the rehearsals, Gizzy said she'd received several texts and emails from Jack. She wanted to ask Jack about Tate, but Casey said no. "He's probably just busy," Casey had mumbled, then returned to her lines.

Right now she was sitting on a quilt with Rachael Wells. Devlin was far downstream, a fishing rod in his hands. He didn't seem to be very practiced at flinging the line into the water.

She looked at Rachael. She was a pretty woman with lots of dark hair, and wearing a sundress that could have been in a 1950s movie. Her bare arms and tan legs were quite thin. "For the camera," she'd told Casey when they first met.

On the drive to the picnic site, Rachael had given Devlin several come-on glances, but he'd ignored them. When they got to the area, he'd slapped some cheese on bread and run off, leaving the women alone.

"You're going back to L.A. tomorrow?" Casey bit into a slice of quiche.

"Yeah, but damn! I wish I'd known Tate wasn't here."

246   JUDE DEVERAUX

"Do you know him?"

Rachael gave a little snort. "Oh, yeah. Tate Landers and I have been friends for a long time. I know his last picture didn't do well and that he thought the publicity of this local play would help, so I assumed he'd be here."

Casey was trying not to let her curiosity show. "You wanted to see him about something?"

"Actually, I have the photos he bought." She glanced toward Devlin, who was well out of hearing distance. "I certainly can't give them to poor Devie. After all Tate did to him, I don't mention his name." She lowered her voice. "In fact, Devie doesn't even know I still do work for Tate."

"What exactly happened between them?"

"Oh. That. Ever hear of a TV show called *Death Point*?"

"No."

"Of course you haven't. No one has. It was Devie's show and Tate killed it. I guess he got jealous of how well it was doing. One star per family seems to be Tate's motto, and he was it." Rachael looked at Casey in surprise. "Hey! You live nearby, so you could give these pictures to him."

"I'm not sure . . ."

"They're not porno, if that's what you think. I mean, not that Tate is above that." She looked around to make sure they were alone. "Just between us girls, if you ever get a chance to go to bed with Tate Landers, do so. I can tell you that an hour or three with him is worth it. You'll remember it always."

Casey swallowed. "So you and he were lovers?"

"Were? Honey, we *are* lovers. You don't think I flew to the middle of nowhere just to deliver photos, do you? Devie's made it clear that he wants his ex-wife back, so I have to make do." She laughed. "I came here to get my Landers fix."

Casey could feel her entire body stiffening. "I think he's seeing someone."

Rachael waved her hand in dismissal. "Tate is always seeing at least two women at a time. Any woman who thinks differently is in for a lot of pain." She pulled a thick envelope out of her handbag. "This was a big job for me. It wasn't easy to set that whole thing up while I stayed in L.A. That kid had to be anchored to the roof, and the cables hidden and released by movie magic. It was a nightmare!"

"Roof? What are you talking about? What child?"

"You didn't hear about it? That rescue Tate and Jack faked? I was told it went off perfectly. I was worried about the kid, but Tate said he'd be okay. Anything for the career, right?"

"Are you saying that the little boy sitting on the edge of the roof and the rescue were part of a publicity stunt?"

"Of course. You don't think two mega-stars like Tate Landers and Jack Worth are going to play hero without a reason, do you?" She was looking at Casey's shocked face. "I'm sorry. I forget that I'm not in L.A. Everyone there is publicity savvy. I didn't mean to burst your Middle America bubble."

"Would you please tell me this entire story?"

"Sure. It was Jack who called me, but then, Tate always has a sidekick. For a while it was Devlin, but ..." She shrugged. "Poor Devie. Tate threw him out of the marriage and got him cut from his TV show, both at the same time. I don't know how he survived it.

"Anyway, Jack called me and said he and Tate were going to some estate sale and they needed something to happen that would portray them as heroes. It wasn't easy, but with the help of a guy I know in Richmond, we set it up. I rented a truck, found a cute kid for the roof and a professional photographer to record it all. No video, just still photos, so it looked more real." She held out the envelope. "You can see them if you want."

Casey knew she shouldn't, but she couldn't stop herself as she pulled the photos out. The top one was of the little boy sitting on the edge of the roof. Gizzy, a rope around her waist, was walking toward him. She looked beautiful, but the child seemed scared.

"Notice that the men stayed inside where it was safe. They weren't going *that* far for publicity!"

Next were two pictures of the boy's mother. Casey held it up to Rachael, her eyebrows raised in question.

"She's a local actress, and the kid belongs to her neighbor. That mother is going to be furious when she sees these photos on the cover of the tabloids!"

Casey went to the next picture. It was of her hanging down the roof.

"That's the other girl. Jack was laughing when he told me that Tate got stuck sleeping with the fat one. Poor guy. But I guess in a small town, even he has to make do with what's available." As she stared at Casey, her eyes widened. "That's— Oh, no! I didn't realize *you* were the second girl they put at risk. I'm so sorry. I didn't know Tate was using you to— I mean, that he's— I have to shut up. Here! Let me have those pictures. I'll ship them to him."

"No," Casey said. "I'd like to keep them."

"Sure." There was sympathy in Rachael's eyes. "After the way Tate used you, you can have anything you want. I'm really sorry about this. And I'm going to kill Devie for not telling me about you and Tate. In L.A. everyone knows what he's like, but out here in the sticks . . . I really am very sorry."

She waited, but Casey didn't speak. "Damn! Now I'm wondering about the next thing Tate wants me to do. He said I should put on heavy clothes and go through some thorn bushes. He said there's a . . ." She checked her notes. "A well house? I'm a city girl. I have no idea what that is. But I'm supposed to peek through a window and take pictures of him inside it. Maybe they're some kind of art photos. Whatever they are, he thinks that if they're published, they'll renew interest in him as a romantic hero. He's worried that younger guys are going to knock him off his pedestal."

Rachael turned to look at Devlin by the stream. "I think we better go. I have a lot to do." She stood up, gave a loud whistle, then motioned for him to return.

Casey was sitting on the quilt, as still as if she were frozen—or dead. All of Rachael's words jumbled together so that she could barely think clearly. The well house. The rescue. That dear little boy. All done for Tate Landers's career? All a publicity stunt?

Rachael looked down at her. "I think I've upset you. Why don't you go back to the car? We'll clean this up."

Casey managed to stand up, and for the first time in her life, she didn't repack what she'd cooked. She stumbled to the car, opened the back door, and got in.

The only thing in her mind was that she must warn Gizzy. The men were in it together. They weren't real. They had come to a small town and found two females willing to go to bed with them. And poor Tate had been stuck with the "fat one." Too bad he hadn't shown up at the theater earlier that first day so he could have had the town beauty.

She watched as Rachael and Devlin put away the picnic things. She seemed to be bawling him out. Rachael was probably chastising Devlin for neglecting to let her know that Casey was the current bedmate of Tate Landers.

Tate had hired Rachael to photograph them inside the well house! Her stomach turned over.

As Rachael and Devlin started toward the car, Casey tried to get herself under control. Okay, so she'd fallen for a movie star's tricks. She could write it off as a learning experience. Someday she might even be able to laugh about how naïve she'd been. For all that she'd thought she was keeping her emotional distance from Tate, she hadn't succeeded.

What was important now was to warn Gizzy that she too was being used. And, also, Casey knew she could *not* tell anyone what was going on. Later, when the "rescue" was on the front pages of some news magazines, she'd be able to say, "Of course I knew it was all a stunt. That child was securely tied onto that roof. No, no, it was all done for publicity and I knew it."

She picked up her phone and sent Gizzy a text. MEET ME AT MY HOUSE IN AN HOUR. IMPORTANT NEWS TO TELL YOU.

As Devlin drove them back to Summer Hill, they were all silent. Rachael seemed to be too angry to speak, and Casey didn't want to. When Devlin stopped at a hotel to let Rachael out, she turned to Casey.

"I am really sorry about all this. I didn't understand what was going on. I think I should tell you that—"

"You've said enough for one day," Devlin said sternly.

"You bastard!" Rachael got out of the car and slammed the door, but she looked back. "Casey, I—"

She didn't hear any more, because Devlin sped away.

At Tattwell, he had to go through a guard at the gate, then he drove Casey to her house. He got out and opened the door for her. "I can't apologize enough for what Rachael told you. But then, it's been very hard for me to stand by and see what my ex-brother-in-law has been doing to you."

"I can't take any more. I've reached my limit."

"I know," he said gently. "But don't worry. I'll take care of you. I'll make you a drink or two and we can sit and talk and—"

Casey stepped away from him. "No. My sister will be here soon and no offense, but I may never want to see a man again." She went into her house and shut the door firmly behind her.

Devlin stood there for a moment staring at it. Damn Rachael! She overdid it. She was supposed to make Casey turn to Devlin in tears. But then, what had he expected? She always was a bad actress. Now that he thought about it, she was probably the main reason his show failed.

But at least Casey wouldn't welcome Landers back with open arms. That had been achieved. And he'd done it all by himself, without any help from anyone. If Rachael thought she was going to be paid for this screw-up, she was mistaken.

He took out his phone and called the PI.

"I was just going to call you," the man said. "You're not going to believe what I found out about this Christopher Montgomery and the former Miss Olivia Paget. This time, you've hit the jackpot."

"It better be good. I've had a rotten day. Why can't people ever do what they're supposed to?"

"You're going to be happy after you hear what I found out."

Twenty minutes later, Devlin Haines was smiling broadly. He felt so good he thought he'd go to Rachael's hotel, let her yell at him some, then get her clothes off. If she was really, really good to him, he might be persuaded to pay her half of what he'd said he would. She should be grateful, since she didn't deserve any of it.

By the time he got to his car, he was laughing. Before long he'd have that Jaguar Landers had refused to buy for him. No! With this news, he wanted a Maybach.

ACT TWO, SCENE SEVENTEEN
Darcy surrenders

"You're sure?" Jack asked Tate. "No doubts about her? None at all?" They were in the back of the car and being driven from the airport to Tattwell.

"Absolutely," Tate said. "I'm tired of the life I live. It's too empty for me."

"That's not a problem. It's just *who* you choose to share it with. You've known this girl for a very short time." Jack was tapping out a message on his phone.

"And who are you texting?"

Jack laughed. "The girl I've known only a very short time." He put his phone back in his pocket. "It's been twenty-four hours since I heard from her. What about you? You get through to Casey?"

"I sent her forty-one texts and emails while I was away, but she never replied. I was pretty worried, but this morning I got a notice that none of them had been sent. I had to go into settings and say, yes, I do want to send all those messages. They all went out at once."

"And?"

"Nothing, but if Casey was in the kitchen she might not have heard the phone." He smiled. "She'll be surprised at the deluge."

"I think something is wrong," Jack said. "Gizzy answered everything I sent her, but I've heard nothing in the last day."

Tate didn't say anything. The photo of Gizzy kissing the fireman still bothered him. Jack had dismissed it, but Tate hadn't. He'd wondered what was in Gizzy's mind. Sometimes it seemed that the only thing she cared about in Jack was his ability to keep up with her wild escapades. Walking along the cliffs, tiptoeing across the roofs, climbing trees. She wanted to do all of that—and maybe not much else. For his taste, Gizzy was too remote, too cool, too reserved. How could someone know what she was thinking or feeling?

She was the opposite of Casey, Tate thought, with her temper and her demands to be treated well. He always knew where he stood with her.

While he'd been gone, he'd thought of nothing but her and what they had together. He'd missed her horribly. Her jokes, her laughter, her eagerness to participate in life, had all become part of him.

Until he went away, it hadn't hit him how much she really meant to him.

In his weeks in Summer Hill, he'd nearly forgotten how the outside world saw him. He was met at the L.A. airport by a couple of fawning studio reps. "May I carry that for you, Mr. Landers?" "Are you comfortable, Mr. Landers?" "If you need anything, Mr. Landers, just tell me and I'll get it for you." The last was said by a pretty girl with a lot of eyelash-batting.

Over the years he'd grown so used to such treatment that he'd come to pay little attention to it. But his time in Summer Hill had been like being at home with Nina and Emmie, with people who saw him as a person, not as a commodity that had to be pampered because it sold well.

Every minute he was away, he'd wished that Casey were with

him. Or that he had her to go home to. At night, alone in his hotel room in faraway Romania, he thought about their time together. Their *life*.

Food and sex, he thought. Casey had given him the best of both. The best food he'd ever eaten and the greatest sex he'd ever had. He'd said that about the food to Nina on the phone just before he flew to Romania.

"Sounds like love," she said. "You don't really believe that the hamburgers you and Emmie grill in the backyard are the best in the whole wide world, do you? They're great because you and my daughter put so much love in them. I bet you like sex with Casey too."

"That's not something I will discuss with my sister."

"When I first knew Devlin and thought I was madly in love with him, the sex was so good that I'd cry. But after I found out what he was really like, I was repulsed by his touch. The only thing that had changed was love."

"You should go on one of those women's talk shows and tell that."

"I don't have to since every woman who's ever lived knows it. It's only men who are dumb."

Tate laughed. "That sounds like something Casey would say. And do *not* give me some platitude about that. Damn! They're here to pick me up. Will you and Emmie come to Tattwell when I get back?"

"Your niece says she needs two more of the eight pink suitcases you bought her, but yes, we'll be there five minutes after you land. Call me as soon as you're back."

"I will. I promise. I love you both. Bye."

All the time he'd been away, he'd thought about Casey and their possible life together. He went over everything in his mind. Where they'd live. If Casey didn't like his house, he'd sell it and they'd buy something cozy. With a great kitchen, of course.

If she wanted to continue catering or open her own restaurant, whatever she wanted, he'd help her do it.

The bad part would be *his* life. Cameras and red carpets and women saying lewd things to him would take getting used to. Over the years, he'd grown nearly immune to it all. But how would Casey react to a hundred cameras in her face and being asked what it was like to go to bed with Tate Landers?

He'd have to protect her. That was going to take some work, but he'd do it!

By the time he got on the plane to return to the U.S., he was full of resolutions—and joy. This was what he wanted, and there was a way to work it out. As Nina said, it just took love.

ACT TWO, SCENE EIGHTEEN

Darcy bares more than his abs

As soon as the driver stopped in front of the Big House, Tate flung open the door and started running. He covered the distance to the guesthouse in record time, but when he got there, he halted.

It was growing dark and Casey had the lights on in her pretty kitchen, so it was almost as if she were standing on a stage. She was at her island, a big bowl in her arm and scooping a dark-blue mixture into a pie shell.

To him, it looked like a beautiful painting, an Old Master where the subject was highlighted and the artist made you feel what he had to say.

Right now he was feeling that he was home. This woman was what he'd thought about, had wanted, and now that he was here, he was absolutely sure that she was his future.

She put the bowl down and swirled the spoon around, then glanced up and saw Tate standing outside. For a second, such joy ran across her face that Tate nearly leaped through the screen. He flung the door open and pulled her into his arms.

He started to kiss her mouth, but she turned her head away and he kissed her face. Her arms were at her side, pinned there by him.

"I've thought about you endlessly. I missed you every minute."

He punctuated his words with kisses. "I want you to stay with me always. I know my life isn't cute and cozy, as you're used to here, and you probably won't like my house, but we can get another one. I was thinking about it, and maybe you should keep the story of your donor siblings private. The tabloids will make an ugly mess of that, and I don't want anyone to be hurt. And I know you'll worry about the public appearances, but there are people at the studio who can do hair and makeup. I don't want you to worry about anything. I'll take care of it all."

She pushed away from him, then she stood there staring at him.

"I'm sorry," he said. "This is too much too fast. I know that, but I've spent days thinking about everything. Come on, let's go in the living room and talk." He reached out to take her hand, but Casey stepped away.

"It sounds like you've decided that you want me, so you've planned my life. Where you live for your job is where I must go. And my real life is a great embarrassment, so it's best to keep it secret. Poof! Dad and siblings gone. And, oh, yes, with professional hair and makeup I might be presentable enough to appear beside a beauty like you."

Tate was stunned. "That's not what I meant."

"I just heard you say that you want me to walk away from my own life to become your arm candy—after I have a full makeover, that is. Is this why you tried to get me to work out with you? So I'd look good beside glorious you? For *publicity*?"

"No." Tate's body stiffened. "I've never considered publicity."

Casey's face changed to a sneer. "You think I'm naïve enough to believe that? Did you think I'd never find out what you did with that little boy? I was told you had him tied on to the roof, but I didn't see any harness. Did you leave that child out there without a safety strap?"

"I have no idea what you're talking about."

"The publicity stunt you pulled at the estate sale, that's what. I know you set up that whole thing. You endangered that child's *life* just to get pictures of yourself looking like an actual hero."

Understanding was coming to Tate. "You think I'd do something like that?" he asked softly. "That I'm that kind of person?"

"I didn't think that—until I saw the photos, then I believed it."

"Might I ask who showed you those pictures? No, wait. Let me guess. Devlin Haines. I should have warned you that he would—"

"*He* didn't tell me!" Casey said loudly. "One of your many girlfriends, Rachael Wells, came here to deliver the pictures to *you.*"

"Rachael Wells? From the TV show? My girlfriend, is she?" Tate stepped back. His face was an unreadable mask. "I can see that whatever I say won't be believed. You have made up your mind about me. I'm sorry to have bothered you. Please forgive my presumption." Turning, he left the house.

Casey went into the living room and collapsed onto the couch. She had certainly told *him*! His arrogance, his assumption about what she'd do with *her* life, was despicable. A makeover! Did he think she was so ugly that she needed to be remade? But then, as Rachael said, she was the "fat one."

Casey dropped her head back against the couch. Of all the mean, hateful things that had ever been said or done to her, this was by far the worst.

But then, as she stared at the ceiling, it went through her mind that if she did, by some impossible chance, go to some movie event, she might, well, actually need a little help with hair and makeup and choosing a dress.

She sat up straight and shook her head. She had to stop thinking like that! What Tate Landers had done to his former brother-in-law, to all the women in his life, and to that dear little boy strapped onto a roof edge was more than she could bear.

She went back to the kitchen to finish cooking. Tonight, she'd go to bed early. Alone. She made herself stop that train of thought. She'd done the right thing and she should be happy about it. She was sure the feeling of misery would soon pass.

ACT TWO, SCENE NINETEEN

Georgiana steps in

As Tate was walking back to his house, his cellphone rang. He didn't answer it. He was too numb, too much in a state of shock, to talk to anyone. How had he been so wrong? How had he misjudged someone and a situation so completely?

When his phone wouldn't stop, he pulled it out of his pocket. It was Nina. It would be better not to let her know anything was wrong. "Hi, baby sister," he said with enthusiastic cheerfulness.

"Oh, no! What happened?"

"Nothing," Tate said. "I'm glad to be back and the play is going well and—"

"Don't you *dare* use your actor voice on me. You're a mess and I want to hear every word of what happened to you."

"Your ex-husband—"

Nina groaned. "I want you to get to a computer and put it on Skype. You're going to tell me all of it, and I want to see your face as you do it."

It was an hour and a half later that Nina closed her computer, and for a moment she gave herself over to quick tears. She well knew the treachery her ex-husband was capable of. His lies, his plots, his manipulations, could destroy lives.

When she was married to Devlin, she'd known he was having affairs, but the truth was that toward the end she was glad for anything that kept him away from her and Emmie. When he was with them, all he did was complain. No one ever gave him enough, did enough for him. She never understood his extreme sense of entitlement, but over the years she'd learned not to confront him. Confrontation made him go into rages that could last for days. Nina could stand it, but a baby didn't deserve it. She'd learned to tiptoe, to be quiet, to agree with him, and especially to constantly, endlessly, without relief, build his ego. Yes, he was magnificent; yes, everyone in the world was too stupid to see what a glorious being he was. Whatever it took to keep his rages under control, she did.

When Tate came home after finishing his fifth movie in a row, he was appalled to see what had happened to his sister. When she was near her husband, every other sentence she spoke was about what a great man he was and how everything he did was better than anything anyone else did.

But Tate saw a man who did no work at all. He didn't support his family, didn't take care of the house Tate had given them, paid no attention to his wife and daughter. Nina was exhausted from housework, childcare, and doing every menial task her husband could think of.

When Tate tried to talk to her, Nina repeated what Devlin told her. Without a good job, he couldn't feel like a man. So Tate had pulled strings, spent money, and made promises to get Devlin a starring role in a TV series. But he'd messed it up. When confronted, Devlin had blamed Nina for the show's failure. He couldn't be expected to succeed when he had a wife who never supported him, who never said a good word to him or about him.

In the end, Tate turned down a movie so he'd have time to oversee the divorce.

But now it looked as if her dear brother was on the receiving end of Devlin's lies. Nina could tell that Tate really liked this young woman, Casey, and she was sure her ex-husband had seen it too.

Nina went to Emmie's room. Her daughter was painting at her easel. "How'd you like to spend the night at Alicia's house?"

"Did she invite me?"

"No," Nina said, "but I'm going to ask her mom if you can stay. It might be for two nights. I have to do something for Uncle Tate, so I have to go to L.A."

Emmie looked at her mother hard. "You're going to save him, aren't you?"

"Yes, I am. When I get back, you and I are going to Summer Hill, and we're going to fix all of Uncle Tate's problems. How does that sound?"

"Great!" Emmie said. "Do you think they sell riding boots in Virginia?"

"Are you kidding? They may have invented them in that state. Meanwhile, think about what you want to eat. Tate's girlfriend can cook anything, and I want her to be very busy with the Landers family."

"Uncle Tate says the best food in the world is peacock and dumplings."

Nina laughed. "My brother is . . ." She stopped. "Deserving of the best," she said. "Now pack, and you're allowed to take only two suitcases to Alicia's house."

"Mom!"

Nina started to leave the room. "Two and that's all," she called over her shoulder.

Smiling, Emmie pulled four pink cases from under the bed.

Everyone suffers

"I am in the right," Casey said aloud. It was what she'd been telling herself for days, but she still felt awful.

After the picnic, Gizzy had shown up and Casey told her everything.

"They did it all for publicity?" Gizzy said, aghast. "How frightened that little boy was!"

Casey had made them drinks and snacks and they'd spent hours sharing—or Gizzy did. She told of every date she and Jack had been on, of the intimacy, the laughter, the adventures they'd had. Casey's eyes widened when she heard of all the things the two of them had done together.

"But we never talk," Gizzy said. "Just plain *talk*. He looks so pleased when I do something like swing from a rope and land in the middle of a pond that I do it again and again. I love the physical and it's great that Jack can keep up with me, but sometimes I want to be still. I want to tell him what's inside my mind. Do you have the same problems with Tate?"

"No." Casey didn't say that everything with Tate had been perfect. She had no complaints at all. He was caring, concerned, an unselfish lover. She could talk to him about anything and he always made her feel better. He—

"Is there any more of this?" Gizzy held up her empty glass.

"Sure." Casey went to the kitchen to get the blender out of the fridge.

"I don't like hearing that you and I were considered temporary," Gizzy said from the doorway, "but it's okay. Jack and I would have broken up anyway. I need more than just the physical side of a relationship." She paused. "Casey, I'm going to leave Summer Hill. I don't know where I'm going yet, but somewhere. I may go back to school to get a license to become a personal trainer. I think . . ."

When Casey looked up, she saw that Gizzy was crying. She set the blender down and went to put her arms around her.

"I'm lying," Gizzy said. "Jack was great. I could have tied him to the bed and *made* him listen to me, but I didn't. He's a movie star, but I'm just a—"

"You're beautiful." Casey meant to stop her from saying anything bad about herself.

Pulling away, Gizzy grabbed a tissue from a box by the cookbooks. "Fat lot of good it does me! Every man in this town is afraid of me."

"The firemen love you."

"Only because I can slither inside skinny spaces."

"I think it's the slithering that they like to watch."

Gizzy sniffed. "Don't make me laugh. How are we going to do this play with Jack and Tate?"

"I don't know," Casey said. "I really and truly don't know."

The two of them ended up crying and hugging and saying that at least they'd learned something. But that was poor compensation for the loss of the two beautiful men they'd come to care about.

Casey had been able to contain her anger about what she'd found out until Tate showed up after his trip. She was like a steam kettle ready to explode. When she first saw him, pure happiness went through her. He was standing in the fading light and looked like he was very glad to see her. For a split second, she wanted to dive through the screen door and go to him. Throw him to the ground and tear his clothes off.

But he got to her before she could move. His arms around her felt so good, and the electrical charge between them made her body hum. For a few seconds she forgot all the terrible things that she'd learned about him.

Then he opened his mouth. Out of it came orders and demands. Everything Casey had heard from Rachael seemed to be in his words. He wanted her to change her life for him, give up all she knew and loved to go to the other side of the country to be at his beck and call. After she had a makeover, that is.

The anger and outrage inside her erupted, and she told him what he could do with his demands.

In an instant, his face had gone from happiness to . . . to nothing. It was like looking at a photograph. He showed no emotion whatever. Not anger or sadness, not even disappointment. Just blank.

After he left, she again talked to Gizzy and they strengthened their resolve to stay away from the men. If they hurt like this now, what would it be like if they continued?

One thing they agreed on was to say nothing about what had happened. If they told even one person about the publicity stunt, it could become local gossip. From there it could go nationwide. The last thing they wanted was some scandal bringing the press to their small town. They didn't want the play tainted with the dreadful news.

Keeping quiet hadn't been easy for Casey. But she said nothing to her mother or to Stacy or to Olivia. She did her best to smile and act as if nothing had happened.

She didn't want to be alone with her thoughts, so she baked.

Pies, cookies, cupcakes, a six-layer salted-caramel cake. She delivered everything to the crew at the gazebo. When they couldn't eat even half of it, her father, Dr. Kyle, took it to a homeless shelter.

"Are you okay?" he asked Casey.

"Sure. Fine. Nothing is wrong with me. How are you? How's the new doctor?"

"Jamie's good. There are problems, but ..." He shrugged. "If you need to talk to someone, I'm always here."

"Thanks, but I really am fine. I have to go and ... uh, rehearse."

"Sure," he said.

The rehearsals were bad. Jack looked as if he hadn't slept in days. Casey saw him and Gizzy talking, but when Gizzy walked away from him, Jack looked like he might cry.

Casey had no mercy. Actors! she thought. Who knew when their emotions were real?

One day, Kit told Casey to rehearse with Tate. It was the scene where Darcy says the ladies want to show off their figures.

"There are only ten yards of fabric in this dress," Casey said. "I hope it'll fit around my hips." Everyone on the stage stopped and stared at her.

Kit ran his hand over his face. "Deliver me from young love."

"What would *you* know of it?" Olivia's voice held an extraordinary amount of anger.

After that, the day went downhill.

Tate and Jack pulled back into shells of coldness, never letting anyone see beneath the surface.

Casey and Gizzy had trouble concealing their anger, and when they spoke their lines, some of the hurt and fury they felt could be heard and seen.

"You're supposed to be *in love* with him!" Kit shouted at Gizzy about her scene with Jack/Bingley.

Her reaction was to walk off the stage, and Casey went after her.

Kit threw up his hands in frustration. "Take a break," he shouted. "Eat some of the hundred and fifty cakes and pies Casey baked."

The only person smiling was Olivia.

Casey ran back to the guesthouse, which had become her sanctuary, her hiding place. She didn't venture out except for rehearsals and necessary errands. No more wandering about the grounds, searching for fruit-bearing plants. She was too afraid she'd see Tate. Or Jack. Or the well house.

She made three meals a day for Tate and Jack and delivered them in a cooler. Only once did she see Tate. He was sitting alone at the table in the breakfast room and he looked as unhappy as she felt.

Probably acting, she thought, and turned away before he saw her.

Twice, Devlin had approached her. Maybe it wasn't fair, but she couldn't bear the sight of him. She wished she could feel some sympathy for him. After all, he seemed to have been thoroughly used as Tate Landers made his way to the top. Devlin's career, his marriage, seeing his beloved daughter, all of it had been taken from him in his ex-brother-in-law's ferociously ambitious pursuit of a career.

But even though it made no sense and wasn't at all fair, Casey didn't want to see Devlin, or talk to him, or even be on the same stage as he was. Before he showed up with his friend Rachael, Casey had been sublimely happy. In one seemingly innocent picnic, it had all changed. Laughter with Tate, telling him secrets about her life, kissing, making love. When she'd been with him, she'd felt more alive than she ever had before. But now all of it was gone, never to be found again.

Maybe it wasn't fair to blame Devlin, but she did. She just wanted to stay far away from Tate *and* Devlin. The anger, the vindictiveness, between those two men was not something she wanted to be part of.

Devlin seemed to understand, because after the first couple of days he kept his distance. He became quieter, almost as though he regretted that he'd been the cause of so much turmoil. Casey often saw him going over lines with young Lori, leaning over her in a fatherly way. It was as though he'd become a mentor to her.

Casey couldn't help thinking that young Lori was having a good effect on Devlin. The girl was a favorite with everyone. She was so quiet, never complaining, always with a book in her hand. In spite of being very pretty, she seemed almost mousy—until she got onstage, that is. Then it was as if a magician waved a wand and Lori went into character. She didn't just play Lydia but *became* her.

Lori had lightened everyone's bad mood when they most needed it.

One day when Dr. Kyle was late, Kit went into the garden to take a phone call. While everyone was standing around grumbling, Lori stepped forward and loudly said, "*I'll* play Mr. Bennet." She looked at Olivia. "Really, my dear," Lori said in a deepened voice, "can you not see that Mr. Collins is an odious little man? Too unlovely for Jane, too stupid for Elizabeth."

The lines weren't in the book or the script, and everyone was bewildered.

Only Olivia understood, and she stepped forward. "Ah, well, then, shall we package Lydia and present her to him? Perhaps roll her in the second-best rug?"

Lori seemed thoughtful as she reached to the fake fireplace and pantomimed removing a pipe. As she lit it and began puffing, she seemed to be thinking hard. "Lydia is too full of life, too exquisitely beautiful, and much too intelligent to be hidden in a rug."

Since Lori was playing Lydia, the spectators let out a muffled laugh.

"I agree," Olivia said. "It would be a shame to conceal hair the color of sunlight for even a moment."

More laughter escaped since Olivia was as blonde as Lori. "Perhaps Kitty?"

Lori puffed on her imaginary pipe. "Kitty is young, silly, and oblivious to the outside world."

At the side of the stage, the high school girl playing Kitty was tapping away on her phone, unaware of anything going on around her. The crowd quit trying to hold in their laughter.

"Then," Olivia said, "oh, wise husband, perhaps Mary. With her books, she could be a match."

"No," Lori said thoughtfully as she looked around at the people on the stage. "I have decided who will marry Mr. Collins and will have this house that is my very soul. The house that is the source of all this beastly marriage rumpus." Lori took a long breath, then whirled around and pointed at the woman playing Hill, the overworked servant of the Bennets.

In real life, the woman was about forty-five years old and was doing the play only because her children had nagged her into it.

"Hill, you are my great love!" Lori said loudly. "And the house will be yours!"

The woman—the only one onstage who was sitting down—said, "Only if Darcy comes with it."

There was an explosion of laughter that didn't end until Kit came back on the stage.

After that little episode, Lori was everyone's favorite.

Other than that one bit of lightheartedness, the rehearsals were unpleasant and they continued to be for nearly a week. By the end of it, Kit and Olivia were hardly speaking. One morning Olivia was to work on the scene where her husband is teasing her. But Dr. Kyle was called out on an emergency and had to leave. Kit stepped in for the part.

"Oh, Mr. Bennet," Olivia said, "you have no feelings for my nerves."

"Your nerves," Kit said softly, even seductively, "your words, your thoughts, your very breath, have been my companions these many years."

"If only I believed that!" Olivia snapped, and walked off the stage.

It took Kit a few moments to recover, then he called for yet another break.

Casey went to the guesthouse to prepare lunch to be delivered to Jack and Tate. When Josh stopped by, she gave him the cooler to take for her. If she could avoid going to the Big House, she did.

Minutes later, he returned with a gift in his hand. It was the size of a shoe box and wrapped in shiny green paper with a pretty pink ribbon. "This is for you."

She gave it a quick glance. "I don't want it."

"It's not from the men. It's from *her*."

Casey looked up from the pie dough she was rolling out. "Who is 'her'?"

"Tate's sister."

"Then I definitely don't want it."

Josh sat down on a stool. "You wouldn't consider telling me what's going on with you and Gizzy, would you?"

"We broke up with some guys," Casey said. "No biggie."

"You four, along with Kit and Olivia, are sabotaging a play that benefits charity, but it's no big deal?"

"Sorry." Casey rolled the dough over her pin.

"Casey!" Josh said loudly as he went to her. "Stop with the pies. You're putting the local bakery out of business." He put his hands on her shoulders and looked at her. "I understand that you and Tate had a falling-out. It happens. But I just met his sister and his little niece and they don't deserve to be part of it." When Casey was silent, he threw up his hands and stepped away. "Nina asked if you'd cook for them."

"Of course. Tate already asked. But . . ." Trailing off, she took a breath. "You're right. I'm carrying this too far. I would be glad to cook for them."

Josh picked up the prettily wrapped gift. "Open it."

"I will."

"No," Josh said firmly. "Open it *now*."

Reluctantly, Casey tore away the paper. Inside was a box filled with pink tissue paper. Buried in the middle was a little blue velvet case, the kind a ring came in. She dropped it back into the papers as though it were poison. "I'm not opening that." She turned away.

Josh picked it up and flipped the lid back. Inside was a small 128GB flash drive. "I have never seen an emerald this big!"

"He'd better not—"When she saw what Josh was holding, she grimaced. "Cute."

"Where's your computer? You're going to see whatever is on here now."

"No, I'm not."

"Casey," Josh said, "I don't know what happened, but I do know there are two sides to every argument, and from what I've seen, you and Tate aren't sharing info. His sister gave me this in private. My guess is that her brother knows nothing about it." He waited until Casey was looking at him. "Sometimes a man doesn't defend himself because he wants to keep his honor. I know that's an old-fashioned concept, and forgive us men, but we still feel it. I once had a girlfriend accuse me of something I didn't do. I walked away and let her think the worst about me rather than put myself on trial. When she found out the truth, she begged me to forgive her, but I couldn't do it. I don't want that to happen to you and Tate."

Casey took a breath. "I'm the one who can't forgive."

Josh went to the door. "I'm going back to the set and I'll tell everyone that you're sick, that for the rest of the day you can't rehearse or cook dinner or even take calls. I want you to swear to me that you'll stay here and see whatever is on that drive. Will you?"

She hesitated. Hearing what Rachael said had hurt a lot and she hadn't yet come close to healing. To see more of the fight within that family, to get more involved, would deepen the wounds.

On the other hand, maybe Josh was right and there *was* another side to what she knew. And besides, wasn't she already buried up to her neck in all of it?

"Okay. No pies, no tarts, no anything. I'll watch all of it."

"Thanks." He kissed her cheek, then left the house.

As Casey wrapped the dough and put it in the fridge, she thought of half a dozen other things she could cook. Of course, she'd have to go to the grocery first. Maybe after that, she could look at the drive. But by then she'd need to . . .

"Oh, hell!" She grabbed the flash drive off the island, went into the living room, and opened her laptop.

At first she didn't know what she was seeing. There were about twenty folders, each one containing documents, photos, and videos. She was glad they were numbered as to what order to open them.

The first folder was labeled DEATH POINT, the name of Devlin's TV show that Tate had ruined. As she watched clips from the episodes, she saw Devlin playing a police detective—but he wasn't the handsome man Casey had met. His eyes were red and he was unsteady on his feet. She could believe that Devlin was drunk or on drugs. Great acting! she thought.

Rachael, playing his girlfriend, came into the scene and started talking to him earnestly, but it was as though she was unaware that he wasn't at full capacity. Maybe that was part of the story, Casey thought.

In the next clip, Devlin looked worse. Bleary-eyed, distracted, pausing between lines.

It began to dawn on Casey that this was *real*. Devlin had played the role while he was high on something.

There were eight clips, each worse than the one before. The last one was for the season finale, and poor Rachael was killed in it. In Devlin's scene, where he was supposed to show grief, he seemed like he couldn't wait to get away. The tears rolling down his cheeks looked as if they were from a bottle of eyedrops.

Besides the clips from the TV shows, there were videos from the set. They appeared to have been taken on a cellphone. Three were of Devlin loudly arguing with crew members. One was of him groping Rachael's backside and her telling him to go screw himself. It was clearly not a happy work environment.

The videos were followed by documents. There were four jeering, laughing newspaper articles about Devlin Haines on the set of *Death Point*. Two *TV Guide* articles speculated on the future of the show. Would it be picked up for season two? Then came a notice saying the show had been canceled and that Devlin was going into rehab.

The next documents were receipts for payments made to Long Meadow, a drug-rehabilitation clinic in Minnesota. They totaled a couple of hundred thousand dollars. The patient was Devlin Haines, and the man who paid the bill was Tate Landers.

Casey got up and walked around for a while, trying to let what she'd seen sink in. This was completely different from what she'd been told!

She sat back down and opened the next file. It contained papers from Nina and Devlin's divorce. Casey felt that these things were none of her business, but she couldn't stop. In return for hundreds of thousands of dollars, Devlin had agreed not to sue for custody of his daughter.

Next was a file labeled RACHAEL. In it was a video of her talking to someone off camera.

"It was the worst thing I ever did," Rachael said. "And he

wouldn't even pay me! That night he came by the hotel and tried to get me to go to bed with him. I slammed the door on his hand and I hope I broke his fingers."

Rachael looked at the camera. "Casey, if you're seeing this, I'm sorry. I've never met Tate Landers and I lied about him. The gossip around L.A. is that he's a really nice man. And as for that story about the publicity stunt, I don't know anything about it. Haines gave me the photos and said he'd pay me to do some acting. I thought it was all a joke—until I saw your face. Devlin Haines is a real bastard."

Rachael glanced over at the interviewer. "Sorry. I know you used to be married to him."

"I've called him worse," said a woman's voice. "Anything else you want to say?"

Rachael looked back at the camera. "Casey, you're not fat. Haines told me to be sure to say that. And again, I'm very sorry for lying to you."

Casey closed the file and got up to make herself a cup of tea. As she reached for the mug, her hands were shaking.

It took hours to go through all the folders. Whoever had put them together—probably Nina—had done a thorough job. The mother of the little boy on the roof had been interviewed. She got very angry when she was told that someone had said the whole thing was a publicity stunt and that the child wasn't hers. Her language became quite colorful!

The man who took the photos of the rescue was interviewed, and he told how he'd been paid twenty grand for them. He had no affiliation to any news media and no one had hired him to take the pictures.

It seemed Tate had told Nina about Devlin's gift to Casey, for there was a sales receipt for the recent purchase of an antique chocolate mold. "So much for his grandmother," Casey murmured.

At eight, she made herself a sandwich and poured a large glass of wine. There was one more file. To be saved for last was the name on it.

Casey didn't know how much more she could take. What kind of person did the things that Devlin Haines had done? The lies, the twisting and turning of facts and history, were beyond what she could comprehend.

She drank half the wine before she opened the remaining folder. What horrible thing had Nina saved for last?

But what she saw on the video was her own house, and what she heard was a little girl giggling.

Casey leaned back on the pillows, pulled the computer onto her lap, and watched Tate Landers put on a silent movie of his war with a peacock.

By the time he got to the pajamas on the floor, Casey was laughing. Tate's pantomimed throat-cutting made her laugh harder.

She heard his stomach growling and saw him scoop up the pie with a big spoon. The look on his face at the taste of the pie she'd made was possibly the most honest, heartfelt compliment she'd ever received.

When she saw herself enter the kitchen and start bawling Tate out, Casey was holding her stomach from laughter. She was like the straight man in a comedy routine. The anger on her face when she saw Tate's shirt hanging from the roof sent her into spasms. And Tate's innocent expression when he asked if she could sew on his button nearly did her in.

It was late when she closed her computer and went upstairs. She needed time to think about all she'd learned.

Lizzy hears a different truth

How do you recover from embarrassment so deep that you never again want to be seen in public? Casey wondered.

The next morning, at barely daylight, she was outside in the herb garden. It was Sunday, so rehearsals wouldn't start until two—and she didn't know if she could bear to go.

How did she face Tate after seeing what she had? What could she possibly say to him? "I'm sorry"? That's what you said when you accidentally stepped on someone's toe.

What words could adequately apologize for the things she'd said? For all that she'd accused Tate of? There were none that could cover it.

Last night, after she'd recovered from her laughter over the Peacock War, she returned to reality and saw her part in the . . . well, the evil of Devlin Haines. Why hadn't she seen through him? Why hadn't she checked out his story? Some of the clips on the drive had been from YouTube, so she could have found them. When Devlin told her Tate had ruined his show, why didn't she look online to verify that?

The answer was, of course, that normal humans weren't used to people who lied on the scale that Devlin Haines did. And there was Casey's assumption that a man who was a movie star must be out for whatever he could get. She had dismissed Tate's talk of staying together, but she'd believed every lie Haines had told her.

Before she went to bed, she'd sent an email to Gizzy: I WAS WRONG ABOUT EVERYTHING. THE RESCUE WAS REAL. I AM AN IDIOT. WE HAVE TO TALK TOMORROW.

She didn't tell Gizzy about what was on the flash drive and knew she wouldn't. So much of it was private. Nina had entrusted those personal documents to Casey, and they weren't to be shared.

She picked some parsley and put it in her trug. Tate's sister and niece had arrived, and she planned to cook them the best food she'd ever made.

As she moved to the little patch of chives, she thought how Nina knew everything. She knew Casey had believed every word Haines said and had assumed that Tate was lying. How was Casey going to face the woman?

At worst, Casey imagined, Nina would sneer at her, curse her, tell her what she thought of her. And Casey deserved it all. She—

"Hello."

She turned to see a pretty little girl with dark hair and eyes that were exactly like Tate's. She had on pink tights, a pink-and-white dress, and sparkly pink shoes. "You must be Emmie."

She nodded. "Uncle Tate said it was okay for me to visit you. Can you really cook? He says you can make dirt and rocks taste good."

"I can," Casey said. "My secret is that I put fried worms on top. I tried red ants but they were too crunchy. I didn't want to compete with the rocks."

Emmie blinked a few times, then smiled exactly like Tate did. "I like sand better than rocks."

Casey laughed. She looked like her uncle and she had his sense of humor. "Are you hungry?"

"Yes," Emmie said.

"Then come inside and I'll make you some breakfast."

Inside, Emmie peered around the kitchen. "Did you really put jam in those jars?"

"I did." Casey was looking in the refrigerator, trying to decide what to cook for this child, who she'd heard was a picky eater.

"I saw the jars when Uncle Tate chased the peacock. He hates that bird! Mom let me buy him a big mug with a peacock handle. It'll make him laugh."

"Has he seen it yet?"

"No," Emmie said. "What's that?"

"Pie dough. I made it yesterday. You wouldn't like to help me make some tiny pies, would you? We can fill them with bacon and cheese, or blackberries, or we can make up a filling. Pizza is nice, or I have some South Carolina peaches we can use."

With every word Casey spoke, Emmie's eyes grew bigger. It took a few minutes to get hands washed, aprons on, and hair tied back before they were ready to begin. Casey showed her how to use the round biscuit cutter to shape the dough and how to put the filling in the middle.

Throughout it all, Emmie kept up a steady stream of talk about everything. Her mother was asleep, Uncle Tate was reading, and Uncle Jack had left the house early that morning. "It was still dark," Emmie said. She said she'd thought about climbing into bed with her mother, but instead she got dressed and went in search of the "food lady."

She and her mother had arrived late the afternoon before. "I wanted to come see you then, but Uncle Tate said no, that you were busy. Do you cook a lot?"

"Lately, I've cooked too much," Casey said. She was putting the first batch of the little pies in the oven. "I thought I'd make a big breakfast and take it over there. When do you think your mother will be awake?"

"Not for a long time." Emmie sighed. "Mom and Uncle Tate talked all night. I went down once and Mom was crying."

"I'm sorry," Casey whispered, and truly hoped she wasn't the cause of Nina's tears. "Do you know why she was crying?"

"My dad," Emmie said. "It's always him. She's unhappy when he's around. Can I use this turtle cutter?"

"I think that's a perfect shape. Want to dye the peaches green?"

"Pink!" Emmie said.

"Good choice." Casey got out her food colorings. She knew she probably shouldn't ask a child, but her mind was so full of what she'd read. How had this lovely child dealt with all that had happened? "When your dad lived with you and your mom, was he gone a lot?"

"Yes, but my mom and I liked it better when he wasn't there." Under Casey's direction, Emmie put a few drops of red coloring on the peaches and turned them pink. "Dad drank whiskey and yelled at us, and that made Mom cry. Uncle Tate was working on movies so we didn't see him except on the computer. Mom said that when he called us we had to lie and say we were really happy. She didn't want Uncle Tate to be sad."

"That must have been difficult." Casey helped Emmie press the edges of the dough together.

"Yeah. It was hard not to tell him the truth. Mom had to put me in another school because Dad wouldn't pay the bill. He said I had to go to school with regular kids, but they weren't nice to me, because my uncle is a movie star. But I couldn't tell Uncle Tate that."

"What happened when your uncle came home?"

Smiling, Emmie used a truffle cutter to make a tiny diamond in the turtle's back. "Uncle Tate went crazy. He was really, really mad. He broke some dishes."

Casey looked up, alarmed. "Were you afraid of him?"

"Naw. It was exciting. Uncle Tate said he was going to murder my dad, but Mom said he couldn't because of the police. He went to my old school and smiled at all the ladies and they let me back in. Uncle Tate is really good at smiling. But my mom said it isn't Uncle Tate's face that makes him a hero, it's that he knows how to pay bills."

Casey laughed. She already liked Nina. "What happened after that?"

"Dad quit being on TV. He said he was glad, because he hated the show. Then he went to a real have."

Casey remembered what she'd read. "Right. Rehab. Did it work? Did he quit drinking?"

"No. My mom said he and his girlfriend were still drinking whiskey. We saw them at a movie. They were kissing and they slid down in the seat. Mom won't let *me* do that at the movies! When we got home, she called Uncle Tate and he came over right away. Mom said we didn't have to lie anymore, so I told him the things Dad said I had to keep secret. When I stayed at his house, there was lots of whiskey and lots of girlfriends."

The child's voice softened. "That's when Uncle Tate started hugging Mom and she cried. The next day she left me with a babysitter, and she and Uncle Tate went to see Mr. Simpson. He's a lawyer and I met him. He has ice cream in his office. He said it kept us brats busy so we wouldn't hear the mothers saying bad words. He was funny."

"Your parents got a divorce."

"Yeah. Lots of kids at school have them, so I wasn't scared. But Mom was really mad. She said it wasn't right that Uncle Tate said he'd pay Dad, that he didn't deserve it."

"Pay him for what?"

"I don't know. His bills, I guess. Uncle Tate bought Dad a red car. And a house. But Dad didn't like them. He said they were cheap and he deserved better." She looked at Casey. "My mom says Uncle Tate is the greatest person alive on the earth."

"I think she might be right."

ACT TWO, SCENE TWENTY-TWO

Lizzy meets Georgiana

After Casey and Emmie finished with the hand pies—and Emmie had eaten hugely of them—they walked around the property together. Emmie wanted to see where her uncle Tate was in the play, so they went to the big gazebo. It was stacked high with chairs and boxes of costumes and props.

Emmie talked constantly. She told Casey about her friends at school, how one little boy was utterly horrible and she hardly ever spoke to him. And how some girls were good one week but bad the next.

"How do you know how to cook?" Emmie asked, as they reached the old orchard.

Casey told the story of her nannies and all the lessons she'd had. "One year while I was in college, I worked in an orchard on weekends and in the summer." To Casey's surprise, Emmie wanted to hear about grafting trees and spraying them when the buds came out. "These poor trees haven't been cared for at all."

"But now you live here so you can do it."

"I think I'll be moving away," Casey said quietly.

Emmie looked at her in alarm. "But who will cook for Uncle Tate when he's here by himself?"

"He'll find someone who can—" Casey began, but stopped. Obviously, the child was truly worried about her beloved uncle

Tate. "I'll cook so much for him that he'll get fat and won't need to eat for a year. Think that will work?"

"No," Emmie said, frowning. "Movie stars can't get fat."

"I won't leave him without food," Casey said softly. "I promise."

Smiling, Emmie went back to asking questions and talking about everything.

But one thing she didn't mention again was her father. As far as Casey could tell, Devlin Haines had no part in the child's everyday life. An image flashed across her mind of the times Devlin had tears in his eyes when he mentioned his daughter, saying how much he missed her and wanted to spend time with her but that Tate had prevented it.

And she had fallen for every word of it!

After about an hour of wandering, they came to the Big House—and Casey held her breath. If they saw Tate, what would she say?

But the house was silent. Casey waited outside as Emmie tiptoed in and came out minutes later wearing a pink swimsuit and carrying a big pink towel. "Pond or pool?" asked Casey.

"Pond," Emmie said, and they clasped hands and began running.

The pond was down a path, through rhododendron bushes, past the big magnolia tree with the stone statue of a smiling woman.

"That's where Letty and Ace saved the world," Emmie said. "They—"

"Fought outer-space demons."

Emmie's eyes widened. "You know about them?"

"Your uncle told me. Did you know that Ace grew up to be my father?"

"Letty is my grandmother, so that makes you my . . . my aunt."

"I don't think that's right," Casey said, but Emmie was running ahead to the pond. Casey had an idea that nothing she could say was going to dissuade Emmie from calling her Aunt Casey.

They walked around the pond and Emmie stuck her foot in, but she liked talking better. When she told the story of Letty and Ace pushing Uncle Freddy in his wheelchair into the pond, Casey thought how she looked forward to getting Olivia and the child together. Olivia had been there!

"Mr. Gates was really upset, but Uncle Freddy just laughed," Emmie said, sounding as if it was a story she'd heard often. "He loved Letty and Ace. What did your father tell you about him?"

"I don't know my father very well," Casey said. "I just met him a few months ago, and we haven't had very many long talks. But I do plan to ask him about when he was Ace."

"I know," Emmie said. "Uncles are much better than fathers. Do you have an uncle?"

"Not a one. I—"

Emmie glanced to the side and her face lit up. "Mom!" she yelled, and went running to hug her mother.

Casey turned to see a tall woman coming toward them. She was quite pretty, with dark hair and eyes, and she very much resembled Tate.

At the sight of her, Casey stiffened. This was the woman who'd let her know how stupid she'd been about Tate. She'd believed a liar and had judged Tate—based on no evidence—to be a bad person.

But Nina smiled at Casey. "Hello." She was hugging her daughter.

"We made little pies," Emmie said. "They have cheese and peaches in them, and mine look like turtles and I ate a dozen of them."

"Why don't you take some to Uncle Tate? I think he's tired of reading his new script."

"Okay." Emmie ran toward the guesthouse, her towel trailing behind her.

When they were alone, Nina turned to Casey. "Thank you for taking care of Emmie this morning. He said he watched her until she found you and . . ." She took a breath. "Tate and I were up late last night. She usually wakes me, but this morning she didn't. By the way, I'm Nina Landers."

Casey's body was so stiff she felt like a mannequin. "I'm sorry," she whispered. "I shouldn't have believed Devlin. I should have—"

Nina's snort of laughter cut her off. "I *married* him! I believed him so much that I pledged to stay with him forever. Anything you did is a poor copy of my idiocy."

"But I . . ." Casey couldn't think what to say.

"Do you really have a kitchen full of food, as Tate says? His fridge is utterly empty."

"Come with me," Casey said, and they began to walk.

"Did I hear you and my daughter talking about Letty and Ace? Tate said Ace is your father. I'd love to talk to him. And Josh Hartman is your brother? He seems nice, very interesting. And understanding. Actually, he has a depth of perception that I find remarkable. I can't believe I didn't meet him when Stacy and I were working together."

As they walked, Casey began to smile. It didn't look like Nina was angry at her—and it seemed that she was interested in Josh. Unfortunately, so were most of the females of Summer Hill. But Casey liked a woman who'd go to so much trouble to defend her brother. Maybe if Casey got together with her sisters, they could push Josh toward this woman.

At the guesthouse, Casey had Nina sit while she made her an omelet of grilled peppers and three cheeses. While Casey cooked, Nina talked and asked questions.

After only a few minutes, Casey's feelings of guilt over what she'd done to Tate began to lessen and she started talking about the rehearsals. "Poor Kit. Everyone is angry at everyone else and he can't get good performances out of any of us. There's some big past secret between him and Olivia."

"Love affair?"

"Of course," Casey said. "Only deep love could make two people as snotty as they are to each other. Will Jack be back for breakfast?"

"Last night he got a call that so upset him I thought he was going to burst. I think it was from his new girlfriend."

"I . . ." Casey began. She'd sent Gizzy the email saying she was wrong. Maybe Gizzy had called Jack and he got angry. "I think that was my fault."

"Which of course means that my ex had a hand in it. Rage trails behind him like damage after a forest fire. Whatever happened, Jack must have left very early and we haven't heard from him since. My guess is that right now he's with Gisele."

Casey was washing a stockpot. "Tate must hate me," she said softly. When Nina didn't say anything, she turned and looked at her.

Nina's pretty face was serious. "I'm not going to lie. He got his male pride hurt and he's not happy. But I think if you're patient he'll get over it." She paused. "Between you and me, his pride could use some bruising. All that fawning isn't good for anyone."

"Thanks." Casey gave a bit of a smile. "And thank you for all the work you did to show me how I misjudged him."

"Oh, well. His pride and your prejudice against him. It's a perfect match."

They looked at each other and laughed.

Lizzy sees through the darkness

Tate didn't show up for the rehearsal. Frowning, Kit said he was the only person who didn't need to work on his part, so he could stay home.

Everyone groaned. They'd been at this for weeks and had seen Kit change from easygoing affability to scowling tyranny.

One of the scenes Casey had to endure was where Wickham told lies about Darcy. Somehow, Casey was supposed to look as though she believed him.

As they got into position to say their lines, Casey saw the bandage on Devlin's left hand. "Did you hurt yourself?" She put as much innocence as she could in her voice.

He gave a sheepish look that she'd seen before, as though he'd been caught doing something he'd meant to keep secret. "You know the saying. No good deed goes unpunished. Let's just say that I won't ever again try to help a woman who is carrying too many packages. She misunderstood my intentions and slammed the car door on my hand. I gave her a couple of tickets to the show, so I hope that made her forgive me. But . . ."

"But what?" She was gritting her teeth at his lie.

"We all know where the spotlight will go in this play. You and I, as regular people, won't be noticed beside Landers."

Now that Casey knew the truth, she marveled at the way this

man twisted the facts. It was as though he were a human balance scale. If Tate, his nemesis, went down, he went up. She forced a smile. "But what about your fans from *Death Point*? If a pretty girl like Rachael would fly out here just to see you, I'm sure more of your fans will show up on opening night."

Devlin gave a genuine smile. "Maybe you're right." He glanced over his shoulder. "Have you seen Lori today?"

"Not yet. Maybe she—"

"Quiet!" Kit bellowed. "Wickham and Lizzy! Take your places."

It wasn't easy for Casey to play the scene with wide-eyed innocence, but she did it—and afterward she felt as if she needed a shower.

Lizzy swallows her pride

At four, Kit called a halt to the rehearsal. By then everyone was worn out from the tension on the set. Casey couldn't keep from glancing at every movement offstage, wondering if it was Tate. Jack and Gizzy had shown up, and she was dying to ask them how they were. During a family scene, Casey had whispered to her father, "I want to hear all about Ace." Unfortunately, that had made Dr. Kyle let out a laugh—which Kit heard.

"Miss Reddick! Is it too much to ask that you do not try to entertain the players while onstage?" Kit said through clenched teeth.

Yet again, Olivia stepped forward. "She only recently learned that her father was Ace, and she wants to know about it."

Kit's face went white and he looked away. When he turned back, he wore no expression. An hour later he let everyone go. "There will be a dress rehearsal tomorrow, so I want all of you here at ten A.M. And, Casey, we'll want lunch. Send me the bill."

"Double it," Olivia muttered as she walked past Casey and Dr. Kyle.

Casey glanced at her father. "Do you know what this is about?"

"I know they had a mad, passionate affair during the summer of 1970. I was only five then, and Letty's and my main goal was to spy on them. We were like Native Americans counting coup. It wasn't until I was an adult that I realized what was happening that summer."

"Who dumped whom?"

"I don't know. I just remember that Kit left in a big black car. I think Letty and I told Livie that his father had come to get him. One thing I remember is that after Kit left, Livie refused to go into the well house. She said Letty and I could have it. We were joyous, and we filled it with treasures from all over the house." He smiled in memory.

"How was Olivia after Kit left?"

"Angry. Quiet. Letty and I missed Kit and kept asking where he was, but no one knew. That fall, my mother . . ." He shrugged. "I quit thinking about Kit and Olivia, and I didn't see her again for years." His cell buzzed and he looked at it. "Sorry, I have to go. Medical emergency." He went down the stairs. "Invite me to dinner and we can talk for hours."

"Wait!" Casey said. "Did you find a diamond ring in the well house?"

Dr. Kyle grinned. "Maybe. Who knows? To Letty, everything was made of diamonds that had been mined on the moon. To her, everything that she saw and touched was magical." He was walking backward.

"Wish I'd known her," Casey said.

"Wish I'd married her." Turning, Dr. Kyle ran to his car.

"Then I wouldn't have been born," Casey muttered. "Or Tate would be my brother. Not good!"

She went back to her house and began making out a menu for the big lunch the next day. It was going to take a lot of work, and she needed to go to the grocery. When she got to the door, she saw Nina and Emmie coming toward her.

"How did the rehearsal go?" Nina asked.

Casey rolled her eyes. "I don't know if my lack of concentration or Kit's bad temper was worse. Whichever, today was a bad experience." She held up her list. "I have to do lunch tomorrow, so I'm off to the grocery. Tell me what you need."

"Fruit, sandwich makings, milk. The regular stuff."

"I want to go with you," Emmie said.

"To the grocery? That's pretty boring," Casey replied.

"You have enchanted her. Would you mind?" Nina asked.

"No, of course not," Casey said honestly. "Ready?"

Emmie, wearing a very cute pink dress with a matching shrug, was already on the way to the car.

Shopping with a child was new to Casey. She was used to concentrating and giving her mind over to what she needed to buy. But Emmie wanted to learn, so Casey answered a lot of questions.

Emmie was intrigued when Casey said she did nearly all her shopping against the walls, not on the inside aisles.

"But my mom buys everything from the middle."

Casey didn't reply to that; she just talked about produce ripeness and cheeses and meats. When they finished shopping, the car was so full that she said it might be too heavy to drive.

"We should have brought Uncle Tate's truck. Do you still like my uncle?"

"Very much."

"Good," Emmie said. "Mom is talking to him."

"What does that mean?"

Emmie shrugged. "Mom says that sometimes Uncle Tate acts like the men in his movies."

"I've never seen one, so I'm not sure what that means."

"Me neither. Mom says I can only see them when I'm thirty-five and have three kids."

They looked at each other and laughed.

"So, uh, what's he been doing?" Casey wanted to sound like she wasn't deeply interested.

"Kicking things and fighting and reading scripts."

"Fighting?" Casey sounded alarmed.

"With swords."

"Oh, I see. Working out. Did you know the trainer is in the play?"

"Yeah. Uncle Tate said he's perfect for the role."

Casey tried to hide her laughter; the trainer was so good at playing the slimy Mr. Collins that when he'd asked her to marry him, Casey hadn't had to act. She really had been repulsed.

"Uncle Tate is angry about the scripts. He wants to do something funny."

"Too bad people can't see the movie he made with the peacock. That was *very* funny."

Emmie looked at Casey with a brilliant grin.

"What's that for?"

"I was just thinking about clouds. They're very pretty."

Puzzled, Casey agreed.

When they got back to the house, Emmie thanked her, then ran away, leaving Casey to haul everything inside and start her prep work. But first she cooked a crab-cake dinner for the Landers family and packed it into a cooler and a big basket. On impulse, she wrote a note.

Dear Tate,

I would like to apologize for believing another person over you. I am angry at myself for not seeing the truth.

When you returned from your trip and spoke of future possibilities, I misunderstood. I feel bad that Nina had to go to so much trouble to show me the truth.

I understand if you cannot forgive me.

Thank you for everything.

Acacia Reddick

She put the note in an envelope, sealed it, shoved it into the side of the basket, then hurried over to the Big House to leave it all on the porch steps.

When she got back to her house, she was shaking. How would Tate react to what she'd written? Would he call her and bawl her out? Appear on her doorstep and tell her she was never to contact him again?

When she couldn't get her mind off what Tate was going to do, she turned on the TV. Maybe a nice scary movie would distract her as she prepped for tomorrow. Counting cast and crew, the lunch would be for about fifty people, so she had a lot to do. She needed to get up no later than five tomorrow morning to put it all together.

She checked the channels to see what was on. To her shock, a Tate Landers movie was just starting. Usually, she'd flip past it—not what she was interested in. But today she pushed the button and put the remote control down. Maybe she should see what so many women were talking about.

ACT THREE, SCENE ONE

Darcy conquers his prejudice—and shows those abs!

There was a naked man on Casey's back porch.

It was five A.M., her alarm had just gone off, and she'd staggered down to the kitchen to start making lunch.

Last night she'd stayed up late because she'd watched three Tate Landers movies in a row. When the first one ended, her heart was pounding and her fingertips were tingling—as was every other part of her body.

The plots of the movies were absolutely absurd. Pretty girl in a jam gets saved by the reluctant hero. Ho-hum. Nothing new there.

But Tate made the pictures so very watchable. His dark good looks were intensified on the screen. When he scowled in annoyance at the heroine, Casey found her own heart beating faster. She'd set down her knife and stared at the screen.

Had Tate ever looked at *her* like that? she wondered. Maybe he had, at first, but she hadn't realized what he was doing. She'd been so angry at him that nothing he did made a good impression on her.

When the first movie ended, all she knew for sure was that she wanted *more*. She searched until she found movies she could stream, and she purchased—not rented—two of them.

By the middle of the second one, she gave up cooking, moved to the bigger TV in the living room, turned out the lights, and watched.

When that was over, she put on the pajamas Tate liked so much and watched the third movie on her iPad while in bed. It was as close as she could get to snuggling with him.

If it hadn't been for the huge lunch she had to cater the next day, she would have stayed up and watched a fourth film. Reluctantly, she turned the iPad off and went to sleep.

When the alarm went off at five, she could hardly get out of bed. She fumbled her way down the stairs, yawning, filled the electric teakettle, and put the leaves in the strainer. A sound made her turn. The back-porch light was on, but she often left it on.

Standing on the stone path was Tate, and as she watched, he took off his T-shirt and sweatpants and let them fall to the ground. Totally nude and facing her, he walked up the three steps, his full male glory in clear view.

He forgave her! That's what went through her mind.

The second thing was lust. His movie! Him on the screen! How much she'd missed him!

She took a step toward the door, her only thought of jumping on him. Ravishing him. Lips and tongues, bodies together. She reached for the buttons on her pajama top, but then she stopped.

No, this was a fantasy. It was being replayed for her, and she wasn't going to ruin it with reality.

Without taking her eyes from Tate's beautiful naked body, she stepped back and fumbled for the electric kettle. As she poured boiling water over the loose tea leaves in the silver strainer, quite a bit missed the mug, went onto the granite countertop, and ran down to the tile floor, but she didn't notice.

She sat down on the stool and studied his body from the toes up. Slowly, taking in every inch of him. But this time, she knew what was to come.

When she got to his face, she looked at his dark eyes under the heavy brows, his lips that she'd grown to know so well. She could remember the feel of his hair when she buried her face in it.

When he got to her door, she drew in her breath. Was he coming inside? But no, he reached out to turn on the water, and his body flexed. Since she'd first seen him, he'd put on more muscle, had trimmed down even more. Casey could feel sweat breaking out on her.

Picking up her mug of tea, she sipped it while she watched him lather himself. He soaped his legs, between them, then moved upward. When he had trouble reaching the entire width of his back, as before, Casey thought of slipping out of her pajamas and joining him.

But she didn't. She wanted this delicious, divine fantasy to play out for as long as possible.

He reached up to the showerhead on the wall, pulled it down, and sprayed water over his entire gorgeous body. Casey was beginning to smile now. Just thinking of what was coming was making her vibrate. Would the electricity between them be in full force? Make all the hair on her body stand on end?

When he turned off the water and looked around for a towel, Casey's smile broadened. This time, would he come inside and keep searching? In one of his movies he'd grabbed a woman's dress and torn it open. Buttons flew everywhere.

Since Casey didn't want the pajamas her mother had given her torn, she unbuttoned the top. Saves time, she thought practically.

When Tate stepped toward the house as though he meant to enter, her heart seemed to stop. He put his hand on the door handle, and her breath halted. She couldn't move. But he dropped his hand and went back down the steps, and she let out her breath. And frowned.

No. This isn't the way it was supposed to go. Tate was to come inside. Didn't he know she was there? Watching him?

Still nude, he picked up his sweatpants. He was about to put them on when Casey flung the door open and ran. Dropping the pants, he opened his arms to her. When she reached him, he held her to him, the two of them clinging together so closely they were like one person.

For minutes they were content to do nothing but feel. Electricity went through them, a soft hum of what was almost peace.

It was Tate who moved first. His lips came down on hers, at first sweetly, but at the touch, the charge that went through them ignited. His kiss became deeper.

Casey's top was already unbuttoned, so her breasts were against the bare skin of his chest.

He backed her against a tree, and as much as she wanted him there and then, she was aware of where they were. She managed to get out one word. "Emmie."

It didn't take more than that to remind Tate that his niece had a way of appearing where she wasn't expected.

To Casey's delight, Tate swept her into his arms and carried her up the steps to her house. With what she knew was a rehearsed gesture—it was in movie number two—he opened the door and carried her inside.

He set her down in the living room. She could see that he was ready for her, but before she could touch him, he had her against the wall, the pajama bottoms off, and entered her quickly.

Passion. That feeling of being desired, wanted, *needed* by a beautiful man was as glorious as the actual sex.

It was as though Tate would die if he didn't have her—and she felt the same way.

She put her head back against the wall, her throat exposed to his lips, as his strokes became harder and more urgent.

When they at last came together, it was a release, but it was also a relief that their separation was over. Anger, misunderstanding, lack of trust, went away. Withholding of secrets and deeper feelings were released.

They clung together, skin to skin. Casey's legs were wrapped around Tate's waist, locking him to her, and his arms held her just as tightly.

When he fell out of her, she felt his smile against her neck. He didn't say anything but carried her up the stairs to her bed.

For a moment he looked down at her in her open nursery pajama top.

Casey had seen the expression he wore in his movies, and for a second it was exciting to think of. But then she saw the man. She had shared a lot with him, from their lonely childhoods to being entangled with a man who plagued his family. In a short time Casey had become enmeshed with Tate's friends, his family, his very *life*.

The movie-star image fell away and she saw the man she'd come to care for deeply. She lifted her arms to him.

The smile he gave her seemed to show that he understood. He stretched out on the bed beside her and pulled her into his arms, her head on his shoulder.

"I'm sorry," she whispered. "I was wrong."

"Shhhh," he said. "It's all right." He stroked her hair.

"I thought you hated me."

"I could never do that."

She pulled away to look at him. "But you were so angry at me!"

Tate gave a little laugh. "I was. I haven't had a lot of women tell me no. It was a shock to me." She put her head back down on his shoulder. "I've committed to this play and I have to honor that. But the second our performances are done, I'll be going back to L.A."

"Oh. I see," Casey said. "L.A. Want me to close up the house here for you?"

"No. Don't take my head off again, but I want you to go with me. But if you don't like that idea, I will come here as often as I can."

Casey let out her breath. "You really meant what you said."

He shook his head in disbelief. "Of course I did! What is it about Haines that makes perfectly sane women like you and Nina believe him?"

She knew it was a rhetorical question, but she answered anyway. "Probably his faked displays of emotion. He says everything with tears and angst, like it's coming from the very depths of his soul. You say, 'Baby, my jet's running. Wanna go with me?'"

Tate laughed. "I think I've been in L.A. too long, because those words are guaranteed to get any other woman there."

Putting his hand under her chin, he tipped her face up to look at him. He was serious. "Acacia, I like you very much. I like the way you see through the outside of me to what's underneath. I like that I can be myself with you, that you have no preconceived ideas of what I should be. I like your enthusiasm for life. I especially love our bodies together."

He took a breath. "I want you to go to L.A. with me to see if you can tolerate my odd life. I made up my mind about you at the first, maybe on that day when you yelled at me about the pie. I've had to wait for you to decide what *you* want." He paused for a moment. "Will you go with me?"

"Yes," she said. "I will." Her head went back to his shoulder.

"Good, but we have to keep it quiet. I'm afraid Haines will take his anger out on Emmie and Nina."

"Can't something be done to stop him? Can't lawyers help?"

"What he does is immoral but not illegal. You can't imprison a man for using words to ruin lives. Not even for lying constantly. It's not illegal to give a pretty girl a gift and tell her it came from his grandmother." Tate sighed. "Why is it that women fall for bad boys, then get angry when they turn out to be bad boys?"

Casey listened more to his tone than to his words. "You're really worried, aren't you?"

"Yes. He's getting worse. He's obsessed with the idea that *I* have ruined his life. I'm going to stop paying him soon, which means that he's either going to have to get a job or figure out a way to get someone else to support him. I dread whatever he's going to do." Tate took a breath. "I don't want to stir him up while Emmie and Nina are here. And you. What he did with that girl . . ."

"Rachael Wells."

"Right. Her. That was defamation of character. When I get back to L.A., and Nina and Emmie are safe on the other side of the country, I'm going to get some legal advice. There has to be something I can do to stop this man's vendetta against my family."

"Does he do this to *all* your girlfriends?"

"No, but he knew I didn't really like any of them."

For all the horror of what Tate was saying, she couldn't stop her smile. She ran her leg between his thighs. "I'll keep us a secret. In the last weeks, my acting ability has improved so much that now I'll be able to make people believe that I can't bear the sight of you."

Tate made a sound that was half laugh, half groan.

She rolled on top of him, her face scrunched into a deep frown. "Are you saying I'm not a good actor?"

"Jack said that yesterday you delivered your lines like you were a robot."

Casey's eyes began to tear, but she blinked them away. "Oh," she said sadly, and started to roll off him.

He grabbed her to him and held her head on his chest. "I'm sorry! I'm sure you were—"

Casey's giggle was muffled by his chest.

He pulled her head away and saw that she'd been teasing. "You brat!" He began kissing her neck.

"Take it back about my acting."

"Or what?" His lips were moving downward on her chest.

"I'll serve you canned soup."

Tate lifted his head, put his hand to his heart, and gave a deep sigh. "'You bruise me to my core. I cannot continue as I have been. Without you I am nothing. I must—'"

She kissed him until he was silent, then broke away to look at him. "You said those lines better on film." She kissed him again.

"You saw one of my movies?" His eyes were alight. "Which one?"

Casey laughed. "Shut up."

"'Your wish is my desire. I live only—'"

He was quoting his lines again. Still laughing, she kissed him again, only this time the kiss didn't end.

They made love slowly, enjoying each other, so very glad to be back together. They exchanged no words, just kisses and caresses.

When they at last finished, it wasn't with the passion they'd felt at first—that seeing-each-other-again fury—but with something deeper, something that came from inside and transcended mere bodies.

They lay in silence, side by side, hands entwined, heads touching.

"Dress rehearsal is today," Tate whispered. "I look forward to seeing you in one of those low-cut—"

Abruptly, Casey sat up. "Lunch! I forgot *lunch!*"

"It's okay. We'll order in and—"

Casey got out of bed. "Listen, City Boy! Bags of grease are not the same as what I cook. Get up, get dressed, go downstairs, and set a stockpot of water on to boil. I have to wash the sweat off."

"I don't have any clothes up here. They're outside and it's now daylight, remember?"

Casey was in the bathroom. "You walk around naked in front of a camera, so make do."

"I am sooooo glad you saw my movies," Tate muttered.

"I heard that!" she yelled from the shower.

Tate opened Casey's closet door, saw nothing he could get into, then decided to go outside and get his own clothes.

Because Casey was in the shower, she didn't get to hear the comments that greeted a nude Tate when he reached the bottom of the stairs.

Emmie giggled and hid her face; Nina handed him his sweatpants; Gizzy said, "Oh, my goodness!"; Jack said Tate needed to work on his pecs; Josh asked if he could train with them.

It took Tate a few moments to recover as he slipped on his clothes. "I take it we're making lunch."

"If you can spare the time," Jack said in sarcasm.

Minutes later, when Casey ran down the stairs in a panic, she was confronted by what looked to be an army of people in her kitchen, all of them busy with food preparation. She wasn't sure whether she was glad or horrified. As far as she knew, none of them knew how to cook, so what were they doing to her food?

Tate put his arm around her shoulders and kissed the top of her head. "You're not alone now," he said softly. "You have a family."

Casey started to smile up at him, but just then Nina dropped a container of chopped onions into a bowl of cake icing. "Oops," she said. "Now I'll have to pick them out."

Tate leaned down to Casey. "On the other hand, you're not alone now. You have a family."

Laughing, Casey hurried forward to sort out the mess.

Later, Nina was chopping peppers—far away from anything sweet—and she asked Josh how he was related to Casey.

"Well," Josh said as he moved to stand closer to Nina. Considering that he hadn't been more than ten inches from her side since he arrived, that wasn't easy. "My parents had me, so of course they wanted *more* kids." He smiled at Nina, who nodded in agreement at his joke.

"But Dad had some physical problems, so Dr. Everett suggested they use a donor. What no one knew was that the donor was his son Kyle, who had funded his many adventures around the world with his ... uh, donations." Josh was grinning in a naughty way. "So anyway, my half sister Stacy was born. We have the same mother but different fathers."

Everyone looked at Casey in question. "My mother couldn't find a man who lived up to her very high standards, so she chose a donor out of a catalog. Dr. Kyle."

Gizzy was next. "No babies came to my parents, so they asked Dr. Everett's advice. He recommended a donor."

Tate laughed. "His son?"

"Yes," Gizzy said. "Of course, no one knew that at the time."

Nina looked at Casey. "So let me see if I get this straight. You and Stacy and Gizzy all have the same father. But if you and Josh don't share a father or a mother, then you aren't related. He could have played Darcy."

Casey's face was serious. "I think the scientific term is called the Ewwww Factor. Yes, that's it. Definitely a yuck."

Josh nodded in agreement. "I think—" He broke off at a sound from the door.

"Hello. I came to help, if you need me."

It was Dr. Kyle, and they couldn't contain their laughter.

Good-naturedly, he opened the screen door. "I take it there's been talk of my dad's obsessive desire to have grandchildren."

They all nodded.

Dr. Kyle looked at Emmie. "I was told that you know all about Letty and Ace. Want to hear how they fooled the grown-ups by faking stomachaches from eating little green apples?"

"Yes!" she said, took his hand, and they left together.

Smiling, Casey glanced at the clock. When she saw that it was almost ten, sheer panic ran through her. "We're going to be late! Kit is going to—" She didn't finish because the thought of Kit's wrath was enough to turn all of them into jet engines.

As they scurried about, Jack gave a quick kiss to Gizzy, and Tate kissed Casey. When Josh passed Nina, it seemed natural that he should kiss her too. The only problem was that the kiss continued. They stopped in the middle of the kitchen, arms about each other, lips locked. If Tate and Jack hadn't caught the dishes falling out of their hands, they would have broken.

Gizzy and Casey moved the kissing couple to the side, out of the way, as they rushed around to clean and pack. At four minutes to ten, the two couples ran out the door. Josh and Nina were backed up to the refrigerator, still kissing. Since neither of them was in the play, the others left them there.

"You Summer Hill people are a lusty lot," Jack said as they ran, and they all laughed together.

ACT THREE, SCENE TWO

Lydia is revealed

Much to Kit's displeasure, it took the cast an hour and a half to get into their costumes. He bellowed that hair and makeup were to be skipped. His words were directed to the two couples playing the leads. "When I said be here by ten, I meant to be ready to *act*. Clothes *on*."

"But you said—" Casey began, but the looks Jack and Tate gave her made her stop. Right. The director's word was the law.

The stage manager, clipboard in hand, interrupted Kit's tirade for a private conversation. From Kit's expression, what she was saying wasn't good.

He turned back to the players, who were in various stages of getting dressed. "Has anyone seen Lori? The girl playing Lydia?"

Everyone shook their heads no.

"Great!" Kit muttered. "A no-show. Probably out with her boyfriend." He looked at the stage manager. "Who do we have for her understudy?"

"Uh . . . Devlin Haines isn't here either."

Kit was so taken aback that he couldn't speak.

Casey looked at Tate, but he shrugged. He had no idea where the man was.

Kit wiped his hand over his face, then announced, "Jack! You'll stand in for Haines, and you, Hildy, will be Lydia for today. Think you can do it?"

"Of course," Hildy said. She was in costume for Lady Catherine de Bourgh, an older woman, so it was going to be interesting to see her try to play a fifteen-year-old girl.

"All right," Kit said. "Places for act one, scene one. The Bennet family's parlor. Kyle, I want you to be laid back. Olivia, I want— Where is she?"

"Here I am," she said, as she stepped onto the stage. She was beautifully coiffed and made up. Her blonde hair had been pulled back and was supplemented with wispy ringlets. Her dress of pale peach and white stripes was embellished with tiny sprigs of forget-me-nots in green and white. With the deep square neckline showing off her ample bosom, she looked utterly divine.

From the expression on Kit's face, he thought so too. Silently, he pointed to the place where she was to stand.

The first scene went off perfectly. Olivia played the neurotic Mrs. Bennet so well it was difficult to remember she wasn't actually that way.

Hildy as a silly, flirtatious fifteen-year-old was absurd. Everyone had to work to suppress laughter.

Casey was pleased to see that her father's performance as Mr. Bennet got better every day. Offstage, she whispered to Gizzy, "This is another talent of his. Maybe an actor brother or sister will show up."

"Jack is helping me enroll in a school in L.A. to become a personal trainer," Gizzy replied. "I'm moving in with him."

"That's wonderful," Casey said as they both went back onstage.

Scene two was at the Meryton assembly hall, and everyone was dancing. Casey had to concentrate to remember the intricate steps they'd rehearsed. When Tate appeared in his glorious tight trousers and midnight-black coat, it was impossible to pretend she didn't like him. She had a vision of them together in her bedroom, in full costume, slowly removing each other's clothes. Maybe there'd be a peacock feather or two involved.

Tate clearly sensed what she was thinking, and he cut a sideways look at her that was so hot, her hair seemed to catch fire.

"Tatton!" Kit bellowed.

Everyone halted. Every actor, Jack included, had been on the receiving end of Kit's bad temper, except Tate. "Could you rein in your carnal imaginings for the length of this play? You are not to show your lech for Miss Elizabeth Bennet until the script says you should do so."

Tate had to suppress a grin as he said, "I will make my utmost effort to not reveal my baser yearnings." The other players smothered laughs, but Kit glared at Tate in silence.

Because of their late start, they only got to Mr. Collins's proposal to Lizzy before the grumbles of hunger made Kit dismiss them for lunch. Cast and crew stopped mid-sentence and ran toward the guesthouse.

"I need to set up," Casey called after them. She grabbed her long skirt as though to run, but Tate caught her arm.

"I sent a text to Nina. Let her and Josh take care of them—if they can stop kissing long enough, that is. Why don't you and I go to my house for a while?"

"Mmmm," Casey said. "Sounds good."

As Tate started to kiss her, Casey stepped back and glanced around. After all, they had agreed to keep what was between them secret—not that they were doing a good job of it. Her father and Olivia were to one side, scripts open in their hands. On the other side of the gazebo, Kit was rummaging through some boxes, but actually watching Olivia with the handsome Dr. Kyle.

"Lori is missing!"

They all turned to look at the woman who came onto the

stage. She was tall, older, and elegantly dressed. "My granddaughter didn't come home last night."

Olivia went to her. "Estelle, tell us what happened."

She just stood there, her eyes bleak, frantic. "I don't know what to do."

Olivia put her arm around the woman's shoulders. "Does Lori have a boyfriend?"

With a shaking hand, Estelle held out a piece of paper and Olivia took it, read it, then handed the paper to Kit.

He read it and groaned. "That's great! Just perfect. Lydia has run off with Wickham. Fiction becomes reality."

Casey drew in her breath, her fist to her mouth in fear, and looked at Tate. He pulled her into his arms.

"Who the hell are we going to get to replace them at this late date?" Kit said angrily. He turned to Tate. "We need some actors fast. Can you call an agent? A casting director? Or—"

"Is that all you care about?" Estelle said. "Who can fill the places in your damned play?"

Kit drew himself up into military stance. "Madam, I am sorry for your unhappiness, but eighteen-year-old girls have minds of their own."

"Eighteen!" Estelle shouted. "Is that what she told you? Lori is fifteen years old." She looked at Olivia. "She's always been tall for her age and she makes people think she's older. She—"

"This is a case for law enforcement." Kit's anger was gone. He pulled out his phone. "I'm calling the FBI."

Estelle shook off Olivia's arm and stalked forward to Kit. "Then what? You turn everything over to them and you go back to your little play? What happens when this odious man hears that he's run off with a child and the FBI is chasing him? What do you think he'll do to her? Dispose of her?" Her voice was a screech.

"I'm sorry." Kit's voice was full of sympathy. "What else can I do?"

"I don't know!" Estelle yelled. "This is all *your* fault, Christopher Montgomery! You and that damned money of yours. Haines found out who Lori is. They called me from Jacksonville and said someone had been asking questions. They said he'd been told the *truth*!"

Kit's voice was gentle but firm. "I'm afraid you have me mixed up with someone else. I've never been to Jacksonville."

Estelle, wringing her hands, her face red, her eyes wild with fear, turned to Olivia. "Tell him! Tell him everything!"

Olivia's face had gone pale, but she kept her composure. "I'm not sure what you mean."

"Lori's mother, my daughter Tisha—short for Portia—was born on the twenty-eighth of May, 1971. Dr. Everett arranged the adoption. Do you remember that date?"

It took Olivia a few seconds to understand what she was hearing. When she did, her knees buckled under her. Tate made a leap and caught her before she hit the wooden floor.

Kit still didn't understand what was going on.

Estelle glared at him. "Lori is *your* biological granddaughter. I believe that man playing Wickham enticed her to run away with him because he found out that she's related to you and your rich family. I think he means to marry her to get money from you. But he *can't* marry her! She's just a child who lies about her age." When Estelle broke into tears, Tate helped her to a chair beside Olivia.

What Estelle was saying was finally beginning to sink in to Kit. When he looked at Olivia, all the blood had drained from her face. Casey and Tate were hovering over her protectively.

"You had our child?" Kit's voice was so soft they could barely hear him. For a few minutes he seemed too stunned to know what to do, but then his many years of dealing with crises kicked in.

His phone was still in his hand and he called a number. "Rowan," he said in a voice of command, "I need you here immediately. This is official business."

Kit turned off the phone and looked at them: Olivia, Estelle, Dr. Kyle, Tate, and Casey. "Need I admonish you to say nothing of this to anyone? My son will be here in a matter of hours, then we'll—" He broke off, and for a moment he stared at Olivia.

She returned his stare with her chin high, almost in defiance.

Kit turned away, started to speak, but then, with his shoulders back, he went down the stairs and disappeared into the garden.

Mr. Bennet confesses his error in judgment

Thirty minutes later, Casey made her way through the blackberry tunnel and into the well house. As she'd hoped, Kit was sitting on the cushions. He looked as if he'd aged a hundred years. Since she had no idea what to say to him, she fell back on her standard: feed them and listen. She poured a cup of hot coffee from a thermos and handed it to him with a toasted bagel with lots of butter on it.

"I haven't been in here in years," he said. His voice was hoarse, raspy, as though he'd been crying. He glanced up at the ceiling. "It needs some repair."

Casey had changed into jeans and a shirt. On impulse, she'd put the cord with the ring she and Tate found around her neck. She took it off and held it out to him. "Is this yours?"

He took it and stared at it. Then tears came to his eyes. "Yes. I left it in here for Livie." For a minute he didn't speak. "I loved her so much," he whispered. "From the first moment I saw her, I loved her." As he held the ring tightly, he gave a little smile. "It wasn't mutual. She had a summer job being housekeeper/cook to a couple of sedentary old men. It was a surprise that I, a nineteen-year-old boy, was also staying here. She called me 'Worthless Boy' and said I was good for nothing but causing her more work."

He looked at Casey, his eyes glistening with tears. "And she was right! I was so young and stupid that I thought an oath I'd taken to my country was more important than she was. I didn't tell her that I was waiting to be picked up whenever our government got around to remembering me. All I really knew about my mission was that I was to be gone for a year and there could be no contact with family or friends during that time. But even knowing nothing, I was so full of my own importance that I didn't tell Olivia anything. I let her believe I was a college dropout, content to live on my family's money."

Kit took a long drink of the coffee and a bite of the bagel. "This ring was my grandmother's. I waited until three days before Olivia was to leave for New York to star in a Broadway production of *Pride and Prejudice* to ask her the big question."

Pausing, he turned the ring over in his hand. "She went to Richmond that day. That's all that happened. A simple, everyday thing like that changed our lives. I was asleep when she left or I would have asked her not to go. But I was worn out from . . ." He waved his hand. "It doesn't matter now. An hour after she left, the agents came for me in a big black car, and I was given twenty minutes to pack and leave."

He looked at Casey. "I panicked. I didn't know what to do. I scribbled out a letter, begging Livie to wait for me, but I was afraid to leave it and the ring in my bedroom. I was scared that the government men would take it. I slipped away from them—something I'm good at, which is why they wanted me—and went to the well house. I knew that no one but Livie and me came in here."

He smiled in memory. "The old peacock guarded the place. Livie and I had peck marks on our legs from his beak. But the good thing was that the creature kept the kids away."

"Letty and Ace."

"Yes," Kit said. "They were everywhere, into everything. No

one had a secret that they didn't find out. But the well house and
its ferocious guardian belonged to Livie and me."

"You left the letter and the ring in here for her?"

"I did," he said. "I thought they'd be safe and that she'd be sure
to find them. The note had contact information for my family,
and I begged her to go to them."

He looked at Casey. "I saw her on Broadway. It was a couple of
months later. The night before I was to ship out, they took me to
New York and put me up in a cheap hotel. I knew that I was
being sent on an undercover mission that I might not return from.
I wasn't supposed to leave the hotel room. I'd been ordered, at the
peril of my life, to contact no one."

His eyes burned in intensity. "But I *had* to see her. If the penalty
had been a firing squad, I couldn't have stopped myself. I sneaked
out a bathroom window, climbed down a drainpipe, and ran to
the theater. I paid a man five hundred dollars for his ticket, then I
sat in the back and watched her. She was an excellent actress, very
natural. I thought that by the time I returned, she'd be the leading
light of Broadway."

When he looked away, Casey reached out to put her hand over
his.

"The mission stretched into three years, and there was a point
where I was more dead than alive. I only survived because I was
sure Livie was waiting for me."

For a moment he stared up at the window. "When I got home
to the U.S., I had healed only enough that I could walk with two
canes. I was shocked that my family hadn't heard from Livie, and
I couldn't believe that her name wasn't in lights in New York. I
went to Summer Hill to find her. I was joyous, thinking of being
with her again. But when I got there . . ."

"You found out that she was married to someone else," Casey
said.

"Yes, and they had a little boy, who I thought was hers—which meant that she hadn't taken any time after I left to find someone else. I saw her in the appliance store and from what I could tell, she ran the place. When I followed her home, I saw her house with its pretty lawn, and I realized that she had what she needed. She did *not* need some damaged military man who disappeared for years at a time."

He looked at Casey. "Oh, hell! I wish I had been that self-sacrificing. The truth is that I was angry. Furious! Why hadn't she waited for me? I could have given her any house she wanted. I could have—" He took a breath. "I felt betrayed, but worse was that I didn't understand any of it."

"Until today."

"Yes, until today." He calmed himself. "I can't imagine what Livie went through. Expecting our baby and totally alone. Her parents were older and fragile. They wouldn't have been any help."

"I think she turned to Dr. Everett."

"Your grandfather," Kit said. "If I'm piecing the story together correctly, he sent Livie to a maternity home in Jacksonville, Florida, to have the baby—our baby. Then he sent a childless Estelle after her. Looks like she said thanks by using Livie's mother's name, Portia." He paused. "Estelle is right. This *is* my fault. I should have contacted Livie to make sure she got the ring. I should have waited outside the theater and spoken to her. But I was afraid the agent in charge of my mission would find out that I was gone. Back then I thought that's what was important. I should have done *something*!"

Casey couldn't bear to see him so devastated. "Did the mission you were sent on help anyone?"

"Yes," he said. "It saved hundreds, maybe thousands, of lives." He took a breath. "I'm sorry I've been so harsh over these last weeks. I didn't mean to be so angry, but it's all gone wrong. Through all those years, my pride kept me from contacting Livie. But when I retired . . ." He looked at Casey and shrugged.

"You returned to Summer Hill."

"Not intentionally. When my secretary heard that the movie star Tate Landers was my distant cousin through little Letty, she nagged me into going to meet him. He told me about his plan to buy our family's plantation. He didn't want to be publicly identified as the owner, so he asked me to put it under my name. I almost said no because that would mean returning to Summer Hill and risking seeing Livie again. But I told myself it had been long enough that the old wound had healed. What an idiot I was! Just the sight of this place brought everything back so hard it was as if I'd never been away."

He paused. "I meant to leave as soon as the paperwork to buy Tattwell was done. But then I saw Olivia on the street and . . ." He lifted his head.

"And you couldn't leave. Not again. What about the play?"

Kit took a moment before he answered. "I bought the warehouse, remodeled it, wrote the play, badgered you and Stacy into helping me, all of it, so I'd have a reason to be near Livie. I thought I knew her well enough that she wouldn't be able to resist trying out for a role. But when she wanted nothing to do with me or my play, it made me furious. I apologize for taking my anger out on all of you." He was beginning to recover himself. "I've told no other person this story."

"Thank you for trusting me with it," Casey said.

"I guess now everyone is going to know." He looked around as though just seeing the little old building. "You found the ring in here?"

Casey reached across him to pull the red metal box out of its place.

He stared at the peacock picture on the lid. "Those kids were fascinated by that bird. When Uncle Freddy told them that somewhere in the attic was an old candy box with a peacock on it, they nearly tore the place apart searching for it." Kit smiled at

Casey. "You know, don't you, that you're a lot like your father. He missed his parents so much, but his father, Dr. Everett, was at the hospital around the clock with his dying wife. Like you, Ace was a good listener."

"Thanks," she said. She wanted to hear more about her father, but there were urgent matters to take care of. "Is your son in the FBI?"

"Yes. Rowan is the product of the marriage that I settled for. It was very unhappy—all my fault—and my children and their mother deserved better." Kit looked back at her. "What happened after I so cowardly left the scene?"

"Only a few of us know about Lori and we're keeping it to ourselves. We told the cast that you had a serious ailment and had to leave."

"Food poisoning."

"Over my dead body!" Casey snapped.

Leaning forward, Kit kissed her cheek. "Thanks. I needed a dose of laughter. How is Livie?"

"After you left, Olivia and Estelle went to the library in the Big House and shut the door. They have a lot to talk about."

"An understatement. What about Haines?"

"Nina is very upset. She says she should have warned people, and Tate and I feel the same way. We should have told what we know about him."

"Warned them of *what*? No, don't tell me now. Let's go back to the house. I want to hear every word about everything."

It took a few minutes to untangle themselves from the briars. When she got out, Casey wasn't surprised to see Tate sitting on the bench by the path, waiting for them.

"I need you to come with me," Tate said to her. "We have to go to Haines's house on the lake to see what we can find out." He glanced at Kit. "Nina knows everything, so she can fill you in. Olivia went to Estelle's house to look at photos and to talk."

There was a flicker of pain across Kit's eyes, but he recovered quickly. "I'll call you when Rowan gets here. He'll want to see you."

"I've already talked to him and given him the facts. He said this is not to reach the press, or Haines might panic."

"I agree," Kit said. "Go on and I'll take care of things here."

Tate took Casey's hand and they walked back to her house.

At last, Wickham is wanted

"What's going on at the house?" Casey asked as soon as they got into her car.

Tate was backing out. "A lot of talk, a lot of tears. How's Kit?"

"Hurt, angry, devastated, shocked. What a waste of years and a mix-up of two lives! I take it you haven't heard anything from Devlin."

"Nothing. Lori's note said that she'd found a man who truly understands her and she wants to be with him forever. It seems that she and Estelle had an argument and . . ."

"I get it," Casey said. "Teenage angst. No one understands her except a thirty-some-year-old divorced man." She swallowed. "Poor kid. I didn't know you knew Kit's son."

"I don't, but it seems he's some big-shot FBI guy, so he has access to all phone numbers. He wanted details about what had upset his father. I think it takes a lot to throw Kit Montgomery."

"Did you tell Rowan that the missing girl is his niece?"

"Yes. I didn't see any reason to sugarcoat things."

"How'd he take it?" Casey asked.

"If he was shocked, he hid it well. He said, 'Good,' then he asked me about Haines."

"What did you say?"

"That he's a complete narcissist. He can't understand why other people are 'given' so much when he's the smartest, most talented, most lovable, et cetera, person on the planet."Tate waved his hand. "Anyway, the good thing is that we're fairly sure that Haines doesn't know Lori is only fifteen."

"If he tries to marry her he'll find out—which is what I assume his intention is. No doubt he plans to do whatever he can to get access to Kit's wealth."

"Yes," Tate said. "That's what we all fear. Rowan will be here with a couple of agents this evening. They're coming in on one of Kit's family's jets."

"Ah," Casey said. "How in the world did he figure all this out?"

"Olivia said she thinks it started when she was at the food tables and mentioned she was allergic to almonds. Lori said she was too. Haines was right beside them. Between that and the physical resemblance . . ." Tate shrugged. "He's always been clever at figuring out things about people."

"I'm the one who first told him about Olivia's allergy."

"I guess it began there, but I was also with Haines when we overheard Olivia and Kit arguing." He told Casey what had happened. "Estelle called someone from the old maternity home where Olivia had the baby. The records were sealed, but it looks like Haines hired the sleazy PI he used against Nina in the divorce. Somebody was paid off to snoop into the records." Tate's mouth tightened. "I'm to blame for this. Whenever I saw Haines and Lori together, I laughed about it. I was so glad he wasn't pestering you or Nina or Emmie that I left that poor kid alone to fight him."

Casey put her hand over his. "I did the same thing." She looked at him. "We have to fix this. You, me, Nina. We have to do everything we can to protect that girl."

"I agree."Tate was driving toward the huge lake beside Summer Hill. He turned off the road that looped around the lake into the driveway of a large, modern house, all glass and natural wood.

Tate pulled a key out of his pocket, opened the door, and they went inside.

The interior had been professionally decorated in furniture with clean lines, and every item had been chosen to stylishly co-ordinate. There was nothing personal about the house.

"Wow," Casey said. "This place must cost him some money."

"Six thousand, two hundred, and twenty-three dollars a month," Tate said. "Plus utilities."

"Do you pay for it?"

"Of course. A lake house for the summer was a bribe to keep him off Nina's back. But he lied to me about where the house was. If I'd known it was near Tattwell, I would have said no."

"I think we should stop beating ourselves up over this. Any idea what we need to look for?"

"None," Tate said. "We can start going through drawers, but I warn you that Haines doesn't leave personal things around. He doesn't like for people to know about him."

Casey opened a glass-doored cabinet in the all-white kitchen and removed a wineglass. "This is mine, a gift from my mother. I asked him about it and he said he left it on the table and that you had probably taken it." She opened a door that led into the garage. "Anything?"

"Just that there's no leaky rowboat in there." She watched Tate open drawers in a cabinet by the dining table. How had he and his sister spent all those years dealing with a man who piled lie on top of lie? Big lies were almost understandable, but not the ones about wineglasses and boats that didn't exist.

Poor Lori, she thought as she started searching with renewed vigor. There were a few cooking implements in the kitchen drawers but nothing else. Not one piece of paper. No old grocery lists, no receipts of any kind, no bills waiting to be paid.

After an hour, they'd looked everywhere. Tate had held Casey up so she could search the top of the bedroom closet. They'd even looked for a concealed panel that led into an attic space. But there was nothing.

The two of them flopped down on the couch, side by side, and stared out the windows at the pretty lake. They had found nothing that hinted at where Haines had taken young Lori.

"If this were a movie," Tate said, "there'd be a matchbook with a hotel name on it."

"Or a pad by the telephone with an imprint of an address. I've always wondered who writes so hard that they mark the page underneath."

"Don't look at me. I'm just cast as a shirtless guy who throws women across his shoulder."

"But you do it so well." She laughed at his expression. "I saw the video of you with the peacock. You were very funny."

"I wish some producers thought so."

"Look on the bright side. If you showed what a versatile actor you are, your ex-brother-in-law would hate you even more."

"Too bad he's going to jail and won't ever have a chance to show the world that he's actually a better actor than I am."

On the coffee table was an oval piece of Lucite on a black stand. Casey picked it up. On the bottom was engraved DEVLIN HAINES. THE BEST. "A bit ambiguous. Was this an award for something?"

"Yeah, and it's his most precious possession. His one and only award, given to him for being a good DJ. I think he chose what was to be written on it."

"What do you know about him personally?"

"During the hell of the divorce, I found out that the story he courted Nina with, about a childhood filled with country clubs and riding lessons, wasn't true." Tate paused. "The truth is that he had a pretty rough childhood. No father, mother rarely sober. He pretty much had to support himself for most of his life. Bagging groceries, mowing lawns when he was so little he had to reach up to hold on to the handle, that sort of thing. But in his last year of high school, he worked as a DJ at a local radio station and he liked doing it. His story is that he was so good at it that it made him go to L.A. to try his hand at getting into the entertainment industry."

"And he became obsessed with the idea of finally getting someone else to support him."

"I guess." Tate took the award from her and put it back on the table. "The irony is that I would have been quite willing to pay his bills if he'd just been good to Nina and Emmie."

"But he wanted *more*. And now he hates you because he couldn't win over you no matter what. Too bad you two couldn't enter a Best DJ contest. He'd leave paradise just to show you up."

Tate turned to her, his eyes wide. "What does he want most in the world?"

"My guess is that it's for you to lose to him. To beat you is probably the only thing he wants more than a life without work. Too bad he can't do that." She drew her breath in sharply as she understood what he was thinking. "An act-off? A challenge? Kit's play? Wickham versus Darcy?"

"That's exactly what's in my mind."

"But how do we make sure he hears of it?"

"He's an obsessive radio listener. He says all the news that's important goes to radio first. Just last year he was trying to get me to buy some local radio station and sign it over to him. He said it was for Emmie's future." Tate stood up. "He always has the radio on. He likes to complain about the DJs and tell how he could do it better, how he would have had a career in that field if he hadn't given it up for Nina and Emmie."

Tate walked to the windows, looked out for a moment, then turned back to her. "We have to plan this. We need to figure it all out before we present it to the others."

"The FBI is going to be involved. Will we have to get their permission?"

"To put on an acting contest? I don't think so. Why don't you and I make as thorough a plan as we can, then present it to Kit's son?"

"I think that's a good idea."

They smiled at each other.

Casey realized that while it was nice to be compatible in bed, in an odd way this sharing of ideas was even more intimate. That they thought alike and dealt with a problem in the same way made her feel closer to him than she ever had before.

"Stop looking at me like that or we'll never keep our clothes on." Tate held out his hand to her. "Let's go home and figure this out."

She took his hand. Home. What a lovely thought.

Lydia learns what she shouldn't know

Devlin was sitting in a plastic chair on the concrete walkway of the sleazy motel and watching the girl Lori do laps in the pool. Running away with her had seemed like such a good idea. He'd been full of thoughts of caviar and champagne on a private jet. Not that he even liked the salty fish eggs—disgusting flavor!—but the thought that he'd soon have anything he wanted had been wonderful.

When the PI told him that the girl was Kit Montgomery's illegitimate granddaughter, Devlin had gone into a frenzy of happiness. All his dreams were going to come true! There'd be no more struggle in his life, no more taking on acting roles that were beneath him, no more people like Tate Landers putting him down.

All he had to do was get the girl to agree to leave with him, and that had been easy. She was astonishingly naïve and dying for some independence. Her parents were out of the country, as her father was some kind of diplomat. Devlin grimaced at that. Wealth could buy excellent jobs! Lori had been turned over to her rich grandmother for the summer to be safeguarded.

Devlin thought how pampered kids today were. When he was eighteen he'd been supporting himself and his mother for years. But this kid still lived at home, was still supervised by adults.

Putting his hand up to shield his eyes against the sun, he watched the girl walk to the low diving board. She looked good in her bikini, but she acted like a child. Before they left, he'd asked her three times if she really was eighteen and she'd said yes. She didn't have a driver's license, but she said she'd get her passport to prove it. When she forgot to pack it, Devlin had been quite annoyed and had told her so. But when she started to cry, he backed off. Until they were actually married, he didn't want to turn her off.

He'd envisioned a chauffeured limo arriving to pick them up. There would, of course, be a dramatic scene. But Devlin could handle drama. He and Lori would hold hands and swear that they couldn't bear to be parted. With triumph, Devlin would show the marriage certificate.

But so far, nothing had gone as he'd planned. The missing ID didn't allow them to marry, so he'd decided to win her in other ways. Until she was fully his, he couldn't risk taking her back to get her passport. That grandmother of hers was much too possessive!

The first night he'd climbed into bed with her, but she'd curled up with cramps and told him in detail about how heavy her "flow" was. It was enough to turn off any man!

That was three nights ago, and he was running out of cash. He didn't dare use his credit cards, since the bills went to Landers. Devlin had been sure Kit Montgomery would use his government connections to find them, but where was he?

Devlin leaned back in the chair and let himself imagine the press coverage of him and the Montgomery heiress as they told the swarming, pushing, excited paparazzi of their great love for each other. He'd become known as more romantic than Tate Landers!

But nothing was happening. *Nothing!* Devlin had the radio on all the time, but there was no news about him. Even local TV hadn't mentioned him. They'd told of the play and how Landers was going to be there, but there was nothing about Devlin. Typical!

And problems were beginning. This morning the girl said she was ready to go home, that she missed her grandmother.

The possible failure of his great plan sent rage coursing through him. Ungrateful brat! Who did she think she was to lead him on like this? He'd had to spend hours listening to her whine about her easy life in her grandmother's big house, and now she *owed* him!

She must have seen the look in his eyes, because she immediately changed her tune. She started talking very fast, saying she was dying to tell all her Facebook friends about her great adventure and how wonderful Devlin was.

He didn't like doing it, but he'd had to be rather firm in telling her that she was to contact no one. He'd already taken away her phone and her computer. And after he found her trying to use the landline in the room in the middle of the night, he'd cut the cord on it. He'd even had to make her stand outside the bathroom door while he was in the shower so he could hear her. She'd become quite untrustworthy!

Scowling, Devlin watched her dive into the pool. She was good at it, which meant she'd probably had a personal coach since she was a kid.

A tall teenage boy slipped into the pool and called out something to her. She started toward him, but then she looked at Devlin, her eyes asking if she had his permission.

When he gave a quick shake of his head, she turned away from the boy. Devlin gave a bit of a smile. At least he'd taught her something! That was better than he'd done with Nina. But then, his ex always went running to her brother, and Landers went against what was morally right and interfered between a man and his wife.

Devlin watched Lori go back to her endless laps across the pool. This time things would be different. Never again would he allow a bully like Tate Landers to intimidate him. This time he'd stand his ground and demand his rights. He'd—

He broke off because he heard his ex-wife's voice on the radio. What now? he thought. Was Landers using Devlin's family to promote himself and his two-bit play? Did the man have no pride at all? If he used Emmie, could Devlin sue?

He turned up the volume. "You're out of your mind!" Nina was saying. "There's no way my ex-husband could beat Tate at anything. Certainly not at *acting!*"

Devlin's eyes widened. The boy in the pool was circling Lori like a shark. Devlin motioned for her to get out and follow him back to their room. He couldn't listen to his first wife's lies while working to keep his almost-second wife from fornicating.

"What do you say to that?" the DJ asked.

"I don't mean to contradict you, Nina, and you know Tate Landers is my best friend, but . . ." It was Jack Worth's voice.

Devlin unlocked the door of the motel room and gave a curt wave to Lori to get inside. He didn't have time to do a hearts-and-flowers gesture. He locked the door behind her, then moved into the shade and listened.

"But what?" Nina demanded.

"I want to be fair. Maybe Devlin and you didn't get along, but he is an excellent actor."

"Ha!" Nina said. "After his performance on *Death Point,* he doesn't deserve your false flattery."

"False flattery?" the DJ said. "Jack, do you agree about—"

"Now, just a minute!" Jack's voice was the growl he used in his movies just before he shot half a dozen men. "There's nothing false about Devlin Haines's acting. There was a scene in *Death Point* when Rachael Wells's character died that nearly put me in tears. I don't know why he didn't get an Emmy for that. He certainly deserved it!"

"In that case, Tate should have been given an Oscar."

Jack gave a little laugh. "Come on, Nina, let's be honest. It doesn't take any real talent to give hot looks to pretty girls. That's not exactly Oscar material. And when Tate was on *Death Point,* he didn't outshine Devlin. Tell me, aren't you at all worried what the New York critics are going to say about the performances tomorrow night? They might like Devlin better. Then what will you say?"

The DJ cut in. "Folks, they are talking about the first performance of *Pride and Prejudice,* which is to be at the Summer Hill Playhouse tomorrow at eight P.M. That show is sold out, but we've been told that three huge screens are being set up outside and everyone is welcome. Outside is free, but they ask for donations, all of which will go to charity. Bring chairs or blankets and a picnic—and your wallet!"

"*If* it will be held." Nina's voice was ominous.

"What does that mean?" the DJ asked.

"Don't start on this again." There was anger in Jack's voice. "You're not an actor and you don't know how it works."

"Am I missing something?" the DJ asked.

"Devlin disappeared," Nina said. "Ran away is my guess. He always was scared of my big brother."

"Are you kidding me?" Jack sounded fighting mad. "Through the whole play, Devlin Haines has worked twice as hard as anyone else. He was there from the first day. Tate didn't even arrive until the auditions were nearly over. But Devlin stuck around and helped the young amateurs, like that girl playing Lydia. He practically held her hand through every line. That kid got the credit, but Devlin did the work. All done while Tate was running off with the local cook. He wasn't helping *anyone!*"

"So where is Devlin *now*?" Nina asked.

"Recharging," Jack shot back. "Gearing up for the play. Doing what he did on his TV show and tapping into his deepest emotions."

"And, folks, that's—"

Nina cut the DJ off. "I'm the one who *knows* him, and I say that he won't show up for tomorrow's performance. He is much too cowardly to face my brother in a live performance."

"Ten grand!" Jack said. "I'll donate ten thousand dollars to charity if he shows up. Anybody out there want to take bets on this?"

"Okay!" the DJ said. "That's all we have time for now, but it looks like the, uh—what do we call this?—the Great Acting Challenge is on. If you're out there, Devlin Haines, and you hear this, we hope you show up tomorrow night so Jack Worth will have to donate ten grand to charity."

"Make it fifty," Jack snapped.

"Whoa," the DJ said. "You heard it here first. The great Jack Worth is donating fifty *thousand* dollars to charity if Devlin Haines, star of the former hit TV show *Death Point,* shows up to perform in the play tomorrow night. And now I'm going to play a little music that Jane Austen herself might have heard."

The DJ turned off his mic and looked from Nina to Jack. "You two aren't going to fight, are you? I mean, I wasn't expecting to start a feud. I just—"

"It's fine," Nina said as she stood up. She was smiling. "You were great. Jack?"

"Yeah, terrific." He was grinning. He got up, went to Nina, and put his arm around her shoulders. "You deserve an award for that."

"I did okay?"

"Haines couldn't have done better."

Nina laughed. They waved at the DJ, then left the building.

In the car, she put her hands over her face. "I didn't like saying those things. And I got genuinely angry when you were so against Tate. I'm afraid his feelings will be hurt."

"After what the critics said about his last movie, he can stand anything. So where to now?"

"We have to escalate this thing," Nina said. "I'm meeting Gizzy at the printer's to get the posters, and you're to go with Josh to a lumberyard. He needs to start building the bleachers. Tate's got a crew flying in to put up the screens."

Jack took Nina's hand and squeezed it. He hated to see her so nervous, so frightened. "You did really well on the radio, and this is going to work."

"I hope so. Pray so. It all depends on whether Devlin hears about it or not." She looked at Jack. "Do you think that poor child will be all right?"

"Yes," Jack said. "I do. Haines isn't given to physical violence. Come on, let's go." He started the car and pulled out of the parking lot. Neither of them mentioned what was on their minds—the sexual aspect of it all.

ACT THREE, SCENE SIX
Darcy to the rescue

Tate stepped into the tiny dressing room and closed the door behind him. Casey was sitting before the makeup table and staring at the lighted mirror. She glanced up at him. "Anything?"

"Not so far," he said. When Casey looked like she might start crying, he picked up a chair, set it by her, then turned her around to face him. He took the brush out of her hand and began applying the pink rouge to her cheeks. "It takes practice to put on makeup so the audience can see you but you don't look like a clown. There. Now you're perfect."

"What if Devlin doesn't show up? What if something has happened to Lori? What if—"

Tate put his lips to hers to cut her off. "Haines will be here. He loves drama. He'll think if he appears at the last minute to save the play from my ineptitude, he's the hero."

Casey put her forehead against his shoulder. They were both in costume, ready to go onstage in a few minutes. Even though the room they were in was under the stage, they could hear the people outside. The stage manager had told Casey that the theater was packed, every seat filled, and the aisles were lined with people. "And outside!" she said. "You wouldn't believe the number of people who are sitting on the grass and waiting for the screens to light up. Hundreds of them! The front lawns of all the houses for five miles have been turned into parking lots. But nobody in Summer Hill cares, because everyone is *here*."

In normal circumstances, Casey would have been a nervous wreck about appearing in a play. When it came to food, she was confident in her abilities. But not in acting. Nina had told her that three well-known critics had flown in, one from New York and two from L.A. "Those people have never been kind to Tate," Nina said, "so I doubt if they'll be any different over this."

But Casey's concern about her performance in a local play had been eclipsed by her worry about Devlin and young Lori. She'd spent the last two days running around with Nina and Gizzy, doing all they could to promote the Great Acting Challenge. Tate had flown his publicist in, and she'd managed to get some national media attention. Casey had been so busy that she'd barely made it to the theater by six-thirty to start getting ready to go onstage.

She looked back at Tate. "How is everyone?"

"Your dad gave Estelle a tranquilizer and she's resting. Kit and Olivia are concentrating on the play. I don't think they've really talked about the past."

"What about Kit's son?" She'd met Rowan yesterday and she'd immediately understood why Stacy had said he was "too serious." That was an understatement. The young man was as businesslike as a machine. He quietly told everyone what they were to do—and they obeyed.

"I'd hate to play poker with that guy," Tate said. "I can't tell what he's thinking, and he never tells us what he's doing. He's on the phone a lot, but—" Tate broke off because he could see that he was upsetting Casey more. He put his hand on her chin. "Haines will be here. He couldn't possibly turn down an opportunity to show me up."

"And when he arrives, he'll be put in handcuffs."

"No," Tate said. "That's not the deal."

"But he kidnapped a fifteen-year-old child!"

Tate took her hands in his. "Rowan and I worked this out. If Haines appears, he'll be allowed to perform. There are about twenty federal agents in the audience, some of them FBI and some retired friends of Kit. There's no way Haines can escape. And besides, we don't think he has any idea of the enormity of what he's done."

"The play must go on, that sort of thing?"

"It's more that the charities must be helped. You've seen Josh as an actor. He can't remember half his lines. If he plays Wickham, we worry that people will demand their money back. That won't help your mother's clinic."

His joke didn't make her smile. She was looking into his eyes. "This isn't about money, is it? This is your doing. Did you ask Rowan to hold off on the arrests so Devlin can have one last performance before his life falls apart?"

For a second, Tate looked surprised, then he laughed. "Caught. How did you figure it out?"

"I'm beginning to know you. How difficult was it to persuade him?"

Tate stood up. "It was hell! Rowan Montgomery is made out of steel, unbreakable. He wanted to slap Haines into chains the second he appeared. But damn! I couldn't do it. He's Emmie's father."

"And a man who has made your life hell, who blames you for every bad thing he's caused."

"If I retaliate in kind, it makes me no better than he is."

"And that belief of yours is one of the reasons why I love you," Casey said, then gasped. "I mean ... I should ..."

Tate pulled her into his arms and held her tightly. "It's okay. I've fallen hard for you too. I think I knew I loved you when you trusted me to hold you while you were hanging down the side of a roof. That you'd risk so much to help a child told me everything about you."

He kissed her long and lingeringly.

The dressing-room door swung open and hit Tate in the back. "Ten minutes," the stage manager yelled. She glanced around Tate to Casey. "Remember that you're supposed to hate him."

"I do," Casey said. "I'm only interested in his body."

"I can understand that!"

With a groan, Tate pushed the door closed. "You two make me feel like a piece of meat."

"Now you're trying to turn me on. Go! I have to repair my lipstick. If Devlin shows up, let me know."

Tate kept kissing her while he backed up, talking between each one. "Does this mean you'll go to L.A. with me? Live with me? Go with me to those publicity things I have to attend? Make pies for me?"

"Yes to everything." She had her hand on his chest and was pushing him out the door. She paused. "Do you like me or my cooking better?"

Tate halted on the way to her lips. "I'll have to think about that." He went forward with another kiss, but Casey drew away.

"Get out of here! And don't take your shirt off for anyone but me."

He was backing down the hall. "What do you think Hollywood is going to say when I have a girlfriend who is a mere cook? The headline will be HE COULD HAVE DONE BETTER."

Casey looked at him in horror.

"Maybe you could take night classes and become a lawyer. That's what Clooney got." He turned away and went down the hall to his own dressing room.

Shocked, Casey stepped inside and closed the door behind her. Of all the vain, egotistical— When it hit her what he'd done, she shook her head. He had put her in the mood of Elizabeth Bennet meeting a man she thought was too full of himself.

Casey went to the table, picked up the big powder puff, and

stared at herself in the mirror. She had on a lot of makeup, her hair was piled up on her head, and her dress was cut lower than her nightgown. "I am Elizabeth Bennet," she whispered, "and I think Fitzwilliam Darcy is a snob."

She stood up, took a deep breath, and left the room.

ACT THREE, SCENE SEVEN

Wickham can't resist

Onstage, with the curtain drawn, all the actors took their places. In spite of her lovely clothes, Olivia looked haggard, torn up by the events of the last few days. Sitting in a chair by the fake fireplace was Dr. Kyle. There were circles under his eyes that makeup couldn't cover. He looked as if he hadn't slept in days.

Gizzy, as Jane, was so pretty in her pink-and-white dress that she fairly sparkled—but her eyes were haunted. To one side of Olivia was Nina. She was subbing for Lydia, but she was too old for the role. From the grim expression on her face, she wasn't going to be able to play a frivolous young girl who cared only about men in uniform.

The only people who didn't seem miserable were the two high school girls playing Mary and Kitty. They were tapping away on their phones, oblivious.

All in all, it was not a happy atmosphere. There was an overriding sense of gloom—and of having lost. They had gambled and lost everything.

It was eight P.M., music was playing from the small orchestra Kit had hired, but the curtain didn't go up.

The stage manager ran to Dr. Kyle and whispered to him. He stood up. "Sorry," he said. "Medical emergency." As he hurried off the stage, everyone slumped in place. Now what?

In the next minute, they heard Josh speaking to the audience. As always, his easy way with people came through. He made some jokes about Dr. Kyle having to rush off to save lives, so they'd be a few minutes late.

Behind the curtain, Kit came onto the stage dressed as Mr. Bennet. But his waistcoat was misbuttoned, and the tie at his neck was askew. Nina and Casey hurried forward to straighten him, but the costume was intricate and they couldn't quite figure it out.

"Let me," Olivia said, and brushed them away. Deftly, she fixed Kit's costume. "You always were worthless," she whispered.

Kit started to say something, but instead he pulled her into his arms and kissed her. It was a kiss of such passion, such longing—and apology—that everyone felt it. Even the teenagers quit tapping. They all stared at the couple.

When Olivia began to return Kit's passion with enthusiasm, eyes widened. One of the girls whispered, "I didn't know old people still did that."

"Nobody's ever done that to *me,*" the other one replied.

Everyone was so transfixed, frozen, in watching the kissing couple that they didn't see who walked onto the stage.

The voice of the girl playing Kitty broke the trance. "Lori! You're back!"

Nina and Casey turned to see Lori, in costume as Lydia, taking her place onstage. Their first reaction was to run to her with hugs and tears of joy. But Jack and Tate were at the side and waving their arms no. They'd worked hard to keep the real reason for the disappearance quiet, and they couldn't blow it now.

Casey had to get herself under control and go back to her place. Josh was waiting in the wings, and when Nina ran to him, she released tears of relief and he led her away.

Kit and Olivia broke apart, and for a moment they stood together, holding hands and staring at Lori, who was smoothing her hair and dress. This tall, pretty young woman was their grand-daughter, and it was the first time they were seeing her with this new knowledge.

As the director, it was Kit's job to be sure that they got into their places before the curtain went up, but he couldn't take his eyes off Lori or leave Olivia's side.

"Places!" the stage manager said loudly, then had to repeat it twice before everyone obeyed.

Casey looked toward the side and saw Tate, and he gave her a thumbs-up. Haines was there.

When the curtain went up, the audience saw a happy family at home. Olivia, as Mrs. Bennet, was complaining that her daughters would never get married because her husband refused to visit Mr. Bingley.

Kit played the role of Olivia's husband with great fondness. His line about her nerves having been his concern for so many years was said with such affectionate teasing that Olivia blushed.

Casey delivered the very famous line that "a single man in possession of a good fortune must be in want of a wife." When the audience laughed, she was startled. She'd worked to try not to remember that she was being watched by what could be hundreds of people. But the laughter at a line *she* had delivered felt very good.

While Olivia and Kit batted lines back and forth, Casey glanced offstage and saw Tate. The way he smiled at her said he knew how she felt. The laughter and applause were a heady experience.

He winked at her, and Casey gave her attention back to the play.

The next scene was at the assembly hall, where the Bennets were to meet Darcy and Bingley and their entourage.

In the quick interlude, while Josh and his crew changed sets, Tate stopped by Casey's dressing room. He fastened the Velcro under the line of buttons down the back of her pale-blue ball gown, which had been made by Stacy's mother. "By the way," he said as he kissed her neck, "I met a beautiful lawyer and I asked her on a date. She's impressed that I'm a movie star."

It was a ridiculous statement, but it was just enough that when she got onstage, Casey was ready to let him know she thought he was a snob.

They all had to pause for the deafening applause that greeted the sight of *both* Tate Landers and Jack Worth. Kit had prepared them for this, and they knew exactly how long to wait. Tate had his back so straight and looked so arrogant that Casey had no problem believing he was eaten up with pride.

Next came a scene in the Bennet parlor, then one at Mr. Bingley's house, Netherfield. They went well.

In the fifth scene, Mr. Collins showed up. The trainer overplayed his role by half. He was so sleazy, so unctuous, and fawned so heavily over Lady Catherine de Bourgh that the audience loved him.

Casey was truly repulsed. When he put his hand on her forearm, her whole body recoiled. The doors to the theater were open, and while the audience inside behaved itself, many people outside hissed loudly. It felt as if at any moment they might start throwing rotten tomatoes.

At the end of the scene, Wickham was to arrive, and Casey did her best to calm her nervousness. When Devlin Haines stepped onto the stage, the crowd roared with yells and applause.

Casey had no doubt that Tate had arranged these accolades. When she glanced offstage, she saw Rowan, flanked by three men in suits. They were just waiting. But from the radiant smile on Devlin's handsome face, he had no idea what was about to happen to him.

While Jane was exchanging small talk with Bingley, Casey watched Devlin moving about the stage. Kit's direction had been that Wickham was to show his attraction to the pretty young Lydia, and she was to return it.

Casey was curious as to what had gone on between the two of them. They'd been away for days. But what had happened? Was Lori's crush still strong?

The girl played her part perfectly. Lydia looked Wickham up and down in the age-old way of attraction, and he gave it back to her. It was perfect—except that when Devlin walked past Lori, she moved her skirt aside so it didn't touch him.

In that small gesture, Casey felt that she'd seen everything. Whatever had happened, that poor child had hated it.

Casey looked offstage to Rowan. Had he seen the subtle gesture? When he gave a curt nod, she was relieved that, yes, he'd seen and understood. She knew all too well how slick and convincing Devlin's lies could be. She didn't want him talking his way out of what he'd done.

Mr. Collins returned to Lizzy, then at last Casey was confronted by Devlin. It took all her inner strength, but she smiled at him in welcome.

Her attitude caused a flash of surprise, but then he returned her smile with a hint of secrecy. It was as though he thought she was genuinely glad to see him.

The scene where Wickham tells Lizzy how horrible Darcy is seemed to go on forever. Casey had to fake her look of shock, had to pretend to believe him. Worse, she had to cover her anger at her character for taking this man's word without proof.

She couldn't help remembering that it was exactly what she'd done to Tate. One time he'd said to her, "Some people want to believe that the only difference between achievement and failure is luck. They like to sit on their couches and say that some sort of predetermined fate was why others made it and they didn't. They never want to admit that hard work did it." Unfortunately, she had experienced the truth of that.

When Wickham glanced at pretty Lydia, who was standing just a few feet away, a knot rose in Casey's throat. She wanted to slap him. What had he done to that poor child?

When the long scene finally ended and the stage darkened, emotion so overcame her that she had trouble standing upright. Tate's strong arm caught her. "You did well. Perfectly. Hold it together now," he whispered as he led her offstage and down to her dressing room.

"What about Lori?"

"Kit and Olivia have her. Some of Kit's friends got Estelle out of bed, and she's in the front row drinking gallons of black coffee to counteract whatever your dad gave her. She is a very happy woman."

While they were talking, he'd peeled the everyday dress off her and helped her step into the ball gown.

"Thank you," she said. "You're the best dresser anyone ever had."

"That's what the lady lawyer said too."

"You touch her and I'll throw a pot of boiling sugar on you."

Laughing, he took her hand and they ran up to the stage. "That's the spirit! When you bawl me out, pretend I'm Haines and let me have it. But then, I've been on the receiving end of your temper, so maybe you should soften your blows. Have pity on poor me."

He had succeeded in making her smile. "Go on, get out of here," she said. "And thanks."

The next scene was the ball at Netherfield, which Wickham didn't attend. It wasn't easy for Casey to run lines with Tate and act disdainful of him, but he kept looking down his nose at her in such an arrogant way that she hardly recognized him. The scene ended with Mary singing very badly—which was why Kit had cast the girl, saying she was a natural.

There was another quick costume change, then Lizzy had to

turn down Mr. Collins's marriage proposal. Casey's revulsion was so real that the audience felt it right along with her.

Olivia's hysteria over Elizabeth's refusal of Mr. Collins was loud and desperate. Kit played the scene with regret in his voice. It seemed to hurt him to go against his beloved wife.

Next came another scene between Lizzy and Wickham. At the end, Lydia spoke to him and, per Kit's direction, there was a definite flirtation in her voice. They walked offstage together.

When Mrs. Bennet heard that their neighbors' daughter Charlotte was to marry Mr. Collins, Olivia tongue-lashed Lizzy so hard that Casey almost started crying.

For the sake of fewer sets and a shorter play, Kit had combined some scenes. Charlotte—played by a young woman Casey didn't really know—and Lizzy were shown on a dark stage with a spotlight on just them. Behind them, Josh and his men, wearing soft slippers, silently changed the set to become a drawing room at Rosings.

When the lights came up, Hildy, as Lady Catherine de Bourgh, was fabulous. She was haughty, disdainful, and utterly perfect. She was so good that Casey had difficulty delivering her lines as though she wasn't intimidated by the woman.

When Hildy said that if she'd ever learned how to play the piano she would have been a great proficient, Casey believed her.

In the scene, Lizzy was to play the piano. Since Casey didn't know one key from another, Kit had set up a tape recording that she was to pantomime. But it didn't work. She pressed on the keys of the fake piano Josh had built, but there was no music.

The audience moved restlessly. Outside were some jeering calls from hecklers.

With panic on her face, she looked at Tate. What should she do?

He stepped forward and calmly said, "May I assist?" He then began to sing in a truly beautiful voice. If not a song of Jane Austen's time, it was close. It was about love that had been found, then lost. A young man had to watch the woman he loved be taken from him by death.

The melody, the words, and Tate's tenor voice were so beautiful that the audience inside and out grew utterly silent. Even the kids who'd been running around like hooligans stopped and listened.

When he finished, the other players didn't know what to say. What he'd done wasn't in the script, so the lines they were to say wouldn't make sense.

It was the audience that reacted. They spontaneously came to their feet and applauded Tate's singing. Outside, they yelled and cheered.

Casey knew that her lines were next. She was to tease Mr. Darcy about how he'd snubbed them at the dance at the assembly hall. When the applause quieted a bit, Casey said loudly, "Perhaps, Mr. Darcy, if you had honored us in this way at Netherfield, you could have saved my sister Mary from any hint of impropriety."

With a swish of her silk skirt, she turned away from him and went to Colonel Fitzwilliam. But before she left, she had the great satisfaction of seeing shock on Tate's face. He wasn't the only one who could ad-lib.

The scene finished with Colonel Fitzwilliam telling Lizzy that Darcy had broken Jane and Bingley apart.

During the quick break, Tate didn't go to Casey's dressing room. Coming up was the scene where she tells him what he can do with his marriage proposal. Earlier, he'd said that pre-scene kissing didn't inspire anger onstage. "And you know this how?" she'd asked, but he'd just laughed.

Olivia helped Casey with the dress change.

"How is Lori?" Casey asked.

"No one is questioning her until the play is over." Olivia's hands were shaking as she fastened the back of Casey's dress.

"Does she know that her mother was adopted?"

"Yes. Portia found out when she was seventeen. Estelle said the news made her very angry. I don't know how the girls are going to feel about . . . about us."

Turning, Casey hugged Olivia. "How could she not be pleased to know you and Kit? And Lori . . ." She didn't know what to say about her.

"Let's go," Olivia said. "Give Darcy hell."

Casey kissed her cheek, then ran up the stairs.

Onstage, she was alone in the parlor of Charlotte and Mr. Collins's home when Darcy entered. Tate looked so good and his eyes were so full of love that Casey wanted to throw her arms around him.

But then he picked up a prop. It was her wineglass—the one Devlin had stolen. The glass was an antique, one of a set of four that her mother had given her to celebrate her graduation from the cooking academy. Casey used them only for special occasions, but that's what she'd thought the dinner with Devlin was going to be. She'd been so attracted to him and he'd been so charming that she'd had visions of a future with him. Instead, he'd left her asleep on the table and had taken the wine and her pretty glass. And when she'd asked him about it, he'd flat-out lied.

Casey glanced from the wineglass to Tate's eyes, and when she delivered her refusal of his marriage proposal, all the venom she felt came out. She practically spit the words at him.

When he left the room, he looked like a man who'd just lost everything he valued in life.

The last scene of the act was of Lizzy sitting at a desk and reading the letter from Mr. Darcy. A prerecorded tape of Tate's voice told of Wickham's lies. Casey remembered the video Nina had prepared and how bad she'd felt when she saw what a fool she'd been—and that memory showed on her face.

When Tate's voice stopped, Casey put her head down on the desk and genuine tears came to her eyes. The curtain came down. End of act two.

Lydia confesses

"You're sure?" Casey asked Tate. They were in her little dressing room and she was again changing her costume. "I did all right?"

"You were great. Excellent. I was impressed. When you turned down my marriage proposal I was genuinely hurt."

"Like you didn't plan that! How did you sneak that wineglass out of my house?"

"I didn't. You left it in the car."

She was pinning up pieces of her hair that had fallen down. "I guess I did, but then, I was hurrying to get started on the acting contest." Her face turned serious. "Did you talk to Rowan?"

"No. He's not talking to anyone except Kit. The last time I saw them, they were arguing. I think Rowan wants to slap handcuffs on Haines right now and the play be damned."

Casey looked at him in the mirror. "I almost feel sorry for Devlin. Since Lori lied to us about her age, she probably lied to him as well. I guess it could be argued that she led him on."

"I don't think that makes a difference. Legally, age is pretty cut and dried, and if he kept her against her will . . . I'd like to hear Lori's side of it all." He paused. "What bothered me so much during the divorce was that nothing bad ever happened to Haines because of his lies. He always ends up the winner. The things he did to Nina were horrific, but they weren't illegal and couldn't be prosecuted."

"And you ended up paying his bills," Casey said.

"Hey! Why are we talking about him? We have time before you have to be back onstage. Let's do something else." He pulled her into his arms and they began kissing. Tate was guiding her toward the wall, his hand sliding up her bare leg, when the door flew open.

Lori, in full costume, burst into the room, slammed the door behind her, and leaned on it. "No one cares!" she said. "No one even *noticed* that I was gone."

When Tate released Casey, she went to the girl and led her to sit on the chair by the dressing table, and handed her tissues.

"No one's said anything to me since I got back! Grams is in the front row, but she looks like she's drunk." She looked up at Tate, her eyes pleading. "I know you're related to Devlin, and I know you're best friends, but I don't know who else to talk to. He says that Grams isn't a blood relative because she adopted my mother, so that makes *him* my legal guardian. Through *you*. And Mr. Kit—who I think is my grandfather. Maybe. None of that makes any sense to me, but—" She broke off, her hands over her face. "Devlin says I have to leave with him after the play."

Tate had to swallow a couple of times before he could speak. "I'm not his relative or his friend, and you're never again going anywhere with him. I want to know everything, including about the note you left."

"What note?" Lori blew her nose.

Casey sat down and took the girl's hands in hers. "Your grandmother isn't drunk. She's full of tranquilizers because she was hysterical with worry over you."

"Was she?"

"Tell me why you left with him." Tate was looming over her.

"Devlin invited me to a party in Richmond that he said would be full of movie stars. He said even Taylor Swift would be there and that she was his friend. I believed him, since he's part of that world and stars know each other." Lori looked at Casey. "It was the girls. I only went to school in Summer Hill for six weeks, but I had a lot of girlfriends. We had fun together. Then the play was announced and we all said that we'd try out. But we knew Ashley would get the role of Lydia."

"Let me guess," Casey said. "She was the first girl who tried out to be Lydia. The cheerleader."

"That's her. She's been the star of all the school plays since she was in the sixth grade. Her father owns the Bank of Summer Hill. She's very popular."

"But you got the role," Tate said.

Lori sniffed. "I didn't mean to win over Ashley, but I don't know what came over me. I just thought of what Lydia was like and I sort of became her."

"It's called talent," Tate said. "Great, deep, natural talent."

"You think so?" Lori asked.

"Yes, he does," Casey said. "I take it that afterward your so-called friends turned nasty."

"They said I'd betrayed Ashley and they quit speaking to me, then they posted some horrible lies about me online. I couldn't tell Grams about any of it because she worries so much, so ... so ..." She glanced at Casey.

"Devlin was there and he listened to every word you had to say," Casey said.

"Not at first, but suddenly he became my best friend. At least I thought he was. When he invited me to go with him to a party that would be full of movie stars, I thought it was a solution to all my problems. If I could get some autographed CDs for the girls, maybe they'd forgive me and we could be friends again. I didn't want to go with Devlin because I didn't really know him, but he said we were related so it was okay. Then Grams started saying that I was spending too much time with the theater people, and we had a fight and . . ." Lori gave a helpless look. "I was so angry that I stopped thinking. I just threw things in a bag and went. It was stupid of me. Really, really stupid."

Tate knelt down beside her, took her other hand, and stared into her eyes. "We all do things that aren't very smart. It's part of growing up. Right now you need to tell us the facts about when you left with him."

"Devlin said I'd need my passport to prove my age to get into the adult party, but I couldn't let him see that I'd lied. Did you know that Taylor Swift and I are exactly the same height? My friends said that boys hate tall girls and that's why I never have any dates."

Tate stood up. "Lori, heterosexual boys love any and all girls. And I'll get you a date with a six-foot-two pop star if you'll just tell us what happened."

"Oh," Lori said, and blinked a couple of times. "Devlin took me to a motel. He said we had to wait for the others to arrive, but they didn't. I told him I wanted to go home, but he said we couldn't leave. He wouldn't let me leave! He watched me every minute. He . . ."

Casey took her hand. "Did he touch you in any way?"

"No," Lori said. "I think he wanted to. The first night, he lay down beside me on the bed, but I started groaning. I said it was the wrong time of the month. I've never, you know, with a guy, and he's really old. Too old to do *that*. Sorry, Mr. Landers. I know he's your age."

"That's all right," Tate said, smiling. "What about the note you left for your grandmother?"

"I didn't write one. I wanted to, but Devlin said I shouldn't. He said that if I left on my own it would show Grams that I'm an independent being and that I'm tired of being treated like a little kid." She looked down at her hands. "The girls were posting that I was a spoiled brat, so he was saying what I wanted to hear. He told me to pack a party dress and a bikini and that's all I'd need. I put a lot more in my suitcase, but when we got to the motel, he took away my cellphone and my laptop. He wouldn't let me talk to anyone. I tried to use the phone in the room, but he cut the line. By the second day I was really scared of him." She started crying again.

Hugging her, Casey looked up at Tate.

"Lori," he said, "listen to me. Did you see those men in suits backstage? They're FBI agents, and they're here because Haines took you away. He is *not* related to you; he has no rights of guardianship over you." He glanced at Casey. "I think you've had enough of all this. We're going to the FBI now."

"But what about the play?" Lori asked.

"Forget it," Tate said. "We can't put you through any more of this."

Lori stood up. "No! I can't do that to people. The whole town is looking forward to this. And there are the charities and . . ."

"And if you're the cause of stopping the play, the girls will butcher you," Casey said, and Lori nodded in agreement.

Tate gave a one-sided grin. "Besides, you love the spotlight, don't you? You like to hear the applause."

"I do," she said, staring at him as though daring him to contradict that.

"If anyone understands, it's me," Tate said. "So here's what we're going to do. For the next hour and a half, you're going to be a professional actor. You're going to be Lydia. Not Lori with her problems, but Lydia. Got it?"

She nodded.

Tate continued: "After the play ends, you're going to be asked a lot of questions. Hundreds of them. And through it all, you're going to be strong and answer everything honestly." He put his hands on her shoulders. "It might help to imagine that you're playing a role. It's a cop show and you're a fifteen-year-old kid who has escaped a kidnapping by an older man. Does that sound like something you can do?"

"I think so."

Outside the room, the stage manager yelled, "Five minutes to curtain. Everyone onstage *now!*"

Tate didn't release Lori's shoulders. "I want you to remember that you are a born actor. It's in your blood from your grandmother Olivia, and you need to live up to your talent. No more lies, no more feeling guilty. You did nothing wrong or stupid. Understand?"

Lori nodded again, and Tate stepped back. "Now go, both of you. I'll see you on the set."

Casey made more swipes at Lori's face to remove the last trace of tears, then held the door open for her.

As they started down the hall, Lori said, "Is Mr. Landers actually my cousin, and do you think he could introduce me to Taylor Swift?"

Standing at the door, Tate rolled his eyes. But he was glad that the child hadn't been physically molested. He went in search of Rowan.

ACT THREE, SCENE NINE

Wickham gets what he deserves

The first scene of act three was when Lydia found out she was to go to Brighton with the Forsters. As Casey watched Lori laughing and talking about the clothes she was to take, she marveled at how the girl actually seemed to *be* Lydia.

Casey had few lines in the scene, so she stood aside and watched Olivia beside Lori. How had she not seen the resemblance? Lori was taller and had that wonderful agility of youth, but the two women looked alike. Their pale blondeness and their blue eyes—which could instantly go from laughter to cutting a person to size—were the same. When Lori moved her hand to dismiss her sister Kitty, Casey knew she'd seen the same movement from Olivia.

Kit sat to one side of the stage, his face hidden from the audience by a newspaper, but Casey could see that he was watching Olivia and Lori. There was so much regret in his eyes that Casey could almost read his mind. He had missed out on the life that had produced this beautiful girl. Olivia, their daughter, Portia, and Lori had all eluded him.

Offstage, Rowan came to stand behind the curtain. He looked like an angrier version of his father, but he too watched Lori's happy performance. They were closely related, but they had missed out on knowing each other.

Kit kept his paper up until only he and Casey were left on the stage. Lizzy was to say that Mr. Bennet could *not* allow Lydia to go to Brighton. To get in the mood, Casey thought of what Lori had told them in the dressing room. Devlin stretching out on the bed beside her! How quick-witted she'd been to say what she did. And how well she'd analyzed his personality to know that he'd be repulsed by her statement.

When Lizzy asked Mr. Bennet to say that Lydia couldn't go, her voice was pleading, desperate. It was as though Casey was trying to stop what had already happened. As for Kit, he delivered Mr. Bennet's words of permission, but his eyes were full of angst.

There was a break while Josh and his men did their magic to turn the set into a beautiful parlor at Pemberley. When Tate came into the scene, Casey was glad she no longer had to pretend to hate him. But then, he was utterly charming. When he smiled at Mr. and Mrs. Gardiner in a way that made the outdoor audience go "Ooooooh" in a chorus of female voices, it was hard for the players not to laugh.

In the next scene there was a change. The high school girl playing Darcy's sister, Georgiana, had been replaced by Nina. A quick glance at Rowan, standing offstage and glowering, answered Casey's question of why. It looked as if Tate had told Lori's story of the bullying high school girls. Maybe after they were questioned by the FBI, those girls would think twice about attacking someone else in a jealous fit.

With Nina there—a person Casey genuinely liked—it was easy to play the role of Lizzy. They left the stage arm in arm.

Casey didn't hurry down to her dressing room but stayed behind to watch Tate with the woman playing her rival, Miss Bingley. After the woman tauntingly said hateful things about Lizzy Bennet, Darcy put her down with so much contempt in his voice that the poor girl almost started crying. She worked in a local shop, and Tate's size and his professional anger directed at her were almost too much for her to withstand. When the curtain came down, she ran offstage.

Smiling, Casey grabbed her long skirt and ran down the stairs. She had to change while Josh made the set into an inn.

Back onstage, when Lizzy delivered her lines about Lydia having run off with Wickham, there was real fear in Casey's voice and tears in her eyes. She knew she was to tell Darcy that it wasn't his problem, and she said the lines, but her eyes begged him for help.

Tate understood what she was saying. This was about what Lori had been through and what she would face in the coming months. His ex-brother-in-law would be arrested, and later there would be a trial. It was going to be hard on the girl.

Tate said his lines perfectly, but at one point he reached out to touch Casey in reassurance. It was an inappropriate gesture for the time period, and he dropped his hand before it connected.

The scene changed to the Bennet parlor, and Mrs. Bennet was coming apart in worry. In rehearsals, Olivia's frantic fluttering— her "nerves"—had been almost laughable. But not tonight. Not in this version. They felt as real as they actually were.

Olivia was to say that her husband was away, looking for their daughter, but Kit threw them off balance by striding onto the stage. His bearing showed his military background. He was Christopher Montgomery, not the wimpy Mr. Bennet, and he put his hands on her shoulders. "I will find her. I will bring her back and we will protect her forever," he said, his eyes on hers.

Olivia, tears blocking her voice, nodded.

"This is all my fault," he said. "I am the one who caused this. I alone allowed it to happen, and I will work until my last breath to make it up to you."

By this time, their heads were almost touching, and again all Olivia could do was nod.

Kit let go of her shoulders, stepped back from her, then turned.

Everyone onstage was confused by this interruption. Olivia stood in silence, her eyes on Kit as he walked away.

He reached the edge of the stage, then halted and turned back to look to Olivia. In a few long strides, he went to her, pulled her into his arms, and kissed her.

It wasn't a stage kiss of closed mouths, meant to imply more than it showed. It was a deep kiss. Porno, X-rated, watch-it-after-the-kids-go-to-bed kiss.

Audiences inside and out stopped. The people onstage opened their eyes wide in shock as they watched The Kiss.

When Olivia nearly fainted, Kit held her in his arms, not letting her fall—and kept kissing her.

After minutes, he pulled away and stood her upright. He kept his hands on her shoulders until she was self-supporting. Then he gave a curt nod, as though to say, "There! Think about that while I'm gone," and strode off the stage, leaving behind a silent audience, crew, and players.

Olivia recovered first. She said her line about how Mr. Bennet would surely fight Wickham and be killed and they'd all be thrown out of their house. In the book it was meant to show the woman as self-centered and unloving, but Olivia's delivery was of a woman sending her beloved off to war. The anger and fear in her voice, following a kiss that could only have been between two people who had loved each other for a very long time, put tears in people's eyes.

When she'd finished, Olivia looked to Mr. Gardiner, Mrs. Bennet's brother. He was to tell her to calm down, but the actor, a local man, was still staring in silence.

Spontaneously, the audience came to their feet with applause and cheers and lots of whistles.

Olivia kept her place, as though she meant to stand still and wait for the applause to stop. But Casey wasn't going to allow that. She grabbed Olivia's hand and turned her around to face the audience.

For a moment Olivia just stood there in silence, then she took a well-deserved bow. She gave several of them before she stepped back into place and everyone grew quiet and the play continued.

What followed was a short scene that wasn't in the book, of Lydia and Wickham together. Casey was supposed to change for the next scene, but she stood behind the curtain and watched. She wasn't surprised when Tate came up behind her.

The rehearsals had been of Lydia giggling and teasing, flirting with Wickham, glad they'd run away together. But that wasn't the way Lori played it onstage. She seemed to mimic how she'd felt when Devlin kept her imprisoned in the motel room. Outwardly, she was nice to him, but she let the audience see the fear that was inside her. The reality of a fifteen-year-old girl being seduced by a thirty-something-year-old man was more than creepy.

The twist on the scene had the audience enthralled—and it made Devlin very angry.

When the scene ended, he stomped off the stage in a fury. "Did you see that?" he said to Casey and Tate. "After all I've done for that little bitch! Has she been telling people lies about me? I spent hours listening to her whining about how her grandmother was abusing her. Since I'm related to the kid, I felt it was my duty as a responsible adult to get her away from the old hag. I would have called the authorities, but I thought I'd better find out the truth first, so I took the kid away. Is there anything *bad* in that?" Devlin glared at the stage, where the men were changing the set. "She acted like *I* had seduced *her*! Look, Landers, if I lose this contest, it's *not* my fault. Got it?"

He stormed away, his rage making the whole stage vibrate.

Tate and Casey looked to the other side to see Rowan. He had heard it all. He didn't say anything, just walked down the stairs to the dressing rooms.

The next scenes dealt with the aftermath of Lydia and Wickham being married. When Mr. Bennet returned home, Mrs. Bennet greeted him with quiet relief, and Kit and Olivia walked away, arm in arm.

When Lydia and Wickham arrived at the Bennet house, Lori wasn't laughing in triumph, as Lydia was in the novel. She looked like a girl who'd learned her lesson—but was too late. Lori delivered the lines in the script, but not with the happiness that was in the novel. Instead, she put a modern twist, a politically correct slant, on the words. She was a fifteen-year-old girl and she was now *married*.

Her words to her sisters weren't gloating but showed her knowledge of what she was going to be missing. No more giggling with them. No more flirting at parties. No more hope for her future.

When Lydia told Lizzy that Mr. Darcy had found them, it was said in the terms of a rescue, that Darcy had made the best of a very bad situation.

From the far side of the stage, Devlin—out of character as Wickham—sent glares of threat to Lori. She knew the audience had seen them, so she stepped almost behind Casey, who put her arm around Lori's shoulders and shot Devlin's looks of threat back at him.

At the end was a bit of dialogue between Elizabeth and Wickham, and Casey let the man—and the audience—see what she thought of him.

The next scene was much-needed happiness, as Jack as Mr. Bingley asked the beautiful Gizzy as Jane to marry him. After the sadness of Lydia and Wickham, the audience burst into happy applause.

In the next-to-last scene, Hildy, as Lady Catherine de Bourgh, came on and gave a marvelous over-the-top performance. She was so outrageously snobbish that the audience laughed. Encouraged by them and by all the disruption in previous scenes, Hildy put extra drama into telling Elizabeth how unworthy she was of a rich, aristocratic man like Mr. Darcy. She seemed to be talking of the cook and the movie star.

Casey replied that she agreed but that he wanted her, so what was she to do? Say no to him? Impossible!

Hildy delivered her long speech of shock with such conviction that Casey almost said she'd stay away from Tate. But she put her shoulders back and said that if he again asked her to marry him, she wouldn't say no.

At last came the final scene. It began with only Lizzy and Darcy. There was a bit of talk of blaming themselves, then Tate said he loved her.

"From the first moment, you have seen me as a man," he said while holding her hands, his face close to hers. "Not as how the world sees me, with the riches I have acquired, but as I truly am. I have grown to love you with all my heart."

His lines weren't as they were in the script, but by that time Casey was used to impromptu. She opened her mouth to reply, but Tate stepped back and held his hand up so the audience could see. On the little finger of his left hand was a staggeringly beautiful ring with a big diamond in the center.

He pulled it off, went down on one knee, and asked Casey to marry him.

The appearance of the ring and the look in Tate's eyes so jolted her that she couldn't remember her lines. All she could do was nod yes.

With a smile, he slipped the ring onto her finger, then stood up and drew her into a kiss. The curtain came down. The end.

The audience rose to its feet, and when the curtain went back up, Casey and Tate were still locked in an embrace. Staying in character, the other players rushed onto the stage to congratulate them. But Tate and Casey didn't break their kiss.

One by one, the players went to the front of the stage and took bows. When Olivia and Kit stepped forward, hands tightly held, the audience went crazy. Outside, car horns were blowing, and a couple of police cars set off alarms in appreciation.

Kit stepped back to give the audience a clear view of Tate and Casey wrapped in each other's arms. But Kit shook his head and gave a thumbs-down. His meaning was clear. A youngster like Landers didn't know how to kiss!

Following Kit's lead, Olivia batted her lashes at him, flipped her hip, and sashayed off the stage with a panting Kit running after her. Everyone laughed loudly.

Lydia and Wickham came next. When Lori wouldn't let Devlin even touch her hand, he had a flash of anger, then he twirled his imaginary mustache and leered at her.

Their act was a relief from what they'd done in the play, which had seemed so very real.

Finally, everyone stepped aside to show Casey and Tate, who were still kissing. They broke apart and took bows. Casey held up her diamond ring, blew on it, and polished it on her shoulder. She raised her arm in triumph, as though to say that she'd just won first prize at the fair.

Tate grabbed her hand and pulled her off the stage, acting as though he couldn't wait to get her alone. They stopped just behind the curtain to watch the audience and the other players, who were taking second bows.

Casey was looking at the ring. It flashed even in the dull light. "This looks real. I think the whole proposal was a great addition to the play. Why didn't you warn me?"

"It is real, and no man warns of a proposal. Hear that?"

The audience was chanting something, but Casey was still staring at the ring. "Real as in how? Diamonds?"

"They're saying 'Lizzy! Lizzy!' They want *you*."

Casey didn't know what he meant.

"Go! Take your bows. You earned them." He pushed her back onto the stage.

By herself, Casey walked to the edge. It was hard to believe, but the audience really was yelling for Lizzy. For her. Emmie ran across the stage, nearly outweighed by an enormous bouquet of pink roses, and handed them to Casey. The child, smiling hugely, started to leave, but Casey took her hand and they both bowed to the applauding audience.

Emmie, young but an old pro, stepped back, her arms extended, and looked toward the curtain to her uncle. In the next moment she started running and Tate caught her. He picked her up and walked out with her to stand beside Casey. The applause, the whistles, shouts, and horns were deafening. It was a long while before they left the stage.

What greeted them offstage was a bewildered Devlin in hand-cuffs. "I didn't know she was so young, and she *wanted* to stay with me. And now she's saying I held her against her will?" He was sputtering. "I can't be held responsible for her lies. If she'd told me the truth I would have helped her—which is what I was trying to do in the first place. How was I to know she was a pathological liar? *She* should be in handcuffs. Not me! I was trying to—"

He broke off because the crowd was calling for him and Lydia. "You have to remove these! They want me."

Rowan gave a snort of derision and clamped down on Devlin's upper arm.

But Kit stepped forward. He said nothing, but he gave his son a glance that said everything. Rowan released Devlin—but he didn't remove the handcuffs.

When Devlin, with Lori beside him, appeared onstage in hand-cuffs, the audience went into peals of laughter and cheers. The villain was being punished. They all thought it was part of the play, and they appreciated the twenty-first-century slant on the story.

Devlin's face lost its sulky expression and he played to the audience, even to chasing Lori around the stage, before finally disappearing behind the curtain. Rowan lost no time in grabbing him, but he stopped when Devlin paused near Tate.

"So who won?" Devlin's voice was a sneer, and it said that there was no doubt that he was the winner of the Great Acting Challenge, something that everyone else had forgotten about.

"You did," Tate said. "I concede to you." With that, he gave a formal bow to his ex-brother-in-law.

Devlin put his chin up and was led off the stage, his hands in cuffs.

ACT THREE, SCENE TEN

Darcy and Lizzy reflect on life

Tate and Casey were in her bed and he was nuzzling her neck. She could feel the ring on her finger, and as soon as her senses were her own, she planned to ask him about it. But right now all she could think about were his lips on her body, his skin against hers.

Last night they'd returned from the play full of energy and hunger, for food and for each other. In between lovemaking and talking, they'd eaten whatever they could find. The play, Devlin's fate, what awaited Lori, and what was going to happen with Kit and Olivia, had occupied them so completely that Casey didn't ask about the ring. But she certainly didn't take it off!

They didn't get to bed until after three A.M. and had fallen into a deep sleep, wrapped around each other.

The clock on the bedside table said it was now ten A.M., and Casey needed to get up and start cooking. Everyone would be wanting breakfast.

When Tate's cellphone began playing Katy Perry's "Roar," he immediately rolled over and picked it up. "Emmie?"

"No, it's me," Nina said, and Casey could hear her. "I have her phone. She said she was on her way to you. I was just checking. My usual smothering."

Tate sat up, the covers falling away from his bare chest. "When did she leave?"

"About a minute ago." Nina drew a breath. "Emmie is upset because she thinks you're going to be mad at her."

"What has she done now?" He was watching Casey as she got out of bed and pulled on her clothes, which she'd discarded on the floor.

"That's not the question," Nina said.

"Let me talk to Nina." Casey took the phone as Tate pulled on his boxers under the sheet. "Tell me what happened."

"Josh took Emmie home right after the play, but when I got there, she was still awake. She was saying that Uncle Tate is going to be really mad at her."

"Do you think it's because of her father?" Casey asked. "Emmie must have seen him in handcuffs."

"I don't think so. She's never expected much from him. Tate is everything to her."

"I'll go look for her," Casey said, but just then Emmie, in head-to-foot pink, stepped into the room. "She's here."

Nina let out a sigh. "Tell Tate to fix this. I'll come and get her in about an hour." She clicked off.

Tate was frowning at his niece, who was standing with her head down, as though in apology. "Just so you know," he said, "when I find out what you did, I'm going to be furious."

"Tate!" Casey said in horror. "She—"

But Emmie knew her uncle well, knew his acting voice from his real one. He wasn't angry and wasn't going to be. She made a leap and launched herself onto him. He caught her to snuggle against his chest and smoothed the hair out of her eyes. "What's this about?"

"I put it online. On the cloud."

"What is 'it'? The play?"

Casey went to the door, meaning to go downstairs to start breakfast, but Emmie's iPad was leaning against the wall, and she picked it up. "Does this have anything to do with it?" She sat down on the bed and handed it to Emmie.

"Show me what you've done," Tate said.

She pushed the button, swiped the screen, and up came the video of Tate in Casey's bedroom, chasing the peacock.

"You posted that silly thing?"

Emmie solemnly nodded, looking as though she'd done something awful. "And the one about Mr. Collins."

"What are you talking about?" Tate asked.

"I saw Gizzy with the phone," Casey answered, looking at Emmie. "You mean when we were at the picnic, don't you? When Uncle Tate played Mr. Collins."

Emmie nodded, still seeming worried.

Tate was finally understanding. "I think you know too much about technology." He tossed the iPad aside and began tickling his niece.

Casey picked up the tablet. "Those two videos have nearly a million hits. Look at the comments. People are saying they had no idea you could be so funny. I wonder if this 'Ron Howard' is the director?"

Tate quit tickling his niece, took the tablet from Casey, and quickly scrolled down the comments. There were several names he recognized. "This couldn't be real." He grabbed his phone and checked the emails. There were ninety-one of them. Wide-eyed, he handed the phone to Casey.

She read the addresses of the senders. "Joel Coen sounds familiar."

Tate fell back against the headboard. "The Coen brothers," he whispered, his voice sounding reverent.

Casey looked at Emmie. "I take it this is good?"

"Oh, yeah," the child said. "Uncle Tate loves them."

They heard the downstairs door slam, and Jack yelled, "Landers!" He was running up the stairs. "Your agent called me. She wanted to know where the—" He stopped when he saw Emmie. "She wants to know why in the world you don't answer your phone." Gizzy was behind him.

Tate seemed unable to speak.

"He has it set so only Emmie and Nina's calls come through," Casey said. "What does his agent want?"

"That video with that stupid bird and the one I sent Emmie have gone viral. Some big shots want you to do something in a movie besides smolder. Harvey called."

Tate gasped.

"Harvey who?" Casey asked.

"Weinstein."

Even she had heard that name. Leaning over, she kissed Tate's cheek, and again she started for the stairs. But this time Nina blocked her. She had a piece of paper in her hands and she thrust it at her brother. She looked too astonished to speak.

Silently, Tate started to read it, but couldn't seem to do so. He handed it to Casey.

It was a review of last night's play, and it was from *The New York Times*. She began to read aloud.

> My editor sent me to some small town no one has ever heard of because her favorite actor, heartthrob Tate Landers, was in a local play. *Pride and Prejudice,* no less. My first thought was that being Darcy onscreen wasn't enough for him? He had to repeat it in a live performance? I complained incessantly for two days—ask my wife. Her reply was, "If I can carry your kid—" Etc. So I went.
>
> But I'm very glad I did. What I saw was a relatively politically correct version of *Pride and Prejudice.*
>
> I know I'm of the proverbial one percent, but Jane Aus-

ten's book always annoyed me. A man runs off with a half-grown child and he ends up richer for it and she's happy. Today he'd end up in handcuffs. And that's the way this was played. Devlin Haines, of the late, unlamented *Death Point,* even came onstage for final bows wearing cuffs. Perfect.

But what was great about the whole production was that the actors—nearly all of them locals—made that tired ol' story almost believable. Performances that are usually played for laughs were done with such seemingly true feelings of misery that we the audience gasped and clutched our throats and at times even got teary-eyed.

Christopher Montgomery and Olivia Paget as Mr. and Mrs. Bennet didn't snip and snap but played a couple who still deeply loved each other after long years together. It was a nice change to an old trope.

Lori Young, playing Lydia, was so good it was like watching pure talent being hatched from an egg. She took her character from a flirty girl to an adult who faced a lifetime of repentance for what she'd done. Her performance was nuanced, heartrending, and oh so very believable.

Devlin Haines was nearly overshadowed by the girl, but he was excellent as the lying, deceitful Wickham. Too bad the TV industry keeps casting him as the good guy.

Jack Worth, rarely seen on film outside a racing vehicle, looked so in love with the beautiful Gisele Nolan—who played the part of Jane with a delicate subtlety—that I felt it. Could he be the next Tate Landers?

As for Landers himself, all I can say is, Who knew?

Something that's always bothered me about every version of *Pride and Prejudice* is that I could never see why Darcy was falling for feisty little Lizzy Bennet. But Landers let us see it.

His cutting looks at the sycophants around him, the way he hid smiles behind pretty Lizzy's back, made me understand.

As for Acacia Reddick as Elizabeth Bennet, she was a fireball! She bawled out poor Darcy so well that I felt sorry for him. Whatever she does in real life, she may want to reconsider.

There are to be twelve performances of *Pride and Prejudice* in the little town of Summer Hill, Virginia, which is halfway between Richmond and Charlottesville. If you're in the area, I suggest you go see it. If you're not in the neighborhood, charter a jet.

Bill Simons, your—for once—happy critic

Casey put the paper down. "Wow," she said, but could think of nothing else to say.

Gizzy held out her hand for Emmie. "Let's go downstairs and I'll scramble a dozen eggs."

"Peacock eggs?" Emmie asked as she took Gizzy's hand.

"We wouldn't have anything else."

Jack and Nina went with them, closing the door and leaving Tate and Casey alone.

"Are you okay?" she asked.

He was still leaning against the headboard, and he held out his arm to her. She snuggled against him.

Tate entwined her fingers with his. "It's all because of you."

"What is?"

"This," he said. "Everything. Jack and Gizzy. Nina and Josh. Kit and Olivia."

"You and Harvey Weinstein?"

Tate laughed. "The true-love match."

"Do you think you'll be asked to play other parts?"

He pulled back to look at her. "I think it just might happen. And you brought it all to me."

"Sure it wasn't Colonel Peacock in the well house?"

He knew what she was doing. She didn't want to take credit for the good that she'd done. He picked up her hand and looked at the ring. "You like it?"

"Very much." Her heart increased its speed. "Where did you get it?"

"My manager sent me some photos and I chose one. We can trade it for something else if you don't like this one."

"I don't understand about this ring. I know you proposed, but it was onstage and not real."

When he slid down in the bed, he took her with him. "A lot of people saw you nod in agreement. I'd really hate to have to sue you for breach of promise. Since I have so many witnesses, you'll lose for sure."

"Guess I better not try it, then." He was kissing her neck. "This is where we started this morning."

"Uncle Tate!" Emmie yelled through the door.

"And this is where it went," Tate said with a moan. "What do you need, Emmie?"

"Mom said she's going to make pancakes."

Casey and Tate looked at each other.

"Sorry," Casey said, "but this is an emergency. Your sister is in my kitchen!" She started to get up, but Tate pulled her back.

"I am the happiest man in the world," he said. "There were things missing in my life, but the gaps have been filled. I love you."

"I love you," she whispered.

"Uncle Tate!" Emmie yelled again, her voice now frantic. "Mom wants to know how much salt to put in the pancakes."

Casey stared at Tate with wild eyes.

"Go!" he said. "Anyway, I need to answer some calls."

After half a dozen quick kisses, Casey ran down the stairs.

Tate pulled on his jeans and went to the window. It was a new day, the beginning of a new life. He heard a crash from downstairs—a bowl broken—and he smiled. Sauntering across the drive was the old peacock, its glorious tail dragging behind it. "Thanks, old man," he said.

Disdainful, the bird didn't even look up.

ACKNOWLEDGMENTS

This book was difficult to write. Think "screaming pain." Too often, I was on the floor pounding fists and feet and yelling sacrilegious things about Jane Austen.

Since I'd read *Pride and Prejudice* so many times and seen every TV/movie version, I thought it would be a cinch to rewrite it.

Ha! Looking at a book from a writer's POV is very different from that of a reader/viewer.

How could I make my heroine believe a man's lies when they could be checked on the Internet? How did a man run off with a fifteen-year-old girl and not have criminal charges brought against him? And why, oh why did Wickham get to do so many rotten things but was never punished?

It took a lot of thinking—and a massive rewrite—to bring the story into the modern world and make it close to being the dreaded "politically correct." Endlessly asking permission wears a romance author out!

At the end I was so brain-dead that I decided not to put in the play. Jane ended her book with "I love you," so I could too. But I put on my must-do hat and wrote the play with three versions of *Pride and Prejudice* going on: Jane's, the one in the script, and the one offstage.

When I finished the book, I sent it to my dear editor, Linda

Marrow, without a final read-through. I fully expected the ol' let's-have-lunch response: the death knell over chocolate when she told me the book was awful.

When she said she loved it, I argued with her. I still think Ms. Austen should have taken up a hobby other than "making up characters."

I would like to thank Linda for her praise and for listening to me complain so much. My Facebook buddies are always great with their many comments.

Thanks to Mary Bralove for saying in horror, "But she *has* to be fifteen!"

And thanks to all the people at Random House who read the book and said, "I loved the opening scene." I'm not sure, but I don't think that was a truly scholarly choice.

ABOUT THE TYPE

This book was set in Bembo, a typeface based on an old-style Roman face that was used for Cardinal Pietro Bembo's tract *De Aetna* in 1495. Bembo was cut by Francesco Griffo (1450–1518) in the early sixteenth century for Italian Renaissance printer and publisher Aldus Manutius (1449–1515). The Lanston Monotype Company of Philadelphia brought the well-proportioned letterforms of Bembo to the United States in the 1930s.